INVASION OF PRIVACY

Ian Sutherland

ISBN: 0-9930056-0-8
ISBN-13: 978-0-9930056-0-2

For Cheryl, thanks for sticking around to see my unexpected announcement that sunny lunchtime in St Catherine's Dock finally fulfilled.

CHAPTER 1

Anna Parker wished she'd paid attention to the doubts buried deep in her mind. That they'd put two fingers in each cheek and whistled. Cried foul. Screamed. Anything to have made her listen to sense. To have helped her see through the charade. For she now knew that's all it was — an elaborate sham that had lured her to this abrupt ending.

"What will you play?" the man named William Webber had asked ten minutes before, when the three-day old illusion was still in full swing and Anna was completely oblivious.

"Elgar's *Concerto in E-Minor*," she replied. Her voice cracked as she spoke, her nervousness sneaking past her lips, betraying the confident image she hoped to portray. She inhaled deeply, knowing from other auditions that this would help calm her nerves.

"Please begin when you are ready," Webber said.

She sat on a lonely chair in the centre of the meeting room, her cello propped on its endpin, the neck resting reassuringly on her shoulder. Anna looked around. Desks lined the edges in a large horseshoe shape. Webber sat cross-legged at the head of the room, in front of an imposing wall-to-wall whiteboard. Overhead a huge projector was suspended from the ceiling. In one corner a sprawling fake plastic plant bestowed upon the insipid space a pretence of life. Anna glanced through the window that spanned the length of one wall. In the distance, she could just see the London Eye slowly rotating, each glass pod packed full of tourists.

Bravely, she gave voice to her concerns. "This is an odd place to hold an audition?"

His eyes flashed briefly. Annoyance perhaps? But then he fingered his beard, offering an air of contemplation.

"Yes, I suppose it is," he smiled tightly. "But the acoustics are good enough for our purposes. Please begin."

Anna wasn't sure she concurred. A meeting room in an office building wasn't exactly designed for musical recitals. But the environment was only half of what had been bothering her.

"From your email, I thought someone from the ROH would be here?"

Webber paused, considering her question.

The email inviting Anna to audition for a place in the Orchestra of the Royal Opera House had arrived in her inbox three days ago. It explained that she had been selected for audition on the recommendation of Jake Symmonds, one of the viola professors at Trinity Laban Conservatoire of Music and Dance, where she studied cello. Although Anna wasn't taught by Jake she knew who he was. She briefly considered that perhaps the email was a prank by one of her four student housemates, all of whom knew it was her dream to play professionally. She dismissed this thought — surely her friends wouldn't be so cruel. No, it was just a straightforward email with a potentially life-changing offer.

Anna's flattered ego soon took over, suppressing her doubts. Of course it was standard practice, she reasoned, for the Royal Opera House Orchestra to consult one of London's leading musical conservatoires as to which of its students to audition. Of course it was normal, she convinced herself, for a viola professor she'd never met to know of her virtuosity as a cellist. Teachers discussed their students with each other all the time, didn't they? Of course it was fair — no, more than that — it was *fitting* for Anna to be given the chance to fulfil her lifelong dream of playing in a professional orchestra years ahead of her peers.

After a few minutes of consternation — or maybe it had been only a few seconds — she embraced the email for what it was: an official invitation to audition for one of the most prestigious orchestras in the country. She felt the excitement build in her and, like a dam made of matchsticks, it quickly burst. With tears cascading happily down her cheeks she jumped up and down on her mattress, screaming for joy, just as she had done one Christmas Day morning years before, when Santa had left an exquisitely laminated maple cello at the foot of her bed.

"As I said to you in the lift on the way up, Miss Parker," Webber responded, "I'm simply the first round. An initial screening, so to speak."

"But —"

"Put it this way. Impress me today, and next Tuesday you'll be in the ROH at Covent Garden for the final stage of the audition."

Anna paused for a moment and allowed his words to sink in. She imagined herself in the orchestra pit, tuned and ready for the conductor to lift his baton, the ballet dancers waiting in the wings, the audience hushing, and finally, the curtains opening. It was a delicious image and she desperately wanted it to happen. To happen to her: the cellist who had evolved from that little girl with the best ever Christmas present. The girl who had worked so hard, first learning the basics — bowing, rhythm, and reading notes — and, in time, attempting to recreate euphonic perfection. Countless hours of solitary practice. Daily sacrifices. A childhood spent observing her school friends through the living room window playing forty-forty, kerbie and later, kiss-chase, while she practised her scales over and over, her bow movements across the strings becoming autonomic as muscle memory took over, the melodies becoming more complex and harmonious.

Anna forced a smile onto her face. "Okay then. I'll do my best."

He nodded. "Whenever you're ready, Anna."

She took two more deep breaths, drew back the bow and launched into the concerto, her favourite piece. The music, as Elgar had planned, came slowly and hauntingly at first. Within a few bars she was lost to the stately rhythm of her part. Webber disappeared from her thoughts, even though she could see him immediately opposite her. It was as if someone else was observing him through her eyes, so lost was she in the music.

Webber began to wave his arms as if conducting her. Although his timing was slightly out, he became quite animated, his eyes closing in rapture.

Anna, too, closed her eyes and within a few bars, had completely surrendered herself to the magnificent piece. She felt as though she was achieving a level of grace that she knew was denied her in any other aspect of her life. The bow in her right hand elegantly flew left and right over the strings. Her left hand moved up and down the fingerboard, rapidly depressing the strings, the positions fluent and clear, each note perfect.

She reached the final crescendo with a flourish. She knew that she had never played better and that Tuesday would see her in Covent Garden. A bead of sweat trickled down her back. She opened her eyes, smiling expectantly.

Webber was nowhere to be seen.

She swivelled on the chair, scanning the room in panic. He was right behind her, one arm raised high, holding what looked like a large dagger, a maniacal grin spread across his face.

Uncomprehending, she asked, "What are you . . ."

Webber rapidly swung his arm downwards, twisting his wrist at the last second to cause the solid base of the dagger's handle to strike Anna cruelly across the side of her face. Her head exploded in pain, whiteness obscuring her vision. She dropped to the floor. Her cello and bow fell from her hands, clattering on top of her, numbed notes emitting from the instrument's strings as it fell to the floor beside her. Alongside the pain Anna instantly became nauseous, as if she'd downed too much tequila too quickly. Tears streamed from her eyes, mingling with the blood oozing from a gash on her cheek. She covered her head with her hands and crunched into a foetal position.

The image of Dorothy from *The Wizard of Oz*, her favourite movie as a child, flickered into her mind. She saw Dorothy holding back the curtain, exposing the charlatan behind the illusion, and accusing him of being *a very bad man*.

Anna forced her heavy lids to open. Her own version of a *very bad man* was leaning down towards her, the point of his gleaming dagger held out in front of him, the illusion he had held her in for three days now completely shattered. She glimpsed past the sharp point and into Webber's eyes — black, lustful and full of malicious intent — and saw her death in them.

Fathoming that she had just given her final performance, yet oddly grateful to have played so perfectly, Anna felt her eyelids droop again as she allowed herself to drift towards welcome blackness.

MONDAY

CHAPTER 2

"I'm here for a 9:00 a.m. interview with Richard Wilkie. My name is Brody Taylor."

The pudgy receptionist pushed her glasses further up the bridge of her nose and checked her computer screen. She squinted in confusion.

"We don't have a Mr Wilkie based in this office."

"Yes, sorry. It's a video interview. He's calling in from Dubai."

"Ah, I see. Yes, here you are. The ground floor video conferencing suite is booked for you, Mr Taylor."

The receptionist printed off a security pass, pressed a button to open the gate, allowed him to pass through and escorted him to a meeting room labelled 'VC1'. She pushed open the door and allowed him to enter.

Impressive. She was efficient and security conscious. It made a pleasant change.

"When Mr Wilkie dials in, it should answer automatically. Is there anything I can get you? Tea, coffee perhaps?"

"I'm fine, thanks." Brody gave his best sheepish smile. "Maybe you could just wish me luck?"

She smiled obligingly. "Good luck, Mr Taylor." She shut the door behind her.

Brody quickly surveyed the room. An oval board table took up the length of the room, but looked like it had been cut in half lengthways, with six black leather seats on the curved side facing onto a massive elongated video screen, actually made up of three widescreen monitors placed side-by-side. Above the centre screen was a unit housing three cameras angled to capture two seats each. Brody knew from experience that when the Cisco TelePresence system activated, the screens would display a similarly furnished room located somewhere else in the world, giving both parties the optical illusion of one complete boardroom.

Brody dropped his leather laptop case on the table and rummaged around inside. He removed his tablet computer and placed it in front of him, flipping it open to reveal its detachable keyboard. He then pulled out a roll of silver duct tape and peeled off three strips, sticking them over the cameras. Grinning to himself at the irony of employing such a low-tech solution, he pushed a panel set into the board table and revealed the touchscreen tablet that controlled the TelePresence system. Deftly he muted the microphones in the room he was in and then searched through the address book. Twenty other Atlas Brands Inc. video conferencing suites were listed by city name. Brody chose Dubai and pressed the green button.

The screens jumped to life. Suddenly, an image of six other people sat opposite him, chit-chatting with each other. The older man in the centre noticed that someone had dialled in. His brows furrowed. "Who's that dialling in from Birmingham? Is there something wrong with your video system? It's just a black screen here."

Brody used the touchscreen control panel to send a text message to their system in Dubai. *Yes, it's Rich Wilkie here. I can see and hear you guys fine. Must be a glitch. Don't worry, I'll message you like this if I've got anything to say.*

Brody watched the older man read his message displayed on their screen three thousand miles away.

"Okay Rich. No problem. How's the weather in the UK?"

Brody typed out his answer. *It's raining, Andrew. It's April. Would you expect anything else?*

Andrew Lamont, Chief Executive Officer of Atlas Brands Inc., laughed. The woman on his left said, "Look, here's Chu in Sydney."

At that moment, the image in Brody's room shrunk to just the middle monitor, destroying the illusion of them all being in the same room. The right hand monitor suddenly displayed another room, with just one inhabitant. It was labelled Sydney. A few moments later, the remaining left-hand screen was taken up by

Munich, with three people.

Spread across the globe, the board of directors of the world's fourth largest restaurant chain and hospitality company greeted each other amiably.

"Okay, it looks as though we're all here," said Lamont. "Let's get this meeting started. For you folks in Sydney and Munich wondering about the black screen, that's Rich Wilkie in Birmingham. Seems to be a problem with the system there, but he can hear us all fine. Right, let's get down to business. Ulf, can you take us through the agenda?"

Ulf Lubber, the middle of the three people in the Munich office, walked everyone through the agenda. The item Brody was here for was fourth on the agenda, at least an hour away. He zoned out of the meeting and connected his tablet computer to the Internet via its built-in 4G SIM card. He might as well use the time productively.

Brody worked his way through his emails, spread across numerous accounts, most of which were newsletters and blog posts from the various technology and computer hacking websites he subscribed to anonymously.

While he worked, he kept one eye and one ear on the meeting. Heather Bell, Atlas Brand's Chief Financial Officer, presented the prior month's financial performance of each of their major restaurant chains, all famous brands in their local regions. Walter Chan, who managed the property portfolio, took them through expansion plans by country. Heng Chu, the Chief Information Officer sitting on his own in the Sydney office, struggled his way through his plans to integrate the IT systems of four recent restaurant chain acquisitions Atlas had made in Asia, frequently interrupted when it became clear the synergy savings the board had promised the shareholders would take much longer to realise.

"What's next, Ulf?" asked Lamont.

"We've got Marketing and the launch plans for a brand new concept." Ulf turned to the man on his right in Munich. "Over to you Tim."

Brody looked up from his computer and focused on the meeting. Adrenalin began to pump through his bloodstream.

Tim Welland, Chief Marketing Officer, began his presentation. He had connected his laptop to the TelePresence system and its screen took over the central monitor, forcing the images of the other meeting rooms to tile next to each other, now even smaller. Welland took them through a polished PowerPoint presentation, illustrated by concept artwork.

"Welcome to Barbecue Union, a brand new mid-range dining concept for the UK, Canada and Germany. Every table in our Barbecue Union outlets will have a live barbecue grille embedded within it, which customers will use to cook their own food. The food will be presented on skewers along with a selection of marinades. It will be a mix of Mediterranean, Indian, Oriental, and American cuisine. Imagine, if you will, all the fun of having your food cooked in front of you, just like the Japanese Teppanyaki restaurants, but without the expensively trained chefs. Yes, you guessed it, our customers will be those chefs."

Welland paused and surveyed his colleagues on the screens. Lots of nodding heads.

He continued his presentation, dropping into lower levels of detail, eventually hitting target market demographics, pricing strategies, menus, and launch costs. "And the best bit is that much of the marketing will be word-of-mouth; the best kind. As customers experience this totally new concept, they will mention it to everyone they know."

With a touch of triumph, Welland concluded his presentation and began taking questions. While they debated the pros and cons of this new chain, Brody pressed a button on the control tablet and the image of his room was added to the others. Just a black screen. He stood up and peeled the duct tape from the webcams in his room, revealing his face in close up on the screen, his swept back white blond hair, green eyes and carefully groomed beard filling the screen. He sat back down, his every move mirrored on the screen, and unmuting his microphone, waited for someone to notice.

"What about hygiene? Surely we'd be liable to local food safety regulations if the customers don't cook the ingredients properly?" asked Annabel Fielding, their Head of Legal, located in the Dubai office.

Just as Welland began to answer, Ulf Lubber in Germany exclaimed, "Who's that?" He pointed at his screen, the others following his direction.

Brody waved and said, "Hi."

On his tablet, Brody absent-mindedly noticed a new email arrive.

He automatically clicked it open.

"Who the hell are you, young man?" demanded Andrew Lamont. "And where's Rich Wilkie?"

"Me?" said Brody innocently, forcing himself to ignore the email. It could wait.

"I know who it is," said Chu in Sydney. "He's a 'white hat' security consultant called Brody Taylor. I recently contracted him to carry out a pentest. But what he's doing there I've no idea!"

"What the hell is a pentest?" asked the CEO.

Brody stepped in. "A penetration test is a simulated attack on your organisation's security defences to identify weaknesses. It's done through computer hacking or social engineering or, as I've done, with a combination of both."

"Social engineering?" prompted Lamont.

"The art of manipulating people into performing actions or divulging confidential information to give me the access I need. And, as you can clearly see, I've successfully broken through your security defences and have been sitting in on your board meeting for the last hour. But fortunately for you, the last part of a pentest is to report back the findings. And that's what I'm here to do."

Lamont turned on the CIO. "Did you agree to this, Chu?"

In Sydney, Chu visibly squirmed in his chair. "No. Mr Taylor was supposed to meet with me next week to present his findings. From there, I would block any holes he found and make sure we're completely secure from a real cyber attack."

Lamont turned back to Brody. "Okay, Mr Taylor, you've proved your point. Thank you for what you've done. Why don't you leave us to our board meeting and report back to Chu as planned."

"Hold on a second," said Fielding. "Did you get him to sign a confidentiality agreement, Chu? He's just heard all about our recent performance and future plans!"

"Yes, of course I did," said Chu.

Brody nodded in agreement. Rising from his seat, he paused halfway and asked. "Before I go, do you mind if I ask you one question, Mr Chu?"

Lamont splayed his hands in exasperation and shook his head in disbelief.

"Why did you hire me for a pentest right now?"

"What do you mean?" asked Chu.

"Why now? Why not a year ago? Or in three months from now?"

"It's part of our security improvement programme. We do this kind of thing all the time in IT."

"From the vulnerabilities I've exposed, I very much doubt that, Mr Chu." Brody looked at Lamont. "Mr Lamont, why don't you ask Mr Chu the same question? Maybe you'll get a straight answer."

Lamont's intent expression showed that he knew there was more going on here than was immediately apparent. "Chu?"

Chu shrugged. "I was talking with Welland about the plans for launching the new restaurant concept. He was worried that one of our competitors might break in and steal our ideas. As I've explained previously, IT doesn't have anywhere near the budget necessary to put in place a comprehensive threat protection programme. So Welland offered to pay for a pentest to at least determine how exposed we are. Who am I to turn down a gift horse like that?"

"That makes sense, doesn't it?" asked Brody. "No more to it."

Tim Welland, the man who'd waxed lyrical about his new restaurant concept a few minutes before, was strangely silent. He clasped his hands together.

"Welland, what's going on?"

"It's as Chu said."

"It's called corporate espionage, Mr Lamont." Brody said, sitting back down. "And your company is guilty of it right now. The last time I heard about a case like this was in the hotel industry. Hilton settled out of court with Starwood for $85 million."

Lamont blew his top, spittle flying everywhere. "What the fuck is going on here?"

All the executives silently studied their hands.

"The funny thing about the presentation you've just heard from Mr Welland is that I've already read about an exceptionally similar concept for a grille-based barbecue restaurant chain. But in the documents I read there was one significant difference. Your number one competitor's logo was all over them. Would you like to know where I found these documents, Mr Lamont?"

"Go on . . ." said Lamont tightly.

"As I've already mentioned, your security defences are so weak I was able to give myself access to each of your email accounts and —"

"You've read our private email?" shrieked Fielding.

"Well, yes. Fascinating reading. But the most interesting were the documents I found in Mr Welland's account."

"I can explain . . ." pleaded Welland.

As Welland attempted to defend himself under constant barrage from his CEO, Head of Legal and most of the other board members, Brody zoned out and read the email that had popped into his inbox earlier. It was from one of the members of CrackerHack entitled, *Favour Required - Will Reciprocate*. CrackerHack was an online forum used by computer hackers from all over the world to brag about their exploits and swap ideas, tips and techniques. Brody spent much of his spare time on there. The message was from a member called Crooner42, a username that Brody vaguely recognised from some of the discussion threads. Crooner42 had blasted it out to all of the subscribers to a forum entitled 'Advanced Pentest Techniques'. In it, Crooner42 explained that he had built an experimental live video-feed based Internet site that was likely to attract unwarranted attention from law agencies around the world. He'd hardened it as best he could, but needed someone deeply skilled to pentest it thoroughly, to ensure it couldn't be broken into or brought down.

Brody wondered what the 'experimental' site was for.

Crooner42 requested that members of the forum declare their interest in carrying out the work. He would then choose from one of the respondents. Brody expected that Crooner42 would select someone based on reviewing his historical activity on the site. Brody knew he would be a strong candidate and, with the Atlas Brands job now pretty much finished, was sorely tempted to offer his services. In return, Crooner42 was bartering a week's worth of his own coding services. That could always come in handy. It wasn't a bad trade for what would probably amount to just a few hours of work.

"Do you have proof of this allegation, Mr Taylor?"

Brody looked up. Lamont had asked the question.

"Well, yes of course. Give me a second."

Brody opened a new browser tab and brought up an email he had drafted earlier. He pressed send.

"I've just forwarded you all some emails sent to Mr Welland from a Janis Taplow. I believe she's a relatively new employee within the marketing organisation. Where did you hire Janis from,

Tim?"

Tim Welland replied flatly. He named their number one competitor.

"The email contains the whole launch campaign for their grille restaurant concept, presentations, financial plans, target countries, demographics, everything. And, if you open up the main presentation, you'll notice that even the concept art is very similar. In fact, the only main difference is the name of the restaurant chain."

"Got it," said Lubber, Chu and Fielding in concert, from three different locations around the world.

As they read through the offending material, Brody flipped back to Crooner42's request. He was tempted by the job, but hesitant to put himself forward until he reviewed the site in question. It was the reference to it receiving unwarranted attention from law agencies that intrigued him.

Incredulity rang in the voices from the screen as they absorbed the material Brody had just emailed them.

He checked Crooner42's profile. He presented himself as more of a coder than a hacker, someone who spent far more time programming than trying to identify exploits in systems. He'd been active on CrackerHack for three years. Satisfied, Brody clicked on the hyperlink to the so-called 'experimental' site. It was called www.SecretlyWatchingYou.com. It seemed to be a random collection of network camera and webcam feeds. Brody clicked on one, making sure his computer's speakers were muted. It showed some people working in an office, layers of desks and desktop computers. Another feed showed some fish swimming around in a fish tank. Not particularly interesting.

The Internet was full of webcam sites, the majority of which were either for viewing public places from afar in real time or for pornographic purposes. But this site claimed to have hacked into private network cameras in peoples' homes and workplaces. It was certainly unusual. It charged fees for access beyond the free taster webcam feeds on the front page. Brody couldn't really see why anyone would want to pay or what all the fuss about law agencies was about.

Surely Crooner42 was over-egging the protection the site needed to have? Who would bother to attack it? And publicly requesting help like this on CrackerHack was definitely out of the ordinary. But then Brody remembered that after this meeting, his diary was looking concerningly clear. If Crooner42 selected Brody over other forum members for the job, his elite status in the hacking community would intensify — doubly so if he quickly broke through the website's security countermeasures.

Ah, what the hell!

He returned to the original email and pressed the link Crooner42 had provided. In the blink of an eye, he had registered his interest in carrying out the pentest on SecretlyWatchingYou. Now it was down to whether Crooner42 chose him over another offer.

Brody returned his attention to the video conference.

"Looks like I'm done here," said Tim Welland, getting to his feet in Munich.

"That's the understatement of the day," commented Chu.

"You'll have my resignation in your inbox within the hour, Mr Lamont." They all waited while Welland gathered his belongings and left the room in Germany.

"Well, Mr Taylor," said Lamont. "A bit unorthodox, but I'd like to thank you for saving our company from a very embarrassing predicament, not to mention the potential law suits."

"Just doing my job."

"I think we should delay the presentation of your findings report until I'm back in the UK, which will be Monday week. I'd also like to personally shake your hand. And if everything is as insecure as you describe, it looks as though Chu will see a lot more budget going his way."

"Sounds good to me," said Brody.

"And me," said Chu, his relief evident.

Ten minutes later, Brody drove out of the Atlas Brands car park in his metallic orange and black, custom-designed Smart Fortwo coupe. It would take a good few hours to get back to London. His phone vibrated. He slowed, looked down and glanced at the message header. It was from Crooner42 and entitled 'Pentest Outcome . . .'

Brody stopped the car and clicked on the message, fully expecting to see his name in lights.

He couldn't believe what he read.

* * *

Breathlessly, DI Jenny Price lowered her umbrella and flashed her warrant card at the police constable blocking the entrance to the tall, glass-clad office building. The PC acknowledged her as "Ma'am", a phrase that always made her feel like an old maid. She pushed the revolving door.

The entrance was imposing, with high ceilings, a large, stone reception desk, and three cream leather suites placed to one side. In the centre of the foyer, a spherical water feature drew the eye momentarily from a large glass block structure standing proudly behind the reception area. Set in a brickwork layout, each rectangular glass tablet had a different company logo etched into it. There were about thirty in total.

Regaining her composure, Jenny recognised DS Alan Coombs leaning on the reception desk, his back to her. He was attempting to interview the receptionist sitting behind, but she was talking to someone on her headset.

Alan turned around and saw Jenny. "Ah Jenny, you're finally here." There was no sarcasm, just genuine relief in his voice.

Jenny automatically formed a catalogue of reasons for her lateness in her mind. She could list at least five traffic black spots she'd inched her way through in the journey across London. But she should have accounted for the Monday morning rush hour. Or she could blame the satnav, which had outsmarted her once again, taking her to South Wharf Road instead of North Wharf road. Hence her recent battle with the elements as she'd been forced to negotiate a wet and windy footbridge over Regents Canal. But blaming the satnav was akin to admitting her technophobia.

"I swam all the way," she offered, shaking out her umbrella.

Alan looked her up and down. "You're soaking. You'll catch your death."

"Al, don't worry, I'll dry off quick enough."

The fifteen years Alan had on Jenny seemed to define the fatherly manner he adopted with her, overriding any seniority she had over him in rank. She found this trait in him endearing when it was just the two of them. But when he exhibited it in front of other coppers, she wanted to scream at him.

"What's the situation, Al? All I've heard from Karim is that a young woman's body was found here this morning." She was referring to DC Karim Malik, another member of her team, who'd phoned her earlier.

Alan filled in Jenny with what he knew. The corpse was in a meeting room on the top floor. From her belongings, she had been identified as Anna Parker, a second-year Music student from Trinity Laban Conservatoire in Greenwich. Her throat had been slit with a knife. No weapon found. Initial observations were that she had probably been brutally raped before being killed.

He concluded, "Poor kid."

Jenny's barriers had instinctively risen as she listened to Alan's dispassionate recount of events. She'd survived two years as a Detective Inspector in the Camden Borough Murder Investigation Team by projecting an invisible, impenetrable shield that kept the horrors of the job out and the emotions buried inside.

"Any idea when she was killed?"

"That's what I've just been checking at reception. According to this," he held up a large transparent evidence bag, a visitor's book inside, "she signed into the building last Friday at 5:20 p.m. The pathologist just arrived a few minutes ago. He should be able to confirm time of death."

"Does the visitor book show who she was here to see?"

"Yes, a W. Webber of WMA Associates for a 5:30 meeting."

"Does the receptionist recall the victim?"

"No, she only works mornings. Job share. I've got the details of Friday afternoon's receptionist." Alan handed her the evidence bag. "Here, you take this upstairs. I'll track down the other receptionist."

"Thanks, Al, you're a real gem. Where's his lord and master?"

"Da Silva's upstairs pissing off the crime scene team with inane questions."

Da Silva had been their DCI for the last two weeks. He'd been promoted from a DI in the Kidnap Unit in Scotland Yard to run the Camden MIT. On a murder case, his rank made him the Senior Investigating Officer in name, but not yet in action as far as Jenny and the other members of his MIT were concerned. He seemed inexperienced in how to effectively prioritise the lines of enquiry and balance the limited resources within his team. Jenny was not alone in wondering if he'd been fast-tracked through the ranks too quickly; another minority officer benefiting from the Met's positive discrimination policies. Although, why a black man from Birmingham had a name like Raul Da Silva, Jenny had yet to find out.

The doors to one of the four lifts slid open. The occupant made a beeline for them. "Not more police?" the man said, tetchily.

"And you are?" asked Jenny.

"Clive Evans. I'm the building manager here." Evans held his hand out, very business-like. Jenny shook it and introduced herself and Alan.

The building manager's lanky frame towered over both her and Alan. Jenny assessed that the grey pinstripe suit Evans wore must have been custom made. There was no way you could buy such a long suit in your average high street shop.

"Can you lead the way?" asked Jenny, walking purposely towards the lifts.

He overtook her in three gangly strides. "Uh, ok. This way."

Jenny followed Evans to the lifts, hoping the squelching in her shoes was less noticeable than it felt. They stood side-by-side.

When the doors slid to a close, Evans asked, "How long will the top floor be cordoned off? The officers upstairs won't tell me anything. Most of our meeting rooms are located on that floor and they're all booked out this morning. I can see this is a serious situation but my tenants are already complaining. I need to tell them something."

Jenny watched his reflection in the lift's mirrored doors as he whined on, but it was the way he looked down his nose at her that wound her up.

"Mr Evans, you do realise that there's been a murder? A *murder*. That's a damn sight more important than a few business meetings being cancelled."

"I do understand that, Detective Inspector. But what should I tell the tenants?"

"Seems to me that most business meetings take place in Starbucks these days. I believe there's one just around the corner."

Evans opened his mouth to respond indignantly and then thought better of it.

They stood in silence as the lift glided upwards. Jenny checked her shoes, half-expecting to see a puddle oozing out from the shiny black patent heels. She noticed that, in her struggle through the downpour, one side of her white blouse had come loose and was showing below the line of her fitted grey jacket, which had also come undone. She tucked the blouse back into the grey skirt and glanced self-consciously at Evans' reflection, only to discover he was staring straight at her reflected breasts, his lips slightly parted. She was used to it, but most men immediately looked away when they realised they had been caught staring. She looked down and understood. Her blouse had become transparent from the wet and her bra was on full show, leaving little to the imagination.

"Seen enough?" she demanded, buttoning up the jacket. She felt her face redden.

He switched to staring at his feet and mumbled something that might have been an apology.

As the lift slowed, Jenny ran fingers through her wet shoulder-length auburn hair in an attempt to get it back under control and recover some sense of professionalism.

The doors parted on the eighteenth floor, revealing a uniformed PC with white overshoes covering his boots. Immediately he said, "Sorry, this floor is closed . . ."

"It's okay, Constable," said Jenny, flashing her warrant card.

"Okay, ma'am. SOCO says you'll need to wear these." He handed out paper slippers to them both, which they obediently put on.

"This way," Evans said, turning left. Jenny followed.

"You said 'tenants'. What do you mean by 'tenants'?"

"The companies that rent office space within this building. Customers of Flexbase, the owner of this building."

Jenny thought of all the logos behind reception. "So this Flexbase just rents office space then?"

Evans paused. "Well no, there's a lot more to it than that. Many of our clients are small companies who can't afford to lease their own permanent office, what with the multi-year contracts and all of the infrastructure costs required. Even if they signed a lease somewhere, they'd need to furnish it, install the IT infrastructure, staff a reception desk or switchboard ... It all adds up, you know. Thousands, if not tens of thousands just in setup costs alone."

Jenny guessed that Evans had probably given this sales pitch many times before. His hands motioned animatedly as they walked. "That's where Flexbase comes in. We provide ready to use offices with no upfront costs and no long-term lease. Our switchboard even answers the phone in their company's name, presenting the illusion of a much larger company. And we take care of everything. From printers and photocopiers right through to AV equipment and meeting rooms."

Jenny looked around. The long corridor was sparsely decorated, just two inoffensive pastel shades of green, the lighter tone on top. Door after door broke the monotony, with the odd framed print in between, each one showcasing more swathes of pastel colours. Not proper pictures. None of the offices had windows onto the corridor and the doors were solid wood. Anything could go on behind them. They rounded a corner and Jenny saw the crime scene tape three doors down.

"So really, you're like a hotel with concierge and room service facilities, but for companies instead of people."

Evans spluttered at her deliberately crass comparison.

"Is WMA Associates one of your tenants?"

"Yes, they're on the third floor. Been with us for about five years."

She changed tack. "Who found the body? You?"

"No, Barry Pitman from Trendal. They're located on the tenth floor."

Jenny halted just before the door to the crime scene.

"Okay, thanks, Mr Evans. No need for you to come any further."

"Uh, sure," he said hesitantly and then, looking relieved, said, "Yes, I'll leave you to it then." He turned back the way they'd come.

She had attended numerous murder scenes, all of them hideous. Even when the victims were criminals themselves, falling foul of their own kind, the sight and stench of lifeless, mutilated bodies always shook Jenny's view of the world. Murder wrenched someone's life away unnaturally. It stole their future. In a way, it was a theft of the most grievous kind.

Jenny steeled herself and stepped around the tape into the room.

A surreal sight confronted her. Not the photographer flashing his camera every few seconds. Not the three-man SOCO team kneeling down in their white, hooded bodysuits, scraping trace evidence into envelopes and plastic bags. Not the pathologist taking rectal temperature readings from the body of a young girl, naked from the waist down, lying face down under a nearby table. Not even the blood that had spewed from beneath the poor girl's neck, spread into a vast dark stain before being soaked up by the carpet tiles. No, all of these details were normal. Well, for a murder scene. What was surreal was the cello in the centre of the room, neatly balanced on its endpin and leaning against an office chair.

In the sterile surroundings of the corporate meeting room, the large musical instrument was completely out of place. Fifteen or so desks were joined together in one long, extended curve around three sides of the room, surrounding the upright cello in the centre. Together with the bow lying on the floor next to it, Jenny had the impression of some kind of musical recital gone terminally wrong; the audience long since departed.

One of the crime scene investigators was examining the legs of the table that the dead girl lay under. He looked up, noticing Jenny. The bright blue eyes between the hood and the respiratory mask narrowed. Jenny recognised Jason Edmonds, a crime scene manager well known for feistily protecting the integrity of crime scenes.

Edmonds signalled Jenny to stay where she was and came over to her. "DI Price, if it wasn't for your fucking boss and all his bollocks about . . ." he lowered his voice and put on a Brummie accent in an impression of Da Silva, "'needing your feminine insights', the nearest you'd have got to my crime scene would have been the reception downstairs."

"You're softening up, Jason. I'm just surprised you haven't emptied all eighteen floors and kicked everyone outside in the rain."

"Don't think it didn't cross my mind. You know I can't have all and sundry traipsing through here like it's some macabre fairground sideshow. It's the integrity of the evidence we gather here that will be used to convict someone."

"I'm sure that's true, but only if we catch him first. And for that to happen we need some insights into the how and the why of it. That's where me and my weird, womanly ways come in."

Reluctantly, Edmonds removed his mask, revealing a slight smirk. His eyes sparkled with humour. "Alright, alright. Let me tell you what we know so far and then you can piss off more quickly."

"Only if I can come in."

"Bloody hell, Jenny. Okay, but be careful and don't step on anything."

Jenny made her way towards the centre of the room, donning a pair of latex gloves she retrieved from her coat pocket. Edmonds followed her, watching her every step.

"Where is the DCI anyway?"

"He's gone off to interview the bloke who found the body."

She paused by the cello.

"Don't . . ." warned Edmonds.

Jenny had been tempted to touch it. It was the way it was so finely balanced that enticed her. Instead, she walked around to the rear of the chair, out of its way. She knelt down on one knee, to get her eye-line closer to the victim's. Edmonds stood to one side of her. The pathologist finished up and retreated to Jenny's other side. Edmonds introduced him as Dr Gorski.

He nodded his head in a formal manner, as if meeting royalty, and stated, "I am pleased to make your acquaintance, DI Price." The pathologist's accent was Eastern European and shed some light on his uncustomary social graces. Unlike Edmonds and the other crime scene officers who all wore standard white over suits, Gorski's mauve suit was unconventional.

Jenny returned the pleasantry and then turned to Edmonds. "Her name's Anna Parker?"

"Yes. In her handbag we found a student photo ID."

Gorski said, "I believe she was struck over the head with a solid object and she fell to the floor there." He pointed to the front of the chair, where a dark spot stained the flooring.

"We've not found anything that fits the bill," said Edmonds.

"I will present some theories later when I carry out a detailed examination of the head wound at the morgue," Gorski continued, pointing at some dark streaks running from the chair towards where the body now lay. "Her hands were tied in front, like this." He held his wrists together by his thighs. "Then she was dragged to the table there and forcibly positioned across it, face down, and very likely sexually assaulted from behind. I will determine that for sure after the post-mortem. He cut through the clothes, right up her back. As you can see, the blouse is sliced in half from behind and the panties and skirt have been thrown in the corner over there. There is a run of cuts from her left buttock up to her neck, indicating he used a blade with two sharp edges, like a dagger or some other kind of double-edged knife."

Jenny saw Anna had self-consciously held on tight to the front of the sliced apart blouse right through to the end. She had been a pretty girl, not tall, but slender, with wavy, long brown hair. Her eyes were dark and lifeless. Tear-tracks had dried on her cheeks.

"Once he was done, he pulled her head back with one hand, probably by her hair, and sliced her throat with the other. Most likely the same knife, but I will confirm later."

On the table and splattered all over the floor and walls beyond was more blood than Jenny had ever seen. She closed her eyes momentarily. She needed to feel, but not let the feelings get the better of her. The violence was overwhelming, but it had a controlled air about it. The way the cello had been stood upright leaning on the chair. That would have to have been done after she'd been killed.

Jenny's eyes blinked open again. Her imaginary shields needed to stay up for her to function and be useful.

"Then her lifeless body slid down to the floor where it is now," concluded Dr Gorski.

They stayed silent for a few moments, standing side by side, each lost in thought. At the rear of the room, the photographers and two other SOCOs had stopped what they had been doing. They'd listened respectfully to the pathologist's dispassionate interpretation of Anna Parker's terrible last few minutes of life.

"She was here as a visitor. I think he made her play the cello for him first," said Jenny. She made a mental note to check whether anyone had heard music on Friday evening. It would have been memorable in such bureaucratic surroundings. "He would have sat over there to listen." She pointed at the head of the room where there was an absence of plastic yellow numbered evidence markers. "He may have sat behind that desk or on the edge of it. There may be prints or trace evidence."

"Hmm," Edmonds said, doubtfully, "Okay, we'll check."

"Then, as she got into the piece, he moved behind her. Perhaps she closed her eyes while playing. Then he struck."

"But why?" asked Gorski.

"One step at a time," said Jenny. "There's a far more pragmatic question to be answered first."

"What is that, then?"

Jenny looked around. Her mind's eye passed beyond the walls of the meeting room, expanded to take in the whole top floor, the lifts and then the seventeen floors below full of businessmen and women, ties, shirts, blouses, pin-stripes, hands shaking on deals done; the formality and etiquette of commerce, pound signs and spreadsheets, stocks and shares, managers and secretaries, printers and photocopiers, computers and graphs, and desks with the token family photo from real life.

Music had no role in this sober and dreary environment.

"Why here?"

CHAPTER 3

Brody slowed to a stop in the middle of Upper Street and indicated right. He was adjacent to an empty residents-only parking space outside his apartment block. Cars backed up behind him as he waited for a gap to appear in the oncoming traffic. He recalled how drunk his flatmate had been last night, and it dawned on Brody that Leroy would be up by now, grumpy and belligerent. He glanced over to his left and noticed a small gap between parked cars outside Bruno's Coffee House, located directly across the road from his flat. It was as if fate was telling him something.

After all, having completed the Atlas Brands job that morning, it wasn't like he had a load of other jobs lined up. Especially as the message he'd read earlier had announced that Crooner42 had awarded the pentest job to someone else. Brody had to admit to himself that he'd only wanted to win the job in order to further reinforce his elite status in the global hacker community. He didn't actually need a week's worth of anyone's coding services. The real prize would have been to make sure that Crooner42 let everyone on the forums know that he had selected Brody for the job. It was the online equivalent of word-of-mouth, one of the few forms of publicity available within the hacker community. Brody had taken years to be recognised as elite and little wins like this reinforced his status in the minds of his fellow hackers. Not being a malicious 'black hat' hacker, Brody didn't have access to the other main form of publicity available to the most notorious in that field, which was to see their codenames on the front page of the news after breaking into a famous website, an approach that certainly achieved infamy but ran the risk of being hunted down vigorously by law enforcement agencies.

The message he'd received from Crooner42 had only told him he'd been unsuccessful, without announcing to whom he'd awarded the work instead. Although Brody's ego was a little bruised, he felt compelled to add insult to injury by trying to find out the identity of the chosen hacker. He would log on from Bruno's.

Brody swapped the indicator to point left and drove directly into the space outside Bruno's, parking his Smart car with the front bumper facing towards the kerb in the way only a Smart car can park. From behind, Brody heard the screeching of rubber on wet tarmac as the car behind impatiently accelerated away.

At the very least the coffee would be good; better than having turned right and ending up facing Leroy in the throes of the morning after. Earlier, Brody had been woken by Leroy and Danny returning from their first night out as a couple in over a fortnight. He had listened to Danny slur loudly that he needed to be up early for a business meeting and then heard his footsteps rebound off the parquet flooring as he made his way to the guest bedroom. Leroy called out that he'd make them both a nightcap and then proceeded to bash his way around the kitchen, slamming cupboard doors while swearing profusely at the kettle boiling noisily, before eventually settling himself in front of the television, volume on maximum, playing his beloved Xbox, Danny apparently forgotten.

When the snoring began a few minutes later, Brody forced himself out of bed to find Leroy sprawled asleep on the sofa, an untouched mug of steaming tea on the glass coffee table. Brody half-cajoled, half-carried Leroy to his room and dumped him unceremoniously on his bed, next to his neatly tucked-in partner, who failed to stir at the commotion. Brody turned off the Xbox and returned to his own room, now completely awake. It had taken at least twenty pages on his Kindle before Brody's eyelids became heavy enough to drop off again … only for his alarm to go off a couple of hours later for the drive up to Atlas Brands in Birmingham. As he left, he heard another alarm sound in Leroy's room and placed a silent bet with himself against Danny making it to his business meeting on time.

Brody entered Bruno's, shaking the rain from his leather jacket. He loved that the independent cosmopolitan coffee lounge wasn't one of the coffee chains that had taken over every busy street in London where baristas operated in little more than factory lines, giving minimal thought to the quality or style of their craft. He particularly loved that, in Bruno's, they waited the tables European style, bringing the coffee to you. But most of all he loved it for being located opposite his home.

"Mr Brody! Welcome. Welcome." It was Stefan the head barista. Brody had never met the eponymous Bruno, assuming he even existed. Stefan, who was at least a foot shorter than Brody's six foot two, wore an immaculately clean black apron over a white shirt and black trousers. His black hair was slicked back with wax. He whipped the white cloth from his shoulder and wiped the already clean table in the window recess by the front door. "Look, your favourite seat is free. The gods are being kind today, no?"

Stefan indicated the scratched, studded leather high-back chair next to the now sparkling table. Brody thanked him and sat down. Bruno's boasted a collection of colourful, worn leather chairs and sofas, randomly arranged in groups around plain brown tables. It was about half full, a few small groups talking quietly and five or six loners reading newspapers or swiping their tablet devices. Italian accordion music piped discreetly from ceiling speakers.

"What will Mr Brody have today? No! Don't tell me . . . " He stared intently at Brody as if trying to read his mind. Brody smiled. It was their usual game. "It's cold and raining out there, so nothing iced I think. Hmm . . . and it's before lunch so nothing filling . . . I know – a caffè macchiato!"

Brody stroked his stubbled chin, as if considering.

"I have it now," said Stefan, "A double macchiato. Am I right, Mr Brody?"

"Spot on, Stefan. You're like an Italian version of Sherlock Holmes."

A few minutes later the barista brought Brody a perfect double caffè macchiato, accompanied by a tall glass of tap water. Brody complimented him on the coffee. The barista, his job done, left him. Brody knew that he could spend hours here without feeling the need to order again. Stefan would occasionally stop by and refill his glass with iced water from a jug.

The shop offered wireless Internet access, but Brody only connected to public Wi-Fi hotspots when desperate. They were completely unsafe. Instead, he'd installed a directional Wi-Fi antenna by his living room window, pointing across the road towards the coffee shop. It boosted the signal of his own private wireless network so that he could securely connect to the Internet and drink high-quality coffee at the same time. The seat by the front window was his favourite because it gave him the strongest signal, not that Stefan was aware of this.

He'd masked his home wireless network from broadcasting its presence to discourage other casual coffee drinkers from picking it up on their devices. However, a literate computer user could easily overcome that so he had also enabled full WPA-Enterprise security to give him the highest levels of authentication and encryption.

Brody opened his tablet PC, connected to his private network and logged in.

The browser was conveniently displaying the CrackerHack forum from when he'd closed the computer in the Atlas Brands meeting earlier. He skim-read the chat logs to see what had been posted since Crooner42 had awarded the pentest work earlier.

Soon enough, Brody spotted a relevant discussion thread. The counter in the top corner showed thirty-two members of the forum were currently online. The actual conversation thread had been started by Matt_The_Hatter and was now between seven or eight of them collectively trying to deduce who had been awarded the job. That meant the rest of them, Brody included, were passively listening in without declaring their presence. Of course, like Brody, no one was admitting to having registered an interest in carrying out the pentest, in order to avoid being shown up as not having been selected by Crooner42. New posts appeared in real time.

Crooner42: Thanks everyone for the offers of help on SWY.

Matt_The_Hatter: It's okay Crooner-boy, you can let them know who you've asked to do the work. I'm not modest.

Crooner42: Didn't think you'd want everyone to know, Matty-boy. But okay, yes. It's official – you got the job.

Brody allowed himself a self-satisfactory smile and sipped his coffee, appreciating the strong flavour and smooth viscosity.

Crooner42 must have chosen Matt_The_Hatter based on the self-penned profiles on the forum. If he'd bothered to look through the posts written in the various forums, he'd have realised that Matt_The_Hatter was arrogant, confrontational, rude and probably the last person you'd ever choose to help you do anything. But Matt_The_Hatter's arrogance wasn't unfounded. He was damn good, possibly even in Brody's class. It was just that his hostile nature and self-importance got in the way. Brody inferred from Crooner42's 'Matty-boy' retort he may already be regretting his choice of penetration tester.

A few members offered Matt_The_Hatter their congratulations. Brody sportingly offered his, as well.

Fingal: Yes, well done Matt

Most hackers carefully devised their online monikers, which had to be completely unique. Few had any similarity to their real name; usually a closely guarded secret, but the chosen username would often reveal something about their interests or style. Two of the most famous hackers in history were 'Cha0s' and 'MafiaBoy', their names chosen to reflect their antisocial approach to the world. Numbers were often used instead of letters to reflect geek-speak and to achieve uniqueness, but Brody believed it showed a lack of imagination.

Brody had based his Fingal username on the hero of some old Scottish poems, secretly referencing that Brody's ancestry was from Scotland, something that was very visible in the real world because of his blond hair and freckled skin. And if that wasn't enough, the meaning of the name Fingal was 'white stranger', which Brody mentally linked to his own chosen profession of being a white hat hacker. There was one other reason for choosing Fingal, but only his best friend Leroy was privy to this.

He was about to click away, when —

Matt_The_Hatter: So come on then Crooner. Who else offered their services? We all wanna know.

Brody waited. Surely Crooner42 wouldn't be dumb enough to list everyone? That was against online etiquette.

Mawrpheus: Yeah, Crooner. Who else offered?
Random_Ness: Sure. Let's see. Who did Matt beat for the job?

Brody knew that Mawrpheus and Random_Ness wouldn't have responded to Crooner42's request for penetration testing help because they didn't have the skills. They were 'script kiddies', whose hacking skills were limited to using pre-packaged tools written by others: proper hackers, like Brody. They were just stirring up trouble. He wanted to type something that would deter Crooner42 from replying, but couldn't think how to word it without giving away that he had been one of those who had proffered his services.

Crooner42: Well, there was only one other . . .

Brody couldn't believe it.
Just one? Shit, that was him.
He was about to be named. And worse, shamed into losing to that arrogant prick, Matt_The_Hatter. And the forum members all knew he was online because, just two minutes ago, he'd naively offered his congratulations to Matt_The_Hatter.
No one posted anything.
Brody and thirty-one — no, word was spreading as the total now showed thirty-five — other hackers from all over the world held their collective virtual breath.

Crooner42: . . . it was Fingal

"Fuck!" shouted Brody loudly. "Crooner, you fucking idiot!" He became aware of other customers in the café turning to stare at him. Behind the coffee counter, Stefan paused from frothing milk and looked over. Brody apologised, lifting both hands in the air in supplication.

Matt_The_Hatter: Awww, unlucky Fingal. The best man clearly won.
Mawrpheus: Loser!
Doc_Doom: Fingal, ignore them. They're just fucking idiots. Crooner42, you should be banned from these forums. I'm reporting you to the moderator for breaching forum etiquette. Matt, grow the fuck up.

Brody appreciated Doc_Doom stepping in. He was a good friend.

How could Crooner42 have named him like that? Stupid things like this could negatively affect everyone's perception of him. And perception was the only reality in cyberspace.

Matt_The_Hatter: Fingal? We all know you're there. Got anything to say?

Brody considered his options. Attack or bow down gracefully? Brody's fingers flew over the keys.

Fingal: Fuck off Matt. I offered my congratulations earlier. That should be enough. The fact that Crooner chose you over me for a job like this already shows how dumb he is. And if he's that dumb, that means SWY will have holes so big in it that even you might be able to help him.
Matt_The_Hatter: Fuck you Fingal.
Random_Ness: Fight! Fight!
Crooner42: Shit, I'm sorry everyone.
Matt_The_Hatter: There's no way you're better than me, Fingal.
Fingal: Matt, you couldn't hack your way into a lidless jam jar.

Brody was indignant. In all his years online, he'd never found himself in such a ludicrous predicament. And in full view of his hacker peers. This whole episode reminded him of the school playground. After his older brother had died, Brody's childhood had been full of bullies with him as a defenceless victim. This type of goading brought it all back. The only difference was that, online, he could fight back. But the emotions were still the same. His fingers shook as the adrenalin coursed through. He downed his coffee in an attempt to calm himself. It had gone cold.

Crooner42: Perhaps if you both did it?
Matt_The_Hatter: No fucking way. You already made your choice.
Doc_Doom: Crooner does have a point. I believe there's an obvious way to settle this. Matt. Fingal. We treat it as a pwning competition. The first one of you that gets root on Crooner's SWY site reports back here. . .

'Pwning', derived from typing in 'owning' incorrectly — the 'p' and 'o' keys being next to each other on a standard Western keyboard — was geek-speak for hacking in and taking ownership of a system. 'Getting root' was taking full administrator control of it and achieving the highest level of security access: meaning you could do anything to it. Brody had done both many times, but these days it was becoming much harder as website security defences became stronger. Crooner42 may be an idiot, but he was bright enough to have done a thorough job in protecting his webcam site before publicly asking for a pentest from some of the world's best hackers.

Doc_Doom: . . .and then, live with us all watching, you run a script to replace SWY's front page with your own username in massive fonts. Then we'll all know for sure who pwned the site and, once and for all, we'll all know who's the better out of the two of you. Do you both accept the challenge?

Brody laughed out loud at the puerility of the situation. Stefan looked up from behind the huge coffee machine, and two nearby patrons stopped talking. Brody held up his hand in apology again.

Crooner42: Come on everyone, there's no need for this.
Doc_Doom: Crooner, keep out of this. Anyway, you're the one who came on this forum asking for a comprehensive pentest. Now you could get two for one, from two of the best.
Matt_The_Hatter: I'm in.

Brody was caught and he knew it. Failure to accept the challenge would look bad, especially as he really had offered to carry out the pentest in the first place.

Doc_Doom: Fingal, you in?

But if he lost the challenge, it would irretrievably ruin his elite status in the hacker community, something every hacker prized far more than anything else. He typed his answer, deliberately flippant, although he felt nothing like it.

Fingal: Sure, sounds like fun. I'm in.

* * *

Jenny found DCI Raul Da Silva on the twelfth floor in an empty office he'd temporarily requisitioned as his base of operations. Leaning all the way back in a leather executive chair behind an impressive oak desk, he'd swung around to take in the view of a dank, grey London. The incessant rain caressed the floor-to-ceiling windows, rivulets of water streaming downwards. He chatted loudly on his mobile, his back to her.

"I don't care what they're complaining about, DC Malik, you make damn sure that the constable at the front door understands that he's not to let any press in. Got it?"

Jenny walked around the desk and pressed her head to the window. She welcomed the bracing cold on her forehead. It helped clear the brutal images of the murdered girl six floors above. Far below, a colourful bunch of umbrellas had gathered outside the entrance. Media vans were double-parked on the road nearby. Television cameras poked out from under rain covers and pointed at the building.

Da Silva noticed Jenny, straightened his chair and ended his call.

"Can you believe this? The press has arrived and want to be allowed in the building — our crime scene — so that they can get out of the rain."

"It is very wet out there," she said absently. A barge powered slowly along Regents Canal, a barely perceptible wake behind it.

"What's with you, DI Price?"

"Nothing, guv." Jenny pulled herself together and took a seat on the other side of the desk. Da Silva pivoted round, placed his massive hands on the table and leaned forward. On the desk stood an improbably huge Starbucks takeaway cup.

"Have we tracked down the other receptionist yet? Looks like she's the last one to have seen the victim alive."

Jenny didn't bother correcting him with the fact that surely the killer last saw Anna Parker alive.

"Alan . . . I mean DS Coombs is picking her up now."

She'd corrected herself because Da Silva didn't like using first names. Being both newly promoted and newly transferred to lead Holborn's MIT, addressing everyone by rank and surname was a technique he employed to reinforce his seniority. Hopefully, he'd one day figure out that facing adversity as a team, day after day, forged a natural closeness that necessitated the informality of forenames and nicknames.

"What about time of death?"

"One of the tenants on the floor below recalled hearing music on Friday evening just as he was leaving for home. Even though it was faint, he remembered as it was out of the norm. He just assumed it was part of a computer presentation"

"What time was this?"

"About six-thirty. He knows because he made his usual train at Paddington."

"So she was alive at six-thirty."

"And dead not long after, according to Dr Gorski, the pathologist."

"What about CCTV?"

"It only covers the reception area. Mr Evans, the building manager, says it's stored and managed remotely at the Flexbase headquarters in Docklands."

"Next of kin?"

"Trinity College gave us her home address. She's originally from Torquay. Devon police have been informed and they're informing the parents. She lives with some other students in Charlton, just round the corner from Greenwich. I'll send DC Malik there in a minute. I'm going to head there too when I finish here."

"That's fine with me."

She hadn't asked his permission, but he acted as if he'd deigned to grant it. He took a sip of his coffee through the hole in the plastic lid. Jenny took the opportunity to jump in and ask her own question before he could hit her with another of his.

"Anything from the guy who found the body?"

"Barry Pitman? He says he had the meeting room booked first thing this morning, showed up, discovered the body, reported it and then buggered off. I tracked him down to the Starbucks round the corner. He'd relocated his meeting to the coffee shop as if nothing serious had happened. Can you believe it? There were eleven of them huddled around his laptop. He didn't like me taking him to one side in the middle of his sales pitch, that's for sure. Wouldn't stop moaning about some big deal he was trying to close."

"Anything to link him as a suspect?"

"I doubt it, but let's check him out fully." Da Silva leaned forward and lowered his voice, conspiratorially. "Pitman was really insensitive about the murdered girl. Talk about self-obsessed. Know what I did? I dragged him back from Starbucks then and there on the pretext of getting his prints to eliminate him. It could easily have waited. He moaned all the way back about how I'd ruined the deal he was doing. Certainly made me feel much better!"

Jenny was astonished. Not at Da Silva's actions — she probably would have done much the same — but that he'd let his barrier slip a little in front of her. She couldn't decide whether he was opening up a little or if he was just showing off. The fact that he'd somehow had time to order himself a grande caffè latte made her think he'd stretched the truth a bit.

Someone knocked at the door behind them. DC Fiona Jones leant on the doorframe, her black bob neatly in place, precision-cut fringe unaffected by the weather. Fiona had been appointed to Da Silva's team just a month ago; her first detective post. She was eager to please, worked long hours, and seemed to have already become 'one of the boys' without losing her femininity – a rare achievement.

Jenny still felt bedraggled from the soaking she had endured running between her car and the Flexbase office building. As she'd arrived on the twelfth floor to meet up with Da Silva, Jenny had spotted the ladies' toilets and dived in, relieved to spot a hand dryer rather than paper towels. She'd contorted herself under its downwards blast of hot air, and managed to dry out her blouse, grey suit, shoes and even her hair. A retouch of lipstick and mascara and she'd felt ready to re-join the investigation. But seeing Fiona still made her feel inadequate. Jenny wondered how she managed to stay perfectly pristine all the time.

"I checked out WMA Associates as you asked, Jenny," said Fiona. "They've got nothing to do with music. They're a tax audit firm. Apparently, WMA stands for Wilfred MacDonald Advisors. I've got Lawrence MacDonald here. He says he runs the London practice. His dad is Wilfred MacDonald, but he retired years ago."

"Okay. Bring him in," said Da Silva.

Fiona returned with a middle-aged man, so dull and grey that if Jenny had had to guess his occupation, accountant would have been top of the list. The only exception was the flash of luminescent green from the frames of his designer glasses.

"Is it true about the poor girl? Some kind of murder?" he asked.

Jenny looked Fiona in the eye, but she shook her head.

"What makes you say murder, Mr MacDonald?"

"Only because of the questions the press asked me as I arrived at the office a few minutes ago."

"Shit!" Da Silva stood up, leaned on the window and stared down twelve floors. Jenny had never heard him swear before. "I'd better sort this out before it gets out of hand. Detective Inspector Price, you take it from here. Excuse me, Mr MacDonald." Taking his mobile phone from his pocket, he left the office. His coffee was left on the desk.

"Did the press say her name?" asked Jenny, standing so as not to be the only one left sitting down.

"No? Please tell me it wasn't one of my employees."

"No, we don't believe so. Her name was Anna Parker. Do you know her?"

"Sorry, no."

"What about a W. Webber?"

MacDonald thought for a minute. "No. Not a name I recognise. Should I?"

"The signing-in book has a W. Webber from your company down for the victim's arrival last Friday evening. Do you know anyone with the surname Webber? A friend? A client, perhaps? A supplier? Someone who knows WMA?"

MacDonald thought for a moment. "None that comes to mind. But we can go downstairs and check our contacts database if you like."

Fiona said, "Thanks. Let's do that in a few minutes."

Jenny walked up and down the length of the window. She slowly articulated a line of thought that was forming in her mind. "Okay, let's assume this Webber person was pretending to be from your company. How could he do that? He's booked a meeting room. And yet you know nothing about it?"

At that moment, Jenny saw Alan through the interior glass wall of the office, accompanied by Evans. She waved them over.

"No, why should I? Any of my staff can book a meeting room. We just phone reception."

Alan and Evans entered the office.

Jenny said to the building manager, "Walk me through how you book a meeting room in this place."

Evans ignored Jenny. "Hello, Mr MacDonald. I'd like to apologise for this inconvenience. I'm sure we'll have everything back to normal in an hour or so."

Jenny wanted to slap him. He acted like a tube driver announcing a short delay to his passengers. "As I said to you in the lift earlier, Mr Evans, someone has been murdered. It's a very serious situation, and not one we can take lightly. I think you'll find it might take more than an hour or so to get back to normal."

Out of Evans' line of sight, Alan winked at Jenny and said gravely, "Maybe as much as the whole day. Perhaps two."

Evans' face whitened.

MacDonald mediated. "The more you can do to help the police, I'm sure the quicker they'll be done."

"Well, uh yes. I'm sorry. I know it's more than an inconvenience, but what I was trying to say was —"

Alan persisted, "Meeting rooms, Mr Evans. How do they get booked?"

"Uh, yes. Let me see." He took a breath. "Meeting rooms can be booked by any of our customers already leasing space in this building or any Flexbase customer leasing space in any of our other serviced offices around the country. Well, saying that, anyone could phone up and book a meeting room. All they'd need is a credit card. We have this concept called Local Meeting —"

"Credit card?" interrupted Jenny, spotting an angle to follow here. "You mean we can see the credit card details that were used to book the room on Friday?"

"Well, yes. That's assuming it wasn't an existing Flexbase tenant with an account. Like WMA here. If it was an existing customer, no credit cards are needed. Just their customer account number, phone number and email address of the person from the company. Then we add it to the company's bill and invoice at the end of the month."

"Can you get me the details of the booking for the room on Friday?" Jenny then forced herself to add, "Please."

"Sure, I'll just go and ask my assistant..."

Jenny picked up the phone on the desk and handed the receiver to Evans. "Will this work?"

"Uh, actually no. It's an IP phone. It doesn't work until someone logs into it first."

Spotting the look of malice in Jenny's eyes, Evans pulled out his mobile phone. He asked his assistant to pull up the records for meeting room eighteen-twelve for the Friday just gone. A pause, then, holding his hand over the mouthpiece, he said to Jenny, "Sorry, not a credit card booking. It was booked out to WMA using their account number..."

MacDonald exclaimed, "That's not possible!"

Fiona placed a hand on MacDonald's arm.

Evans continued, "...In the name of a William Webber. He booked it from 4:00 p.m. through to 7:00 p.m. He gave his phone number as the main switchboard number that WMA uses."

"How do you request a room?" asked Fiona. "Phone? Email?"

"You can book by phone, email or even through our website. Whichever method you use, we always ask for an email address for the booking confirmation to be sent to."

"Which method was used?"

Evans repeated the question into his phone. "They can't tell. Perhaps the IT people in headquarters can tell?"

"Okay, we'll check that later," said Fiona. Jenny knew the DC was doing a far better job dealing with these technology-related issues than she ever could. "What email address was given?"

Evans relayed the answer: "William.webber@wmallp.co.uk."

"But we don't have a William Webber, I tell you," MacDonald persevered. "Hold on, I'll phone my IT guy to see if that address is on our email system." MacDonald pulled out his mobile, dialled a number and started issuing instructions.

Fiona asked Evans, "Can you tell when the booking was originally made?"

Evans relayed it into his phone. The answer came, "Two days before." His eyes widened. "No way! Apparently, the same person also booked the four other meeting rooms on the same floor for the same times. That's the whole damn floor!"

A chill ran through Jenny's body.

"I suppose being that late on a Friday afternoon meant they were all available?" Alan surmised.

"Well yes, I suppose. It's typically the quietest time of the week. Everyone wants to get home for the weekend."

MacDonald then spoke, "No, we don't have an address with that name on the WMA email system. And my IT guy says that, as he doesn't have it set up, it doesn't exist and never has."

Jenny summarised, to make sure she had it right. "So, two days prior, someone with access to WMA's Flexbase account number booked the whole top floor on Friday from 4:00 p.m. onwards. And they gave a fake name and email address that made it look like it was someone from WMA."

"So, what would happen if the email address used for the booking was fake?" Fiona asked Evans.

Evans said he didn't know and relayed the question into his phone. "My assistant doesn't know either. She's just patching me through to IT in Head Office." A minute later, Evans repeated the question and listened. "Apparently, we just type it into the booking system. As the domain name — you know, the bit after the '@' sign in the email address — matches the customer's, no one would have questioned it. The booking system sends out a confirmation email." He listened some more and then relayed the next bit with a fatalistic tone. "But if the email address didn't exist, it would bounce back to the booking system's own email address and —"

"— no one ever looks at that," finished Fiona for him.

Evans nodded.

MacDonald turned to Evans, indignant. "So what you're telling me is that anyone could book a meeting room in my company's name just by phoning in with a fake email address? Right, that's it. I'm going through every invoice for the six months we've been here at Flexbase!"

"But they would have to know your Flexbase account number as well," wheedled Evans, "and only your employees would know that."

"*And* anyone working for Flexbase, Mr Evans," said Jenny, firmly.

Brody's fingers were shaking over the keyboard. He wasn't sure if it was too much caffeine or an adrenaline rush from the challenge he'd foolishly got himself caught up in. He wondered whether Doc_Doom had manipulated him into taking on the challenge against Matt_The_Hatter. He scanned back through the chat logs but there was no real evidence of that. Like any hacker — white, grey or black — Brody's reputation online was built up over time, through publishing new exploits, sharing code, blogging, tweeting and answering questions on the forums from other hackers. Brody had spent years getting his reputation as Fingal to its current elite status. And here he was putting it all on the line in a childish race to gain root access to a website. If he failed, then word would spread rapidly across the global hacker community. That was one of the downsides of the Internet; it only took seconds for news and gossip to spread. His online reputation would be in tatters.

Brody slammed the tablet PC shut, looked up and caught Stefan's eye. The barista came over immediately.

"Ah, Mr Brody," said Stefan, "Let me think . . . "

"— same again," said Brody, in no mood to play Stefan's guessing game.

"Oh! Okay . . . as you wish, Mr Brody." Stefan shuffled off.

Brody wondered if he could have avoided trapping himself in the challenge. The root cause was his perfunctory approach to reviewing Crooner42's original request for help during the Atlas Brands pentest at that morning. He should have waited until he'd returned to London, when he would have gone thorough due diligence before offering to help. He would have carried out an initial set of penetration tests before responding to make sure that he knew there were some holes he could quickly take advantage of once he was formally given the job. He would also have devoted time to checking out Crooner42's online background more thoroughly to make sure the request for help was legitimate. After all, no one other than Matt_The_Hatter and he had responded to the Crooner42's unusual broadcast for help. Perhaps all the others had figured out this was a tough job and didn't want to risk their reputation.

Now he was in the unpleasant situation where not only did he have to take on the challenge, but failure would be very public. He just hoped he had a few more tricks up his sleeves than Matt_The_Hatter.

A fresh cup of coffee was placed on his table. Brody looked up to say thank you to Stefan, but it was Stefan's trainee waitress who had brought it over instead. Stefan was behind the counter, wiping it down and deliberately avoiding eye contact. Brody thanked the girl anyway and made a mental note to apologise to Stefan before leaving. Maybe a larger tip than normal would help.

Brody rolled up his sleeves and began.

The first step was to familiarise himself with the website in the way a normal online visitor would do. Well, not quite a normal visitor. First of all he would disguise who he was and from where he was connecting. He logged into TOR and two additional proxy connections, one in Russia and the second in Bulgaria. The proxies slowed down his speed a little, but it was worth it to make him impossible to trace. Anyone tracking his address would think he was accessing the Internet from Bulgaria rather than his apartment in Islington. And even if they somehow tracked him down through the first proxy, they'd then think he was really from Russia. And after that, they'd have to take on hundreds of randomly selected relays within the encrypted TOR network.

Brody remembered Crooner42's concern that police around the world might take an interest in the site. Double-proxying should handle that.

He clicked on the site.

The site Crooner42 had built was called www.SecretlyWatchingYou.com. Its name and description implied that it was serving live webcam footage without the knowledge of the inhabitants. Brody knew enough about webcam sites to know that this was very rarely the case. A whole new industry had popped up the day a redheaded American student called Jennifer Ringley chose to broadcast her day-to-day life over the Internet, clothed or naked. Fully aware that she was watched all the time, JenniCam had become an Internet phenomenon at much the same time that *Big Brother* was beginning to take off in the UK. Millions of voyeurs paid to watch and Ringley became very rich, spawning thousands of copycat sites. Brody couldn't understand why anyone would want to watch someone else's life like that, never mind allow it to be watched in the first place.

At first glance, SWY — the techie in Brody had automatically shortened SecretlyWatchingYou to a more usable acronym — seemed harmless enough. Brody was able to look at a few taster videos without registering any personal details. One of the teaser clips was of a girl taking a shower, with the camera directly above. Brody couldn't see her face and the steam blocked out anything interesting. Another was of a man doing the washing up. His back was to the camera. There were five or six others. Big deal. It all seemed boringly innocuous.

He clicked through to the registration pages. Eight US dollars a month or $66 for a year. And that was just for the 'basic' locations. There were newly added 'premium' locations available where users needed to pay more. The site was quite expensive. Who the hell would pay these rates?

The fastest way for Brody to check out the website was to pretend to be a customer. He quickly registered with a brand new anonymous and untraceable email address. The default payment option was PayPal, which meant only needing to disclose his PayPal email address to the website. Although PayPal would never share those details with the website, it was traceable and so not something Brody wanted to use. However, there was one other payment method — bitcoin — and Brody was impressed to see it listed. It was a cyber-currency, which used a peer-to-peer network coupled with cryptography to control and secure the transactions. But most importantly, it was completely unregulated by any government. For Brody, bitcoin's main benefit was that it was virtually untraceable, especially for smart people who masked their credentials when creating accounts. Brody always set up a new account for every job he took on, just to further confuse anyone who attempted a trace.

He pressed submit. His account was created. He was inside.

The man who called himself Crooner42 on the CrackerHack forums scanned the SWY system logs in real time. Every action that users took on the website was recorded in the system logs. Crooner42 often whiled away time watching the logs fill with the activity of tens of thousands of paying subscribers. It was amazing to observe how addictive the site was. His site. It made him feel proud.

It was also making him very rich.

A new entry appeared in the log. Damn, it was just one of the regulars logging back in. A few more entries appeared as the same user navigated through the site and chose a video feed. The log entries highlighted that this user had all the options turned on for the location he was viewing. Perfect, a high-paying customer. Crooner42's favourite type.

But Crooner42 was growing impatient. He'd set the trap perfectly. Fingal had taken the bait and then he'd had no choice but to accept the challenge. He knew Fingal would waste no time.

Crooner42 was fully aware that the first step on any pentest was to passively scan the target. In the case of SWY the only information available in the public domain was the site itself. Unlike websites for bricks and mortar businesses, SWY had no published list of employees, office addresses or any contact details from the physical world.

That meant Fingal would have to jump to the next step and familiarise himself with the site itself. Crooner42 had set the site up so that some of the webcam locations had looping teaser video feeds, just enough to give future customers a taste of what was inside if they parted with their money. As a non-registered customer, Fingal wouldn't really be able to find out much. Certainly not enough to pull together enough information to formulate an appropriate pentest strategy.

No, Fingal would have no choice but to register as a new user on the site. That's what Crooner42 was looking out for in the logs: the creation of a new account. The only problem was that the site was becoming so popular that he was getting hundreds of new user registrations every day. But whoever registered in the next few minutes was bound to be Fingal, hiding behind a fake email address. After all, that's what Crooner42 would have done.

So where the hell was he?

Crooner42 glanced at his Breitling. It had been thirty minutes since Fingal had accepted the challenge on the CrackerHack pentest forum. And, so far, no new users had registered in that time.

Crooner42 had snorted out loud when Fingal had tried to lighten the seriousness of the challenge with his impudent, "Sure, sounds like fun" acceptance. That hadn't fooled Crooner42 at all. He knew that Fingal would be shitting himself.

And so he should be.

Public humiliation in the global hacker community wasn't trivial. It takes months, if not years, to fully recover. Crooner42 knew this better than anyone. He'd been through it, and much, much worse. All thanks to Fingal.

Now it was payback time.

Come on Fingal. Register for fuck's sake.

Crooner42 was in his two-bedroom penthouse apartment that overlooked the Thames to the south. Not that he ever went out on the balcony to take in the expensive views. He had used some of the income from the site to buy the flat. He'd hired an interior designer and given her the brief to design the world's best bachelor pad. She'd not let him down. Everything was stone, leather or glass. The colour spectrum supposedly ranged between ecru and burnt umber, which turned out meant off-white to dark-brown. Huge prints of French art-house movies dominated the walls. A reconditioned *Adams Family* pinball machine sat next to classic *Asteroids* arcade machine. He enjoyed playing those. But the American-style pool table in the centre was purely for show.

The main bedroom had a huge circular bed, with masculine covers and cushions. It had seen plenty of action over the last few months. The second bedroom, however, was hidden behind a false wall. None of his guests even knew the room was there. He'd had the doors ripped out and replaced with a fake, modern looking bookcase. The interior designer hadn't even asked why. She'd taken it as a challenge and had delivered a neat solution. When he keyed the code into an app on his iPhone or pressed the button on his key fob, the bookcases swung outwards to reveal a state of the art home office.

Here he observed and controlled every aspect of SWY via thirty-three LCD computer displays mounted floor-to-ceiling on the wall opposite his glass desk. He'd arranged it like a CCTV control room. The screen in the centre was a massive sixty inches. It was surrounded with smaller thirty-six-inch screens in a six-by-six grid. The displays slowly cycled through the hundreds of video feeds from the website, allowing Crooner42 the opportunity to freely survey what his customers paid for.

Most of the webcam locations held little personal appeal. His attention was generally focused on ensuring the feeds kept on working. But there was one location that held his interest. It was the one that had given him the idea for SWY in the first place and he retained a soft spot for it. For this location, he reserved the four top centre screens of the grid to permanently display its webcam feeds. On the public website, he'd assigned the moniker *Student Heaven* to it.

The log display on the large screen in the centre scrolled upwards. New lines of text appeared at the bottom.

A new account had been created.

Just as Crooner42 was about to congratulate himself, more log entries appeared. Within two minutes there were eight new user accounts. Damn, which one belonged to Fingal? Or was Fingal being extra clever? Perhaps all eight were his.

Crooner42 rolled up his shirtsleeves. He had some work to do to check out the email addresses, payment details and IP addresses of all eight accounts to see if he could narrow down which of them belonged to everyday users, and which belonged to Fingal. Any typical Internet user should be relatively easy to trace back to the real world. Fingal's user account would be the one that was absolutely impossible to trace.

Crooner42 raised his hands in the air, as if conducting an orchestra.

One or more of the eight was Fingal, he was sure of it.

You slowly cycle down the affluent residential street as if you're one of them. No one gives you a second look. You pass within inches of a woman pushing a baby stroller. She is under an umbrella and is plugged into some white earphones. You catch the tinny sound of music. You look back as you pass. Naturally, you want to see if the swivel of her hips has returned following childbirth. You want to see if she's back on the market, asking for it already, but the music — and the baby, if you're really honest with yourself — puts you off. You ignore her. You choose not to take an interest.

Yes, you choose. You are the one who decides. You're like a Roman Emperor selecting who lives and who dies. Thumbs up or thumbs down? Regardless, you've already chosen your next one. She's been really begging for it. She might even be The One. You can't wait. The anticipation is a pleasure. You can feel it forming between your legs. You try to push it away, back down through your black cycle-shorts but, as usual, it seems to have a life of its own.

You spot a residential green on the corner opposite your destination. You dismount and sit on the bench under a tree. The tree gives a little shelter from the rain. You cross your legs and wait patiently for the hardness to subside. You try to take your mind off it. You look up and concentrate on the wind blowing through the branches. You focus on the dampness of the bench seeping through your Lycra shorts. You hear the slow tap tap tap of raindrops on your cycling helmet, larger for having first collected on the leaves and branches before falling.

You recall the last one.

The cellist.

It wasn't as good as you'd expected. As you'd planned. She'd wanted it too much, the slut. You knew that now with hindsight. Someone like that could never make the grade.

Even in the middle of her 'recital' the tart was trying to tease you.

The way she spread her legs either side of the cello – such a blatant come-on. And then her hand movements with the bow. She knew damn well they were suggestive. She wasn't just playing the cello. She was trying to play you too, but her music was so fucking boring. She was into it though. She closed her eyes tight as she concentrated, her body swaying, arm sliding backwards and forwards.

You didn't waste the opportunity. You snuck up behind her and smashed her over the head just as she finished playing. You even laughed out loud as she fell to the floor, the crappy music silenced once and for all.

It took ages for her to come back round.

You'd already tied her hands together, dragged her up onto the table, sliced off her clothes and entered her. You weren't far off coming when she regained consciousness. It hadn't even been a minute. Nowhere near long enough. You tried to hold back, but you wanted her to scream.

It was so much better when she screamed.

She wailed loudly when you grabbed a clump of hair with one hand and yanked her head back. She shrieked even louder when she felt the sharp blade you held at her throat with your other hand. You felt it then, the tightening of her muscles around it. But that was too much. You couldn't hold on anymore. You climaxed and scythed open her neck at the same time.

A double release.

But you'd rushed it. You weren't sure why. You could have prolonged it. Strung it out. Made it last like it should have.

Next time you wouldn't knock her out cold. Or if you did, you'd wait until she came round before getting it on properly. There really was no need to hurry. After all, you'd planned it that way. The whole point was to enjoy it. Enjoy it slowly. For her to experience pleasure and pain intensified by the dawning realisation that she was at death's door. Combined with the sex, it was overpowering. For her too, you briefly wonder? And then you chide yourself. Who cares?

Opposite from where you sit you can see the house numbered 85. The next slut lives there. It's time to invite her to the best experience of her life.

And her last.

CHAPTER 4

As a paying customer, the site now presented Brody with a graphical
menu of purportedly live webcam locations listed by vague but
mostly humorous names. These included, *Wannabe Lesbians, Au Pair
Affair, Boring Fart Toiletcam* and many, many others. Brody clicked on
Au Pair Affair and was presented with three video streams. No
audio. He was surprised at the sharp resolution and smooth motion
quality. Video is one of the hungriest consumers of bandwidth —
the amount of network space that a data stream has to be squeezed
through — and, as a result, many CCTV and webcam feeds suffer
from poor image quality or resort to sending still snapshots every
few seconds. The site must be employing a codec with high
compression similar to YouTube, the popular video site.

One of the three video streams displayed a modern, well-
appointed kitchen. A young woman wearing a white dressing gown
was feeding a baby in a highchair from a bottle. The camera was up
high, probably hidden in the ceiling. Another image, again from
above, showed a bedroom with a single bed. It was empty. Brody
thought he could make out U2 posters on the wall. The third image
showed what looked like the baby's bedroom. A cot in one corner,
teddy bears everywhere, and a playpen in the centre with plastic toys
in it. But no sign of life.

There was movement on the kitchen cam. Brody clicked in and
the video feed filled his screen. The image quality lessened a little,
but it was still very clear. A tall, middle-aged man in a navy suit had
walked in. He kissed the baby on the head. He looked out the
kitchen window quickly and then leaned forward and kissed the

young woman hungrily. She responded eagerly, opening her dressing gown to reveal that she was naked underneath. The man fondled her breasts while the baby watched obliviously. Abruptly, the man withdrew and pointed to his watch. He spoke a few words, but the audio was silent. He leaned in for one more quick kiss with the young woman, patted the baby on the head and left the room. The girl tied her dressing gown around her and resumed feeding the baby.

The scene captivated Brody.

He shrunk the video footage back to thumbnail size and looked around the rest of the *Au Pair Affair* webcam location. He noticed that there were upgrade options. One option was to pay more to receive footage from the four remaining webcams at that location, labelled as premium. These claimed to be the master bedroom, its en-suite bathroom, the main bathroom and the living room. Each had a still picture hinting at what the live feed would contain. Another upgrade option was to receive audio from the webcams at this location. Both upgrade options were fifty-nine pence each. Or the two for ninety-nine pence. The price was certainly low enough to tempt. Undoubtedly the same upgrade approach was repeated on the other video feeds throughout the site.

Brody realised he was intrigued by the two people he'd just spied on. Three if you included the baby. And if *Au Pair Affair* was an accurate description then there would also be a fourth to increase the drama: the unsuspecting wife. Just that thought alone made Brody realise how addictive this site was likely to be.

And how financially successful.

Brody forced himself to click back to the main menu. He skimmed through the webcam locations. There seemed to be about two hundred or so locations, each with two or three feeds and all with at least two or three additional premium feeds for anyone tempted enough to upgrade; for the additional fee of course.

If the other webcam locations were as intriguing as *Au Pair Affair*, then SWY was a money-making machine.

He chose some locations at random. The first few seemed to be from other homes, although they all seemed to be deserted. Perhaps they were all at work. That notion made him click on one that looked like an office. People were sitting behind computer desks, most with two screens side-by-side, typing and talking into headsets.

It looked like a call centre. Clicking on, he found the fish tank location he'd noticed when he'd first looked at the site during the Atlas Brands presentation that morning. The fish still swam peacefully.

None of the streams seemed to be showing people sat at their computers, which meant that there were no webcams of the type integrated within laptop computers, typically used to make video calls. They all seemed to be from dedicated standalone network webcams, mostly mounted high in the rooms they surveyed.

Brody hypothesised whether SWY was a scam; fake feeds to get you hooked and take your money. But the call centre location looked genuine. It would certainly cost too much to pay twenty actors every day to fill out a call centre scene. So, if it was fake, that only left one other option: repeating pre-recorded footage day after day, presenting it as live. But in that case, surely the site's regular paying subscribers would spot the repetition and complain?

Which only left one other alternative. The feeds were live.

How could he confirm one way or the other?

Although Brody was analysing the site like a normal user, in his mind he was already jumping ahead to identify potential exploits he could use to gain root access. If the feeds were truly live it meant they most probably came from sources external to the SWY site, which meant potential backdoor routes into the site. If they were fake, then the site was little more than a catalogue of repeating video files, which meant it would be self-contained and harder to crack.

Brody continued clicking around for another twenty minutes, getting a feel for it. Occasionally, he switched modes to read the site's native HTML, the code that the browser interprets to display the content as a graphical web page. This enabled him to gain a limited understanding of how site was architected. Most modern websites were simply a gluing together of scripts and open-source widgets from all over the world. Each could have known vulnerabilities he could exploit. But, from an initial scan, he noticed nothing with an obvious exploit.

From the HTML and the scripts, he could determine the underlying technology components used to make the site work. There was an awful lot of Java, which was being used to give the site its interactive feel and manage the video feeds, along with some python and PHP. Java is a programming language where the human readable source code is compiled into a machine code, which the computer can execute but is impossible for humans to understand. Brody tried a decompiler to reverse engineer the machine code back into a source code format but Crooner42 had professionally obfuscated it, preventing the decompiler from working. The implications weren't lost on Brody. This challenge might be tougher than he'd originally anticipated.

It was time to get serious. He would head across the road where he had access to more equipment. Also, the Italian muzak was starting to annoy him. He liked to hack to orchestral music played very loud. One of his movie soundtrack playlists should do it. Stefan was chatting with other customers, his back to Brody. The trainee waitress was making coffee. Brody estimated how much he owed and doubled it. He placed a £10 note on the table.

Just as he was about to close the PC, Brody noticed something. The call centre location was still on his screen and he'd spotted some pixelated letters moving from right to left in the bottom left corner of one of the webcam feeds. He clicked in and the webcam's stream filled his screen. The webcam observed the comings and goings of a doorway. He saw a man wearing a business suit exit through the door. But, more importantly, mounted on the wall above and to the right of the doorway was what looked like the bottom corner of a massive digital display. Brody squinted his eyes but it was impossible to make out the text scrolling across it. He was aware that these readerboards were commonly used in call centres to display status summaries about the number of calls in progress, operators free, total calls resolved that day and so on.

He clicked back to the location summary, hoping to find a better view of the readerboard in one of the other feeds. The last stream was the one. It was from a webcam pointed solely at the readerboard. However, it was a premium stream requiring him to pay an upgrade fee to receive the remaining feeds as video. He clicked his consent and a charge of fifty-nine pence was added to his account. All five of these premium images converted from still to moving videos.

He maximised the stream focused on the call centre's digital readerboard. Now filling his screen he could easily read the scrolling text. As he'd thought, it was a massive electronic LED ticker with scrolling call queue metrics displayed for all the call centre operators to see. However, on the left area of the readerboard the time was displayed digitally. Brody compared it to the time being shown on his watch. The readerboard was a minute behind his own. He put that down to the delay of transferring and processing video streams across the Internet. This suggested two things. Firstly, the call centre was situated in the UK, or at least in a country within the same time zone. Secondly, it wasn't incontrovertible proof of a live feed. If a 24-hour pre-recorded feed looped, then the timeline could easily be synchronised.

He focused on the information scrolling across the readerboard, waiting patiently. The metrics may have been relevant to the call centre staff, who could presumably look up from their desks to observe their progress against their colleagues', but they were fairly meaningless to him. He waited, hoping . . .

. . . and then he saw it. The scrolling text now displayed a date moving slowly from left to right across the board.

Satisfied, Brody closed the tablet PC and threw it in his khaki man-bag. Stefan was now behind the counter. Brody stood up, pointed at the money on the table and called over to him, "Thanks Stefan."

The barista nodded hesitantly and then spying the £10 note, formed a toothy smile. "No problem, Mr Brody. See you tomorrow."

Brody turned away with a wave, his mind full of the implications of what he'd seen.

Today's date.

Brody whistled to himself in disbelief.

The feed really was live.

Which strongly indicated that all two hundred locations were live. At an average of five cameras per location, that equated to around a thousand live feeds. The magnitude was enormous. Especially if, as the site claimed, the people being observed in the feeds had no idea they were being filmed.

I'm really worried about Anna now, Kim Chang typed into the Facebook chat box on her mobile phone.

She had said the same thing numerous times since Friday, but she meant it now. *She never goes an hour without texting me or updating her status on Facebook. Never mind three whole days.* She pressed 'Send'.

Patrick's response came back. *She can take care of herself.*

Kim paced up and down the kitchen floor. Seeing a mark on the kitchen counter, she grabbed the cloth and wiped it clean. Normally, the kitchen was piled high with used plates, empty takeaway cartons, and unwashed cups and glasses. The kitchen hadn't been this clean since she and the other four girls had rented the house together eight months ago. Cleaning was all she could do to distract her mind from worrying about Anna.

She tapped into her phone, *If only I'd written down the address of her audition. Then I could go see if she turned up or if they know where she went afterwards.*

Kim racked her brains. She could remember that an agency working on behalf of the Royal Opera House orchestra had invited Anna to an audition somewhere near Paddington Station. On Saturday afternoon, a day after Anna had left, Kim had googled 'Royal Opera House' and 'Paddington' but only the famous landmark in Covent Garden came up. She had phoned them anyway but they told her they were not currently auditioning for their orchestra. That was odd. And no, they had no offices near Paddington. Odder still. Yesterday, Kim had even called Shirley, Anna's mum, but Anna hadn't shown up there either. Of course, that had set Shirley off as well. Yesterday evening, she finally rang the police.

Patrick's words appeared on the screen. *I bet she met some other people at the audition, most probably some bloke – you know what she's like – and went off partying for the weekend.*

Automatically, Kim felt the need to defend her friend. *Anna's not really like that, Patrick.* Her thumb hovered above the 'Send' button.

But, he had a point. Pretty much ever since Kim had got together with Patrick a year ago, Anna had been blatantly putting herself about. Lately, her behaviour with men had been getting even worse. She'd brought back at least four different men over the last few months – all one night stands. And then there were countless nights where she didn't come home at all. Anna was completely blasé about it all. When talking about it with Kim, she openly shared the sordid details of these nights of passion, with no apparent regret and certainly no desire to form a more substantial relationship with any of her partners.

Kim backspaced through the message she hadn't sent and replaced it with, *You could be right. I hope that's all it is.*

The year before had been different. It had been their first year at Trinity College and she and Anna had met as neighbours in the halls of residence. They had quickly become firm friends. The relentless studying and practice associated with their respective courses — Kim's was dance and Anna's music — kept them apart during the day. But most evenings, when the social side of university life kicked in, they went everywhere together. They mixed with larger groups of friends, but it always came down to the two of them at the end of the night, frequently propping each other up as they giggled and staggered their way home from the campus bars. Their first year was relatively tame as far as the other sex was concerned. Just the odd brief encounter, not much to speak of. Then in the second year, they had had agreed to move off campus with three other friends. Five girls. They had found the delightful five-bedroom house near the centre of Greenwich that they now shared. It was a far better standard than everything else they'd seen for the same money and so, deposit paid, they moved in immediately. The three other girls turned out to be much more studious and so it was still mostly Anna and Kim that partied regularly.

After a few months of a similar lifestyle to when they'd been in the halls of residence, Kim had met Patrick, and everything started to change with Anna. Whenever Kim and Patrick stayed in Anna would go out, coming home very drunk or stoned. She and Kim even began to argue, usually over Patrick.

Patrick Harper was not Kim's normal type. Most of the men she went out with were other dancers, fit and incredibly strong, but mostly dull. She found she'd been drawn in by his intelligence but had been captured by his intenseness. His unwavering focus on her needs and wants. He seemed to innately know her innermost desires. And they had so much in common. Everything from their taste in music, ballet and opera, to their political views, to the places they wanted to visit someday, to walking across Greenwich Park, and even down to their sexual likes and dislikes. Anna often joked that Patrick must be a closet homosexual to have so much in common with Kim.

Even the night Kim met Patrick was based on a common interest. She and Anna were in a karaoke restaurant in Plumstead with a group of friends, taking turns with the other diners to sing. At one point, she heard the introduction to Natasha Bedingfield's 'Unwritten', her favourite song. She looked up, surprised to see a young man, instead of a woman, holding the mic. He was average height and quite plain-looking, with pockmarked skin, dark cropped hair and round wire-framed glasses. He must have noticed her staring because he overtly began to sing to her, ignoring the rest of the restaurant. His voice wasn't bad, considering the song was an octave higher than most men's voices could reach. She found herself captivated by his singular focus and the passion in his smile. As he finished, Anna, who knew it was Kim's favourite, pushed her up onto the floor and she fell clumsily into his arms. Initially embarrassed, with everyone staring and clapping, he led her by the hand to the bar area and they began chatting. He explained that it was his favourite song of all time. She couldn't believe the coincidence. And over the rest of that night, and the year since, she and Patrick discovered they had so much more in common.

Would you like me to come over? messaged Patrick.

That was so like him. He was supposed to be allowing her time to rehearse for her final end-of-year dance performance. They'd agreed to only see each other twice a week until the end of term.

Through the kitchen window her attention was caught by a dark blue saloon parking up. An Asian man wearing black trousers and a dark grey raincoat exited the car and walked towards her front gate, hunched under an umbrella.

The phone in her hand vibrated. *Kim?* asked Patrick.

She waited a moment. She prayed it was for next door. They shared the same front gate after all.

The bell rang.

She froze solid. It was her bell. A sense of foreboding overcame her. Don't answer the door.

But she forced herself to walk down the hall.

Taking a deep breath, she opened the door.

"Hello. Is this the home of Anna Parker?"

Unbidden, tears welled up in her eyes. "Yes."

"I'm DC Malik from the Met police. I'm sorry . . . " the man began, solemnly.

And then she knew.

* * *

Derek Saxton returned to his office, a little light-headed but happy with his lunchtime's work. His prospective client — Arthur Aguda, the London Olympic British bronze medal winning middleweight boxer now turning professional — had taken some convincing that Saxton's company was the best agency to manage his career. Saxton won Aguda over eventually. It took all of his charm, with a liberal dose of rags-to-riches stories of the many famous sportspeople he managed. A couple of the stories were even true. The message he portrayed was that talent, diet and training only got you so far. To become a household name required access to the best opportunities. And Derek Saxton had the tightest of relationships with the best boxing promoters in the industry. Two years of careful management would lead Aguda to a shot at the WBA title.

Not that he'd put any guarantee in the contract.

They shook hands and cracked open a bottle of champagne. Then a second and a third. In Saxton's rugby-playing days, a few bottles of champagne wouldn't have touched the sides. Now, walking into his office, he was feeling surprisingly merry.

And horny. Success always turned him on.

Jude Parker, his secretary, looked up as he walked through the door. She closed her *Perfect Wedding* magazine and looked at him over the rim of her thick-rimmed black glasses. Her bright green eyes registered his unsteady progress across the room.

In her interview a year before, Jude had come across as sexy and voluptuous. She had worn a tight red dress that pushed up her more-than-ample breasts. A couple of months into the job, he finally gave up flirting with her. She was engaged to 'Her George', a window cleaner of all things, and nothing was going to distract her from their Caribbean wedding in the summer. She still wore tight dresses, but these days he no longer thought of her as shapely and curvy; instead she'd become more plump and chunky. He wished George good luck. He had thought of replacing her but it turned out that Jude was highly efficient at running the office, calmly kept the clients sweet and methodically organising him and his busy schedule.

"Hey Jude," he said to her as he passed her desk. She had stopped smiling at the joke months ago, but he kept saying it anyway. "No calls or interruptions for an hour if you don't mind."

"Not even a cuppa, Derek? My George loves strong black coffee after a business lunch."

What the hell was a window cleaner doing having business lunches?

"No thanks, love." He yawned conspicuously. "Got a lot to catch up on."

"Ah, I see," she said, knowingly.

Saxton closed his office door behind him and pulled down the blind. It gave complete privacy. He hung up the jacket of his grey Paul Smith suit and opened another button on his black Hugo Boss shirt. He had an idea far better than an afternoon nap.

He moved the mouse on his desk and the computer screen came back to life. He brought up an Internet browser. He chose www.HomeWebCam.com from his list of favourite sites and entered his email address and password when prompted. Up popped seven small video images. He squinted his eyes to work out where she was. Ah ha. In the baby's room. He clicked on the image and it enlarged to fill the screen.

Audri was busy changing Isabel's nappy. He could hear her gently murmuring to the baby. Having once changed one of his daughter's nappies, Saxton was pleased that video was restricted to image and audio. Audri still wore the same white, terry cloth dressing gown he'd seen her in when he'd left home that morning.

He fished out his mobile phone and texted her: *I'm watching ;-)*

While Audri finished with the baby, Saxton decided to check the other webcams to make sure that his wife was definitely out. It was rare for Hilary to come home from work early, but it was sensible to check. No. They were safe.

Saxton clicked back on the baby's room. Isabel was in the playpen, happily pressing some buttons on a toy. No Audri.

His phoned beeped. She had texted him back. *It's my bath time. Come and watch :-).*

Saxton smiled at her deliberate innuendo.

It had started innocuously, or so he'd initially thought. But then he realised she'd orchestrated everything. The way she kept leaving her bedroom door open when she was getting changed. Or the bathroom door when she was in the shower, naked. How she'd trapped the belt of her bathrobe in the utensils drawer in the kitchen one morning and, as she'd walked towards him carrying two mugs of tea, it had pulled her robe open for him to see her beautiful body. She'd not shown any embarrassment, just smiled coquettishly, put the mugs down on the table and slowly did herself up, while asking him if he liked what he'd seen. Just when he'd begun to write it all off as a series of coincidences that just happened when people cohabited, she'd upped the ante. She'd stretch out on the sofa in front of the TV or while reading a magazine, her skirt riding up her long legs, exposing the fact that she wore no underwear, pretending not to notice it had happened, allowing him to ogle her to his heart's content. She took to being overly tactile, her fingers always lingering whenever she accidentally touched him. Everything she did like this happened when Hilary wasn't around. For a couple of weeks, he even took to avoiding being alone in the house with her. He told himself he didn't need that kind of complication in his life. He'd promised Hilary, hadn't he?

And then, one evening, he was innocently walking past her room having just put Izzy down to sleep himself. Hilary was out with friends and, as usual, Audri had left her bedroom door open. He couldn't help looking in. She lay naked on her bed, noisily pleasuring herself with a vibrator. As it happened, he'd already seen her do this a few times via the webcam he'd had secretly installed in her room, but she was so much more alluring in the flesh. She caught his eye, licked her lips sensually and carried on. On autopilot, he walked into her bedroom and closed the door behind him.

Now, four months later, their fling was still in full flow. She was amazing. Full of inventive ideas and games for them to play. And with no strings attached. She wanted nothing from him. She didn't want to break up his marriage. She told him he was *convenient*, which he'd been angry at initially, but then he realised it really didn't matter why she kept wanting to have sex with a much older man.

At his desk, he clicked on the video feed for the main bathroom. There she was, looking up directly into the webcam. She waved and then spoke. "Hello Derek." Her voice was seductive, but her expression showed she was unsure. After all, she couldn't see him.

Audri turned the bath taps on and poured in some bubble bath.

Saxton was pleased with himself. Although he'd watched Audri bathe many times, this would be the first time she would participate knowingly. Only yesterday, Saxton pointed out to her exactly where the webcam in the bathroom was hidden. She'd been surprised when he'd explained about the cameras and was delighted that he was finally stepping up with some inventive games himself. She immediately figured out that he must have watched her many times, both before and after their relationship had begun, and lightly teased him that he was some kind of pervert. Then she reminded him that, being Swedish, she was far more sexually liberated and that being naked in public was only natural.

Saxton licked his lips and unzipped his flies.

She turned off the taps and faced the camera. Slowly, she slipped the robe from her shoulders. She held it to her, seductively rubbing her breasts hidden underneath. She exposed one, then both, passing her hands over them repeatedly.

Saxton paused for a moment and considered how wonderfully exclusive his situation was. He was only four miles away but could easily have been four thousand. He was in his own office, enjoying his own private peep show, by his own nanny, from his own house and his wife had no idea. And the security on the HomeWebCam website ensured that no one else could sneak a peek.

Oh, how he loved the Internet.

Brody leaned back in his cream leather executive chair and forcibly lifted his hands away from the keyboard. He realised he was wasting time simply observing the unwitting inhabitants of yet another SWY webcam stream, which only served to repeat what he'd already learned from all the other streams throughout his reconnaissance of the site. Not a lot.

He wondered if he was subconsciously procrastinating; delaying the start of his actual hacking session in order to defer potential failure. He was no armchair psychologist, but he knew that a self-diagnosis like that didn't really make logical sense. He was in a race to get root. To race, he had to take part. But was he in a sprint or a marathon? He didn't know that yet.

Brody sat at his desk in his living room. He had got rid of the formal suit he'd worn for his 'interview' earlier and was now dressed in smart black jeans and a casual white shirt, all bought from Ted Baker, like the majority of his wardrobe.

His computer was connected to a bank of three widescreen monitors, each displaying different windows. The left and right screens displayed Internet browsers logged into different parts of the SWY site, multiple video feeds running without audio, the inhabitants silently going about their lives. On the centre screen, he opened a command line interface. The cursor prompt flashed, expectantly awaiting his command.

He typed *"WhoIs SecretlyWatchingYou.com"* at the prompt and then, just as he was about to press 'Enter', realised something was missing. It was completely silent in his living room. He grabbed his smartphone and brought up the *Sonos* app that controlled the speaker system installed throughout the apartment. Brody selected his favourite movie soundtrack playlist, set it for random with the volume high and pressed play. The opening bars to John Barry's *Dances With Wolves* boomed from floor-standing Bose speakers either side of the huge wall-mounted television.

Then, like a concert pianist about to perform a solo, he rested his fingers on the keyboard in front of him and centred his right thumb on the mouse trackpad. He hovered his right pinkie finger over the 'Enter' key.

He was ready.

"Turn it off you fucking knob!" It was Leroy, shouting from his bedroom.

Shit. He quickly grabbed his phone, fiddled with the *Sonos* app and realised that he'd neglected to ensure the speakers in the guest room were off. He quickly muted them and, for good measure, lowered the volume in the living room. Brody whispered a curse and waited for the fallout.

"Morning." Leroy's accusatory voice behind him, full of gravel.

Brody turned around. Leroy stood barefoot by the leather sofa, his bloodshot eyes squinting at the daylight, wearing the same clothes as he'd worn last night: a high-collared white shirt open one button too many, revealing black skin stretched taught over huge pecs, rumpled from being slept in, and dark trousers, also creased, from a slim-fitting two piece suit, the jacket of which had been slung across the back of the sofa. He held his head in his right hand and simultaneously scratched his balls with his left.

The image of Leroy hung-over first thing in the morning was a familiar sight to Brody, repeated hundreds of times over the years, dating right back to when they were two of five student housemates thrown together while attending university in London. The other three students in the house that first year had been girls, all studying academic subjects and with the sociability of The Three Witches from *Macbeth*. Forced into each other's company, Brody and Leroy had eventually hit it off and became the very best of friends.

"Afternoon."

"It is? Fuck me, must have been a good night then." He climbed over the back of the sofa and allowed himself to fall into the cushions. "Mornings are overrated anyway."

Reaching for the remote control on the coffee table, Leroy pressed some buttons and the massive wall-mounted television burst into life. A kids' cartoon.

"Leroy, I'm working."

"Yeah, well I was sleeping until you put a fucking orchestra in my room." Selecting *Little House on the Prairie*, he turned the TV volume up high, trying to compete with John Barry and his orchestra. "Loved watching reruns of this as a kid back in Wales."

"Turn it off, Leroy."

"Turn it off, Leroy," he imitated in a high-pitched voice.

"Now!"

"Bloody hell," he moaned. He muted it instead, not quite giving in completely.

"You act like a spoilt teenager when you're hung-over."

"Yeah, well you act like a nerd when you're sober. Wait a second, you are a nerd!" He laughed at his own joke and then grimaced as pain shot through his head.

"Careful, Leroy. This nerd might hack into Facebook and screw with you. Let me see, who's that guy who keeps trying to come on to you. Joe? John? No, Jordan, that's right. I can see his post on your wall now: *Leroy, last night's show was soooo good, especially when you sucked my cock dry between act one and act two.* You never know who might see it. Danny perhaps?"

"You bitch!"

"And then this same nerd might send a friend request from your Facebook account to your Dad, now that your sister's bought him an iPad. Imagine his reaction to all those photos posted of you and Danny together."

Leroy had grown up in a small village in North Wales where he had been forced to suppress his sexuality completely; his only confidante as a teenager being his younger sister, Hope. Leaving

Wales to attend university in London, Leroy felt unleashed. He made up for his closeted childhood by having a string of relationships with men of all shapes, sizes and colours. In the first few weeks of their blossoming friendship, Leroy even made a drunken pass at Brody. Brody had reacted instinctively and punched him in the stomach as hard as he could; an action he'd never done to anyone before or since. While Leroy was writhing on the floor, Brody made him promise never to try it on with him again. In a strange way it cemented their friendship completely.

Most other university students had assumed Brody was also gay, predominantly based on rumours spread by their three boring cohabitants who quickly become frustrated with the two party-animal housemates stumbling noisily into the house at all hours of the night. It had the effect of cutting down Brody's ability to successfully approach single female students within the university. Brody and Leroy took to going out together, helping each other meet potential partners. Some nights Leroy would pretend to be heterosexual and would chat up pairs of girls in the hope that Brody would strike lucky, which happened enough times to make the charade worthwhile. Leroy was naturally extrovert and loquacious, making up for Brody's tongue-tiedness when in the company of good looking women. On other nights, Brody would begrudgingly return the favour, pretending he was gay with a camp performance that had Leroy in stitches. The minute Leroy looked like he was in luck, Brody would magically disappear in an effort to avoid being on the receiving end of unsubtle gropes and passes from oversexed men. But, after a few nights of this, Brody refused to re-enact his homosexual sham and played it, quite literally, straight. He still had to fend off just as many advances from gay men who took his presence in their midst as a challenge, contending that he wouldn't be in their club if he wasn't at least a little bit interested.

After a few weeks, Leroy started inventing fake occupations for themselves during their nights out. They started off with the classics: firemen, policemen and lawyers. In character, Brody actually found it much easier to talk to women, and even men when out on a Leroy night. Justified by the need to strengthen his improvisation skills for his Drama degree course, Leroy kept upping the stakes, coming up with obscure professions for them both; micro-biologists, key grips – they had seen the job title in movie credits – zookeepers, rocket scientists, politicians and even circus clowns. Brody's degree had been Film Studies and so he didn't have the same incentive as Leroy to keep inventing new characters for their nights out. But it had amused him to see how far he could go with the games. So much so that all these years later, false backstories remained a key part of his life. It was strange to consider that Leroy seemed the one who had grown up first. Although looking at him now, slumped on the sofa, he didn't seem any more mature than the version Brody had first met.

Leroy finally turned off *Little House on the Prairie*. "Okay, okay. I give in. I'm sorry."

"Thank you."

He stood up, tentatively. "You want a cuppa, darling?" A peace offering.

"No ta. I've already had way too much coffee."

Leroy disappeared into the kitchen and banged about. Brody knew better than to try and begin his hacking session until he settled. Eventually, he returned to the living room, carrying a mug and a plate of buttered toast. He perched on the edge of Brody's desk. Brody sighed audibly, but Leroy ignored it.

"Thought you had that job in Birmingham today."

"I finished it, but I've got stuck with another one already."

"Since when do you get stuck with anything, Brody? We both know you don't *have* to work."

That riled Brody. Leroy knew full well that it hadn't always been that way for Brody, not like Leroy whose parents had been rich enough to fund his university course, his ever growing collection of video games and his expensive social life. Brody had come from a working class family in Hertford, his father a civil servant in the county council and his mother a hairdresser. He had always been deeply into computers and the hobby became a necessary source of income during university. Initially, he did what other capable programmers did and built websites for local businesses. But it was time-consuming and mundane, it didn't challenge his skills and the income was minimal.

Then Brody stumbled across online poker and spotted an opportunity. He created poker bots, programs that automated playing poker hands to a standard set of scenarios that he programmed in from books he loaned from the library on poker strategies. The bots would impersonate humans in the online poker rooms, their human opponents having no idea they were playing *Texas Hold'Em* against a computer. Individually, the bots held their own against inexperienced players, but stronger players who bluffed more effectively, would beat his bots consistently. It was while watching a rerun of an old *Star Trek: The Next Generation* episode with the 'Borg', a collection of species that functioned as drones of a collective hive mind, that gave him the money-making idea of having his bots gang up as one. He would partially fill an online poker room with the artificial bots, leaving one or two seats free for gullible humans. He upgraded their programming so that the bots secretly shared with each other which two cards they had each been dealt, massively enhancing their odds as a group. Five bots in a poker room meant that between them they knew ten of the cards dealt from the pack, whereas the human opponents only knew the two in their own hand. Humans in these bot-filled online poker rooms had no idea what they were up against and only ever won with an outrageously lucky hand. To avoid drawing attention, Brody only let them play until they had amassed enough winnings to cover his personal outgoings for the next night. In order to fool the poker site administrators, who actively traced Internet addresses to ensure there was no collusion amongst players, Brody logged in each bot via Internet proxies located all around the world, giving the impression that the players, his bots, could not possibly know each other.

Only Leroy had known about Brody's secret source of funds that got him through university. He decided to ignore Leroy's comment about not having to work.

"This job's different."

"Yeah, sure." He clearly didn't believe Brody. "So that means you'll be head down and boring all afternoon and night, just like usual."

"Depends. I might be able to crack this in a couple of hours – if I had some peace . . ." Maybe he would take the hint.

"It's my day off, darling."

"Come on Leroy, you know I can't work with you distracting me. And I've got to get this done straight away."

"I'm not your only distraction today, or have you forgotten?" He took a large bite of toast. "You've got that date later."

"Oh fuck. Yeah, I nearly forgot. What was her name again?"

"I should be asking you that. Come on, bring up her profile."

Brody opened the dating website he'd been using for the last two years and logged in. He found the long list of matched dates and scrolled to the bottom. Leroy looked over his shoulder. Brody clicked on the bottom entry.

"Harriet, eh? She's nice," said Leroy. "Well, nice for a girl I suppose. What's that? A property lawyer. Ha! She'll rip you apart."

"Don't worry, I'm a big boy now."

"Yeah, sure." He pulled a doubtful expression and pointed at a framed poster on the wall. "So you're going to introduce yourself as Brody, computer hacker, wanted in fifteen different countries!"

Brody didn't really like the term computer hacker. He had certainly never intended to become one, deliberately taking a Film Studies degree instead of Computer Science in order to offer him an alternative career path. And anyway, the level of technical proficiency he had gained programming computers from such a young age meant there was little he was likely to learn by formally studying computing. It was this technical prowess that gave him the taste of the financial fruits of what he could achieve with computers during his degree course. And, after graduating, he'd never really found a good use for his Film Studies degree. So, his first job was working in the IT security department of a major high street bank chain. After a few years he gave it up, having found corporate life too monotonous and the job unchallenging. He set up as an independent security consultant, completely separate from his online persona as Fingal. At one time he flipped to poacher-turned-gamekeeper and advised some of the online poker sites on how to redesign their systems to make it harder for automated bots to work effectively. As part of the assignment, he had tracked down some of the people running similar scams to his own and the poker companies had brought the police in, arresting them for fraud.

By then, he had discovered a new completely legal source of income: Internet-based betting exchanges, where gamblers competed against each other rather than against bookmakers, backing or laying the outcomes of sports events. He developed statistical betting and laying systems for horse races and tennis tournaments, which he then automated with bots so that they ran themselves. He felt much better about them as there was no ganging up on unsuspecting opponents. It was simply his statistical betting strategy versus lots of other anonymous gamblers willing to accept his proffered odds to test whether their own betting strategy or, more often, their hunch was a better prediction of the event's outcome. While his system didn't win every bet, it won more often than it lost. Within a few years, the regular tax-free winnings had amassed into a fund so large that it freed him from the necessity of working for a regular salary.

To keep him busy and current with technology, Brody branched into white-hat hacking and penetration testing services. He enjoyed the work and would gladly have done it for free but, as a matter of principle, he always charged very high rates to substantiate the value the multinational corporations gained from his work.

In his early hacking days, he particularly relished the intellectual challenge of identifying zero-day exploits — coming up with a brand new attack vector that exploited a previously unknown vulnerability in a vendor's operating system or application — and then publishing them so that the vendor could block the hole. More recently, Brody had found himself exposing unknown Advanced Persistent Threats — cyber attacks that employ advanced stealth techniques to remain undetected for long periods of time while they replicate themselves and carry out their work of sending compromised data back to their authors. In most of the cases large corporations, usually banks or utility companies, had hired him. Unknown APTs have no signature because they have not been discovered, and so remain invisible to traditional countermeasures. Brody usually uncovered their existence by analysing network activity to identify anomalous traffic, especially heading in the direction of known Command and Control servers. Once installed on a target system, APTs needed to 'phone home' to a CnC in order to receive instructions or to send back compromised data. Once he detected the existence of an APT, he then narrowed down on the infected computer and analysed the APT. Under his Fingal handle, he always posted full details on the Internet, where the anti-virus vendors would pick them up and write new signatures to detect them, foiling the malicious aims of the APT authors, all of which served to increase his credibility and infamy in the online hacking communities.

But hunting zero-days and chasing APTs was nothing compared

to the rush he got from carrying out social engineering based pentests. The buzz was like nothing else, especially when he physically conned his way into a secure facility like he'd done with Atlas Brands that morning. He supposed that his proclivity to trick and deceive must be rooted in his nights out with Leroy all those years ago. And the combination of the two sets of skills, computer hacking and impersonation, made social engineering his true vocation in life.

And while Leroy's passing comment about being wanted in fifteen different countries was said in jest, there was, unfortunately, some truth to it.

Over the years, Brody had enraged a lot of black hats around the world, many of whom were members of organised crime rings. These cyber-criminals applied their hacking skills to steal or launder money, facilitate sex trafficking of women and children, aid the smuggling of drugs and a number of other illegal activities. Brody had interrupted many of their schemes — sometimes deliberately but mostly inadvertently — by exposing many of their lucrative APTs, enabling their targets to defend themselves, anti-virus vendors to create signatures that detected their existence and software vendors to block the exposed vulnerability completely. Halted in their tracks, the black hats were then forced to devise alternative techniques.

In the online forums, Fingal had received numerous death threats. Secure in the stealth tactics he employed to protect himself online, Brody flagrantly laughed them off, frustrating them further. All of which fed Fingal's online infamy and strengthened his status in the global hacking community. If any of the cyber-criminals somehow found a way to track him down in the physical world, where his defences were weakest, they would exact a terrible revenge.

Vorovskoy Mir, one of the leading Russian cyber-gangs, had become so enraged at him that they had added him to their infamous 'most wanted' list. They were parodying the American FBI's 'cyber most wanted' website, which published the names of suspected cyber-criminals. On the FBI site, headshots and real names were provided, along with a description of their alleged crimes, aliases and reward amounts in exchange for information that could lead to their arrest (usually upwards of $100,000). On the

Vorovskoy Mir list, the online handles of eight well-known hackers in the cyber-community were listed beneath blacked-out head silhouettes. At the bottom of the page were four others, but this time displaying real faces. Only they each had the word 'ELIMINATED' in red splashed diagonally across them. The third silhouette in the list of eight was labelled 'Fingal'. The reward for information leading to his capture was $1 million in bitcoins, no questions asked.

As a very visible reminder to always be careful online and mask his identity and IP address, Brody had printed off the Russian cyber-gang's 'most wanted' website, blown it up into a massive poster, had it framed and mounted it on the living room wall.

"I'm not wanted anywhere, you fool." Brody always made light of the death-threats against him. As long as he maintained his anonymity online, he was completely safe. And so was anyone associated with him. "Anyway, Harriet the lawyer thinks she's meeting Brody Taylor the cinema photographer, just back from shooting a *Bourne Identity* movie sequel in Morocco. In the UK for one night and then flying out to Rome tomorrow."

"Brilliant! I especially like the time limit." Leroy laughed and then shook his head sadly. "You know something, darling. One day you're going to repeat what happened with Mel and you'll be completely screwed, caught in your usual web of lies, broken, lonely and miserable all over again. Why can't you just be yourself?"

Mel had been Brody's last serious girlfriend, a relationship that had ended just over a six months ago. They had met via the dating site, but for once a one-night-stand wasn't enough, not that they'd had sex on that first night. She was zany and funny. She spoke with a French accent that he could listen to all night. But the clincher was her altruistic nature. She wanted to fix the world, joining any good cause that caught her attention. She fitted them in around her shifts as a nurse in a care home. She stood outside pharmaceutical offices protesting about animal cruelty. She fed London's homeless in a soup kitchen. She took disadvantaged children to the countryside on her spare weekends. And she helped out in her local Oxfam shop. Her relationship with Brody was the only thing in her life that was about her.

After two months, Brody decided that he couldn't continue the charade he'd caught himself within. He finally revealed the truth, explaining that he wasn't a location scout, and his parents and siblings hadn't died in a car crash. He told her about his life as a computer hacker and how he made his income from pentest consultancy assignments. She'd left before he'd even had a chance to explain that he'd concocted it all to protect her from the real world dangers of his hacking life. How he had made many enemies within the organised crime syndicates littering the underworld of the Internet, any of whom would absolutely love five minutes with him if they could somehow track him down in the real world. He had been trying to protect her; that was all.

But the truth had come too late. Wounded, Mel had accused him of being a manipulating cheat and a compulsive lier. She declared that she'd never been so betrayed. And with that, she turned and walked out of his life.

Brody answered Leroy's question, "I choose to live my life this way. It's a price I have to pay."

"No strings. Yes, I know. It's just a shame . . ." Leroy faltered when he saw Brody's glare and changed tack, " . . . Are you going to dazzle this lawyer lady with a visit to Bromptons?"

He was referring to the private members' club in South Kensington, a well-hidden destination for those in the know. Brody had become a member three years previously, although he mostly frequented when trying to impress his dates.

"Probably, but we'll have dinner somewhere else first."

"Good. I'll probably be there later with Danny."

In two days time, Leroy and Danny would be celebrating their fifth anniversary, which Brody still found incredible. At university, Brody had watched Leroy have fling after fling right up until the last few months, when he'd finally fallen deeply in love with a fellow student actor called Jed. Leroy had followed his new partner out to Hollywood where they both attempted to break into the movie business. Leroy's father even cut his allowance in an attempt to bring him back to the UK to 'find a proper job'. Leroy and Jed waited tables and eventually Leroy made a few television pilots, but none got picked up as a series. He blamed his Welsh accent and so cultivated an English one instead, which ultimately became his day-to-day speaking voice. After eighteen months, their relationship ended when Leroy found out Jed had secretly made a few porn movies. Jed's on-camera sexual infidelities bothered Leroy, but nowhere near as much as his lowering his standards to work in the porn industry.

Eventually a more grown-up version of Leroy returned to London, and Brody and Leroy carried on where they'd left off, but happily without the chaos of their university days. Leroy won occasional bit parts in TV soaps and stage productions, but rarely anything with a regular income. He frequently turned up on Brody's doorstep, desperate and penniless, and Brody would put him up in the guest room for a while, before some new acting role swept him off to the latest glamorous destination.

Five years ago Leroy met Danny while on holiday in the Florida Keys. Danny was a fellow Welshman and ran his own modest recruitment business in Cardiff, which was not quite the centre of the professional acting universe for Leroy, otherwise they'd have got a place together years ago. As it was, they managed to spend most weekends with each other, either in Cardiff or London. This time, Leroy had been staying at Brody's for three months, but a few weeks ago Leroy had landed a part in a new stage production. It had a limited West End run and in a few more weeks it would begin a nationwide tour. And Leroy with it.

Brody was looking forward to the peace and quiet.

Leroy said, "Don't worry, I'll remind Danny you're a big shot Hollywood cameraman. He'll play along and we'll make your cover story even more credible."

"Yeah, well make sure —"

"Bloody hell, you pervert. What kind of weird shit are you working on?"

Brody followed Leroy's pointing finger to the left hand screen still displaying thumbnail video feeds from the SWY website. He recognised the dark haired girl from the *Au Pair Affair* feed. Only now it looked as though she was naked in the bath. Brody clicked the image and it enlarged to fill the screen. He pressed un-mute. The camera looked down from ceiling height, a wide-angle lens positioned to take in the shower, bath and even the toilet.

The young woman arched her back, her pelvis rising above the water revealing a neat strip of black pubic hair. Hungrily, she rubbed herself between her legs, deep panting breaths coming faster and faster. The noise was tinny, echoing from the tiled bathroom walls. She lifted one leg over the side to spread herself more widely.

Frothy water spilled on the floor.

"So that's how girls do it, then," said Leroy through a mouthful of toast, "Seems much more complicated."

Brody gaped at the image, completely mesmerised.

She reached a crescendo, panting giving way to a hoarse, guttural scream. Then a deep, contented sigh. Slowly, her lithe body retreated back under the water.

"So this is your next job, is it darling?" Suspicion punctuated Leroy's clarification. "Do you want me to leave you two alone?"

Brody ignored him. SWY really was full of surprises. Pleasant ones as well. He'd already proved the site was fed from real locations. Which meant somewhere in the world right this minute, this particular girl lay in a bath having just finished pleasuring herself.

"What is this site then?" asked Leroy.

"It's called SecretlyWatchingYou. Hundreds of private webcam feeds from all over the world."

"Secret, eh? So you're saying she has no idea she's got an audience?"

Almost as if she heard Leroy, the young woman opened her eyes, tilted her head, looked straight at the camera and smiled.

"Well, well. I guess she does know. That's very interesting," said Brody.

"Can she hear us?" asked Leroy excitedly. He leant towards the laptop and barked to the naked girl. "Don't forget to wash behind your ears, young lady!"

"Leroy, you fool, the audio is one-way only."

"Oh." He leaned back, disappointed. "What is this job you're doing, then?"

"Just a favour for a mate."

"One of your hacker mates?"

"Yeah, kind off."

"Have you ever met this *mate*?"

"Sure, loads of times."

Leroy stood up and drained his mug of tea. "In the real world? You know, in the flesh. As in, *offline*?"

"Makes no difference to me."

Leroy sprawled on the sofa. "You talk such shit sometimes, darling. You can't truly get to know someone just from talking to them in a chat room."

Brody didn't answer. They'd had this argument before. What did Leroy know anyway? Brody had built up plenty of friendships with people he'd never met in person. And not just other hackers. Online, people were a lot more open about themselves, cutting to the chase, brutally honest. In the real world, there was so much dancing around, never quite saying what they meant, always holding back. The anonymity of the Internet made everything possible. It was one of the reasons he loved it so much.

"Just ignore me, Brody. It's my hangover talking. Making me tetchy. I think I'll go back to bed."

"Yeah, sure."

Leroy raised himself up and delicately shuffled back to his room. He opened his bedroom door, paused and said, "What makes you think they're from all over the world?"

"What?"

"The private webcams in your pervy website. You said they were from all over the world."

"It's the Internet." Brody couldn't keep the condescending tone out of his voice. "It's a global phenomenon."

Leroy turned around and lumbered back to lean on Brody's desk. He pointed at the girl in the bathroom, who was now drying herself off with a towel.

"Bet you a foot massage she's in the UK somewhere."

"How can you tell that?"

"You taking the bet, darling?"

"Fuck off, Leroy."

Leroy chuckled to himself, "Back in a mo." He ambled off down the hallway. Brody heard the bathroom door open.

Brody stared at the screen, confused. The girl wrapped one towel around her hair and the other around her body. She grabbed a mobile phone from the window mantle and pressed some keys rapidly with two thumbs. She looked up at the camera again, pointed her phone upwards and pressed a button. Smiling, she left the bathroom. This girl definitely knew she was being watched.

Brody recalled her voice from earlier in the day when he'd observed her talking nonsense to the baby. He'd formed the impression that her accent sounded Scandinavian. So how did Leroy come up with the UK?

Leroy returned and slammed a plastic bottle of toilet cleaner on his desk and said triumphantly, "Asda, you knob."

Brody instinctively recoiled from the yellow bottle in disgust. It lived behind their toilet and probably had dried urine all over it. Perhaps that's why the packaging designers had chosen yellow.

Yellow bottle.

Yellow bottle, red lid with a black and white label.

He stared at the motionless bathroom video feed. Although very small on the screen, there, by the toilet, was exactly the same shape yellow bottle with a red lid and a black and white label.

Leroy ambled off to his room. "Much to learn, you still have . . . my young Padawan. Good night."

Brody smiled at Leroy's use of Yoda's line from *Star Wars: Episode II – Attack of the Clones*. But then he frowned. How did the presence of toilet cleaner connect the webcam location to the UK? And then he realised. *Asda.* Asda was a UK-only supermarket. It was owned by Wal-Mart, the American giant. In every other country, Wal-Mart traded under its own brand, but in the UK it was Asda. And the toilet cleaner was Asda's own brand.

The location of this video feed was somewhere in the UK.

He clicked back to the office location webcams and selected the feed with the readerboard. The date and time scrolled by again. Sure enough, it was still one minute out. He'd noted earlier that it was in the same time zone as he was, but there were plenty of other countries on Greenwich Mean Time. He'd looked them up: Ghana, Iceland, Ireland, Morocco, Liberia, Portugal, Senegal, Sierra Leone and some others he'd only vaguely heard of.

But, with *Au Pair Affair* located somewhere in the UK, he had a sneaking suspicion that the office location was in the UK as well.

Her window wipers at full speed, Jenny Price turned her silver Audi A3 into Troughton Road in Charlton, the address Trinity College had provided for Anna Parker. Pastel colours and fake cladding sporadically broke the redbrick monotony of the long Edwardian terrace. The original town planners could never have predicted that the inhabitants of the two-up two-down houses would one day own their own cars and park them proudly in front of their homes, shrinking the usable width of the road to a single slalom track. Jenny zigzagged her way past two oncoming cars, the passing places formed by houses that had exchanged their personal patch of lawn for a private concrete driveway. Fifteen or so houses beyond the house Anna Parker had shared, Jenny finally found a space and then groaned as she spotted the dropped kerb outside warding strangers from parking there.

Sod it. She parked anyway, the continuous downpour overcoming her civic morals. Partially protected under her extendable umbrella, Jenny bolted back up the road, through the gate and up the path. With perfect timing, DS Karim Malik opened the front door and Jenny charged into the hallway. She shook the rain off herself and the umbrella.

"Thank fuck you're here, Jen."

"What's going on, Karim?"

"Got one of the victim's flatmates in the kitchen in floods. What am I supposed to do? I'm a copper, not a fucking counsellor."

"Tea and sympathy, Karim. That's all you can do."

Jenny had long ago stopped picking up Karim on his foul language, although she found it amusing that he managed to curb it whenever Da Silva was in earshot. Being a Muslim police officer was tough and Jenny supposed Karim's foul language was some kind of defence mechanism, a way to make him appear less noticeable to his colleagues. And, even though it often seemed exaggerated, it worked. Karim was well liked within the squad. Jenny had no idea what the *Qur'an*'s position on swearing was. If it was a problem it was Karim's problem, not hers.

"What's the flatmate's name?" she asked.

"Kim Chang. She's a dance student."

"Where're all the other flatmates?"

"It's some kind of study week, so the other three flew off on holiday together last week. Imagine it. One house, five students. All birds. Fucking fantastic."

"Have a bit of decency, Karim. One of them's the victim."

"Sorry boss."

"What have you told her?"

"Nothing really. I didn't get much past telling her that Anna had been found dead before she started wailing."

Jenny followed Karim into the kitchen. A dark-haired girl sat at the table, puffy eyes almost masking her delicate Oriental features. She looked up, hope on her face. Karim introduced Jenny and her features collapsed once again. Jenny made the standard noises about how sorry she was, feeling utterly false. Karim leaned against the sink, out of the girl's eye-line.

"Poor Anna," the girl said, her voice cracking as she reached for another tissue.

Jenny sat down opposite her. "I know it's devastating, Miss Chang, but I need you to answer a few questions."

"Kim," she said, blowing her nose.

"Okay, Kim. When did you last see Anna?"

"Friday morning. When I left for college, she was practising for an audition she was going to that afternoon."

Karim opened his mouth to jump in but Jenny raised a hand enough for him to notice. He held back. Jenny had also realised the significance of the audition.

"What was she auditioning for?"

"A summer work placement in the Royal Opera House Orchestra. That was her dream, you know, to play for a ballet company. She never thought she'd ever get a shot at the Royal Opera House."

"She was that good?"

"I think so." There was hesitation in her voice. "I'm no expert. I'm just a dancer. But we both go to Trinity Laban Conservatoire. It's a specialist college for music and dance. You have to be pretty good to go there."

"And dedicated?"

Another pause, and then she gathered herself. "Of course. We all are."

"Was the audition in Covent Garden?" Jenny didn't know much about opera but she knew where the Royal Opera House was. And even though Jenny knew the answer before Kim spoke, she wanted to understand how open Kim was being.

"No. That was strange actually. It was somewhere near Paddington. We looked it up on Google Maps. Some kind of office building, which was a bit odd."

"Did she phone the Royal Opera House to double-check?"

"No way. She didn't want to give them any chance of changing their mind. In case they'd chosen her by accident or something. Anyway, Anna said the invitation was from an agency working on behalf of the ROH."

Jenny was about to ask if she had a copy of the invitation when Kim abruptly asked, "Was it a car accident or something like that?"

Jenny was thrown momentarily. She glanced over at Karim, who held up his hands behind Kim, as if to say, "I told you."

"I'm sorry, Kim, I thought DC Malik had told you already. Anna was murdered."

"*What?*" There was sudden outrage in her voice.

Jenny didn't answer, sensing more was to come.

Kim continued, her voice now shaking. "Murdered? Who? How? Not some bloke she picked up? I told her she was asking for trouble."

"What do you mean?"

Kim turned her head, catching sight of Karim to one side of her. "Nothing. It's not important."

"Kim, do you mind if DC Malik takes a look in Anna's room?"

"Sure, go ahead. First floor, first on the left."

Karim took the hint and left them in the kitchen.

Jenny asked Kim to explain her comment again, adding, "It could be important."

Kim folded her arms. "It's just that ever since me and Patrick got together — he's my boyfriend — Anna's been out partying a lot. Too much. We always used to go out together, before Patrick, but nowhere near as much as this. And lately there's been a string of one-night stands. It's so embarrassing when you come down in the morning and there's yet another bloke there with her. Once, she introduced me to one and she couldn't even remember his bloody name."

"So you think she may have picked up someone who killed her?"

"I guess? A year-and-a-half ago she only ever got it together with other music and dance students, and even then only occasionally. Nothing serious. Usually when I met someone as well. And she only ever went for the good-looking ones. She can, you know. She's gorgeous. But recently? They've been all sorts. Short. Ugly. And mostly older, middle-aged men. Yuck."

"Can you remember any of their names?"

"Maybe. Let me see . . ." She listed three or four names. Jenny wrote them down and then asked, "Do you recall a William Webber? Or any William?"

"No, I don't think so. Why, have you arrested someone already?"

Hope filled her face.

"Not yet, but I'm sure we will soon." But Jenny was starting to think the opposite. She changed tack. "If she was partying so hard, how was it affecting her studies?"

"She's pretty much stopped going to Trinity. She's stopped practising her cello. She used to play upstairs for hours at a time. It was so nice to hear. But nothing for the last few months. Well, except for this week, practising for her audition. She says she'll make it up before the end of year recitals. I tried to talk to her but there was no getting through. She always turns it back to me and Patrick."

"What did she have against Patrick?"

"I think she's just jealous. He's so attentive towards me. But she thinks he's . . . what's the word she used . . . *fawny*. She said it's not normal for a bloke to be so slavish. And for us to have so much in common. She says that anyone who has that much in common with a girl must be gay. Well he's not gay! I think it's because she's never really had that kind of relationship."

Jenny thought back to the crime scene and realised she'd probably gone too far off-track. There was no need to have Kim rake her friend through the muck, when the killing was obviously related to the audition. And Kim referenced Anna in the present tense, which meant she'd not fully absorbed her friend's death yet.

"When we were talking about the audition a few minutes ago, it felt that you were holding something back. Was it to do with Anna's recent behaviour?"

"I guess. In a way. She was invited to the audition based on a recommendation from one of her music lecturers. But she's hardly been to the college lately. It seemed such an unlikely recommendation."

"Which lecturer?"

"His name's Jake Symmonds. But he's just Jake to us. We call all our lecturers by their first names. Not like school you know." Kim smiled weakly. The smile revealed the girl's attractiveness. She had shapely cheekbones and full lips, and was short and petite; a ballerina's body with a ballerina's poise. Almost the opposite of Jenny, who had the height of a supermodel but all the grace of a grounded albatross. "I remember, Jake Symmonds."

"When did Jake tell Anna about the audition?"

"He didn't. Anna got an email a week ago from someone working on behalf of the ROH, inviting her to the audition. The email said that Jake had made the recommendation."

"Did she talk to Jake about it?"

"No, the invitation implied he'd done it off-the-record and so she didn't want to drop him in it. Or find out that he'd recommended anyone else."

"I see. The agency you mentioned earlier. Have you got a copy of his email?"

"It'll be on Anna's Mac. It's up in her room. Why are you asking so much about the audition?"

"Because that's where she was when . . . you know."

"Oh. Was it horrible?"

'Horrible' was such an understated word for what Anna had been put through. Inwardly Jenny shuddered at the memory of her discarded body.

"Yes."

Kim sobbed and put her head in her hands. "Poor, poor Anna."

Jenny put a hand on her arm.

Kim looked up suddenly, tears halted. "So this audition. Was it fake? Was she set up?"

"It's certainly starting to look that way."

"But that means she was targeted! Someone planned this in advance. The email proves it. You can trace it, surely? I'll get her Mac."

Kim ran out the door before Jenny could stop her. Footsteps ascended the stairs two at a time, noisily for someone so nimble.

Jenny sat back down, considering what she'd learned. A promising musician turned promiscuous student. A dubious recommendation leading to a fake audition. A gruesome rape and murder. A premeditated plan that exploited Anna's dreams. Anna must have known her murderer. Or, at the very least, her murderer must have known her.

Jenny heard a key rattle in the front door. She stood up and returned to the hallway. A young man with dark hair and round, wire-framed spectacles walked through the door, shaking out a golf umbrella. He stopped short when he saw Jenny.

Jenny held up her warrant card and said, "Detective Inspector Price, Met Police. And you are?"

The man withdrew his key from the lock and closed the door. "Patrick Harper. What's going on?"

"Oh Patrick, you shouldn't have come!" Kim rushed down the stairs, carrying a thin silver laptop. She shoved it into Jenny's hands and threw her arms around Patrick. "But I'm glad you did." She buried her head in his coat and wept forlornly.

"What's wrong, Kim?" He stroked her hair but stared steadily at Jenny.

"It's Anna. She's been . . . she's dead."

"*What? Dead?* Good God. I'm so sorry, Kim." He hugged her close, kissing the top of her head.

Karim came down the stairs. He indicated that he needed to talk to Jenny. They returned to the kitchen and spoke in low voices. Karim closed the door.

"Look at this," Karim said, holding up a plastic bag. Latex gloves now covered his hands. The contents of the bag were obvious.

"Drugs."

"Yup, marijuana, and I reckon the white tablets are speed."

"Anna's?"

"They were under her pillow."

"I'm not surprised, given what I've just been told. Seems like she was on a downward spiral."

"Who's the Harry Potter lookalike?"

"Kim's boyfriend."

"*Him?* You've got to be taking the piss. She's Premiership. He's Conference at best."

Jenny was no football fan, but she understood the reference. They were certainly mismatched.

"Perhaps he cast a spell over her."

"Well his magic wand is parked right outside." Karim pointed through the window.

A Porsche 911 Carrera GTS, sparking white exterior, red leather interior, was parked directly in front. Right in front. Not two hundred yards away through rain and wind like her car.

Lucky.

And rich, although Kim hadn't come across as a gold digger. But she *had* described Anna as being jealous of Kim's relationship with Patrick. Jenny wondered if there was more to it.

She put Anna's laptop on the table. "Let's get a crime scene team down here. And ask for Harry O'Reilly from Computer Crime as well. There's an email on that computer we need to trace."

Karim pulled out his mobile phone.

Through the rain-soaked window, Jenny looked up and down the street. No other spaces to park. He really was lucky.

Maybe Patrick was a wizard after all.

Brody was still astonished by what he'd seen.

Spying on a beautiful young girl masturbating in the bath had really brought home how real this was. He shouldn't have been surprised. People got up to all sorts of stuff in the privacy of their own homes. But it had still been an eye-opener.

And, he had to admit, very enjoyable.

So much so that he'd connected a spare laptop to his wall-mounted, 56" LCD television and left it displaying the *Au Pair Affair* streams in the background. Perhaps the girl would repeat the show later on. Or maybe the wife would catch the husband and the girl at it. Or maybe there were other locations on the site that were just as interesting.

As these thoughts passed through his mind, he realised how clever the whole SWY concept was. It had the drama of a soap opera crossed with the allure of secretly spying on a stranger. The global, long-standing success of the *Big Brother* television show had amply demonstrated how voyeurism hooks the public. Each series, contestants lived together for three months, with their every move observed by cameras and broadcast live to the public, who then voted to evict contestants each week. But the contestants were all too aware of the cameras and often played up for the audience. SWY was *Big Brother* for real. No cheap games and gimmicks to spice up the activities, just intimate, real-life moments on display from hundreds of contestants all over the world.

Brody checked the television screen. Not much was happening in the *Au Pair Affair* household. The Scandinavian girl was fully dressed and leafing through a magazine in the lounge. The baby was sleeping soundly in the cot in the nursery. No sign of the baby's parents anywhere.

Brody restarted his randomised movie soundtrack playlist, careful to ensure it didn't wake Leroy again. This time it picked 'Gabriel's Oboe' from Ennio Morricone's *The Mission*. Perhaps a bit too gentle, but good enough for now.

Brody pressed 'Enter' on the *WhoIs* lookup command he had typed in earlier. It ran with the parameter of the website's domain name: SecretlyWatchingYou.com. Every domain name on the Internet is unique and registered in a central database along with certain key information such as IP addresses and contact details for the site's administrators. Brody read through the results, which showed that the IP addresses for SecretlyWatchingYou.com were located in Russia. The contact details were for a Russian Internet Service Provider. This did not necessarily mean that Crooner42 himself was Russian; just that he was being smart by hosting the site there. Internet Service Providers in the Eastern Bloc countries did little to help police forces.

Armed with the IP address, Brody could begin his pentest — he corrected himself — he could begin his *attack*. Simply identifying and reporting on the site's weaknesses was no longer his objective. He needed to break in and take control. He looked at his watch and automatically drew air in through his teeth. He had wasted too much time. Matt_The_Hatter could be way ahead of him by now.

Brody's standard approach was to sneak through the outer perimeter of the site, find a vulnerability within its local network and then exploit it. The first defence of any network is the firewall, which is designed to only let certain types of traffic through on certain 'ports'. His first task was to scan the firewall to identify which ports were open. He had to be careful to ensure the firewall did not detect it was being probed. It would automatically block the originating IP address. To counter this he, like many accomplished hackers, had set up his own 'botnet', hundreds of remote programs on servers distributed around the globe, ready to carry out his instructions.

On every system Brody had compromised over the last few years, he had left a small remote Trojan horse program running, known as a daemon. The daemon sat idle awaiting Brody's bidding. The administrators of these networks had no idea the daemons were there. In his penetration test result reports that he presented to his clients, he conveniently forgot to inform them that he'd left a little piece of code behind. Brody thought of it as a tip automatically added to a bill for providing a good service. Not that he declared it or offered them an option to remove it.

Brody coordinated the activities of his remote daemons from a program running on his computer. He kicked it off, instructing the remote daemons to cycle through all ports on the firewall protecting the SWY site. The firewall had no idea this was a coordinated probe as the individual port scans were coming from hundreds of different IP addresses all over the world. Acting as one botnet, they sent their results back to Brody's computer.

In the black hat community, botnets are used maliciously to run Distributed Denial of Service, or DDOS, attacks. Instead of subtle probing, the botnet would be set up to fully interact with a target website and flood it with legitimate looking communication requests. The website, unable to determine which were real and which were fake, would attempt to respond to them all, ultimately leading to degraded performance or even a complete system crash. Even when restarted, the DDOS attack would resume, crashing the site over and over. Many famous sites have fallen victim to DDOS attacks, including Twitter and Facebook.

Brody read through the logs from the port scan and frowned.

The scan had run smoothly, but the results gave Brody the first indication of the considerable strength with which Crooner42 had secured SWY. All non-essential ports were blocked, which meant he had no way to take control of the firewall itself and open up any port he needed. Instead, he would need to mask all his activities through port 80, the standard port used for website traffic.

He thought of himself as an archer trying to fire a grappling hook from a crossbow at the keep of a castle across a moat at night. Instead of firing over the walls to the keep in the centre of the castle, he had to fire through the huge gate, the firewall, which was closed to most traffic. But there was a small access hatch open within the gate, port 80, that he could fire the hook through. If he could snag the grappling hook onto the keep beyond, the web server, he might then have a something to work with. The question was, were the granite walls of the keep hardened to an impenetrable, smooth diamond, or were they rough slate, with small cracks that his grapple hook could snag onto?

To figure that out he first needed to map the grounds of the castle, the network, behind the firewall. He tried a simple *trace route* command but, predictably, the firewall blocked it. Instead, he fired up an advanced network sniffer program. He set it to work through port 80, and pointed it at the SecretlyWatchingYou.com IP address.

Brody left it running and went to the kitchen to make a coffee. The kitchen had every conceivable appliance installed and the bean-to-cup automated coffee maker did a fair job, but not good enough to prevent Brody popping over the road to Bruno's Coffee House a few times a day.

Brody rented the flat fully furnished. The owner was a City broker who had spent a year refurbishing it, sparing no expense. A month after it had been completed, the broker's bank had relocated him to Hong Kong, forcing him to arrange a quick lease.

Conveniently, Brody had walked into the letting agent's office just minutes before they were about to publish the flat's details on their website for all to see. The letting agent had stressed how incredibly lucky Brody's timing was, as the area was very popular and flats like this were snapped up very quickly. Little did the agent know that Brody had surreptitiously hacked into their desktop computers a month before, and every time any new digital picture was added to their computers, a hidden program covertly emailed a copy to one of Brody's anonymous email accounts. He spotted the flat within minutes of the agents transferring the pictures from their digital camera to the computer. Their camera even had a GPS positioning feature enabled and so the location of the flat was encoded within the JPEG file. He converted the GPS longitude and latitude to an address in Upper Street and checked it out. Within minutes, Brody knew this area was where he wanted to live. He fell in love with the lively vibe, the unusual restaurants and the proximity to central London. And the two-bedroom flat itself was the ultimate bachelor pad. It was a no-brainer. His higher than requested rental offer had sealed the deal, without it ever being advertised by the agent.

Espresso in hand, Brody returned to his computer in the living room.

The network scan had finished. It had found a router, a web server, a proxy server and three other unidentified servers. They were all Unix based, which were usually slightly harder to crack than Microsoft Windows-based servers. Brody's priority was the web server. He ran some scans to work out the versions and patch levels of the Unix operating system. Knowing this would allow him to figure out if there were any published weaknesses that he could exploit. A few minutes later the results were displayed.

Brody took one look and buried his head in his hands. It was patched to the most current versions: the defences were solid. The walls of this keep were a smooth diamond. There was nothing to hook onto. He hoped Matt_The_Hatter was finding this as troublesome as he was.

He decided it was time to get creative. No more shortcuts.

He would dig a tunnel.

CHAPTER 5

"Okay everyone, can I have your attention, please."

Jenny looked up from her desk. DCI Da Silva stood alone by the far wall of the Murder Investigation Room, a whiteboard stretching from one side of the room to the other behind him. Grisly shots of Anna Parker's body in situ were grouped in the centre, held in place by magnets, captions written in marker pen underneath. A map of Paddington and a floor plan of the top floor of the office building were mounted to the right. Plenty more space was available on the left, but Jenny knew from experience this would fill up quickly. Once the post-mortem was completed later that day, a grotesque art gallery exhibition of Anna Parker's corpse would appear, close-ups of her fatal wounds taking top billing.

Jenny looked around to see if anyone else had taken any notice of Da Silva. Uniformed officers and an interweaving of plain clothes detectives and civilian staff had begun to shuffle towards the front of the room, dragging chairs behind them or perching on the edges of desks. Jenny sighed, stopped making notes in the incident management log, decamped to the front of the room and stood facing the gathering in her place to Da Silva's right.

Da Silva waited patiently until everyone was settled. The general hubbub gradually died down, as the group waited expectantly for Da Silva to take charge. Jenny saw that her core team sat in a huddle together to her left. DS Alan Coombs whispered something to DC Karim Malik, the back of his hand shielding his lips. Karim sniggered under his breath and passed on the witticism to DC Fiona Jones, who smirked briefly then resumed her straight face.

"Thank you," Da Silva said. "I think it's time we gathered our thoughts." His words wouldn't have been out of place in a church service.

Jenny wondered how Da Silva was going to pull this off. The last time he'd addressed the full Holborn Murder Investigation Team, on his first day in charge, he'd instantly damaged his credibility. It had been a fatuous speech full of empty corporate-speak: how he was assured he could rely on the same professional standards the team had given to his predecessor; how he needed two hundred per cent from everyone each and every minute of the day; how, under his leadership, they would quickly cut down their team's monumental backlog of outstanding lines of enquiry, which, he stressed, was very visible in HOLMES — the computer system used by all forces nationwide to aid in the investigation of serious crime; and how, together, they would positively improve their team's ranking on the dashboard of statistics reviewed monthly by the Met Commissioner, whom he happened to know personally.

Jenny heard Da Silva cough deliberately. An obedient hush fell across the room. She stared down at her feet.

"DI Price, would you be so kind as to take us through the case so far?"

"Me, sir?"

Shit, what a fool. Why had she asked that? She caught sight of Karim whispering to Fiona again, but Fiona ignored whatever it was he had said. Alan mouthed silently to her, "Go on." Goaded, she continued speaking before Da Silva had a chance to reply. "No. Of course. Right."

As a delaying tactic, she turned her back on the audience and selected one of the coloured whiteboard marker pens, tested the ink ran smoothly on the board, wiped it with her wrist to make sure it was non-permanent and turned back to the crowd.

"Anna Parker," she stated, her voice catching. She cleared her throat and continued, far more clearly. "Second year music student at Trinity Laban Conservatoire in Greenwich. Raped and murdered by persons unknown during a fake cello recital held in a meeting room on the top floor of an office building in Paddington Basin." Jenny paused and then said, almost to herself, "You know what, saying that out loud makes you realise how bizarre this case is."

Nods of agreement around the room. Da Silva took a seat at the front of the crowd, facing her along with everyone else. She noticed that Jason Edmonds, the Crime Scene Manager was at the back of the room. He nodded at her; his usual smirk still evident.

"I see three main lines of investigation. The first is the crime itself." She scrawled 'CRIME SCENE' on the whiteboard. "Second, there's the location choice. We'll dig into each of these in a minute; let's just get the headings for now. Lastly, is the way Miss Parker was lured to the location." Jenny had written two other headings: 'LOCATION' and 'LURE'.

She had their attention now. Not bad for someone thinking on her feet. At least no one had disagreed.

Karim spoke up, "Jenny, what about a catch-all for all the other lines of enquiry? You know, other witnesses and suspects not linked to those three areas. Like her flatmates and the all the dodgy one night shags she's had?"

She spotted Da Silva frown at Karim's choice of language, but he said nothing.

"Good thinking, Karim." Jenny wrote a fourth heading: 'OTHER'.

"DC Jones," said Da Silva to Fiona, "would you mind taking over the pen from DI Price?" He looked at Jenny and explained, "Struggling to read your writing."

"Oh, sorry," said Jenny, a flush of red rapidly spreading across her face. Bastard.

"Looks fine from here," said Alan, coming to her rescue as always. "You can borrow these if you like, guv." He held his glasses towards Da Silva by one of its arms. A few snickers sounded around the room.

"I can see fine, DS Coombs," said Da Silva.

What an arse. Just as she was getting going, Da Silva had to reassert his authority by humiliating her in front of the whole team. Fiona joined her at the front and accepted the pen, shrugging to indicate she was just following orders.

Jenny put Da Silva's comment to one side. "Let's start with the crime itself and then work backwards." She caught the Crime Scene Manager's eye. "Jason, would you mind summarising what you've found so far."

"Sure," said Edmonds.

Jenny had rarely seen Edmonds without a crime scene suit and respiratory mask covering all but those bright blue eyes. Uncovered, his closely-shaven head was evident, which Jenny guessed was designed to defocus attention from early onset baldness.

"Based on initial assessments, the victim was killed between 6:00 and 8:00 p.m. last Friday evening —"

"It was definitely after 6:30," Fiona jumped in. "We've got a witness to classical music being heard after then."

Edmonds stared down Fiona. "As I was saying, based on crime scene evidence, absence of rigor mortis, body temperature, and a hundred other little things, that is my initial assessment. But thank you, it's great that good detective work can corroborate my team's findings."

Someone whistled a sarcastic woo-wee. Fiona held her hands up in apology to Edmonds.

"Being a meeting room, lots of people have used it. At this stage, we cannot narrow down from fingerprints and other trace evidence how many people were in the room at time of death." Edmonds looked at Jenny and then Da Silva. "We'll need your team to go through the room bookings, find out everyone who's been there in the last month or so, and obtain samples for elimination purposes."

Da Silva nodded. Fiona dutifully wrote the action on the board.

"But won't we need to go wider than just the people who work in the building?" asked Karim.

"Absolutely," said Jenny. "We'll get Flexbase — that's the company who runs the building for all the paying tenants — to give us a list of who booked each meeting room. Then we track them down. Take their samples for elimination. Find out who else was in their meeting, which could well be visitors. Track them down. Eliminate them. A lot of work."

Fiona scribbled further actions across the whiteboard.

"If we're really lucky," continued Edmonds, "Dr Gorski will be able to lift prints from the victim's body during the post-mortem and we'll be able to match them to the surroundings. But don't hold your breath. With the air conditioning, the humidity levels are low, which makes it harder."

"Have you figured out the order of events?" asked Jenny.

Dr Gorski gave a slightly updated version of the same

monologue he'd given that morning at the crime scene, describing the ordeal that Anna must have endured at the hands of the killer. As before, a hushed silence fell across the room.

And then, almost as one, everyone began talking. Offering thoughts, comments, ideas. Jenny took control and flowed them through to Fiona, one by one, for noting on the whiteboard. The contributions came from everyone, some of the best from the uniforms and the civilian staff. Jenny was pleased that the team was beginning to work as one, despite Da Silva's unorthodox leadership style.

The list of actions under 'CRIME SCENE' reached the bottom of the board.

"Okay everyone, let's move on to the location," said Jenny. "As we all know, the choice of any location tells us a lot about the killer, particularly when it's pre-planned — as it most certainly was in this case."

Alan joined in. "Yeah, this has to be someone familiar with the way Flexbase operates. But that could be anyone. Flexbase staff, the tenants, ex-tenants, visitors and so on. That's an awful lot of people."

"Especially when you consider that Flexbase runs over forty office buildings like this all over the country," added Fiona, "each sharing a central booking system."

Jenny asked Alan, "Did you track down the receptionist who was on duty on Friday afternoon?"

"Yes." Alan pulled out his pocket notebook. "Leyla Seidov. She remembered Anna mainly because of the cello case. Apparently, she struggled lugging it through revolving doors and tripped over, falling flat on her face in the middle of the reception area." He looked up from his notes. "Miss Seidov thought it was an amusing story until I pointed out the girl was now dead."

Alan gazed about as if expecting a follow-up comment. None came.

"Was Anna picked up from reception?" Jenny asked, trying to keep the momentum flowing.

"About half an hour before Anna arrived, Miss Seidov received a call from the meeting room on the eighteenth floor. It was a man's voice. Identified himself as William Webber. She doesn't recall any particular accent, but she is from Azerbaijan after all."

"What did the man say?"

"Only that he was expecting a visitor at 5:30 p.m. He asked for the receptionist to phone him directly in the meeting room rather than the WMA offices."

"Which presumably she did . . ."

"Yes, and when she phoned through, Webber asked the receptionist to send her straight up to the eighteenth floor, where he said he would meet her at the lifts."

"Was there no security? Surely, that was an unusual request, Alan?" asked DS Harry O'Reilly, the MIT's computer specialist, from the back of the room.

"Apparently not in that building. There's no security barriers or anything. Just the reception. The receptionist said she worked in other higher security Flexbase buildings where guests need to be escorted, but not this one."

"What about CCTV?" asked one of the PCs that Jenny didn't know. "Surely the killer must have arrived earlier that day?"

"Only in reception. But it's all controlled centrally from the Flexbase HQ in Docklands. We need to get someone over there to start going through the footage. Fiona . . ." Alan nodded at Fiona who took the hint and added the action to the list.

"This is a priority line of enquiry," contributed Da Silva. "The perpetrator could be recorded going in or leaving afterwards. And I cannot believe, DI Price, that we have no one chasing this down already."

Jenny immediately felt her shackles rising. The cheek of the man. That was why the team got together like this, so that they could collate all lines of enquiry and prioritise them. Which would be done at the end of the session. She was about to say this when Alan spoke.

"I'll head off down there now, Jenny. I think I'm all done here anyway."

"Thank you, DS Coombs," said Da Silva.

"Yes, thanks Alan," said Jenny.

Alan stood up and made his way through the throng to the exit at the back of the room. Da Silva folded his arms.

"DS O'Reilly, what have you learned about how the meeting room was booked?"

"I've been on the phone to yer man from their help desk for

hours already." Harry had the soft lilt of an Irish accent. "Those beggars know nothing at all. Best I could get out of them was that yer man booked it through the Flexbase public website."

"Can they trace where the booking was made from?" Fiona asked, more comfortable with IT than Jenny would ever be.

"Not the eejits I was talking to. The admin app they're using doesn't display source IP addresses from whoever booked. Now that doesn't mean it's not stored in the database itself, just that they've no idea how to check. I've got the name of the vendor who wrote the booking system. I'll follow up after this."

"Is it true the email address used to make the booking was fake?" Jenny asked, recalling Lawrence MacDonald's outburst at the Flexbase building manager earlier.

"Completely made up. It's just an open text field to be filled in on the web page. No logic built in to verify if it's even in a valid email format, never mind a check to see it's real. The confirmation email that the booking system sends out just bounced and no one ever checks the logs. Bad design if you ask me."

"The meeting room booking was made the Monday before?"

"Yes, at 3:14 p.m. And he booked out all four rooms on the eighteenth floor with the same fake email address."

"Which is one of the reasons we know this murder was pre-meditated," said Karim.

Jenny summarised for the group. She made sure that Fiona captured all the actions. In fact, she rather enjoyed having someone else do the writing. Perhaps Da Silva had a point. Her handwriting *was* pretty illegible, especially compared to Fiona Jones' neat block capitals.

"Now the most interesting part," Jenny stated. "The lure."

The murder itself felt secondary for solving this case. The rape and murder were key components of the killer's ritual, but that was as far as it went. Criminal psychologists might disagree, but understanding the killer's physical actions wouldn't necessarily help Jenny make a break through. And anyway, HOLMES would have thrown up a similar case if the modus operandi had been recorded already. And it hadn't.

To Jenny, the use of the meeting room for the location was unusual and would certainly help to narrow down suspects, but all the techno-gabble around vendors, booking systems and IP addresses confused her.

She was convinced that victim selection was key, especially so far in advance. This was no stranger. It had to be someone close to Anna. Someone who knew enough to exploit her private dreams of playing in the Royal Opera House Orchestra. It was the smart use of the Royal Opera House that had overruled any reservations Anna should have had when confronted with a strange, corporate office block in Paddington for her audition.

Jenny summarised this line of thinking for the room. There was general agreement all round.

"O'Reilly, have you retrieved the killer's email from Anna's laptop yet?"

"Technically, it's on a mail-server in . . . ah, sure never mind. Here's a printout." He handed her a sheet of paper.

Jenny scanned it and then read it aloud to the group.

Dear Ms Parker,

I have been given your details by Jake Symmonds, one of your music lecturers at Trinity Laban. He has done this off-the-record as he and I are old colleagues. I work for WMA Associates, an independent agency that identifies up-and-coming talent for professional orchestras around the world. I am currently carrying out a confidential search for a cellist on behalf of the Royal Opera House Orchestra. Initially, this would be a temporary position, filling in for someone going on maternity leave. But it could lead to greater things.

Jenny paused and then commented, "Can you believe this shit?"

"Sadly, Anna Parker did," said Da Silva.

"Yes, she did." Jenny knew she deserved the gentle rebuke. She continued reading.

Jake has given you a strong personal reference and so I would like to invite you to audition for this exciting opportunity. Due to urgent time pressures, the only slot I have remaining is on Friday 20th April at 17:30. The address for the audition is at the WMA Associates offices, which are located at Tower 2, Paddington Basin, London, W1 9OL.

Please be prepared to play two solo pieces of your choice.

I would very much appreciate it if you could keep this under wraps at this stage, given the publicity surrounding my client. I look forward to meeting you in person on Friday afternoon.

Kind regards,
William Webber.

The room pondered the note silently.

Jenny offered her thoughts, "Okay, this gives us at least three strands. Who was he to know so much about her? Does this lecturer Jake really have any involvement in this? And the email itself – can it be tracked?"

Fiona added further actions to the whiteboard.

"I'm after looking into the email," said Harry. "It's from a spoofed email account. It's the same fake address as yer man used when booking the meeting room. Now then, underneath the display headers, it's a completely different email address. It's one of those disposable ones that you can get without registering any personal details. The only line of enquiry left is to trace the IP address via the email service provider, from when it was initially registered and when this email was sent. The only problem is that could take a fierce long time and depends if they are forthcoming or not."

"So, does that mean we're dealing with someone really IT savvy?" asked Jenny.

"Not necessarily. If you google 'fake email address' there's a feckload of sites that explain step-by-step how to do it without being traced."

"Okay, so we're back to the list of people who would have known enough about Anna to compose something like this, playing on her dreams so well. What about Facebook?"

"I've already checked," said Fiona, standing beside Jenny. "She's got over five hundred friends listed. We'll need to eliminate all of them. And we're checking Facebook and Twitter to see if anyone has been cyber-stalking her."

"Who has five hundred friends?" asked Verity, one of the civilian indexers, a rotund middle-aged woman.

"Come on, Verity," said her colleague, an older gentleman whom Jenny recognised from around the station but didn't know, "You know what the kids are like these days with their friends. Quantity over quality, not like in our day, eh!"

Jenny agreed with the sentiment. Online connections were no substitute for the proper intimacy that real face-to-face friendship offered.

"What about cross-referencing everyone on her Facebook and Twitter accounts with every name we end up getting from Flexbase?" suggested Fiona. "If someone shows up on the list of people who know something about Flexbase and also on the list of Anna's friends, then we'd have a strong suspect."

"Great idea, DC Jones," said Da Silva.

Jenny agreed; it really was a good idea. She'd never have thought of it herself. But that was why they were a team.

"Can you set that up, Harry?" Fiona asked.

"I can," he replied. "It'll only take a minute. Just get me the names from Flexbase, ideally with email addresses, and I'll be after organising it."

"This is good," said Jenny. "What about this lecturer? Jake?"

"Yup, I'm on that," said Fiona, capturing the action anyway.

"Anything else?" Jenny asked the room.

Karim put up his hand and said, "What about checking with the Royal Opera House? Just in case they really *were* auditioning?"

Fiona wrote down the action.

"Okay. Last strand. Other witnesses and suspects. You know, the basic legwork we're all so good at. Let's trace Anna's steps from leaving her house to arriving at Flexbase. Did she go anywhere else first? Meet anyone else? Let's talk to her family and friends. Anyone who had something against her? There's a list of one-night stands over the last six months we need to talk to. Perhaps there's something there."

Karim added, "Yeah, and we've yet to confirm alibis for the other flatmates. And then there's Kim Chang's boyfriend. There's something not right there."

"What do you mean, Karim?" asked one of the other DCs, with a smirk.

"Karim's just jealous," said another to the room. "He mentioned it earlier. He can't understand how come a looker like this Kim Chang would lower her standards so much. I think Karim's hoping he's in with a shot if we nick the boyfriend."

Laughter erupted around the room. The light relief at Karim's expense eased the tension of the workload they all knew was going to be immense over the next few days.

Da Silva stood up. "Thank you DI Price. The only thing missing is the media engagement strategy. We need one, following the impromptu interview I was forced to give this morning in Paddington. I'll pick that up with DS Schuster, our press officer. He'll be here later. Okay folks, let's get this list of actions prioritised, listed on HOLMES and assigned owners. I want to regroup in two hours."

Jenny thought about Da Silva. She'd never seen a DCI be so hands-off before. And yet, he maintained his authority, made decisions and kept the media to himself, where he would be most visible to his superiors. Perhaps this high-flying, fast-tracked, overly promoted detective had more to him than was initially apparent.

The problem with creating a tunnel through the Internet is the necessity to dig from both sides. A daemon should be running at the other end, working in tandem to set up the tunnel. Once the tunnel is in place, any kind of protocol, instruction or data can be sent through and the firewall has no idea. All it sees is more traffic on port 80. The daemon at the other end of the tunnel relays these instructions from its privileged location behind the firewall, launching data against any of the servers. In this way a hacker can run far more sophisticated scans for weaknesses and ultimately take control of any of the servers.

But the key was identifying an initial vulnerability through which to set up a remote daemon. Brody had tried and failed dismally for the last two hours. This web server was secure. Incredibly secure. As was the router and the other servers behind the firewall.

He was frustrated. And he had the shakes. The latter he put down to far too much caffeine. He always overdid the coffee during a marathon hacking session. He knew the stereotype Hollywood hacker was a young kid with acne, who drank too much cola. Maybe that was him fifteen years ago, but continued access to a decent income had given him a taste for some of the finer things in life. Good quality coffee was his modern-day cola substitute. The only downside was that the caffeine count was much higher. And decaffeinated coffee was no substitute for the real thing.

Brody wondered if Matt_The_Hatter had some tricks up his sleeve that Brody didn't know about. Paranoiacally, Brody checked back into the CrackerHack forum pages, dreading a post from Matt_The_Hatter already announcing his success over Brody. But nothing had been published.

Crooner42 had done an impressive job in setting up SWY's defences. Maybe his naive public approach to requesting a pentest was a smart move after all. If both Fingal and Matt_The_Hatter were seen to fail, then there was no way any police force would ever succeed. And Crooner42's status in the hacker community would immediately notch up a few levels while theirs would plummet.

Brody's smartphone beeped twice. He checked it absently. It was his calendar reminding him to head for his daily workout at the gym. That could wait.

But then he noticed another calendar item. It was for his date with Harriet that evening.

Damn, he'd been looking forward to that.

Harriet was a lawyer, aged twenty-nine, five feet four inches, and lived in Bermondsey. She was a brunette with long, curly locks. She'd even spoken with an upper class accent in her pre-recorded video on the dating site. But it had been her dimply smile that had been the clincher.

He looked at his watch. He considered where he was up to in the attack. Nowhere near far enough. He had no choice. He'd have to cancel the date. And their dinner reservation. And the hotel room, which had probably been optimistic anyway.

He thought through a list of excuses and settled on one about delays filming in Morocco . . . only just got back to a place with mobile phone reception . . . first chance he'd had to text her . . . really sorry about the short notice . . . could they reschedule for the weekend?

Brody typed it all in and pressed 'Send'.

A few minutes later his phoned beeped. Her response was to the point.

No, thanks. Your loss.

He groaned and decided to leave it there. He'd work on Harriet again once he got SWY out of the way.

Without a foothold on the other side of the firewall, Brody's tunnel attack had failed at the first hurdle. He would have to find an indirect route.

For bricks and mortar companies, the public facing website was just one of the numerous routes into their corporate networks. Companies also needed to provide controlled access for customers, suppliers, business partners and employees. A month ago, Brody had broken into a major retail company's systems by first breaking into a third-party logistics company used by the retailer for store deliveries. Unlike the retailer, the logistics company had very basic defences and, once hacked in, Brody discovered login credentials back into the retailer's supply chain system. Once logged in there, he identified a vulnerability ripe for exploitation and quickly gained full administrative access.

The problem with SWY was that there were no obvious indirect routes in. There were no suppliers or business partners. He was already signed up as a paying customer, but that route had already proved barren. And Crooner42 was probably the only employee.

As he mulled the situation over, Brody's eyes flicked over to the huge television screen displaying the *Au Pair Affair* video feeds.

Few sites exist in a bubble. Nearly all use widgets and data from external sources. Every time an external source is used, access has to be granted. Surely there must be an external data source?

Following this line of thought, Brody began a thorough review of the website itself, viewing the source HTML on every page. Line by line he searched for external references.

Time passed in a blur.

Leroy resurfaced but found Brody uncommunicative, buried in his computers. He clunked his way around the kitchen for a while making lunch, or maybe dinner, then he showered in the bathroom and then eventually Brody heard the front door slam as Leroy left, saying something about going to the cinema with Danny.

The HTML scan was getting him nowhere. The external widgets were few and far between and he found no vulnerabilities.

Another front door slammed.

"Audri! How many times do I have to tell you that the living room is out of bounds?" A woman's voice.

Brody jumped, looking around his room for the voice's source. No one was there.

Belatedly he realised it came from the TV, displaying the *Au Pair Affair* feeds. It had been quiet in the household for so long he'd forgotten it was on.

His movie soundtrack playlist was still going. He muted it and focused on the TV.

He saw movement in the thumbnail image labelled 'Living Room' and so clicked it to maximise it on the screen. The wife he'd observed that morning had returned home. The au pair, whom he could still picture naked, jumped up from the sofa. The baby, who had been asleep across her chest, woke up at the abrupt movement and cried out cheerfully, "Ma! Ma!"

Brody wrote *Nanny = Audri* on a notepad.

"I'm so sorry, Mrs Saxton. I was just —"

"No excuses. You have a TV in your own room and in the kitchen."

Brody wrote down *Mrs Saxton*. Next to Audri's name he wrote *Scandinavian?*, confirming his earlier thoughts about the girl's accent.

Audri lowered the baby to the carpeted floor and she crawled towards her mother. Mrs Saxton crouched down and held her hands out. "Do you want your mummy, Izzy? Do you want your mummy?"

The baby reached her mother and was lifted up into the air.

Audri left the room and Mrs Saxton remained on the sofa, talking nonsense to the baby. Brody lowered the volume.

Brody realised he was hungry. He didn't have the time to cook. And he fancied more than a few packets of crisps. He brought up the website of the local Thai takeaway and submitted his regular order: Pad Thai, Panang Beef and Coconut Rice. They estimated thirty minutes for delivery.

Back on the TV, all was quiet. The living room was now empty. He minimised it to display all seven feeds, searching for movement. Spotting activity in the kitchen, he maximised its screen and chose to receive sound from there instead.

The baby sat in the high chair, playing with plastic keys. Audri filled a kettle at the sink. Mrs Saxton opened a pile of letters at the kitchen table.

Brody squinted his eyes to try and make out the address on the envelopes, but the image resolution was too low. Perhaps if a letter was held close to the camera he might be able to read it.

Mrs Saxton held up two envelopes. "I hate the way American consumerism is ruining this country. Look at this. Two adverts for credit cards at discounted rates." She put on a fake American accent. "'You have pre-qualified for our amazing new discount. Sign today and receive a free watch.' Why can't we just go back to trusting our banks to look after our interests? Is it the same in Sweden?"

Brody scribbled out *Scandinavian* and wrote *Swedish*. Pleased that he'd been in the right ballpark.

"It is becoming the same. We have four or five main banks and they are learning to fight against each other. In Stockholm, you can see all of the European banks starting to invade."

"That's sad. Next it will be McDonald's."

"Oh no. There are already lots of them."

Audri turned the kettle on and leaned on the counter. She was a pretty girl, but not a conventional Swedish blonde. She had dark hair in a bob that hid part of her face. She had a lithe figure, which Brody already knew. Brody could see why Mrs Saxton's husband was tempted, but not the other way around.

"Oh. Here's a letter for you, Audri. Strange. No stamp." With a shrug, Mrs Saxton handed over the letter.

Brody wrote *Audrey?* next to the word *Swedish*, wondering if the Swedish spelling would be different. He'd google it later.

"Thank you." Audri grabbed the letter and stuffed it into the back pocket of her jeans.

"Not going to open it?"

"Oh it's just . . . what is the word?" She thought for a moment. "It's just a magazine article that my friend Ornetta promised to let me have."

Brody was getting bored. It was all so domestic. He wished they'd do something interesting. And it was diverting him from attacking the website properly.

Audri made two filter coffees with a carafe, gave one to Mrs Saxton and said she was going to her room. Mrs Saxton turned her attention to the baby and started cooing.

Brody clicked back to the menu and chose *Au Pair's Room*.

Audri entered and closed the door, locking it. She jumped on her bed and ripped open the envelope. A single piece of white paper with typed print fell out. It didn't look like a magazine. She read it and immediately looked at her watch.

She lay back on the bed and stared up. It almost looked like she was looking straight into the camera at Brody.

"Enough of this," said Brody to himself.

He pointed the remote control at the TV and muted it.

Brody logged into CrackerHack and skim read the chat logs. Nervously, he scanned for Matt_The_Hatter's ID to see if he'd got root already. As he reached the bottom, an electric jolt passed through him.

There, on the screen, was a post from Matt_The_Hatter.

This time, Jenny managed to park only a few doors down from Anna Parker's home, right in front of a Crime Scene Investigation Unit forensic response van. This late in the evening, far more gaps had appeared in Troughton Road; the commuters from the train station around the corner having returned en mass and jumped into their cars for their last leg home. Determined not to let the weather get the better of her, Jenny grabbed her umbrella from the passenger footwell.

When Jenny left Holborn earlier that evening, she had meant to go home. She wanted to put her feet up, vacantly watch some mind-numbing television, order in Thai or Chinese and slowly finish the half-full bottle of red wine she knew was sitting on the counter in her kitchen. But as the morgue was en-route, she decided to stop by to hear the results of Anna Parker's post-mortem from Dr Gorski. She soon wished she hadn't as he was only mid-way through the post-mortem. The wretched sight of Anna Parker's half-dissected body, the putrid smell of decay, and the contrast of the pathologist's over-the-top cheerfulness had wiped out her appetite in seconds. She was forced to watch and wait, but left as fast as she could afterwards.

On the journey from the morgue to her flat in Richmond, she had found herself thinking through the many threads to the case, always coming back to the line of enquiry she believed was key: the way Anna had been targeted and then lured to her death in the Paddington office block. Her killer had exploited her ambition of playing cello in the Royal Opera House Orchestra. To do this, he must have known her. At least well enough for Anna to have shared her hopes and aspirations with him. The promiscuous party girl that Kim Chang had described certainly didn't sound like the kind of girl who exposed her innermost dreams in idle chitchat. Which meant her killer must have taken the time to get to know Anna intimately.

As Jenny reached Lambeth Bridge for the fast stretch along the north bank of the Thames, she concluded that she too needed to get to know Anna. If she could gain some insights into her life, perhaps it would expose who knew Anna well enough to construct such an elaborate snare. Instead of continuing straight on in the direction of home, she turned left over the bridge and followed the roads along the south bank parallel to the river, winding her way eastwards towards Charlton.

Parked up, she bolted up the garden path aiming for the shelter of the arched porch of number 93. The front door opened just as she held her finger over the bell. A crime scene technician, not expecting anyone to be there, walked straight into her. She jumped to one side.

"Whoa," he said stepping back, holding steady a pile of labelled bags of evidence. "Sorry 'bout that."

A second tech walked up behind him, carrying plastic cases of equipment. The first looked her up and down and smiled. She recognised him from the earlier crime scene in Paddington.

"Alright, DI Price." She had no idea how he knew her name. "We're done here. Just heading off actually."

"Hi," she said, unable to dredge up his name. "Long day, eh?"

"Yeah." He let out a big sigh. "Look, once we drop this lot back at the ranch we're heading down to The Dolphin." He was referring to the pub a few doors down from Holborn Police Station. Most of her team would probably be in there by now. "Need to after a day like today. Fancy joining us?"

It was disguised as a matey offer, but the flush in his cheeks gave him away. She was flattered, but her automatic reaction against mixing business with pleasure kicked in.

"Thanks, but I've still got loads to do."

"No worries." He shuffled past her into the rain.

"Anyone around?" she asked the second technician.

"Don't think so. There was a girl here earlier. She made us a cuppa then left us to it. Went off with some guy in a white Porsche."

Kim Chang and Patrick Harper.

She nodded past him into the house. "Find anything useful?"

"Maybe. Hard to tell right now. Lots of prints and trace evidence." He shrugged. "If we're lucky, we'll get a fingerprint match against the murder scene earlier. And I don't mean the victim's."

"Yeah, we could do with a break. Keep me posted."

He held the front door open for her with his foot and, once she had entered, caught up with his colleague by the van. As she let the front door close, she heard them squabbling over who had the keys.

She was alone in the house. Other than the dripping rain outside, it was silent. And spooky. But she put that down to feeling uneasy about trespassing in someone else's empty home. She knew it was also because the image of Anna Parker's battered body, being violated further in the name of scientific investigation at the morgue, was still fresh in her mind.

Jenny tugged her coat tighter and headed for the stairs.

Dr Gorski had established the cause of death as exsanguination – bleeding to death because Anna's throat had been sliced open, severing the jugular veins and carotid arteries. From the length and depth of the single, effortless gash across her neck, the pathologist confidently stated that the blade was about eight inches long and razor sharp. The victim would have taken two or three minutes to die, certainly enough time for the killer to finish the rape he was performing at the same time. This too had been confirmed from bruising and traces of semen. Her assailant certainly hadn't worried to use a condom, which probably meant he was confident of not being listed by name on any DNA database.

They would check anyway. They always did.

Anna had also sustained other injuries before the final, fatal slice through her neck. The first trauma was to the side of her head. A hard, blunt object about an inch in diameter had struck her from behind, instantly cracking her skull. SOCO had found nothing at the crime scene that matched the shape of the wound. Jenny suggested the butt of the killer's knife and the pathologist agreed it was a possibility, especially if it had been an all-metal handle. Gorski explained that she probably lost consciousness for a short time from the violent blow. Holding still in hopeful anticipation, Jenny asked if it were possible that she had not regained consciousness. But her hopes were immediately crushed. Like a child showing off a new toy, Gorski had excitedly drawn Jenny's attention to the bruising on Anna's wrists, evidence that the victim had struggled against the rope that bound them together. And, he continued, as she could not have played the cello with her wrists tied, the logical conclusion was she had been bound up while unconscious and had came too at some point after. Jenny had been sickened by Gorski's detachment; his ability to get excited by the deductions he could make from examining a corpse, while suppressing any compassion for the person that had once inhabited the body or for the suffering endured that had caused death.

At the top of the stairs, Jenny saw Disney princess cut-outs mounted on the bedroom doors with the forenames of the housemates pre-printed on them. Undeniably practical, but presumably done as some kind of in-joke between the housemates. Kim's was Belle from *Beauty and the Beast* and Anna's was Jasmine from *Aladdin*. Jenny wondered if there had been any rationale behind who was which princess. And if it had been malicious in any way, assuming that being likened to a Disney princess could even be done unkindly.

Jenny reached in her coat pocket, found some latex gloves and pulled them over her hands. She pushed open the door to Anna's room.

It was smaller than she expected, though maybe that was the dark purple walls lending a claustrophobic feel to the room. A double bed in one corner took up much of the floor space. The cream covers were thrown back, as if the occupant had just got up. She noticed squares had been cut out of the sheets: the work of the crime scene team. Brightly coloured clothes were strewn across the back of a chair by a desk in another corner. Shoes, some with impossibly high heels, were piled up randomly underneath the desk.

Evidence of Anna's musicianship was everywhere. A cello leaned against one wall. She owned more than one, then. Next to it, hanging from their necks on wall mounts, was a violin and an acoustic guitar. A mouth organ lay discarded on the desk. On the printer, Jenny picked up some papers. A half-completed essay about someone called Dvořák. Jenny scanned the text and deduced he had been a 19th century composer. Lots of posters, mostly of music bands or album covers, brightened up the dark wall beside the bed. She recognised The Beatles, but the rest she'd never heard of. On the side table next to the bed, an empty iPod dock sat next to, of all things, a record player. It was a sixties style red box, open with a record in place. The round lever in the bottom corner was set to 33 rpm and, although Jenny had only ever owned CDs herself, she innately knew that meant it was set to play an album rather than a single. She lifted the arm. Automatically, the turntable rotated. She placed the needle on the record. The volume was set quite high.

There was some audible crackling in the background, but the sound quality wasn't too bad. Despite the haunting classical music not being to her taste, she left it playing anyway.

Jenny continued to nose around.

She sifted through the clothes hanging in the wardrobe behind the door. She saw well-worn denim jeans and baggy jumpers next to short dresses and see-through tops. Her student life and her nightlife. Were they two separate lives or one life completely intertwined? Was her killer from Trinity College or from the nights out that Kim had mentioned? Or both? Or from some other aspect of her life that she kept secret?

The room had a fireplace, but with only an empty glass vase within its recess. On the mantel were three photos in matching frames. On the left was a studio style portrait of a middle-aged couple. From the likeness, especially the woman, Jenny guessed they were her parents. In the centre was a nice one of Anna and Kim in Trafalgar Square, their arms around each other's waists, huge toothy grins plastered on their faces and pigeons perched on their heads and shoulders. The last picture was of Anna herself, picked out within an orchestra, serious concentration on her face, playing her cello and wearing a stunning lime-green ballgown.

Jenny sat down on the bed, disturbing a giant teddy bear, and studied the three photos of Anna's life from a distance. The parents from her past, her closest friend from the present and her love for performing music, her stolen future. Anna Parker's whole life summed up in three images.

Jenny wondered if three images could sum up her own life. She herself had not gone to university, unlike both her older brothers who had studied academic subjects like Engineering and Politics. Instead, she had been naturally artistic and, following A-Levels, had become a trainee hairdresser in a top salon in London, believing it was the most practical way to earn a living from her impractical skills. After two years, she had decided that she enjoyed working with the public but found washing, brushing and styling hair meaningless. At the same time she had just been ungracefully dumped by her first love, a trainee officer in the City of London police whom she'd dated since the age of seventeen. In a fit of rage or a bout of inspiration – she'd never really worked out which – she applied to join the Met. She'd never looked back.

Jenny wondered how different her life would have been if she'd gone to university like her brothers and most of her school friends. She'd probably have chosen one far away from her childhood home in Kent. Perhaps as far as —

She caught sight of movement out of the corner of her eye.

The door was slowly being pushed ajar.

She felt the hair lift on her arms and nape. A knife blade glinted in the gap between door and frame. She felt the colour drain from her face.

She rapidly looked around.

There was nowhere to run to.

CHAPTER 6

Half-empty aluminium foil trays lay strewn about Brody's desk. Thai spices, initially bright and fragrant, had dissipated, transmuting into a sticky fug that attached itself to Brody's cotton shirt and denim jeans. Slowly, a queasy feeling forged in Brody's stomach. He wasn't sure whether to blame the takeaway meal or the growing dread from hours of continuous failure.

SWY's defences were amongst the best he'd ever seen. It was as if every security precaution he'd ever recommended had been collated and applied to this one site.

He was running out of ideas.

For the umpteenth time that evening, Brody logged back into the CrackerHack forum. He scrolled through that day's chat logs, tentatively scanning for Matt_The_Hatter's announcement that he'd got root already.

He reached the bottom. Nothing there.

Thank God.

Earlier, he'd spotted a new post from Matt_The_Hatter and had thought the game was up already. But it had turned out to be nothing more than Matt_The_Hatter arrogantly picking on a newbie for asking dumb questions on the forum. Matt_The_Hatter must still be overly confident of pwning SWY if he felt able to take time out to torment new victims.

A few of the members had been chatting to each other about the challenge, quickly polarising into Fingal or Matt_The_Hatter supporters. Some pointed out that Fingal must have a massive ego if he thought he could outwit Matt_The_Hatter in a get root challenge. Gratefully, he saw that some more experienced forum members had fought his defence, denouncing Matt_The_Hatter as little more than a script kiddie. His friend, Doc_Doom, had gone one step further and pointed out that Matt_The_Hatter exhibited borderline personality disorder tendencies. Which was effortlessly summarised by another member, who commented that Matt_The_Hatter was just a forum bully and that anyone supporting him was only scared shitless of his infamous vengeance.

Other than losing the challenge, Brody personally feared little from Matt_The_Hatter. He had the experience and knowhow to make himself completely untraceable back to RL – real life. Other weaker forum members, hackers with limited skills, had been known to fall foul of Matt_The_Hatter's wrath. In one extreme case only two months before, a newbie forum member called Queen_Xoltan had accused Matt_The_Hatter of claiming credit for her friend's hack. In an online fit of rage, Matt_The_Hatter declared that Queen_Xoltan was dead in the online world and that he would track her down and publicly 'out' her. Four days later, Matt_The_Hatter cheerfully posted Queen_Xoltan's real world name and address for all to see, including the numerous law enforcement agencies that anonymously prowled the hacker forums trying to track down black hat hackers. To Matt_The_Hatter's evident delight, Queen_Xoltan turned out to be a confused teenage boy from the Faroe Islands.

Brody's Samsung Galaxy phone beeped. It was a message from Doc_Doom, checking to see how he was getting on with the challenge. There was a link to a private secure online chat site in case he "wanted to knock about any ideas or just needed some moral support". He'd be there for the next hour or so.

Brody genuinely appreciated Doc_Doom reaching out to him like this. It wasn't the first time either. Brody doubted whether his friend would have any ideas that he hadn't already tried, but he was gratified by the moral support from someone who understood more than anything else. Perhaps just talking things through for a few minutes would help.

He switched to his tablet PC and clicked on the link. The chat screen took over the centre monitor, the ones on either side still displaying network maps and dumps of the SWY site.

Fingal: Hi Doc.

Doc_Doom: You winning?

Fingal: Not yet. SWY's a tough nut to crack. I think Crooner knew what he was doing all along.

Doc_Doom: Yup. Think you're right there, man. It certainly was a strange way to ask for help. You think this is all about him showing off on the forums?

Fingal: Yeah. Looks like it. Just hope Matt_The_Pratt is having as tough a time as I am.

Doc_Doom: He's all talk. Not a squeak from him since the challenge. Anyway, why'd you offer to help in the first place?

Fingal: Bit stupid, really. I was on a high from a job I'd just finished.

Doc_Doom: Yeah, I've been there too, man. You feel like you can do anything.

He was spot on. The bravado whipped up from successfully completing a hack was addictive. But, for Brody, the biggest high came from social engineering, where he combined hacking computers with hacking humans. They added the extra dimension of putting his physical, real world self in the firing line, hugely increasing risk, but exponentially intensifying the euphoria from success. Last week's Atlas Brands job had been one of his slickest yet and he now realised that his ego had got the better of him. In the Atlas video conference he'd hacked into this morning, he'd shown off. A lot. The euphoria had become arrogance and he'd allowed it to affect his judgement. And one impulsive click later, he'd registered his interest in Crooner42's pentest without doing any of the normal due diligence.

And so here he was.

Stuck.

Fingal: Any ideas, Doc?

Doc_Doom: Does the site use Java?

Fingal: Yes

Doc_Doom: Have you decompiled the Java bytecode?

A bit obvious. Of course, he had.

Fingal: Yes, but there were no passwords, application paths or anything sensitive.

Doc_Doom: I've heard about a new exploit for Java on the Eastern European forums. Give me a minute, I'll search for it . . .

This could be promising.

Brody waited, drumming his fingers on his desk. He looked up at the TV screens to see if anything interesting was happening in the Saxton household. Mrs Saxton sat next to the cot in the baby's bedroom, reading aloud from a picture book. The baby lay quietly in the cot. Audri was in her bedroom, getting changed.

Now *that* was interesting.

He wheeled his chair over to the laptop connected to the TV, maximised the video stream from Audri's room and unmuted the volume.

Audri dropped her bathrobe onto her bed, revealing white bra and panties. She opened her wardrobe and withdrew a bright red coat. She held it against her and stood in front of a mirror, checking the length. Satisfied, she dropped it on the bed and quickly removed her bra and stepped out of her panties.

Brody licked his lips and then realised he'd done so. He'd never have guessed that voyeurism could be so thrilling. A moment like this, a girl undressing, was the reward for hours of monotony. The whole thing was beguiling.

Audri picked up the red coat from the bed and put it on, directly over her naked body.

Now Brody was intrigued. And, he realised, quite turned on.

She stepped into a pair of black high heels and grabbed a matching handbag. She picked up something from her bedside cabinet. Brody looked more closely. It was the unstamped letter she'd received earlier that day. She opened the envelope, glanced at the letter it contained, stuffed it back in the envelope and slid it into her coat pocket. Checking herself once more in the mirror, she nodded and spoke something in Swedish to her reflection.

Brody thought he heard a slight noise, like a car driving over gravel. Audri obviously had, as well. She looked down out the bedroom window, then turned and flew out of the room.

Brody swiftly minimised the screen, revealing all seven feeds from around the Saxton household. No cameras covered the stairs or hallway, but he saw light appear in the baby's bedroom from the doorway. He clicked on it to hear the audio. Mrs Saxton paused her reading and looked towards the light. Although not visible onscreen, Audri's voice whispered, "My taxi's here, Mrs Saxton. I'll be late tonight."

Hilary whispered back, "Okay, Audri. Have fun with Ornetta."

"Will do. And don't worry; I'll make sure I'm up by 8:00 a.m. tomorrow. I haven't forgotten."

Mrs Saxton smiled. "Thanks, Audri." The room grew darker again. Then she added, "Don't forget your keys."

"Got them. Bye."

A few seconds later Brody heard a large door bang shut. Hilary Saxton paused a moment, checked on the baby and then resumed reading aloud.

Brody muted the audio again and mused over what he'd seen. There was no way the au pair was going out to see her girlfriend dressed, or more literally undressed, like that. The mysterious letter she'd received earlier that day had something to do with it. Brody recalled Mr Saxton kissing her that morning. He didn't need to be Sherlock Holmes to work this one out. She was off to meet the husband somewhere else for a night of illicit sex.

Brody wondered what she saw in the man. He was probably twice her age and married. But then, as Leroy always pointed out, he was hardly an expert on understanding what made relationships work.

He looked back at the online chatroom to see if Doc_Doom had finished his search. A string of messages awaited him.

Doc_Doom: Got it. It's an exploit based on Java applet same-origin policy being bypassed via a HTTP redirect. You heard of it?
Doc_Doom: Fingal, you there?
Doc_Doom: Earth calling Fingal . . .

Just as Brody was about to type a response another entry appeared.

Doc_Doom: Fine, I'm off.
Fingal: I'm back. Sorry about that. Pizza delivery just arrived.
Doc_Doom: Ah, the food staple of champion hackers. Pepperoni and mozzarella? Or do you Brits not do pizza like we do here?
Fingal: Told you before, mate. I'm Australian. Which means shrimp and

bbq sauce toppings.

Doc_Doom: Not buying it Fingal. But don't worry, I understand your need for stealth. I'm the same really. But wouldn't it be great to actually meet in person one day and actually talk to each other, f2f, over a Bud or something. No typing. Online is great, don't get me wrong, but . . .

Brody had had a similar conversation with Doc_Doom a month ago. He'd been taken aback at his suggestion then. After two years of building their friendship online — knocking around hacking challenges like this one, amiably debating whether the Empire from *Star Wars* could kick the Federation from *Star Trek's* ass, whether Marvel's superheroes were more rounded characters than DC's, or exploring how limiting it would have been in the eighties to write assembler programs on the old eight-bit chipsets used by Sinclair and Commodore — Doc_Doom had proposed meeting up in person.

Brody had briefly been tempted. Their online friendship was great. They shared opinions on many subjects. They convivially disagreed on others, each defending his corner with deep personal knowledge or rapid searches on the Internet to unearth facts and examples to bolster his viewpoint. It had become a real friendship and Brody was confident it would survive the transfer from the online to the offline world.

And he was tempted again now.

Instinctively, Brody looked up at the framed poster of Vorovskoy Mir's most wanted list and his gaze fell on his own online name, Fingal, listed under the third silhouette.

Fingal: You know my policy, Doc. It's just too dangerous to mix physical and virtual.

Doc_Doom: I understand. One day maybe, eh? Anyway, what about that new exploit? Any use?

Brody hadn't heard of anyone using HTTP redirect to bypass Java's same-origin policy. He quickly searched on the phrase and found more details of the hack, first published only two weeks ago. It was quite an interesting approach. Yes, it might work. Excited, he dropped over to Oracle's website, the vendor of Java, and linked through to the pages listing their latest versions. The most current patch for Java was released just four days before. Shit, they might have plugged it. He searched through the accompanying release notes for details of what had been fixed and, sure enough, there it was.

The hole was blocked.

But, if he was lucky, there was still one chance. If Crooner42 hadn't installed this newly patched version of Java onto the SWY site, he could still use the exploit. After all, the patch had only been released four days ago. He ran one of his utilities against the web server to identify the version of Java.

Damn. It was at the latest patch level. The hole was plugged. Deflated, Brody replied to Doc_Doom.

Fingal: Thanks Doc. But Crooner's already blocked it.
Doc_Doom: Jesus, that was fast. Very fast. He's better than I thought.
Fingal: Tell me about it.
Doc_Doom: Have you tried session hijacking?
Fingal: I can't, he's got server side session id tracking enabled.
Doc_Doom: Dictionary attack?

They carried on for another half-an-hour, back and forth, throwing ideas out for consideration, and quickly knocking them down. Brody felt even more disheartened. He hadn't really expected Doc_Doom to come up with anything, but going through everything like this had reconfirmed his predicament.

Doc_Doom: Jesus, this site's more secure than Fort Knox. Who the hell is this guy?
Fingal: You'd know better than me.
Doc_Doom: What's that supposed to mean?
Fingal: Just that you seem to get on better with the other forum members.
Doc_Doom: Better than you, you mean? Yeah, well that's because I'm less of a threat to them than you are.
Fingal: Don't be so modest, Doc. Do you know anything about Crooner? I'm thinking if I can identify another website he's built, maybe it'll be less secure but some of the configuration will be the same. Which means I could use what I learn there to aid in cracking SWY.
Doc_Doom: I like your logic. But all I know about Crooner is what you see on these forums. He's been around for a couple of years. He's never been that

forthcoming about what he does. As far as I'm aware, this is the only site he's mentioned. I guess he's just one of those who mostly stay in the background, mopping up everyone else's thoughts and ideas. Looks like we all underestimated him.

Fingal: True enough.

Doc_Doom: If it helps, I think he's British.

Doc_Doom: Like you :-)

Fingal: Okay, let's have this out once and for all. What makes you say that? About me and him?

Doc_Doom: The letters 'u' and 's'.

Fingal: ?

Doc_Doom: Color. Flavor. Personalize. Realize. Recognize.

Fingal: Ah, because I don't use Americanised spelling like you do. Maybe it's a deliberate ploy by me. Or, as I said earlier, maybe it's because I come from Australia. Or New Zealand. Or any other ex-British colony.

Doc_Doom: And then there's your use of slang. Or your lack of use of Australian slang.

Fingal: Strewth. And there's me thinking we were just chewing the fat. Fair dinkum, mate. So you think Crooner's a Pommie, then?

Fingal: (That enough Oz-talk for you?)

Doc_Doom: Okay, okay. I'll stop over-analyzing. But yes, I think Crooner's a Brit.

Fingal: Interesting. But not sure how it helps me.

Doc_Doom: Would help if you're a Brit too and you could somehow track him down in meatspace.

Fingal: Hmmm.

Brody bristled at Doc_Doom's shrewd analysis of his spelling and slang usage. He made a mental note to better disguise himself going forward, especially on the more public forums on CrackerHack. He'd google a list of obscure Australian slang terms and occasionally insert them into his future posts.

As for Crooner42 also being British, that was interesting, but unlikely to be of any use. The technical ability he exhibited in securing SWY meant he was most likely every bit as good as Brody in protecting his real world identity. Which meant tracking him down in meatspace — real life — would be next to impossible. And supposing he did, what could Brody actually do? Threaten him? That would only work if he turned out to be a meek teenage kid.

And even then Brody wasn't confident. He had no training or experience in any form of physical combat. He certainly had no idea how to physically coerce anyone against his or her will.

No, he just needed to keep going as he was.

Or admit defeat.

Or wait for Matt_The_Hatter to announce he'd got root first, and face the inevitable fallout. The public humiliation. The wrecking of his hard-earned elite status.

No. He needed to keep going. Surely there must be a way?

Of course there was. He needed to come up with a new zero-day exploit, something he hadn't done in well over two years. He needed to identify a brand new vulnerability that no one had ever come up with before and use it to crack through the site's defences.

The only problem was that it was incredibly difficult to do. Unless you fluked it, creating a zero-day exploit was incredibly time-consuming. It involved *fuzzing* — an inconsistent technique whereby he inserted random data into memory, attempting to force an application to crash, from which he could then analyse the results to see if there was a flaw he could exploit by substituting his own commands — but it was completely hit and miss. Usually miss. With no guarantee of success at all. And usually days or weeks of work.

And all the while, Matt_The_Hatter could break through.

But what choice did he have?

Brody stared at the seven feeds on the huge TV screen. Hilary Saxton lay in bed, reading. Izzy Saxton slept in her cot. Audri the au pair was still out with Derek the cheating husband. Life in Middle England carried on as normal.

Middle England?

England?

He had a thought.

He was approaching this from the wrong direction. Perhaps there was another way after all. He just needed to stop thinking like a typical computer hacker.

Jenny fought to overcome the overwhelming desire to run. To hide. Her eyes darted from left to right as she searched for exits. There were none. She scanned the room for something defend herself with. Nothing obvious. She'd been trained for this, she told herself.

Trained to run towards danger not away from it. To attack not fly.

Attack. That was it.

Jenny pushed herself up from the bed.

Everything seemed to happen in slow motion.

The knife protruding past the door became a hand holding a knife. The door continued to swing open. She rushed for the door, slamming her full body weight onto it. The door slammed against the wrist. The knife clattered to the bedroom floor. A bread knife.

"Argh!" a female voice screamed.

Then the door was shoved back into Jenny's face, knocking her backwards. She fell to the floor. The hand withdrew. Landing on her bum, Jenny kicked the door with both her feet. It banged shut. A clattering noise from the other side.

"Police!" she shouted, realising she should have done that earlier.

Jenny climbed back to her feet and readied herself to open the door. She kicked the knife under the bed, counted to three and threw the door open.

Crumpled in a heap in the hallway and cradling her wrist was Kim Chang. Crying.

Jenny felt helpless. And stupid. "I'm so sorry, Kim!" She knelt down beside her. "Are you alright?"

Between gulps of air, Kim said, "I thought it was Anna. I came home, opened the front door, heard the music and I thought it was Anna." She stared helplessly into Jenny's eyes, tears falling freely. "And then I remembered what had happened to her . . . I grabbed a knife. I thought you were her . . . her killer."

Jenny wrapped her arms around the girl. Kim leaned into her chest and sobbed.

"I'm so sorry, Kim. I thought maybe . . ." she didn't finish her sentence. She had been going to say that she thought Kim was Anna's killer also. "How's your arm?" she asked instead.

She held it up, wiggled her hand around and winced. A red mark had appeared. It would bruise. "I don't think anything's broken." She sniffed.

"That's good."

Kim made to stand up. Jenny stood first and helped her up.

The Disney plaque with Anna's name on it lay on the floor. Kim picked it up with her good hand. From within the room, symbols crashed and drums banged. The music had reached a crescendo.

Jenny re-entered the room and lifted the arm of the record player.

Silence descended.

"Anna bought these for us all," pronounced Kim, leaning on the doorframe and examining the plaque in her hands. "She gave them all out as presents last Christmas. It was a bit of a joke. Joanne got Cinderella because she never stays out after midnight. Polly got Sleeping Beauty because she's always lying in. Denise was given the one from *The Princess and the Frog* because she's always cooking something. Apparently, that's the plot in the movie. I've no idea; I've not seen it. Have you?"

Jenny shook her head, happy to allow Kim to chatter freely. She perched herself on the chair by the desk.

"She said she was originally going to give me Mulan seeing as she's Chinese, but then she gave me Belle instead. She said it was because we both always have our heads in books, but I know it was really a dig at Patrick. You know, Beauty and the *Beast.*"

"How did Patrick react?"

"He thinks the whole thing is stupid and childish."

"And she gave herself Jasmine from *Aladdin*?"

"Yeah. She said it was the only one left. Patrick said it was because she wears loads of see through clothes and acts like she lives in a harem."

Kim hung the plaque back on the door. She grabbed a tissue from a box on the bedside table, wiped her eyes and blew her nose. She sat down on the bed.

"Did he say that to her face?"

"No, Patrick would never do that."

"Did he know about her ambition to play in the Royal Opera House Orchestra?"

"What?" her voice raised an octave with incredulity. "You think Patrick killed Anna?"

"No, that's not what I'm saying, Kim," said Jenny calmly. "But someone who knows a lot about her did this. I'm just trying to understand who might have known her dreams."

"Well, she wouldn't have told Patrick. They're just about civil to each other and that's only for my benefit. They're hardly going to share their hopes and dreams with each other."

"Could you have told him about it?"

"Why are you fixating on Patrick? There's loads of people out there who might have known her ambitions."

"Like who?"

"I don't know, do I?" she said sharply. "She could have written it on Facebook for all we know."

Jenny hadn't thought of that. She made a mental note to ask Harry O'Reilly to check it out.

Kim continued. "And there's her lecturers, music teachers, other students on her course. Friends. Family. Could be anyone." She paused and then finished, "And no, I didn't tell Patrick."

"Did she keep a diary?"

"Not that I know of."

Jenny pinched her lips together and decided to change tack. "When did Anna last discuss her hopes about the Royal Opera House with you?"

Kim cocked her head to one side, as if deciding whether to take affront. She let it pass and answered plainly, "I think the last time was about a month ago. We were at the bottom of a second bottle of wine. Cheap night in. And we got onto the subject of life after college. I think it was because we were being forced to take career advice at Trinity at the time."

"Did she specifically mention the Royal Opera House that night?"

"I guess so. But more as an example."

"Where were the other housemates?"

"I think they were around but in their rooms. Joanne would have been asleep. It was well after midnight, after all." She smiled at her use of Anna's joke. "Denise was in and out of the kitchen as always. Don't know about Polly. She might have been out."

Jenny pointed at the mantelpiece. "I like the photo of the two of you."

Kim studied it, as if seeing it for the first time. She stood and picked it up, then winced and swapped the picture to her uninjured hand.

"Yeah, that was a cracking day out. It was last year, just before my birthday. We decided to be tourists in London. Did all the sights. I've got one framed in my room, as well. The two of us with a Beefeater, outside the Tower of London."

She put the photo back in its place.

"Can we go downstairs? I feel weird being in Anna's room."

"Of course."

In the kitchen, they sat at the table. Jenny asked background questions about Anna. Kim answered them obligingly, happy to talk about her friend.

Anna was originally from Torquay. Her mother was a music teacher in the local secondary school. Her father left them when she was eight, migrating to Canada. Anna had never said much about him. Her stepdad ran a second hand car dealership in Devon somewhere. Two younger stepbrothers, both still in primary school. No problems at home, at least none she'd ever mentioned. Anna had always been happy to go back to Devon in the term breaks.

"Anyone ever come up and visit from Devon?"

"Other than her mum and stepdad, no."

"What about boyfriends from back then?"

"She said she'd had a few, but nothing really serious."

"What were her relationships like at Uni?"

"Pretty good. She was popular with other students as well as the lecturers."

"You mentioned earlier today about the recent string of one-night stands . . . " Jenny paused, waiting to see if there was a reaction. Kim nodded slowly. " . . . Any lecturers?"

She thought for a second. "I don't know all the lecturers at the college and, don't forget, we did different courses. But I don't think so."

"You last saw her on Friday morning when you left for college?"

"Yes."

Jenny felt awkward but asked anyway. "What did you do the rest of the day?"

Kim sat upright, bristling at the question. "So now I'm a suspect too, am I?"

"I have to ask — for elimination purposes."

"You must see some really twisted stuff to always look for the worst in people." She caught her breath and then, like it was an intrinsic proof, blurted out, "*I was her best friend!*"

Kim stood, opened the fridge and pulled out a wine bottle. She held it up to the light. It was white wine and just under half full.

"I think I need a drink."

She pulled two large goblets from a cupboard and poured wine into both. She placed one in front of Jenny as if laying down a challenge and sat back down opposite her.

"I went to college." She gulped a mouthful and continued. "We were rehearsing like mad on Friday, as we had the opening night the next evening. We're doing a production of *La Bayadère*." She saw the frown on Jenny's face. "It's a ballet. We spent most of the day at it. And the evening. I think I left there about 9:30, maybe 10:00 p.m. When I got home, the house was empty. I was dying to hear about Anna's audition. I Facebooked her to ask how it went, but she didn't reply. I just assumed she'd gone out with someone."

"How was the show?"

"It was brill. Really went well. The audience loved it. We did it last night and tonight, as well. That's where I was just now. Wasn't as good tonight though, I think the news about Anna has dampened everyone's mood. Even though some people don't know her, she's from our college. We've got two more performances to go. Tomorrow night, then a break for a few days and then the finale on Saturday. We all said we'd put more energy into it tomorrow. For her."

Jenny took a small sip of her wine. She wouldn't drink it all — she was driving — but she really wanted to. Looking over the rim of her glass, she asked, "And Patrick? Where was he on Friday?"

Kim sighed to make obvious her exasperation, but answered anyway. "He came round when I got home and stayed over."

"And before that?"

"He was working."

"What does he do for a living?"

"Actually, he's doing a Computer Science degree at Imperial College. But he's taking a gap year, working for a TV channel. Channel 4 or 5, can't remember which one. Something to do with upgrading their online catch-up service."

"Must pay well. Young guy like that driving a Porsche."

"He's set up an online business to get him through Uni so that he doesn't come out with a load of debt, like the rest of us."

"What kind of businesses?"

"I've no idea, really. Something to do with making money from adverts on websites. What's the word . . . *click-throughs*, that's it. Apparently that's how you make money on the Internet. All I know about the Internet is Facebook, Twitter, YouTube, Google and Flickr."

"That's way more than me," said Jenny. "Someone set Facebook up for me once but I've forgotten the password."

Kim smirked sympathetically. "I don't know how you can live without them."

"Okay. Give me an example of what I'm missing out on?"

Kim thought for a second. "How about this? I met Anna on Facebook before I met her in person." She gave Jenny a smug nod and sipped her wine.

Jenny tried to work it through in her head.

Kim explained. "Once I knew I was accepted at Trinity Laban and which halls of residence I was in, I jumped on the online student forums to find other people in the same halls. I found Anna, we connected on Facebook and got to know each other ahead of college. We were already close before showing up on the first day."

Jenny was impressed and told Kim so. Finally, a practical use for social media that had nothing to do with telling the world every inane little thing you've ever thought or done.

"I was quite a shy person back then. Getting to know Anna beforehand made settling in here much easier."

"Not so shy anymore, then?"

"Not really. Between Anna and the dance degree, I've been dragged out of my shell."

Jenny and Kim carried on talking for another hour. It had long stopped being a subtle interrogation into a victim's life before her death and had simply become a conversation between two acquaintances, sharing titbits of their lives with each over a large glass of wine. Despite the twelve-year age gap between them, Jenny felt she'd connected with Kim.

And perhaps, through her, to Anna.

Derek Saxton withstood the initial jolt from the bitterly cold water cascading down his sweaty body. He forced his head under the showerhead. A loud involuntary shiver escaped his lips, but he stood there steadfastly. His body temperature cooled and the water temperature became bearable.

His workout had been tough going; each fitness machine defeating him more quickly than the last, each set becoming slower and, towards the end, with fewer reps. After only fifteen minutes on the bike, he gave up cardio and skipped the rowing completely. He managed a proper warm-down, knowing that he'd ache like hell otherwise.

Normally, he would steer clear of the gym after drinking in the afternoon. Especially when the couple of glasses of wine accompanying lunch had turned into an extended champagne celebration. For an Olympic medal-winning boxer, highly attuned to the nuances of his body's metabolism, his newly-signed client could really pack the bubbly away. Saxton made a note to ensure Aguda kept well away from alcohol going forward. The last thing Saxton needed was to find Aguda plastered all over the pavement — and the newspapers — in the run-up to his first professional fight.

Although gym and alcohol didn't mix, he'd needed to kill time ahead of his secret rendezvous this evening.

Jude had left the office at six. She and 'Her George' were off to the cinema — cheap tickets on a Monday night, apparently — to see a French art-house flick he'd never heard of nor likely ever see. What the hell were a secretary and a window cleaner doing watching foreign movies, subtitles and all? She had been suspicious that Saxton was staying back. As far as she knew, there was nothing in the diary that required him to stay late. The cheeky cow shrugged sceptically when he gave the excuse that he had loads of work to catch up on.

Saxton dried himself with a towel, doused his body all over with aromatic body spray and put back on the silky black shirt and the sharp grey suit he had worn all day. He admired what he saw in the mirror. Still the right shape for an outside centre. Tall, broad shoulders, plenty of muscle and, best of all, no beer belly. Well, not yet anyway. It was a shame his knee was completely knackered, or he'd probably still be playing professionally. He missed the game sometimes, although he had to admit that rugby had changed as a sport over the last few years, ever since Jonny Wilkinson slotted that drop goal to secure England's Rugby World Cup win in 2003. He wasn't sure he was cut out for the modern style of professionalism. All muscles and speed rather than brains and talent. And, worst of all, no partying in-between matches — what was the point?

Ten minutes later he was outside his office building, searching through his coat pockets for his pass with one hand while trying to hold up the umbrella with the other. Watford's streets were quiet this time of the evening, especially in the rain. And Monday was always subdued, not like the weekend when the centre became a rabble of teenage kids out on the town, drifting from pub to club, cider bottles strewn behind them, puke left in the gutters like dogs marking territory, and police watching on nonchalantly, occasionally picking off the odd reveller separated from the pack.

Saxton waved his photo-pass to unlock the front door and entered the building. He shook off his brolly and coat. The night security guard, young and podgy with huge bags under his eyes, looked up from his newspaper. He was certainly no sportsman, unless sumo was making a new splash locally.

Saxton said, "Hi, mate. I'm expecting a visitor in about ten minutes. Can you let her in and ring me on extension 2820?"

"Sure will, boss. 2820." The guard wrote the number on the top of his newspaper.

Saxton took the lift up three floors, feeling justified after the workout. And anyway, he didn't want to work up another sweat in his suit.

Checking his reflection in the lift doors, he smiled, reflecting on the day that had started so well.

Signing up Aguda earlier that afternoon had been just the kind of boost Saxton's business needed. Especially after losing two Premiership footballers to rival sports agents last month. He probably should have issued a press release immediately following today's lunch, but he'd been rather inebriated. And anyway, he'd had his private webcam session with Audri. She really was a lot of fun. Completely uninhibited and up for anything. How did eighteen-year old girls become so worldly-wise so fast? It wasn't like that when he was her age.

It was a shame he'd have to end it.

The lift doors opened, splitting his smiling reflection in two.

He unlocked his office and pushed through the door. The lights came on automatically. He realised he was actually a little nervous about the next hour. Perhaps he should have a quick medicinal scotch before his guest arrived, just to calm his nerves.

As he poured the whisky from the crystal decanter, the phone rang. She had arrived. He took a quick sip, savouring the burning feeling as it flowed down his throat, and answered the phone.

* * *

"Mr Saxton's sending someone down for you." The security guard hooked the telephone handset back on its base.

Self-consciously, Audri tightened the belt on her red rain mac even more. Someone else? What the hell was Derek playing at?

"Cats and dogs out there, eh," said the guard, handing her a see-through plastic badge with her name written on the paper placed inside. She shoved it in her coat pocket.

Audri looked back through the glass doors, but there were no animals.

"I mean," the guard explained, sensing her confusion, "it's raining out there."

"Yes," she agreed. "Raining."

Another English idiom to add to her collection.

"Would you like me to take your coat?"

"No!" She'd answered too quickly. "I mean, thanks. But no, I'm okay. Keeps me warm." She was rambling now.

The guard shrugged and pointed at the reception seating area behind her. "You can wait over there if you like." He picked up a pen and held it over a half-completed crossword puzzle.

"Thanks."

She chose a chair that faced away from the guard. She didn't want him to get a glimpse of her bare thighs and put two and two together like the mini cab driver had earlier. It had been her own fault. She'd been careless when she'd sat in the passenger seat, her coat parting a little too much, giving the ancient Indian man an eyeful of her breasts. Throughout the fifteen minute journey he had eyed her legs every chance he got. Sometimes she was such a fool. She should have sat in the rear. But as the car ploughed through the puddles into Watford she found, despite herself, she was becoming aroused. She wasn't sure if it was the anticipation of the next few hours with Derek, or this new game he had her playing. She realised she was also savouring the effect she was having on the driver.

When she climbed out of the car she really couldn't help herself. She turned around to pay the man, leaning down to keep her hair dry inside the vehicle. She fumbled in her pocket for her purse and caused the belt to loosen. The coat spilled open, privately revealing everything to him. His jaw actually dropped open. She laughed and said she was sorry she only had £20, brazenly leaving the coat as it was. He stared unashamedly for a long ten seconds and then shook his head slowly, telling her not to worry about it. She thanked him and told him he was sweet. She rewrapped the coat around her, pocketed the note and trotted towards the entrance of the office building.

Sitting in the reception area, the image of her mother, frowning at her free-spirited daughter, entered her mind. She tried to push it away. She didn't want to feel guilty anymore. She'd left behind her two younger sisters in that suffocating family home. Ever since Pappa and her older brother, Erik, had drowned in a boating accident on the lake, Mamma had become over-protective almost to the point of turning their home into a prison. Audri and her sisters were dropped off at school and promptly picked up again at last bell. She was never allowed out. Never allowed friends round. At the age of sixteen, Audri rebelled and the terrible rows started. She would stay out partying all night, ignoring the missed calls and untold texts from Mamma. She discovered boys. And then men. One night the shouting and screaming and threatening became too much and Audri slapped her mother around the face as hard as she could. She only wanted to knock sense into her. In a rage, Mamma demanded Audri move out. Spitefully, Audri threatened to take the morning ferry out of the country. Minutes later, she left the house with a hastily packed case, her passport and a handful of money emptied out of her piggy bank. The next day she was true to her word and watched the port slip away into the distance. Mamma stood on the pier, a look of wretched horror on her tear-stained face, as Audri disappeared.

The lift dinged loudly and the doors slid apart. A man stepped out, looked around, spotted her and called over to her.

"Miss Sahlberg?" He had a nasally voice, almost like he had a cold.

She stood quickly, checking everything was covered.

"Yes, that's me."

"Mr Saxton has asked me to take you up to the meeting room. He's stuck on a conference call with the States right now."

Audri followed the man into the lift and stood beside him. He pressed a button and the doors closed, the polished steel finish revealing their reflections. He stood rigidly beside her, offering no small talk, his arms by his sides like a soldier. The only movement came from his hands, which he clasped shut and then opened wide, fingers spread fully before repeating the action again and again. He was of average height, with a long gaunt face, a brown mop of hair in some kind of deliberately styled mess. He wore plain black denims and a white formal shirt, open at the neck. Instead of shoes he wore thick black boots, their top line visible through his jeans just above the ankles. Audri surmised that he didn't own a formal suit, which was a little strange, given the high-class nature of Derek's business and the amount of effort, and money, that Derek put into his own designer wardrobe.

The man's eyes strayed to take in her reflection and she looked down to avoid eye contact, her peripheral vision able to observe him purposely studying her. Almost as if assessing her. She wondered if he suspected she was completely naked under the mac. But that was unlikely. Unless Derek had told him for some reason. No, she was just being silly.

"You're working late," she said, breaking the uncomfortable silence.

"Yes, it is late, isn't it? Just been catching up on some paperwork while it's quiet. Lucky for you I was still here, or Derek would have left you sitting in reception with that lecherous night security guard."

"Huh?"

The doors slid open and he marched out, no elaboration on his unwarranted comment. She stayed put, wondering what the hell he'd meant by it. Was he just warning her about the guard? Which was odd, as the guard had shown no interest in her whatsoever. She had a sixth-sense when it came to men being attracted to her. The taxi driver for one. And Derek. Four months ago she and Derek had finally got it together for the first time, but she'd been aware of Derek's desire for her right from her very first minute as the family au pair.

But the guard downstairs? Definitely not. He was more interested in completing his crossword.

The lift doors began to close and she jumped out. She caught up with Derek's colleague and stayed one step behind him as they walked down the empty corridor. After four or five closed doors he opened one and stood back to allow her to pass. She looked past him.

It was a nondescript meeting room. Just an oval beech wood table with six chairs circling it, all green coloured leather with matching beech armrests. There was a window at the far end with its blinds drawn. A fake tree sat in one corner.

The man held out a brown A4-sized padded envelope. Her forename was scrawled in black ink capitals on the front. "Derek asked me to give you this, Audri."

She recalled that he'd addressed her as Miss Sahlberg earlier. Now she was Audri? She thanked him and entered the room.

She could feel something lumpy inside the padded envelope.

"Right, I'm off home now. As you said, it's late. I'm sure Derek will be down in a few minutes. Is there anything I can get you before I go?"

"No thanks. Please go."

"Would you like me to take your coat?" He flashed her a sardonic smile.

He knew. And he wanted her to know it.

"Sure, thanks." Her voice was more cheerful than she felt.

She slowly reached for her belt, not taking her eyes off him. His smile transformed into a leer.

She carefully pulled at the belt.

He licked his upper lip.

"Actually, it's a bit cold in here. I think I'll keep it on."

His shoulders slumped and he turned to leave the room.

"Goodbye Audri," he said over his shoulder. "I hope you have a good meeting with Derek."

He pulled the door shut as he left.

"Pervert," she said to the door.

She realised that he hadn't given her his name. Mr Pervert would do. Wait till Derek gets here. He was in for a massive dressing-down over discussing their relationship with Mr Pervert.

How dare he.

She was surprised though. Derek went to great lengths to keep their liaisons secret from Hilary. Why would he risk discussing anything with colleagues from work? She supposed it had to do with his ego. She knew boys loved boasting about their sexual conquests. And it seemed that men did too.

Idiot.

But he was an idiot who was pretty good in bed. For an older man he kept himself fit. No flabby belly and huge tree trunks for arms and legs. She enjoyed his experienced techniques. He was able to pleasure her in ways she had never dreamed possible. Best of all though, she felt incredibly tiny in his arms, a surprisingly tender embrace for such a muscular man, especially in the minutes after climax, when they lay there panting.

She remembered the envelope in her hands and ripped it open. A sheet of paper fell out along with some folded over black cloth. She opened the cloth. A blindfold.

She smiled. This was new.

Audri read the printed sheet of paper. There was no addressee or signature.

I hope being secretly naked outdoors has turned you on just as much as the thought of you naked in my office has made me rock hard with anticipation. Follow these instructions to the letter. I promise it will be worth it. Tonight, I'll take you to a place you've never been before.

Here's what I want you to do:

1) Take off your coat but leave your shoes on. Leave the coat on the table.
2) Place one of the chairs in the centre of the room, its back to the door.
3) Straddle it, facing the door. You'll be sitting in the chair backwards. Your legs will be wide apart.
4) Put the blindfold on.
5) Wait for me.
6) Don't peek!

Audri giggled to herself. This looked like fun. She'd defer moaning about Mr Pervert until after. First things first.

Obediently, she grabbed one of the chairs and positioned it backwards to the door, then took off her coat and threw it on the table. The air-conditioned office was colder than she realised. On the chair, the armrests looped from the seat base to the back. She'd have to manoeuvre her legs in through each loop. Derek hadn't thought that through! Or maybe he had. She'd almost be trapped in the chair. She nearly fell backwards doing it, but quickly caught her balance. She re-read the instructions. Yes, she'd done it right. She threw the sheet of paper onto the table. It missed, floating under it. She blindfolded herself.

Everything went dark.

Audri waited.

She could hear the hum of the air-conditioning. She felt goose bumps appear on her arms. She wasn't sure if it was because of the cold or because she was excited. And a little nervous.

What if Mr Pervert came back? He'd be in for a huge shock, that's for sure.

Or what if Derek's conference call went on for ages? She couldn't hold this position comfortably for very long. The armrest holes were smaller than she realised and were pressing into her thighs. What if the blood flow constricted and she got pins and needles in her legs? That would be no good.

The draught of air reached her skin before the slight sound of the swinging door reached her ears. She smiled and said, "Derek?"

"Sshhh, Audri." It was his voice. Thank God. She relaxed.

She heard the door click back into place. She could feel him standing in front of her, presumably looking at her naked body.

"Did I do everything okay, Derek?"

"Sshhh, Audri," he repeated.

She felt hands on her shoulders. He stood right behind her. His hands were warm and clammy. She leaned back, trying to rest into where she thought his crotch would be. She felt his hardness press onto her back. She smiled and raised her arms to wrap them around his neck. She wanted to pull him down so that she could kiss him deeply, but he caught her wrists half way and firmly pushed her hands down by her sides. She felt both his hands reach down across her shoulders. He cupped both her breasts, fondling first, then gripping hard and squeezing them like he was kneading bread dough. He pinched both nipples roughly. She gasped, flinching with the unexpected pain. One hand strayed further down, toyed briefly with her neatly trimmed pubic hair and then continued to its objective. She'd been turned on continuously since leaving the house naked, and now two of his fingers glided easily into her. She leaned back on him to make the angle better but he withdrew his fingers and stepped away from her.

Silence.

What now?

Maybe she would hear his flies unzipping. Or maybe he would instruct her to masturbate for him again. He liked that a lot. Or maybe he was just watching and waiting for her to do something.

What should she do?

"Derek?" she whispered.

Nothing.

"Derek, are you there?"

She waited, but nothing happened.

She decided enough was enough. This game was becoming too weird for her. Her nipples throbbed from the pinching. He'd never hurt her like that before. For his massive size, Derek was a gentle giant.

She reached up and removed the blindfold. Her eyes automatically squinted in the bright fluorescent light. The door was closed. She turned her head to look for Derek behind her. Catching a flash of movement out of the corner of her eye, she instinctively recoiled, but it was too late. A dagger was nearing the end of its swipe right at her face. The fist enclosing it didn't extend and so it was the base of the protruding black metal handle that was going to connect rather than its huge double-edged blade. She quickly turned to one side but it smashed into the side of her head regardless, with the force of a battering ram.

Audri's whole body slumped and she felt herself slowly list to one side. Her limbs wouldn't respond to the instructions from her brain. Her scissored legs, still trapped in the chair, and her body's imbalance caused the chair to tip over. The floor rushed up towards her. This time her face took the force full on. She heard rather than felt the bones in her nose crack and crush. One arm was trapped under the chair at a strange angle. Feeling returned to her body. And with it, the pain.

Almighty pain.

Audri cried out and, hearing she was able to make a noise, opened her mouth and took the deepest ever breath to make the loudest ever scream. Swiftly, a hand reached down and shoved a white cloth into it, gagging her. She forced the scream out anyway, but it was muffled and useless. With her working hand, she tried to rip the gag out but the knife flicked at her wrist. Her arm dropped limply to the floor, blood pumping from the clean gash.

Audri sobbed.

What had she done wrong? All those times with Derek had given no indication of this. For the first time she questioned her liberal, free-as-a-bird, risk-seeking attitude to life. She thought forlornly of Mamma crying on the pier as she'd left on the ferry towards Denmark. Audri realised she wanted to go home. She would stop running away. Stop punishing her. Live a normal life. Be with her sisters. Finish school. Meet boys her own age. Get a real job. Grow up.

Most of all she wanted to say sorry.

A boot came rushing towards her face. It was as if she was the rugby ball lined up for a penalty. She knew then that no apology would ever reach her Mamma.

The last thing she heard, before blessed unconsciousness took hold, was Derek's voice quietly saying, "Sshhh, Audri."

TUESDAY

CHAPTER 7

The microwave binged. Jenny removed the bowl of porridge and stirred in a generous helping of honey. She felt she'd earned it, having pushed herself hard this morning during her regular morning jog around Marble Hill Park, which formed the grounds of the nearby Georgian villa, now a tourist attraction. She'd vowed years ago to visit the grand eighteenth-century house but had somehow never found the time. According to the leaflet pinned to the corkboard in her kitchen it had been built by King George II, when he had been the Prince of Wales, for his mistress.

She'd enjoyed the route through the park, especially the riverside stretch with glimpses through the ash trees of boats moored peacefully on dark water and parkland on the opposite bank of the Thames. With so much nature around her, she always found it hard to imagine she was running within the heart of the country's capital. The rain had finally eased off during the night, which had made this morning's run more pleasant than of late, but she had still returned soaked through from a combination of mist and dew, persistent puddles and a well worked up sweat.

The radio on the breakfast bar was tuned to Capital Radio. The DJ handed·over to the newsroom for the 7:30 a.m. bulletin. As Jenny ate her sweetened oatmeal, she heard talk of the failing economy and the Prime Minister's visit to India. As she spooned in the final mouthful, she heard reference to her case.

Police have launched a murder enquiry after finding the body of Anna

Parker, a twenty-year-old music student, in an eighteenth floor meeting room of an office building in Paddington. Speaking now is Detective Chief Inspector Da Silva of the Met's Homicide and Serious Crime Command...

The voice changed to a recording of her boss.

We have carried out initial enquiries and are in the process of forensically examining the scene. There have been no arrests at this stage and enquiries continue. We are keeping an open mind as to the motive. Next of kin have been informed.

The newsreader's grave voice returned.

An incident room has been set up at Holborn Police Station and anyone with information is asked to call in. They gave out the phone number and switched topics. *And now on to the sport . . .*

Jenny zoned out of the radio and picked up her notepad. It was covered in her scrawl and had a series of tasks she needed to do this morning. She'd written the list in the middle of the night, after waking up from a restless sleep. Her dreams had been full of images of Anna Parker's lifeless body, pools of blood, Disney princesses and being stuck in a lift. All to the accompaniment of frenzied cello music. When the lift in her dream had started to free fall she'd sat bolt upright, completely awake.

She knew from experience that if she just laid her head straight back down sleep would escape her. This type of lucid dreaming was her brain's subconscious attempt to make sense of the day's events and organise outstanding issues on the case. Over the years, she'd learned to embrace it. She turned the light on, grabbed the pen and notepad she kept on the bedside table and wrote down all of the actions she could think of relating to the case. It was her way of letting her brain know that it had done its work, everything was written down, delegated safely to paper. It would be there in the morning when she awoke.

She turned the light off and lay back down.

But half an hour later, sleep had remained elusive. She was still wound up from the case and needed to take her mind off it all.

She had just the answer.

A few minutes later, wrapped in her thick, comfy dressing gown, Jenny lay sideways in her living room armchair, her legs draped over the arm. She wore a headset with a protruding microphone. A wire connected it to an Xbox One controller cradled in her hands, her thumbs and fingers a blur of activity, as she controlled what she saw on the television in front of her.

"Hank, he's behind that building," she said into the headset. "I'll draw his fire and then you come up behind him. Ready . . ."

In the headset, she heard an American accent in reply. "Roger that."

On the screen, she jumped out from behind a wall and ran across the warzone. Zombies suddenly appeared out of nowhere, but she took them out with three well-aimed shots right between their eyes. She heard bullets ricochet behind her as she jumped for safety through a broken window.

"Nice work, Jen," said the voice. "It worked. I got him."

"Brilliant," she replied. "Okay, Jackal, where are you?"

"I've got your six," said a female voice, also American. "Turn around and you'll see me."

"Oh right, there you are. Okay, let's clear this building. Last time I fought against Arctic Dragons, one of their team holed out at the top of this building. He stayed silent for ages and then took me out in the open with his sniper rifle. I reckon he's trying the same trick again."

"Okay, let's go for it. Cover me."

Four years prior, in a rare fit of familial support during some leave from work, Jenny had babysat her twelve-year old nephew, Damien. She had not been able to get much more than the odd grunt out of him, as he was engrossed in playing a violent war game on his games console. In an effort to connect with him, she asked if she could have a go. He laughed patronisingly but obliged her. He showed her how to use the controller to move around and shoot everything that moved. The graphics were amazing and she found herself drawn in completely. At the end of the evening, Damien even commented, minus the condescending tone, "Not bad for a girl." It had become a new foundation for their relationship.

That weekend, she borrowed Damien from April, her sister. Together they went shopping for her own Xbox. Back at her flat, Damien set it all up for her and showed her how to use it. A month later, she had completed *Call of Duty*'s single player campaign on the hardest level. Playing against the computer turned out to be straightforward as the enemy soldier's movements were predictable. She offered to babysit her nephew more frequently and together they played split-screen mode, sometimes as a team against the computer and occasionally heads-up against each other. Around that time, Damien explained about online play, where you could compete against other gamers from all over the world in real time, either one-against-all or in teams of four. That weekend, she borrowed her nephew again and he helped her order a broadband connection for her flat. When it was installed he'd connected the Xbox to it and set up her own online username. Two months later, Jenny won her first victory over Damien in head-to-head combat, he at his home in Kent and she in her flat in Richmond, both continuously taunting each other via their microphone headsets. Within six months, Jenny had risen above Damien in the worldwide rankings, much to his embarrassment.

Nowadays, Jenny was an ardent online gamer, a hobby she kept entirely secret from all her friends and especially her colleagues on the force. Only April and Damien knew. Well, plus a few thousand online gamers, but they only knew her as Jennifer3000. Whenever a visitor pointed at the Xbox sitting under her television, she explained that she'd bought it for her nephew for when he came round to stay. Damien now thought Jenny was, "Well cool!" – something her straight-laced sister found highly amusing.

She had upgraded each time the makers released a new version of *Call of Duty*, or *COD* as gamers referred to it. She had also become competent on other first person shooters such as *Halo* and *Far Cry*. She knew a thirty-two-year-old single female police detective like herself didn't fit the typical demographic, but she didn't care. She enjoyed the escapism and the connectedness of being part of a group, even if most of the group's members were spotty teenage boys or grown-up social incompetents.

Jenny wondered if perhaps it was *she* who was the social incompetent. It wasn't like she lived a normal life. The few friends she had stayed in touch with from her distant schooldays were all starting to marry and have kids in their two-up, two-downs. Even most of the female officers in the force managed to hold down long-term relationships, although mostly with other coppers. After being the focus of station gossip during one three-month relationship with her immediate superior some years ago, back when she was in uniform, Jenny had vowed never to date another colleague again. This rule, however, turned out to be a real problem. It was hard to meet decent men in her line of work. The few civilians she had risked dating seemed to be far more interested in the bragging rights going out with a policewoman gave them in front of their mates. One, a good looking advertising executive introduced to her by her sister, had, after a month of romantic meals and nights out, finally showed his true colours by asking her, in the middle of ripping each other's clothes off, to fish out her uniform and handcuffs. Instead, she applied her police training and viciously bent his arms up behind his back and launched him, just in his underwear, out the front door, down the stone steps and onto his arse in a huge puddle that had conveniently formed by the kerb. The rest of his clothes landed next to him a couple of minutes later.

Jenny had spent another hour playing *COD* before she caught herself yawning. She'd finished the game, pleased at the win, logged off and went back to bed. This time, when her head hit the pillow, she had drifted off into an uninterrupted, dreamless sleep.

The sport news on the radio gave way to music. She didn't recognise the song. Jenny reviewed the list of actions in her notebook and picked up her phone. She dialled Alan Coombs, who answered immediately. He was already at Holborn.

"Do you ever sleep?" she asked.

"When you're my age, sleep's less important. Anyway, I only live round the corner."

Alan's wife had died from cancer two years ago. Since then, he had allowed the job to fill the void in his home life. He often came in on weekends, without claiming overtime, to process the never-ending backlog of paperwork. And he was always the first into the station each day, active case or not. Occasionally, she worried he would burn himself out, but he always remained upbeat and cheerful.

After a few minutes of catching up, she placed her finger under the first point on her notepad and asked, "Where have we got to on the CCTV footage?"

"Fiona went up to Flexbase HQ in Docklands yesterday. She got there fairly late, so they said they'd email the video files to her this morning. They may already be in her inbox."

"Did she see what was on them?"

"Don't think so. They just asked for the timeframe and told her they'd send it over."

"Hmmm, sounds strange."

"It's some big computer system that centrally manages the CCTV for all their offices around the UK. It's not like the good old days where you'd have a VHS video recorder out the back of a shop."

"Okay." Jenny moved her finger down to the second point. "What about the other flatmates?"

"Yeah, I finally got hold of them yesterday evening. They're all on study leave since last week. Guess where?" He didn't wait for an answer, but she already knew from her conversation with Kim last night. "Egypt, on holiday. They're flying back in tomorrow, but their alibi looks solid. I'll check them out anyway."

He didn't need to add the last part. Jenny knew Alan Coombs followed up every lead diligently.

"How'd they take it?" Jenny recalled what Kim had said about the dynamics in their house.

"They seemed upset. Shocked. They were on speakerphone their end. One of them was uncontrollable. Broke down crying. It was a difficult call."

"I bet. Anything else, Al?"

"Just one thing. I talked to Jake Symmonds, the lecturer who supposedly made the recommendation to the Royal Opera House."

"And?"

"He claims he did no such thing."

"Well, I think we knew that anyway."

"Yeah. He said there is a partnership between the college and the ROH, but it's more about their professionals coming in to teach at the college."

She thought out loud. "The killer must have known that, to make it more believable to Anna on the email . . ."

"I agree. I'm going up to the Royal Opera House later. Just to check things out. You never know."

"Good thinking. What about the college itself?"

"I'm heading there after."

"Great. Okay, I'm just about to jump in the car. Should be at Holborn by about 8:30. I want to look through the CCTV footage as a priority."

"Right. See you then."

Jenny washed up her bowl, turned off the radio, and looked around for her maroon suit jacket. She grabbed her car keys and black leather handbag and exited the flat.

By the time she was driving over Twickenham Bridge, the car's heating system had begun to take the edge off the cold. Her phone rang. It was a central London number, but not one she recognised. She accepted the call and spoke into the hands-free system.

"DI Price."

"Ah, DI Price, it's Clive Evans here."

Jenny racked her brains to place the name.

He continued, "The building manager from Flexbase in Paddington."

"Ah yes, Mr Evans." She remembered the lanky, whiny man now.

"Sorry to trouble you, but I thought you ought to know . . ."

"Know what?"

"There's been another."

"Another what?" She had no idea what he was talking about.

"Another dead girl."

"Audri?" called a female voice.

A pause.

"Audreeee!" Much louder this time. "Where is that girl?"

"No idea." A male voice answered. "Do you want me to go up and wake her?"

"Don't be stupid, Derek. You can't just walk into her room. I'll do it."

Silence. Thank God. Brody allowed himself to drift back to sleep again.

"She's not here!" The woman's voice again. Annoyed.

"What do you mean, not here? Where else would she be?"

"She mustn't have come home last night."

"What do you mean? Did she go out?"

"Yes, with Ornetta."

"Where to?"

"I don't know. Watford, I suppose."

Watford.

Brody was sure that was a piece of information he needed to know. Only he couldn't recall why.

Watford . . . Watford. A town on the north-western perimeter of London, just inside the M25 motorway. He had been there four or five years ago with Leroy and his sister, Hope, who had also moved to London from Wales. She had met a guy in a nightclub the night before who claimed to be a stand-up comedian. Leroy wanted to check out Hope's potential new boyfriend and declared they had to see him in action. If he made Leroy laugh, then Leroy would grant his blessing to them both. Hope begged Brody to accompany them, if only to keep Leroy reined in, and the next day Brody accompanied brother and sister to the end of the Metropolitan tube line, where they tracked down the dingy comedy club in Watford. Hope's one-night stand was the opening act of the evening's line-up and it was soon apparent why. He turned out to be excruciatingly unfunny and the small audience, sensing blood in the water, heckled him relentlessly, especially Leroy. Initially, Hope was mortified but eventually she gave in and heckled him herself. The comedian promptly exited stage left to a round of rapturous applause. Hope never saw him again.

Watford . . . why was Watford important now?

And then Brody had it. It was an English town. It was a place, a specific location in Middle England, where *life carried on as normal*; the line of thought that had prompted his new hacking approach the previous evening. Watford was the real-world location of the Saxton household's webcam feed inside the virtual world of SecretlyWatchingYou.com.

Brody opened his eyes.

He lay slumped on his desk, his arms curled into a makeshift pillow. He raised himself slowly and felt his back crack. His shoulder muscles ached. His legs had somehow entwined themselves around the wheel spokes of his chair. He disentangled himself and immediately wished he hadn't. Blood gushed to his lower legs and, along with it, excruciating pins and needles. He held his body rigid until they wore off. Finally, able to move without pain, he stood and rubbed his beard vigorously. It needed trimming.

Lying on the desk in front of him, he noticed the disgusting, probably-covered-in-piss, yellow bottle of bleach that Leroy had placed on his desk yesterday — the clue that had helped him realise the SWY feeds were all from the UK; his Middle England line of thought. He screwed his face in disgust as he realised that, in his sleep, he'd somehow wrapped his arms around it and inadvertently used it as a makeshift pillow.

Cursing Leroy, he rushed to the bathroom and scrubbed his face clean. He returned to the living room with some sheets of toilet paper wrapped around one hand as a substitute glove. Carefully picking up the bottle of bleach from his desk, he dropped it and the paper into the wastebasket. He'd rather buy a replacement than touch that one again.

He looked at his watch. 8:15 a.m. He'd been there all night. Just after 1:00 a.m., Leroy had returned home with Danny, both half-cut. They tried engaging Brody in conversation, but he grunted distractedly and then donned a pair of headphones. Eventually, they took the hint and disappeared to the bedroom. A few minutes later, Brody removed them only to immediately reinstate them on hearing porn movie noises emanating from their room. An hour later he'd risked it again and found to his relief that all was quiet. He'd carried on observing the feeds and must have fallen asleep sometime after two.

The large screen in the centre of the room displayed the *Au Pair Affair* location from within SWY. The kitchen feed was selected and the audio that had awakened him originated from there. A man sat on one of three stools at a breakfast bar, crunching his way through a bowl of cereal. Brody recognised him from the day before, when he had first seen him in the same kitchen, illicitly kissing the au pair and fondling her breasts. So, his name was Derek. Hilary stood by the sink, a smartphone in her hands.

Brody added the name to his notes. He had the full cast now. The Saxtons – Derek, Hilary and their baby, Izzy – and their au pair, Audri. And now he had a location. Watford. He should have enough to track down a specific address. He fired up a browser on his computer and quickly navigated to a commercial people-finder site. Even with the limited information he had, he would be able to run a search through loads of publicly available records, all visible online to anyone who chose to look. The site made it quick and easy, centralising information from birth, marriage and death certificates, the phonebook, electoral rolls, company director registrations and the land registry.

As he searched, he heard the Saxtons resume their conversation.

"Have you tried ringing her?" asked Derek.

Brody paused to look at the main screen.

"What do you think I'm doing?" Hilary waved the phone in her hand at him. It looked to Brody like an iPhone. She put it to her ear and frowned. "Ringing tone, no reply . . . Audri, it's Hilary here. It's 8:20 a.m. Where the hell are you? I'm going to be late for work now, young lady. Ring me as soon as you get this."

"You should probably text her, as well. And Facebook and tweet her. Young people seem to take far more notice of that stuff than voicemails."

"Yeah, you're an expert on young people." She spoke with a tedious tone in her voice, not looking at him.

Derek peered at her sharply, his spoon frozen halfway to his mouth. "What's that supposed to mean?"

Hilary ignored him and rapidly tapped out a message on the phone.

On Brody's PC, the search results came up. Negative. Damn, that was unexpected. He tried a few variations — initials instead of forenames, different spellings of Saxton, focusing on Hilary as the primary instead of Derek, expanding the geographic search beyond Watford — but still the search came up empty.

He wondered if he'd somehow misheard Watford. After all, he had been half asleep at the time.

In the Saxton household, the debate about Audri carried on.

"I can't believe she's going to make me late! Can't you look after Izzy, Derek? Surely you haven't got anything important on this morning. Especially after that late meeting last night."

"It's because of that late meeting that I have to get to the office first thing. Tons to do. Sorry, darling."

"Bloody hell. I've got a huge funeral order to prepare this morning. Ten different wreaths." She looked at her wristwatch. "The funeral directors are picking up the flowers from the shop at 1:00 p.m."

"I'm sure Amanda can handle it, darling."

"She won't get back from New Convent Garden Market until about 10:00 a.m. I'll have to ask Joan to come in, even though it's her day off."

"There you go, darling. Problem solved."

"I tell you what. When that girl gets home, I'm going to bloody well kill her."

The feeling of déjà vu was sickening.

Another dreary meeting room inside another characterless office block. Another naked, lifeless young woman, used and discarded like a Barbie doll no longer in favour, the weight of her torso keeping her body on the table, her splayed legs limply hanging down almost, but not quite, kneeling on the floor. Bound arms stretched out in front. Her head lay cheek down on the table, dark hair spilling and merging with a pool of blood. And *so much* blood. Red splatters across walls and windows from the slicing action of the killer's sharp knife, coupled with the last few desperate spurts from the body's once powerful beating heart and then, gravity and time having done its work, blood slowly drained from the gash across her throat and the slice on one arm into a massive red slick, puddling across the oval table and overflowing the sides to the chairs and floor beneath.

"Is it the same?" asked DI Hamid, a note of hopefulness in his voice.

Jenny forced herself to look for differences.

The absence of a cello was one. The lack of clothes either on the body or — she checked around — anywhere in the room was another. Just a bright red coat, thrown across the other end of the table from where the victim's body lay.

"Yes, pretty much the same."

"My guvnor will be really hacked off when he gets here. He's not had a good murder case for ages."

"Really? I'd swap places with you any day of the week if that's true."

Hamid shrugged. "I wouldn't. We might not have loads of murders to deal with every day like you lot in the Met, but we still have plenty of serious crime to keep us busy as hell."

Hamid was from the Bedfordshire and Hertfordshire Major Crime Unit, a joint force set up by the two neighbouring police constabularies bordering Greater London to its north. Watford fell within their territory rather than the Met's. Jenny had gate-crashed someone else's party.

Clive Evans had called an hour ago. He had been alerted by the building manager from the Flexbase offices in Watford. He had no real details to tell her, only that it was a dead girl in a meeting room, just like yesterday in Paddington. He told her local police were already on the way.

"How come your colleague from Watford phoned you so

quickly?" Jenny had asked Evans.

"Because all Flexbase building managers around the country were informed of what happened here yesterday, mostly so that we could reassure any clients in case they heard about it on the news. No one for a minute thought the same thing would happen again."

A sentiment with which Jenny completely concurred. She too had assumed that Anna Parker's murder was a one-off. The way she had been singled out, tricked and lured to her death seemed so particular to her as a target that Jenny had not considered the possibility that somehow this was part of a series. And this line of thinking had swayed the channels of enquiry that she had proposed to Da Silva for the investigation team to follow. An assumption she seriously regretted having made.

Evans gave her the address.

On the way, she had phoned Da Silva, asking him to focus on any potential territory conflict. If this was the second in a linked series, then the Holborn MIT were already one day ahead and, therefore, needed to lead this investigation, as well. Time to see if his connections with the upper ranks were as good as he boasted they were. She also phoned Alan, Karim, Fiona and Edmonds, leaving messages for the first two when she reached their voicemails, and asking Fiona and Edmonds to join her as soon as possible.

She had never been to Watford before. Driving round its own short ring road, she could see the multi-storey car parks and department stores all circling *intu* Watford, an indoor shopping mall. At the northern point, she turned left into Clarendon Road, her destination. It seemed to be the business centre of the town, with a run of large office blocks leading towards Watford Junction station. The tallest was probably only six or seven storeys high, certainly nothing to threaten the giddy heights of their cousins in the City of London or Docklands. Three double-parked patrol cars told her she'd reached the address.

Upon sight of her Met warrant card, the PC acting as guard raised an eyebrow but granted her access to the reception of the Watford Flexbase office. It was far more modest than its Paddington equivalent, more functional and with a guest seating area that actually looked comfortable. She was directed to the lifts. The second floor corridors turned out to have the same two shades of pastel green as in Paddington, as well as the same inoffensive framed prints.

Before entering the meeting room, she put on the white plastic overshoes and gloves she had grabbed from the boot of her car. Two similarly clad men looked up, quizzical expressions on their faces. They'd introduced themselves as DI Deepak Hamid and DS Joe Selby. Jenny explained who she was and why she was here. Once Jenny had stated that she believed the crime to be related to her other case, Hamid said he'd need to inform his guvnor, DCI Jeffries, and left the room, mobile phone at his ear.

"Look at this," said Selby, who was kneeling on the floor, just beyond the pool of blood.

Jenny kneeled down next to him. A ripped open envelope and an unfolded single sheet of paper, with printing on one side, lay discarded on the floor underneath. Blood had reached the envelope but not the sheet. Jenny reached a gloved hand out —

"Don't you dare interfere with my crime scene," said a hoarse, booming voice.

Jenny looked through the legs of the table and chairs in the direction of the voice. Two pairs of legs stood by the entrance to the room. She recognised DI Hamid's faded jeans on the left, shoes still engulfed in white plastic. The other pair of legs was covered by sharply creased grey trousers, which met black shoes also contained within elasticated covers. She raised her head above the eye-line of the table, still kneeling. The trousers were part of a sharp Italian-cut suit, with a plain white shirt open at the neck, silver cufflinks visible at the cuffs. The owner of the suit was very tanned, with deep lines etched across his forehead and in the corners of his eyes. His full head of wavy black hair counteracted his sun-damaged skin and made his age hard to determine.

"DCI Jeffries?" Jenny asked, standing up.

"Yes," confirmed Hamid, on behalf of his boss.

"Deepak tells me you're trying to wade in on my turf with some bullshit about a similar crime yesterday."

"The similarities are way beyond coincidence, sir."

"You sure you're not just trying to get yourself linked to a serial killer case?" His eyes narrowed as he spoke. "A bit of buzz from something like that helps build careers."

"With respect," Jenny looked him squarely in the eyes, "but fuck you. Sir."

Hamid raised both eyebrows and looked up at the ceiling, as if some spot had suddenly gained interest. To her side, Selby, still on his knees, lowered his head back under the table. Jeffries looked at her and nodded to himself, weighing her up. He chuckled.

"Okay, DI Price," he said, sportingly. "You've got my attention. Now what have you got?"

Jenny explained about the Anna Parker case, labouring the similarities. The location being a meeting room in a Flexbase office block. The sliced throat. The bound wrists. The rape.

"We don't know yet that this girl's been raped," said Hamid.

"She will have been."

"And you say that your victim from yesterday was tricked into going to the office?" asked Jeffries.

"Yes. I'm guessing that bit of paper on the floor is something along those lines for this girl."

"Maybe, but let's wait for my SOCO team to get here first, eh."

"Any idea of the victim's identity?" asked Jenny.

Jeffries looked at Hamid, who looked at Selby. Selby shrugged.

"Her name is Audri Sahlberg."

They all turned to the sound of a female voice behind them.

"Thanks, Fiona," said Jenny to her teammate. "Gentlemen, this is DC Jones."

"According to the signing-in book in the reception downstairs," Fiona explained, "Miss Sahlberg arrived at 7:50 last night. She was here to see a Derek Saxton."

Brody had abandoned his full frontal assault on SWY yesterday evening. The site was far too well protected and nothing less than a brand new, indefensible zero-day exploit would break through. And he certainly didn't have weeks of time at his disposal to create one. Doc_Doom and Brody's other friends on the CrackerHack forums had been unable to help. He just hoped that Matt_The_Hatter didn't have access to a relevant new zero-day, either self-developed or from one of his allies.

With no direct attack vector available, Brody was forced to come up with a flanking strategy. His theory was that the video feeds streamed into the site through an alternate route over the Internet, a different way in than the front door used by visitors to browse the site. If he could find this back door, then it might be less well defended. He realised that relying on an *if* and a *might* was not necessarily the most robust approach, but it was all he could come up with. The first step was to follow the route the video feeds took to get into the site. And to do that, he needed to find the webcams themselves. In the physical world.

Which meant he had to track down the Saxtons' home.

The commercial people-finder site gave up no hits for Saxton in London or the Home Counties using Derek or Hilary as forenames. The family seemed to be off the grid. Perhaps they weren't married, though they certainly acted like a married couple. He wondered if they were famous in some way — though he didn't recognise them; not that he was an expert on celebrity culture — as household names take massive steps to hide information about themselves from the prying public, especially their home address. Or maybe the Saxtons were simply ex-directory, rented instead of owned their home and were new to the area in which they lived. That would explain the lack of footprint in the phone, property and electoral records.

By far Brody's easiest option was to just sit and watch, hoping that across the hundreds of virtual locations on SWY, someone would divulge a phone number or address out loud. If he waited long enough perhaps someone, somewhere would order a pizza and state the address out loud for its delivery. Or answer the home phone by repeating the last part of their phone number in a tuneful ditty, like his mother still did to this day. Or give some other clue to their physical location. He only needed to find the real-world location for one of them. It didn't have to be the *Au Pair Affair* location, although at least they were active right now and, he had to admit, their antics intrigued him. Like Hilary, Brody was interested in finding out where Audri had got to, especially after seeing the way she had dressed — or rather *undressed* — to go out last night.

The problem with audio was that he couldn't listen to more than two or three feeds at once before it became confusing. Choosing the right ones to listen out for that kind of titbit would be a lottery. He supposed he could download a speech-to-text converter utility, feed it all of the locations on SWY as different audio inputs and then search the outputted text logs en masse, but that would be prone to transcription error and would take him hours to set up.

And even then, there was no guarantee that anyone would actually give details about their location.

He thought about what he knew so far. He knew their names. He knew their general location in Watford. And then, he realised, he knew something else.

Hilary Saxton was a florist.

Brody's fingers flew to his keyboard.

A few seconds later, his screen displayed a Google map with all the florists in the Watford area plotted neatly. He picked the centremost one and clicked through to its website. It was a basic one-page HTML site that listed the shop's address and phone number in front of a photograph of a colourful bouquet of flowers.

He rang the number.

"Rosita's Flower Shop. Can I help you?"

"Hi. Is Hilary there?" Brody asked.

"Who?"

"Hilary Saxton?"

"Sorry, no one of that name here."

"Oh, I'm sorry, I must have the wrong number."

He disconnected and moved onto the next one.

The same conversation repeated itself. The next two didn't answer, but it wasn't yet 9:00 a.m. He would try them again later when they were open. And then he heard the magic words, "Sorry, Hilary's not in yet."

Brody punched the air in triumph.

Of course she wasn't there. He was looking at her in her home right now, through a webcam connected to the Internet, broadcasting live.

"Oh, no problem, I'll phone back later." He disconnected.

Hilary's flower shop was imaginatively entitled, 'Forget-Me-Not.' It was located in Bushey High Street, in a smaller town on the outskirts of Watford. In an hour, he could be parked outside the florists, staking it out, waiting for Hilary to show or, more importantly, leave so that he could follow her home. That would probably work, assuming she went to work today, but the downside was that he'd lose most of the day waiting.

Forget-Me-Not had a website. Brody checked it out. It was a cleanly designed, static site with tabs to click on for bouquets, weddings and funerals, each with sample pictures and nice, descriptive passages. The site had no online ordering capability; it was just a digital brochure. The 'About' page provided the history of the shop. It had been there for six years and stressed the quality and freshness of the stock and the creativeness of the florists. There was a generic 'info' email address. Not much use.

He ran a *Whois* command on the website address, to identify who had registered its domain name. Hilary Saxton's name came up as the registrant, but the physical address provided was for the shop. He ran an online company check against the shop's name and found the company registration details. Under the company directors was listed a Hilary Bone, presumably her maiden name. It provided an address in Reading, Berkshire.

That must be it. Brody was getting excited now.

But then he recalled another detail and told himself not to get carried away. Last night, Audri had left the family home to go out in Watford, something you were very unlikely to do if you lived in Reading, about fifty miles away. He copied the postcode into Google Maps and used the Street View facility to check it out.

Brody loved Street View. It allowed him to take a virtual walk down almost any street in the world. When he'd first heard that Google were going to send fleets of vehicles through street after street around the world, photographing everything they saw through a unique 360 degree camera mounted atop the car and subsequently making the stitched-together images available to everyone for free, he had been awed at their audacity, the sheer scale of their undertaking. He'd never even noticed the Google-branded car slowly pass through Upper Street but, zooming in to Bruno's coffee shop when Street View was first launched in the UK, he was fairly sure it was him captured that day, sitting in his usual window seat, his head in his laptop.

From the Street View images of the address in Reading, Brody immediately realised he was in an industrial trading estate. He zoomed in and saw from the overhead sign that a firm of accountants inhabited the building. Typically of many small businesses, Forget-Me-Not's company registered address was that of their accountant.

He'd drawn a blank. Again.

Brody decided working on an empty stomach wasn't helping. Twenty minutes later, showered and changed into a fresh pair of jeans and a plain cotton shirt, he sat in the window seat at Bruno's, a perfectly steamed cappuccino and a warmed almond croissant on the table in front of him. As if Brody's abruptness yesterday had never happened, Stefan had greeted him as warmly as ever and had correctly guessed Brody's choice of beverage.

Brody had deliberately left his tablet PC behind to force himself to think. He stared through the window. A blanket of grey cloud lay low in the sky, but at least it had finally stopped raining sometime in the early hours. Cars passed slowly in both directions, most with their headlights illuminated despite it being daytime, clouds of surface spray in their wake. So much water had fallen over the last few days that the drains underneath were overwhelmed.

There were lots of approaches he could take. He could focus on the baby, Izzy, searching through birth records. But Izzy sounded like it was short for something, maybe Elizabeth or Isabel. He could get Hilary's email address and send her an old-school payload, a virus that would open up her PC to him, where he was bound to uncover her home address. The only problem was that most PCs these days had antivirus software running, a strong defence against such an antiquated hack. He could send an email that, when she opened it, gave him her IP address. Armed with that, he could launch any number of forays.

By the time he had finished his Italian breakfast, Brody had thought through three or four lines of attack. Refreshed and refocused, he made a point of politely complimenting Stefan before heading back across the road.

Walking to the pedestrian crossing, his mind planning the order of bombardment, he was suddenly drenched by a huge cascade of freezing cold water, heedlessly thrown up by a passing car. He stopped, looked down at his soaked clothes and, feeling stupid, stared incredulously at the offending car as it drove on, oblivious to its handiwork. In the rear-view mirror, he thought he saw a pair of sparkling eyes spot him and smirk. Foolishness quickly turned to fury. He made a mental note of the number plate and thought of ways to track the driver down and exact revenge. It was an expensive red Maserati. It probably had a vehicle tracking device fitted —

And then he had it. Geotracking. That was how he'd find Hilary's home address.

He rushed back to the apartment, the red Maserati completely forgotten.

Changed once again, this time into a pair of black denims and a plain grey t-shirt, Brody phoned 'Forget-Me-Not'. On the screen in front of him, Hilary was feeding the baby in the kitchen.

"Forget-Me-Not, Joan speaking. How can I help?"

"Oh, hi Joan. Is Mrs Saxton there?" Brody was putting on an East Coast American accent. Partly to spice it up, but also to sound different to his brief call earlier.

"Sorry no. She'll probably be in later. Can I help you?"

"Oh, no problem, ma'am. It's Geoff here from Interflora. We've just completed a rebranding exercise and so I just want to send Mrs Saxton our new logos so she can update the Forget-Me-Not marketing collateral."

"Okay?" Joan sounded confused. Just as Brody had wanted. He'd noticed the Interflora logo on their website earlier and, having personally used the service to send flowers, Brody knew there would be a business relationship between the small independent flower shop in Bushey and the global flower delivery network.

"Tell you what, I'll email them over to her."

"That's probably best, Geoff."

"Let me just check . . . actually I don't seem to have her email address here. Can you let me have it?"

"Yes, it's written down here somewhere. Ah, here it is. It's hilary@forgetmenotbushey.co.uk. All lowercase mind."

Brody knew that the case didn't make any difference but chose not to correct her. "Thanks a lot, ma'am. I'll email her now." He disconnected.

He created a fake Gmail account, yet another free service provided by the ubiquitous Google. He loaded Hilary's email address as a contact within the Gmail account. He then logged into a spare Twitter account he had lying around.

In fact, all Brody's Twitter accounts were spare, as he had never used them for their intended purpose: tweeting. He had never understood why people wanted to share short bursts of information, tweets, with each other in such a public area. At least the forums on CrackerHack had some level of control over who joined. He likened tweeting to shouting at someone you vaguely knew across the other side of a packed stadium. Sometimes they'd catch what you said and shout back. And all the people around, most of them also shouting at each other, could listen in and, if they chose to, join in the conversation. Brody used his anonymous Twitter accounts for one purpose, listening.

Within Twitter, anyone could follow anyone or be followed by anyone. *If they knew their Twitter username.* If his guess was right, Hilary was a tweeter. Derek had mentioned her tweeting Audri earlier and Brody had noticed how competently Hilary used her iPhone. All he needed was her Twitter username.

He pressed the link on the Twitter site that helped him find friends. He ran through the import wizard and allowed it to import all of the contacts stored against the temporary Gmail address he had just set up. It only had one contact: Hilary Saxton's. He waited for the screen to refresh . . . and there was her Twitter username: '@floristhilary'.

He browsed through her Twitter profile. He immediately found what he was looking for.

Links to photos she'd tweeted.

This might actually work.

Most of the photos Hilary had tweeted were of Izzy. He opened up one of them. Izzy looked cute, sitting on Derek's lap in their living room. He recognised the room and furniture from the webcam feed displayed in front of him now.

Perfect.

He downloaded the photo and passed the file into a geotag viewer program.

Brody had observed that Hilary was an avid iPhone user. Like most modern smartphones, the iPhone includes the capability to determine its approximate real-world location, triangulated using information from cellular, Wi-Fi and Global Positioning System networks. Handy for a multitude of innocuous uses, like finding the nearest coffee shop or car park. When photos are taken, this same location data is hidden inside the image file, a process known as geotagging, enabling the photographer to plot on a map the locations of where all their pictures were taken, another innocuous feature to make life better. But when these same images are uploaded to public locations accessed by the likes of Twitter, and if the geotag data is not stripped out, then anyone in the know can reverse engineer where the photo was taken.

He'd heard about celebrity stalkers and paparazzi looking out for famous people tweeting photos from their smartphone and then using this geotracking technique to show up at the celebrity's location minutes later, much to their surprise. Until now, he'd never thought of a reason to use the same technique himself.

Brody allowed himself a self-satisfied smile. Displayed on the screen in front of him was a pointer on a map, highlighting a location in a street just outside Bushey. He switched to satellite view and saw that it was an expensive residential street with huge detached homes. He dropped into Street View and zoomed into the front door of the house pinpointed by the geotag coordinates. Number 85.

Now he had the house number as well as the street name. For completeness, he fed the details into the Post Office's reverse postcode look-up program and was presented with the full postal address.

Brody looked at the large screen in the centre of the room. Hilary was still feeding the baby.

He spoke out loud, aptly adapting Davina McCall's catchphrase back from when she used to host the *Big Brother* TV show:

"Hilary Saxton, I'm coming to get you!"

CHAPTER 8

DCI Jeffries disconnected his mobile and shrugged. He looked across the board table to DCI Da Silva and said, "This is now officially a linked series murder and you're lead SIO. You'll have the full support of me and my team."

Jeffries and Da Silva stood. They shook hands across the table, as if they'd sealed a major deal. Da Silva even thanked him for his professionalism.

Jeffries turned to Jenny. "I'll leave DS Hamid and DC Selby here with you for any local knowledge they can share."

"Thanks, sir," she said.

He bored into her eyes and said, with a smirk, "Remember, DI Price, you've got my attention."

Jenny couldn't decide if she had just been come on to by the suave-looking DCI, right in front of her boss and her whole team. Or if she had just been politely threatened. He turned and left the meeting room.

Following Fiona's timely entrance three hours ago, Alan, Karim and Edmonds had also arrived. Edmonds took over processing the crime scene, leading the local SOCO officers until his own team arrived and assumed responsibility. Jenny had phoned Dr Gorski and he had shown up just a few minutes before the local pathologist, who happily turned around and returned to his office; one less case to deal with. Half an hour before, Da Silva had finally turned up having, he explained, been on the phone to the Met executives all morning, making sure his MIT team were given full control of the crime scene.

Now they all sat in a boardroom two doors along from the crime scene, ready to review what they had learned so far. The building manager had kindly sent up tea, coffee and a plate of biscuits, as if they were valued Flexbase customers.

On the table before them were two documents in sealed, transparent evidence bags. The first was the envelope DC Selby had originally spotted under the table on which the dead girl lay. 'AUDRI' was handwritten on the front in black ballpoint capitals. The second was the letter it had contained.

Jenny picked it up and shook her head at its audacity.

"He got her to do all of the work!" First reading the list of instructions the letter contained to herself, she then summarised for the room: "Arrive virtually naked. Take off your coat. Trap yourself in the chair. Put on a blindfold. And wait to be murdered."

"She must have known her killer to play that kind of sex game," said DC Jones. Some nods.

"Why the blindfold, then?" asked Karim, munching a custard cream.

"Part of the game?"

"Or," Jenny mused, "to hide the fact that the killer wasn't who she thought it was."

"But that doesn't really make sense," said Alan. "If he was going to kill her anyway, why hide his face?"

"So that she was compliant while he tied her hands with the wire?" suggested Fiona.

"I don't think so," said Dr Gorski. "She was knocked to the floor while her legs were trapped in the arms of the chair. See all the blood there." He pointed at a dark puddle by a fallen office chair in the centre of the room. "She broke her nose from the fall. That's probably when she broke her arm as well, from the weight of her body and the chair landing on it, with no ability to break the fall. If her hands had been tied before she fell, she couldn't have broken her arm in that way. That's when he tied her up and dragged her to where she is now." He nodded unnecessarily at her body lying on the meeting room table in a massive pool of blood.

"Was she sexually assaulted, Doctor?" asked Jenny, resigned to the answer she already knew.

"I believe so. I'll confirm for sure at the post-mortem."

"Time of death?"

"Taking into account room temperature, internal body temperature, rigor mortis and so on, I'd estimate between twelve and sixteen hours ago."

"And I take it the cause was the cut throat."

"Yes, I would think so, very similar to yesterday. But it's clear she suffered a lot of other trauma before that."

Jenny shook her head.

She turned to Alan. "What about the security guard from last night?"

"Just got off the phone to him. He was expecting the girl as someone had phoned down ahead of time to let him know."

"Let me guess," said Jenny. "He was told to phone directly through to the meeting room rather than the regular company phone number in the building."

"Exactly. He didn't remember the name of the person, but said he'd written it down in the signing-in book."

"Derek Saxton."

"Yes."

"Which tenant was he supposed to be with?"

"He didn't say."

"Surely the guard would have needed to know which company she was here to visit?"

"Yes, I asked that. But, because he phoned from the meeting room, he didn't think to ask."

"Did Audri not state the company name when she asked for this Derek Saxton?"

"No. The guard said she just asked for Derek Saxton."

"Did he send her up?"

"No, apparently Saxton sent someone down to pick her up."

"What did he look like?"

"The guard doesn't remember. He said he was more focused on his crossword. I'm going to go see him after this to see if I can get more details face-to-face."

Karim jumped in. "So this guard is so into his crossword he doesn't even realise that she's arrived naked under that red mac."

"Not everyone spends all their life trying to picture what's under women's clothes, Karim," quipped Fiona, lightening the mood.

"Not all women are worth the effort," retorted Karim. "I haven't thought about you—"

"Focus on the case," ordered Da Silva, his only contribution so far.

Inwardly Jenny sighed. She loved the banter within her team. It was healthy. Karim's response had been pretty good for him, partly because he'd omitted the usual swear words but mostly because Fiona Jones was absolutely stunning. Jenny was convinced her angular cheekbones, huge hazel eyes and tall hourglass figure could easily get her on the front cover of *Vogue*.

"Anything else, Alan?" asked Jenny.

"Only that the guard noticed that she arrived in a taxi."

Hamid spoke up. "I'll take that if you like. I know all the cab companies round here."

"Thank you, DI Hamid," said Da Silva.

"Yes, that's great. Obviously, we want the pick-up address."

"I'll get straight on it." He downed the contents of his cup and left the room.

Jenny turned to Fiona.

"Anything on this Derek Saxton?"

"As far as I can tell so far, there's no one who works here with that name. I've talked to all the tenants based in this building. But, just as in the Paddington building, hundreds of non-tenant companies use it as nothing more than a postal address and for hosting the odd business meeting. I've still got to get through to all of them."

A mobile phone trilled. Fiona looked at the number. "I need to take this." Jenny nodded and she stepped out of the room.

"So it's nothing to do with *the* Derek Saxton," offered Alan. Seeing confused looks from those around the table, he explained himself. "Used to play professional rugby for Saracens about ten or twelve years ago. Until he broke his knee."

"Is that really relevant, DS Coombs?" asked Da Silva.

"Saracens used to be a local team to Watford until they moved to their new stadium down the road in Hendon. It could be him."

"Well, check it out anyway, Alan. Just in case," said Jenny.

"CCTV?" Jenny asked Karim.

"Same as in Paddington. Just for reception, but all stored remotely at their head office in Canary Wharf."

Jenny had planned to review the Paddington footage that morning, but Audri Sahlberg's murder had taken precedence.

"Right, we need to prioritise this. With two crime scenes, we can search the footage for the same person showing up in both receptions."

The door opened and Fiona returned. Taking her seat, she said, "That was about the meeting room booking. It's the same system as in Paddington. They take bookings over the phone or via their Internet site, as long as you've got a valid account number."

"Do we know in whose name it was booked?"

"I do now. It was booked by a Derek Saxton using the account number of Colnbrook Services Ltd, which is one of the tenants in this building. I talked to them earlier, but I'll go see them again now they've been dropped into this. And guess what . . ."

Jenny said, "The room was booked four days previously along with all the other meeting rooms on this floor."

Fiona's face fell. "How'd you know that?"

"It fits the pattern."

"I guess."

Realising that she had ruined her subordinate's moment in the spotlight, Jenny said, "Good work, Fiona. Anything else, anyone?"

She looked around the room. Da Silva sat at the head of the table; observing the team at work, his hands clasped together. Alan and Karim shook their heads. Selby, who had remained quiet throughout, said nothing. Fiona said, "Nothing from me." Dr Gorski shook his head.

"Let's summarise then. Our killer is someone who knows the Flexbase systems really well. He books these meeting rooms in false names well in advance. He knows his victims and is able to lure them there under false pretences. He knocks them unconscious, ties them up and sexually assaults them from behind. And then he slices their throats with a sharp double-bladed knife."

"Assuming the results of this post-mortem match the previous victim," said Dr Gorski.

"Understood."

"You do realise that," DC Selby spoke up, "if your timings are right he already planned this murder before carrying out first one?"

Jenny hadn't thought of that.

Selby continued. "And if he's done two already, he might have more lined up."

"Agreed. We need to move quickly. Let's summarise who's doing what," said Da Silva.

Jenny look at him, surprised, but then realised he was doing again what he'd done yesterday in the incident room in front of the whole murder investigation team. He was allowing her to do all the work and then taking control at the end during wrap-up and action-setting. He was reasserting his control.

Jenny formed the actions in her mind and was about to speak when there was a knock at the door.

"Come in," said Jenny and Da Silva in unison.

Jason Edmonds, the crime scene manager, entered. He held up three evidence bags and said, "Thought you might want to see these straight away. We found them both in the pockets of the red coat on the table."

"What are they?"

"This one's just the badge she would have been given by security when she arrived last night." He threw it on the table. Karim picked it up to examine it. "This one's her iPhone. It's locked; we'll need to break the code." He placed it on the table and then continued, "But this one's far more interesting."

Jenny stood up and held her hand out before he placed the bag on the desk with the others. He dropped it in her hand and waited, expectantly.

"Thanks," she said.

"No. Read it."

It was a typewritten note, printed on a plain white sheet of A4. Jenny read it to herself.

Audri,

I can't keep you out of my mind. I want you all the time. I want you tonight. I can't wait until Friday when she's next out. I hate sleeping in the room next to yours with her, thinking of you. It won't be for much longer, that I promise you.

Come over to my office at 8pm. Make an excuse to you know who.
Wear the red coat and the black high heels I bought you.
NOTHING ELSE!
I mean it – nothing else!!

I want to imagine you travelling naked under that coat.

Take a taxi to my office at 37 Clarendon Road in Watford. I've got a meeting room booked. Ask for me by name at the reception. They'll call me and I'll come get you.

Don't ring me today. I can't take any calls.

We'll have so much fun tonight.

I can't wait!

D.

"Bloody hell," Jenny said, falling back into her seat. She read the letter out loud to the group, trying to maintain a monotone voice.

"Fuck me sideways," said Karim.

Da Silva either hadn't heard him or simply ignored him, clearly perturbed by what the letter contained.

The door opened and DS Hamid walked back in. He was about to say something but sensed the stunned silence in the room and paused.

Fiona gave voice to her thoughts. "That's way beyond the lure that was used for Anna Parker. Hers was completely fabricated, playing on her dreams. This one seems to be based on an existing affair."

"D stands for Derek, then? Derek Saxton," proposed Alan.

"It reads like they're having an affair under the nose of the wife," suggested Jenny.

"Are you sure these two cases are linked?" asked Selby. "Seems like a simple case of the husband finishing an affair. Terminally."

"I'm not sure now," said Alan. "Well, not one hundred per cent," he said quickly, spotting Da Silva's look of annoyance.

"The individualised lure of both victims to different Flexbase meeting rooms is far more than a coincidence. We will proceed with the two cases being linked," stated Da Silva.

"Right, first job is to track down an address for this Derek Saxton," said Jenny.

Hamid finally spoke up. "Yeah, got that. Found the taxi driver. Said he picked her up last night about 7:30 p.m. He said she was completely naked under the coat. Made his month, he reckoned." Hamid looked around, expecting them to laugh. Receiving no reaction, he hurriedly finished, "The pick-up address is in Bushey.

The taxi driver knows the house. Usually he picks up the bloke who lives there. Apparently, he's an ex-professional rugby player. Used to play for Saracens."

"Derek Saxton," said Alan.

Opposite Number 85 was the entrance to a cul-de-sac. Brody steered into it, turned the Smart car round at its dead-end and then reversed up, parked so that he was facing towards the Saxton household. In his rear-view mirror, he could see an old grey SEAT Toledo, the cheap car out of context with the well-to-do surroundings. Next to him was a corner green with a bench.

The bushes in front of the house had grown much higher in the few years since Google's car had driven down this road, capturing its 360-degree images, but he still recognised the ostentatious property. From one gated entrance, a long horseshoe driveway led past a detached garage block with three double doors towards the main house, and then curved back towards a separate gated exit. The house was more glass than brick: an architect's fantasy home. A massive porch protected the huge double doors set in the centre of the front of the building. Brody knew from the satellite image on Google maps that the rear garden was massive and backed onto woodland.

It was one of many large detached residences in a particularly affluent private road, just a few streets behind Bushey's main thoroughfare of local independent shops, pubs, post office and cafés. He had even driven past the Forget-Me-Not Flower Shop owned by Hilary Saxton.

Inside this house was his target: a computer that received the feeds over the local network from the webcams installed in most of the rooms in the house. If he could hack into the network video recorder PC, then he could determine how it connected to the SWY site. No doubt, it would have a target address for where to send the live video footage, along with a username and password. Armed with these credentials, he should be able to gain access to SWY via a less protected entrance. It would be like attacking the site via its flanks, rather than head on as previously.

Now that he was physically here, he would be able to pick up the home's Wi-Fi network signal. But to obtain access to it, he would need to crack its secure password, which, although relatively easy to do — even with WPA2 encryption enabled — would take him a good few hours. Hours he didn't have. But there was an alternative: he could social engineer his way in.

He had come prepared. In the small boot of his Smart car, he had his fake BT engineer uniform along with a tool box, clipboard and mocked up BT security pass with his photo on it. Even if BT were not the Internet Service Provider that delivered broadband to the house, he could still pretend there was a telephone line fault and that he needed access to all the telephone sockets in the house. He knew the names of the inhabitants, so was sure he could confidently bluff his way in. Once inside, he would physically plug his PC into one of unprotected network ports on the broadband router and hack into the network video record PC via the home's Local Area Network.

It occurred to Brody that, in all of his many social engineering exploits, he had never physically cheated his way into someone's private home before. He'd occasionally hacked into someone's home remotely via an Internet connection, but that was virtual rather than physical. His in-person hacks had always been about finding a way through the secure facilities of large organisations — offices, factories, data centres, shops, warehouses, distribution centres, and so on. To Brody, these targets were faceless, corporate institutions and were fair game. Conning his way into a private home felt like he was stepping over a line. This was more personal, a full-on invasion of privacy.

He thought of SWY, and realised that the inhabitants of Number 85 had long ago given up their right to privacy when they had agreed to broadcast their lives to the world via the Internet-connected cameras all over their house. He recalled naked Audri stepping out of the bath and staring straight into the camera, as if communicating with her audience. If the au pair knew about the cameras, then surely they all knew.

Well, maybe not the baby.

Brody realised he could use SWY to help him see what was going on inside the house, just to make sure there would be no surprises. He took a moment to reflect on the irony that the site he was trying to crack was going to aid him in doing so. That was a first.

He connected to the Internet on his tablet PC via its in-built 4G SIM card. He brought up the SWY site, logged in and selected the

Au Pair Affair location. He scanned all seven webcam feeds. He only spotted movement in the kitchen and clicked on its thumbnail to display the full video feed. Hilary Saxton was loading the dishwasher while talking on the phone. The baby sat in its high chair, playing with some plastic blocks. Brody clicked for audio.

"You've done all ten wreaths already! Oh well done Amanda . . . Yes, tell Joan I said thanks as well . . . No, no sign of her yet. I'm actually starting to get worried now. She's never done anything like this before . . . It just goes to her voicemail . . . No, I don't have Ornetta's number . . ."

Brody considered that if she was still on the phone when she answered the door to him, perhaps she'd be distracted, making it easier for Brody to convince her he really was a telecoms engineer from BT. Brody stepped out of his car and opened the boot. He looked around to check for anyone watching, but the road was deathly quiet. He swapped his coat for a navy blue fleece with an embroidered BT logo. Over the top, he pulled on a yellow hi-visibility vest. The vest didn't have the BT Openreach logo on the back like the real thing, but the logos on the fleece and the fake security pass should do the trick.

He grabbed the toolbox, shut the boot and, crossing the road, walked purposefully towards the house. As he neared, he saw that both gates were shut. He noticed a video intercom next to right hand one. Damn, an extra line of defence to navigate past. He thought it through quickly and concluded a winning smile followed by holding up his fake pass to the camera should do the trick. After all, intercom resolutions were typically fairly low, which should play to his advantage. Hilary would be able to make out the familiar and trusted BT logo. He should be fine.

He pressed the button and waited.

He thought he heard something, but not from the intercom. It was the sound of a distant car downshifting then accelerating. He turned his head in the direction of the noise. The road gently curved to the right. Nothing.

"Hello?" It was Mrs Saxton's voice, tinny through the intercom.

A small Audi flew round the bend. The silver car screeched to a halt right behind him. Car doors flew open and its occupants began to exit. He heard more noise and looked to the left to spot two other cars approaching at speed. One of them was a police patrol car. They pulled up right behind the first car.

The driver of the marked police car looked straight at him.

Brody froze.

You lock yourself away in an air-conditioned room. It's cold, but you know that no one will disturb you in here. They all think you've gone out for lunch, but really you've come for one more look before you make your choice.

You examine the images you've captured. You study their pretty faces. They're all bewitching. You recall the last two encounters. After the overly hurried experience with the cellist, you had vowed to take it much more slowly with the babysitter. After all, you'd set the whole thing up perfectly. So that you could take your time. Allow perfection to be rediscovered once more.

But you failed. Totally.

In the heat of the moment, you allowed yourself to get carried away. The bitch was just too damn provocative in that raincoat, naked underneath, wanting you so badly. You were aroused long before you even walked into the room, even when you stood next to her in the lift. Just the thought of her following your instructions had been overwhelming.

She must have known that too. That's why she had followed them to the letter, the slut. She had wanted you to be quick. To get it over with. Just like all the times before.

You'd spent your teenage years being rushed. "Hurry up," *she* had always said to you. "Hurry up, you stupid boy. I haven't got all day, you know. Hurry up." But it was never something you could control, was it? If you didn't feel aroused, how could you finish quickly? But you always tried to oblige. You closed your eyes and conjured up the pornographic images of naked women you'd stumbled onto on the Internet. Just women, though. Never men. No, that wasn't allowed.

So why did you allow yourself to fall into the babysitter's trap and be rushed all over again? You know you should have walked away. Calmed down. Breathed. Let it subside. And then returned in complete control. Then you could have enjoyed hours of delirium, pleasure and pain, followed by the ultimate climax.

Next time you'd get it right. And the time after that.

You study the photographs in front of you.

Who would be next?

They're all different to look at. But underneath, you know they are all the same. They are all just different manifestations of *her*. Like all sluts are.

It really doesn't matter whom you choose next. The same ending is coming to all of them. In time. What's the difference?

Choices, choices.

You need to choose.

Thumbs-up or thumbs-down?

And you realise it doesn't matter. Eeny, meeny, miny, moe.

When the rhyme finishes, you smile. Your index finger was pointing to one a lot like *her*.

This time you'd get it right. But first you have to organise things. And for this one you've concocted a truly irresistible lure. You know her motivations. You know she'll come to you willingly. Desperately.

Like a moth to a flame.

The last ball shot past both flippers before he had time to nudge the machine with his hips. Damn, he had been caught out *again* by 'The Power', a mode in the *Addams Family* pinball game that employed rotating electromagnets under the board to send the metal ball in unpredictable directions. He watched the end-of-ball bonuses tot up, taking his score just over two hundred million, woefully short of his own high score of three hundred and ninety-six million. One day he'd crack a five hundred. Then he'd be happy.

Crooner42 looked at his watch. The game had taken him nearly an hour. An hour to fail, yet again.

He fished his iPhone out of his pocket and brought up the Remote Home app. A few taps later and the bookcase on the other side of the penthouse apartment silently swung open. He entered his secret room.

At his desk, he logged into CrackerHack. The SWY creator checked for any recent posts about the get root battle he had spawned between Fingal and Matt_The_Hatter. He scanned the chat logs.

Nothing.

Crooner42 couldn't decide whether to become concerned or start to congratulate himself. They were now over twenty-four hours into the contest and, so far, SWY had held up to everything Fingal had thrown against it. And, he chuckled to himself, Matt_The_Hatter. But, right now, there was no system activity from the usernames Fingal had registered under yesterday. He was also completely silent on the forums. How was Crooner42 supposed to interpret this? Was Fingal taking a break? Had he quietly given up? Or was he trying something else that Crooner42 hadn't anticipated?

If Fingal failed to break in then no one could. Which was important, because Crooner42 had no idea how many laws he had broken by launching SWY. And one of the main objectives of this whole exercise was to prove conclusively the site was totally impregnable. The side benefit was to completely ruin Fingal's credibility. In the unlikely scenario that Fingal somehow found a way to obtain root level control, Crooner42 would be made aware of an unknown weakness and could then block it, making SWY even more secure. And if that happened, he still had a backup plan to deal with Fingal. It was a win-win situation.

Crooner42 smiled to himself; a private little pat on the back for his genius. His sheer ingenuity in creating SWY in the first place; his commercial savvy in developing a money-spinning machine; his mastery in hardening the site so well that it had survived a twenty-four hour-long attack from one of the best; and his cleverness about manipulating Fingal into this no-win position.

Crooner42 was desperate to know if Fingal had given up. The silence was killing him. He decided to provoke a response to at least determine if Fingal was still in the game. He composed a post on the forum.

Crooner42: It's awfully quiet out there. Has SWY got you beat Fingal? Matt_The_Hatter? You've had 24 hours already – way more than enough.
Crooner42: COME ON YOU LOSERS – ADMIT DEFEAT!!!

He waited a while. As he'd hoped, some of the usual suspects weighed in.

Mawrpheus: Losers, losers, losers! I agree with Crooner – admit defeat you losers.
Random_Ness: Rubbish. 48 hours is about right for this. Crooner, you can't declare you've beaten them until at least this time tomorrow.

Doc_Doom: Crooner you're an overconfident fool. One of those two will take your site down soon enough. Just you watch. And learn.

Crooner42 was pretty sure Doc_Doom was friends with Fingal. Did that mean that he knew for sure that Fingal was still in the game?

Crooner42: Brave words Doc. But I think not. They are going down...

Doc_Doom: You've changed your tune. Up until yesterday you were a timid mouse on these forums. Now you're an arrogant prick.

Crooner42: Fuck you Doc. I've taken out Fingal and Matt_The_Hatter in one swoop. Name anyone else who's done that.

Doc_Doom: You've done nothing yet.

Crooner42: Yeah, well where are they then?

Mawrpheus: Good question!! Where are they? Come out, come out, wherever you are!

Random_Ness: LOL

He needed to be more patient. The longer Crooner42 let the competition run, the greater Fingal's failure would be and, more importantly, the more sensational Crooner42's victory would be.

He would grant Fingal another day.

While all the unusual network activity was to be expected from a coordinated hacking attempt, Crooner42 did find Fingal's behaviour, when logged into SWY itself, quite unusual. From observing the logs, he'd noticed that Fingal had maintained a focus on a single webcam location – the one that Crooner42 had christened *Au Pair Affair*. Why would he do that? Why pick just one? It didn't really make any sense. And why that one? There was nothing special about it as far as Crooner42 could tell. There were far more intriguing locations on the site.

Crooner42 decided to check for himself. He swiped his tablet computer to select the large screen in the centre of his wall of screens. On it, he brought up the *Au Pair Affair* location. There were seven feeds. All showing various rooms in a huge residential house. Ah yes, he remembered this one. It was a huge mansion just outside Watford. A classic nanny-cam fit out. And he'd named it *Au Pair Affair* because, just after he'd added it to the SWY site about eight months ago, he'd once clocked the husband getting it on with the nanny.

He saw movement in the kitchen. He maximised the feed and turned on the audio.

A woman holding a baby tightly to her chest was confronting six people. He could see the mother full on, and two of the six were men, but from the angle of the camera he could only see the shoulders and backs of the heads of the other four. Even so, he was sure that two of them were uniformed police officers. Interesting.

"Is this some kind of sick joke?" demanded the woman.

"No," said a female voice, softly. Crooner42 couldn't tell which of the four with their backs to the camera had spoken.

"Where is your husband?" asked another. A male voice.

"Derek? What's this got to do with Derek?"

"Where is he, Mrs Saxton? We need to talk to him. Urgently."

"He's at work."

"And where is that?" asked the woman.

"In his office in Watford."

Crooner42 saw two of the figures turn and look at each other, knowingly. From this new side-on view, he could see that the one on the left was the woman. She had shoulder-length brown hair and wore a tight fitting maroon suit, with three-quarter length sleeves revealing slender wrists.

"The Flexbase building on Clarendon Road?"

"No. Why would you think that?"

The same two figures looked at each other again, this time with genuine confusion.

"My mistake. What's the address of his office?" asked the woman. Clearly she was in charge.

"On the trading estate on Tolpits Lane. Halfway to Rickmansworth."

"I know where that is," said one of the men in full view.

What the woman with the baby said next sent a chill down Crooner42's back.

"But it can't be Audri you've found! Surely you've got it wrong? She's just a kid, really. She can't be dead!"

Brody couldn't believe what he was hearing.

What the hell had he stumbled into? The nanny, dead?

In his mind, he replayed what he'd observed yesterday. Audri receiving the hand-delivered letter. Getting ready to go out, leaving the house naked under her red coat. Lying to Hilary that she was off to see her friend, when she was clearly meeting the husband illicitly.

And now she was dead. Murdered even.

Did his knowledge of what he'd seen via SWY make him some kind of witness? Did that mean he had to get involved? Come forward? The last thing he needed was to be forced to explain the webcam site and his involvement with it to the police. If it came up, he'd say he was a normal customer of the website. They'd probably think he was some kind of pervert.

Or should he instead say nothing to the police? It was obvious the perpetrator was Derek Saxton. They'd pull him in, interrogate him and put him away for Audri's murder.

Yes, there was absolutely no need for Brody to involve himself at all.

The last thing he needed was the police poking around in his life.

Ten minutes earlier, when the three police cars had screeched to a halt outside the gates to the Saxton household, Brody had been right in the middle of impersonating a BT engineer, which, like most things he did, was probably illegal in some way.

As the bodies piled out of the cars, Brody thought quickly, checked his clipboard and spoke to the first of them, "You lot here for Number 87 as well?"

The copper said, "No, this is 85."

"Is it?" Brody made a show of looking for confirmation, pointed at the number sign on the wall and then hit his forehead with the palm of his hand, tutting. "You're right, I'll leave you to it." Brody picked up his silver briefcase and started off in the direction of Number 87. After a few steps, he turned back to the policeman. "What's going on?"

"None of your business. On your way, mate."

Brody walked away, attempting to maintain a measured pace, completely against the wishes of his legs, which desperately wanted to break into a sprint.

He stopped at Number 87. It had a solid wooden double-gate for vehicles and separate arched doorway for people on foot. An old-school bell push was mounted on the door. He pretended to press it, waited, and looked back at the police.

Number 85's electric gate started to slide open. Brody's eyes were drawn to one of the two women in the group. She wore a sharp maroon suit with three-quarter-length sleeves, slender arms, skirt just above the knee, bare legs and shiny black heels. Exuding a business-like air, she swiftly entered the premises. The others followed close behind.

With no one left watching him, Brody turned and walked off. Once out of sight, he removed the yellow vest and the fleece with the BT logo, rolled them up in a bundle and placed them under a bush at the border of someone's garden. He turned around and casually walked back to his car parked in the cul-de-sac opposite. From the driver's seat, he was able to observe Number 85. The right-hand gate was now open and a uniformed officer stood guard at the front door.

Brody opened up his tablet PC and reconnected to the Internet, pulled up the SWY site and quickly brought up the feed, which was when he'd heard Hilary Saxton's disbelief at the news of her nanny's death.

"We'll need to get the body formally identified to be sure," said a woman's voice. He was unable to determine which of the seven people in the kitchen had spoken. Two were in full view alongside Hilary Saxton, who was holding her baby to her shoulder, so it wasn't either of them. The others all had their backs to the camera. The voice continued, "Do you have any contact details for her family?"

"Yes, I think so, DI Price. Somewhere."

"Can you get them, please?" From the head movements, Brody had determined that the female voice belonged to the leftmost person. DI Price. He spied the maroon-coloured shoulder, the same as the suit jacket he'd noticed earlier.

"They'll be in the study. I'll go get them."

When the door closed behind Hilary, DI Price began giving orders.

"Right. Al, you get yourself down to the husband's office on Tolpits Lane. Joe, can you go with Alan, a bit of local knowledge and all that."

Brody caught movement out of the corner of his eye. He looked up from the computer. The front door opened and two uniformed policemen walked out, followed by two plainclothes detectives. He presumed that two of them were Alan and Joe. They walked over to one of the marked cars.

But, back on the screen, no one had moved. DI Price was still handing out orders.

"I'd prefer it if you could just verify Saxton's there, make sure he goes nowhere and wait until I join you. I want to be there when we arrest him. Take some uniform with you."

"Where are we taking him?" asked one of the plainclothes officers. Either Alan or Joe, Brody couldn't tell.

"Holborn."

The four men made to leave the kitchen, the same four men he'd already observed exit the house from his vantage point across the road. Brody realised abruptly that the video footage was a minute or so behind real time.

Price said she'd only be a few minutes behind them; she just wanted to secure the crime scene first. Hilary Saxton returned and handed over a piece of paper.

"Audri made me promise never to contact her family. She only gave me the address because I demanded it for emergencies. She said she had fallen out with her mother." Hilary's voice cracked, clearly not far from tears. "God, that's terrible. To be told your daughter has been killed..." She pulled Izzy closer to her and rocked from side to side.

"She's from Sweden?" asked Price, having read the piece of paper.

Hilary nodded, tears falling now.

"Mrs Saxton, can you show DC Jones here where Audri's room is?"

Hilary nodded and wiped her eyes. She left the kitchen. The person on the right followed her. As they moved more into the camera's range, Brody could see that DC Jones was also female.

The front door opened again. Brody looked up from his PC. The attractive detective, in her maroon suit, exited, followed by a man with olive skin. On-screen, they were still in the kitchen. The time lag was confusing.

"Karim, you stay here with Mrs Saxton," she said onscreen. "Make sure she doesn't tip-off the husband we're coming."

In front of him, the same woman walked down the path towards the gate and the cars. As she neared, Brody began to make out her features more clearly. She briefly looked upwards and flicked her hair to one side, a gesture that revealed soft, full lips, a delicate, straight nose, prominent cheekbones and dimples. An attractive police detective. Now that was interesting.

The onscreen Karim said, "Sure, Jenny."

Brody spoke aloud: "Looks like you and I need to get to know each other, DI Jenny Price."

CHAPTER 9

Alan Coombs was waiting for them as Jenny and Hamid exited the lift.

"That's his office, there." He was pointing at a closed door with *Saxton Sports Management* engraved on its frosted window. "I'm pretty sure he's in there, Jen."

"Unless he's done a runner without his car," said Jenny. "I was talking to DS Selby downstairs. He spotted a Merc in the car park with a personalised number plate and ran a PNC check."

"So you've not seen Saxton then?" asked DI Hamid.

"Nah. Just made sure no one came in or out. I can hear voices and movement."

Jenny knocked on the door and entered without waiting. Alan and Hamid followed behind her.

A pretty girl, almost bursting out of a short, green dress, looked up from reading a wedding magazine. She was behind a small, smoked glass reception desk in the centre of the room, her long, tanned legs visible through the glass. Shiny, black rectangular leather sofas were pushed up against the walls offering seating for waiting guests. Above them and all around the room, large, square framed black and white portraits of sports stars — most caught in action, a few posing — adorned the walls, each with messages and autographs scribbled on them in marker pen. Jenny recognised a few of them.

On either side of the only other door in the room, behind the reception desk, were two much larger prints, both showing the same young rugby player in two different strips.

Coombs pointed at them and whispered to Jenny, "That's Derek Saxton in his glory days."

"Can I help you?" asked the receptionist, standing up. She was a little taller than Jenny, but glancing down, Jenny realised the girl's improbable stilettos accounted for most of the difference.

"We'd like to speak with Mr Saxton," said Alan, "Miss . . .?"

"Parker." She flashed a smile. "Call me Jude." She frowned. "But you don't have an appointment?"

"We don't need one." Hamid flashed his warrant card. "We're police."

"Oh! I'll just let Derek know."

Jenny barged around the desk and said, "Don't worry, I'll do it."

Parker, failing in her job, reached out for Jenny's arm. "No, you can't —"

Jenny shrugged her off and opened the rear door.

"Well. Wait till I tell my George about this. How rude!" Parker sat down.

Behind a modern executive desk sat a much older version of the man from the two photos, only a little larger with hair beginning to recede. He was on the phone, reclining in his chair with his shoes up on the desk.

Seeing Jenny, he said into the phone, "Hold on a moment, Arthur. . ." Spotting the two men following behind, he said, "Tell you what, I'll phone you back in a few minutes. Something's come up here."

Saxton set the phone back on its cradle, lifted his legs off the table and stood. "You've just interrupted a conversation with Arthur Aguda. This better be important." Standing, Saxton's height and build was imposing.

"The Olympic boxer?" asked Alan, clearly impressed by the name Saxton had dropped, but foolishly handing control to the agent.

"Yes. My new client as of yesterday." He said this through a huge smile. "He's about to turn professional and I'm —"

Jenny interrupted, "We're here to talk about Audri Sahlberg, Mr Saxton."

"Who's we?"

Jenny dug out her warrant card. "Police, Mr Saxton. Tell me

about Audri."

"Audri?"

"Yes. Tell me about her."

"She's our au pair," said Saxton, warily.

"That's all you have to say?"

"That's all there is to say. She lives in our house and looks after our baby. Dictionary definition of an 'au pair'."

"That's it?"

Saxton cocked his head to one side. "That's it?"

"Alan, caution Mr Saxton would you."

Alan recited, "You do not have to say anything. But it may harm your defence . . ."

As the policeman read him his rights, Saxton sat back down in his chair, a dumbfounded expression on his face. Jenny pulled over one of the wheeled guest chairs and sat down too. Hamid did likewise. When Alan finished, he noticed that the secretary had followed them into the room, so he ushered her out and closed the door.

"Now Mr Saxton. Let's try again. Tell me about Audri."

"What's going on?"

"You're saying you know nothing?"

"About what?"

"Audri?" Jenny was deliberately not giving anything away.

"She didn't come home last night. Shit, has something happened?"

"You could put it that way," said Hamid. "She was found dead this morning."

Jenny glanced at Hamid, but held back the scowl she wanted to throw his way. Saxton brought his fingers up to his open lips. Jenny was impressed. He really did look surprised. Shocked even.

"How?" he asked, finally. And then in quick succession, "Where? Why?" And then, shaking his head, "Fuck me."

"Mr Saxton, she was murdered," Jenny stated.

Saxton continued to shake his head in apparent disbelief.

"Last night, Derek, she left your house to meet up with you. To continue your illicit affair."

Saxton's head stopped shaking. His eyes narrowed and he glared intently at Jenny. "I think I need a lawyer."

"Yes, you do," agreed Jenny. "You better ask him to meet you at

Holborn Police Station."

Brody ordered one macchiato and one cappuccino. He paid and stood waiting by the counter while the barista prepared the two coffees. Out of the corner of his eye, he caught Leroy waving to him, letting him know that he had successfully secured them two seats in the bustling coffee shop.

They were in Monmouth's in Borough Market, located on the south bank of the Thames, just a short walk from the Tate Modern and Globe Theatre tourist hotspots, both located opposite the massive dome of St Paul's Cathedral, proudly towering above riverside building on the opposite bank. Although Monmouth's was one of London's best independent coffee chains, the internal seating area was small and spartan, utilising wooden bench tables and tiny wooden seats to make the most of the limited space. But it was worth it for coffee this good, even though it looked as though he and Leroy would be sharing a table with a pair of elderly couples — American tourists by the look of their bright clothes and shopping bags.

Brody collected the coffees and brought them over to where Leroy sat, squeezing himself into the tight space.

"Out with it," demanded Leroy.

Brody added a spoon of sugar to his macchiato and sipped it, savouring the strong flavour. He listened to their neighbours' voices. Yes, they were Americans.

"Come on Brody," insisted Leroy. "You've got a face as long as a fiddle. Is it this hacking thing? You haven't lost your little competition have you?"

"No, it's not that. I've stumbled into a police investigation."

"Eh?"

"Earlier today, I was at a police crime scene." Brody leaned in close and lowered his voice. "For a murder."

"Fuck me! Who did you kill?" Leroy's exclamation was far too loud. Their American neighbours stopped their conversation and all four turned to stare at him and then, having digested what had been said, at Brody.

"Sorry about that. We were just rehearsing some lines from *Hamlet*," said Leroy amiably, his face completely straight. "Hamlet here," he pointed at Brody, "has just killed Claudius. It's a key scene." He leaned forward, as if letting them in on a secret. "We're understudies from the Globe Theatre and we've only just found out we're on tonight. We both need to get a bit of practice in."

The Americans smiled dubiously, nodded politely and resumed their own conversation.

Leroy smiled at Brody, like a dog awaiting a reward for fetching a stick.

Brody took no notice and said quietly, "I didn't kill anyone, you idiot. But, I think it might be linked to the get root hack I've been working on."

"The webcam thing?"

Brody nodded.

"How's that got anything to do with someone being murdered?"

"Hopefully nothing. A coincidence ... You know that girl we watched?"

"The one in the bath?"

Brody nodded.

"What about her?" Brody waited for Leroy to make the mental leap. Leroy's jaw dropped open. "*Her?*"

The American lady next to Brody turned her head again, raising an eyebrow.

"Sorry, not you love," said Leroy. "We're talking about Ophelia now. Hamlet's girlfriend. Drowned herself."

The woman harrumphed and returned to her own conversation.

Brody explained. "I traced the real world location of that webcam to this mansion in Bushey. I drove up there earlier. I was just about to knock on the door when a shitload of police cars came flying out of nowhere. At first I thought they were there for me, but when I walked away they didn't follow me."

"So how do you know what they were there for if you walked away?"

"I spied on them through the webcams on the website."

Leroy looked up, digesting Brody's story. Brody finished his macchiato, waiting.

"Blimey, did you see the body?"

"No. She was killed somewhere else. The police were trying to track down the husband. I think they think he killed her."

"Why?"

"No idea."

"What are you going to do?"

"Nothing, I guess."

"But what if what you know is crucial to the police investigation?"

"The webcams or the affair?"

"Either. Both."

"I'm sure they'll figure it out themselves. They're police after all."

"But they might not. What have you got to lose?"

"Leroy, I can't. What I do is borderline illegal. I don't need the police sniffing around in my life. I can't just walk up to them and say, 'Hi. You won't believe this but I saw you lot live on camera on some dodgy website and I thought you might like to know.'"

"Why not? At least you'd be leaving out the hacking bit."

"Hmm."

"Probably best not to mention you were sitting right outside the house today when they turned up, otherwise they're going to ask why you were there." Leroy paused as a thought struck him. "Why were you there?"

"I needed to get onto the local area network that the webcams themselves are on, the network within the house. Then I can follow the route the live webcam traffic takes to get to the website itself, hopefully exposing a weakness I can exploit."

"I think I got about a quarter of that," laughed Leroy. "So, you were planning on illegally breaking into someone's personal network in order to hack into a website? Probably best if you don't mention any of that to an officer of the law."

"Well, if I don't say any of that, I guess I'd better not mention I was dressed as a BT engineer so that I could obtain entry into the house under false pretences."

"You weren't!"

Brody was pleased that he had shocked Leroy. "The police turned up when I was in full character."

"I bet you cacked yourself."

"Pretty much."

They both laughed.

The Americans turned their heads once again.

Brody addressed their neighbours this time, "Tragedies like Hamlet are far too depressing in this day and age, so we've come up with a few jokes that we're going to insert into the play tonight.

That one was a rip-roarer. You should get tickets for this evening's performance. It's going to be a blast."

"But keep it to yourself about the jokes," added Leroy, "Can't have our director finding out and ruining our fun."

The woman next to Brody tutted loudly and turned to her husband. Taking his cue, the husband stood and announced to the table, "Right, that's it. I've had enough of this crap. Let's beat it and leave these two English fools to their pretentious delusions."

"Yes," agreed the second woman, "You're not taking us for a ride." She reached into her bag, pulled out a piece of paper and held it so that Brody and Leroy could read it. It was a ticket for the Globe that night, for its production of *As You Like It.*

The tourists gathered their bags and headed for the exit, shaking their heads and muttering about "the damned locals". Leroy turned to Brody and said loudly, for the benefit of the Americans, "Oh shit Brody, we've only gone and learned the lines for the wrong play!"

The door slammed shut.

They high-fived each other and spread out. After a minute, Brody said, "You know what, Leroy? You might have a point. If I did help Jenny, then maybe I could legitimately get inside the Saxton household as part of the police investigation."

"Who's Jenny?"

"Oh, she's the main detective. DI Jenny Price."

"Ooh, *Jenny*," said Leroy, teasing. "You sure this is still about the hacking job?"

"Now you're just being stupid."

"So she's not good-looking then?"

"Shut up, Leroy."

"Maybe you should try for a bit more honesty when you speak to her. You don't want to be caught lying to a police officer."

"Not lying as such. Just not quite telling them everything."

"If this Jenny ever finds out, I'm pretty sure she'll go apeshit."

"I'd just be there to help. After all, I have information they don't have."

"You never learn." Leroy shook his head sadly. "Anyway, how will you approach her? You going to show up at her nick tomorrow?"

"No, I don't fancy walking in off the street into a police station. Too many cops for my liking."

"What then?"

"Leroy, you underestimate me. I'm a social engineer. I've got moves the police will never see coming."

"Uh-oh, that doesn't sound good. You're going to 'social engineer' your way in front of the police officer running a murder enquiry you're somehow involved in?"

Brody beamed at Leroy. "Yes," he said. "Yes, I am."

Saxton lowered his head in concession. "Okay. Okay. I admit to the affair with Audri."

Three long hours had passed since Jenny's first meeting with Derek Saxton in his office just outside of Watford. They were now back in Holborn.

Once Jenny realised that Da Silva wasn't planning on being present, she had ensured Alan Coombs was with her in the interview room. He knew her interview style, unlike DI Hamid earlier. His interruption during her initial meeting with Saxton at his office had annoyed her immensely. Not that she had let her feelings show, especially in front of the suspect. Hamid obviously employed a confrontational approach, blunt and direct. In Jenny's mind this approach typically handed over too much information, and therefore control, to the suspect. She preferred to adapt her technique to the situation and, in Saxton's case, she had wanted to see what he was willing to offer up first. It helped clue her into how she needed to play things later when the questioning got tougher and the answers more evasive.

Although the Audri Sahlberg case had had a quick break with Derek Saxton's detainment, she was very conscious that nothing had so far linked Saxton to Anna Parker's murder, even though the MO's of the two crimes matched closely. There must be some other connection.

She sat opposite Saxton in a large interview room, a wooden table between them. The red light on the recording system was on, picking up audio and video from microphones and cameras concealed in the walls and ceiling. Both DCI's, Da Silva and Jeffries, were watching the live feed in the room next door. Alan Coombs sat to her left. To Saxton's right was Stephen Masterson, his solicitor, clad in a Savile Row three-piece suit, a silk handkerchief peeking out of his top pocket. He looked decidedly uncomfortable, frequently rubbing his thighs. Jenny reasoned that most of his lawyerly dealings related to business – advising on employment contracts, mergers and acquisitions and shareholder disputes. But here, dragged by his client into a criminal situation, he seemed distinctly out of his depth.

"How long has it been going on?" Jenny asked, pleased that her persistence had finally elicited something of note from Saxton.

"About four months."

"And your wife?"

Saxton looked at his palms and shook his head. Then he eyeballed Jenny. "And she doesn't need to know either." He spoke firmly and turned to his lawyer. "This is confidential, right? They can't say any of this to Hilary, can they?"

Masterson shook his head noncommittally. "Depends."

"On what?" he demanded.

Jenny answered. "On whether you killed Audri."

"I told you ten times already. I had nothing to do with it. Why would I?"

"To cover up the affair you're now admitting to."

"For fuck's sake!"

Jenny changed tack. "Tell me about last night."

"I was working late."

"Where?"

"In my office."

"Tolpits Lane?"

"Yes."

"Anyone with you?"

"No. Jude left at about 6:00 p.m."

"Are you having an affair with her as well?"

Saxton glowered at Jenny and turned again to Masterson. "Can she really dish out this kind of dirt?"

Masterson shrugged.

Saxton spoke in a deliberately slow, exasperated voice. "No. I am not having, nor ever have had an affair with my secretary."

"So, you were in the office from 6:00 until well after 10:00 p.m. And no one saw you?"

Saxton thought for a moment and then looked up brightly. "Actually, I went to the gym. Yes, I forgot that. I left the office a few minutes after Jude."

"And where is this gym?"

Saxton gave the address. Jenny asked Alan to note it down and check up on it after the interview.

"Then you went home?"

"No, I went back to the office." He looked crestfallen.

"At what time?"

"About 7:15 p.m. It was just a quick workout."

"And no one saw you? Not even the receptionist?"

"Oh yes, of course." His expression brightened. "The security guard. That time of night, they put a security guard on reception. He saw me."

"At 7:15 p.m.?"

"Yes, about then."

"And he saw you again when you left to go home later?"

Saxton paused for thought. "Actually, no. When I left later he wasn't there. Must have gone to the loo or something."

"That's convenient."

Jenny wondered about Saxton. His thoughts and emotions were all over the place. He wasn't thinking clearly. Nothing stacked up. His defence was weak. And yet, when Jenny wasn't rubbing him up the wrong way, he seemed to be earnestly trying to help. It was time to up the stakes.

"Tell me about the sex games you enjoyed playing with Miss Sahlberg."

Saxton's jaw dropped. She'd hit a nerve with that one. "How — ?" He stopped himself, reformed his thoughts and then said, "I'm not going to dignify that with an answer."

"That's up to you, Mr Saxton. But my advice — and I'm sure your solicitor would agree — is to offer up the truth in advance. It will go down well for you later." It wouldn't make any difference, but Jenny didn't think Masterson had enough experience of courtrooms to know for sure.

Saxton said nothing.

"Is it that you're uncomfortable talking to me about this?" she asked. "You know, me being a woman and all that."

"No. I'm not embarrassed. It's just . . ." He looked at Alan for moral support. "It's private. That's all."

"I appreciate that, but it is relevant."

"I don't see how any of what me and Audri got up to in the sack has any relevance."

"Just answer the question, Mr Saxton. Did you include sex games in your relationship with Miss Sahlberg?"

Saxton let a deep breath out. "She's very uninhibited. Up for anything. Full of ideas."

"Like . . ." prompted Alan.

"Do I have to do this?"

Jenny didn't move a muscle and was confident Alan would remain quiet at her side. Masterson shuffled in his seat, rubbing his legs again.

Saxton spoke slowly at first and then, as he made it through the first few examples, related his encounters with more enthusiasm. At no point did he blush, although Jenny felt her cheeks redden. "She was just great. She'd text me all the time. You know, dirty texts. She'd do things like dig out my old rugby kit and we'd have sex while she was wearing it. Or make me wear it. She'd drag me into the woods for a quickie in the park near where we live. Or she'd put on private peep show. Or just wear high heels. And she got hold of some handcuffs from somewhere . . . Like I said, she was full of ideas."

"And all this under your wife's nose." Jenny fought to keep a judgmental tone out of her voice.

"Yeah," he sighed. "Audri was . . . pragmatic. So matter-of-fact about it. We never did much of anything when Hilary was around. She would wait for Hilary to go to work and then text me to pop back home."

"The way you describe it, everything was her idea. Never yours?"

"I did start to take the lead with new ideas in the last few weeks. She told me that I couldn't leave it up to her all the time."

"Was one of your ideas for her to leave the house naked save her coat and shoes and meet you somewhere?"

"Where are you going with this?" asked Masterson, speaking up for the first time. "Mr Saxton is cooperating beyond the call of duty here."

"Alan, show Mr Saxton the letter."

Alan leafed through the pile of papers in front of him and handed over the evidence bag containing the invitation that had been found in her coat pocket.

Saxton read the letter slowly. Masterson leaned in to read over

Saxton's shoulder. Saxton stood up and walked in tight circles behind his chair. "No way. But this is . . . I mean, how the fuck . . ." Saxton continued, failing to string a sentence together for a minute more.

"Did you write this letter, Mr Saxton?"

Saxton looked Jenny squarely in the eye and said, "No."

"Who else knows about your liaisons with Miss Sahlberg?"

"No one."

"You sure?"

He paused for a moment and then nodded.

"You see my problem? If you didn't write it and no one knows about your private games, then who else could have written it?"

Saxton sat back down in his seat, the wind completely taken out of his sails. He picked up the letter again and re-read it, leaning forward in his seat. "But that's not even my office!" he exclaimed. "See here." He lay the letter down on the desk and pointed. "It says to come to my office in Clarendon Road. That's not my office."

"Did Miss Sahlberg know where you worked? Had she been to your office in Tolpits Lane before?"

"No, she's never been there." He thought a bit more. "I'm not sure if I ever said specifically where I work."

"So, she would be none the wiser," concluded Alan.

Saxton chose not to comment.

"How many au pairs have you had?" asked Jenny.

"Two others."

"Did you have affairs with them as well?"

"No."

"But you wanted to, didn't you?" Jenny prodded.

"No." It was an obvious lie.

"Are they still alive?"

"What kind of question is that?"

"A pretty relevant one given the situation, don't you think?" Jenny didn't wait for an answer and switched to another topic. "Do you know Anna Parker?"

"Who?"

"Does Audri know an Anna Parker?"

"How the hell should I know?"

"Where were you last Friday? Late afternoon, early evening?"

"Friday? Why Friday?"

"I'll ask the questions, Mr Saxton."

Saxton thought for a moment and, with a sheepish look, said, "I was with Audri. Left work early to go home."

"Where was Mrs Saxton?"

"She went out with the girls from work, so Audri suggested . . . well, you know."

"I think I'm getting the picture. So you have no alibi for Friday either."

"Why do I even need one?"

Jenny ignored him and switched tracks again. She thought that if she went fast enough, perhaps he would slip up. "Do you ever go to the Royal Opera House?"

"What the hell are you on about?"

"Just answer the question, Mr Saxton," commanded Alan.

"No. I fucking hate opera."

"What about Greenwich? Trinity Laban college? Ring any bells?"

"Eh?"

"Flexbase then?"

"Flexbase. What, the facilities company?"

"Yes."

"What about it?"

"Are you a customer of theirs?"

"No. They're far too expensive. I looked at them once, years ago. You want one of their offices and it's like renting a hotel room when what you need is an unfurnished flat on a long term lease."

Jenny almost smiled, remembering that she had made the same point the previous morning to the Paddington building manager.

"You know where the Flexbase office is in Watford?"

"I just said I knew, didn't I?" And then it dawned on him. "Oh, I see where you're going with this. Yes, they're in Clarendon Road. But I wasn't there yesterday. I haven't been there in years."

"It seems we only have your word for that. No one saw you after 7:15 p.m. And we have a letter from you to Audri, referring to your on-going sex games and inviting her to meet you at Clarendon Road."

"I told you, I didn't write that letter! I didn't leave my office in Tolpits Lane, two miles away, until after 10:00 p.m. And I certainly didn't kill Audri."

"Is there any CCTV in your building to verify any of this?" Jenny already knew there wasn't.

"No idea."

"What about Clarendon Road?" asked the lawyer. "Is there CCTV there?"

Saxton looked at his solicitor in surprise. "Nice one, Stephen." He turned to face Jenny, waiting for her answer.

"Yes, there is. In the foyer. We're trying to get hold of it now."

Like the Paddington Basin office, the CCTV system was managed centrally from the Flexbase headquarters in Canary Wharf. They were waiting on Flexbase to provide the footage from both receptions. She made a mental note to put pressure on them to hurry up.

"And when you see I'm not on there, what then?"

Alan answered. "Means nothing. There are other ways in and out of the building. Delivery entrances and so on."

"Christ on a bike, what do I have to do to prove I had nothing to do with this?"

"Nothing Derek," advised his lawyer. "It's the police that have to prove you killed Miss Sahlberg. It's not your job to prove you didn't."

Saxton glared at Jenny and then formed his lips into a smile. It was stone cold.

You love the planning stage: making sure you've thought through every eventuality, leaving nothing to chance. You know that doing what you do on a whim would be foolish. You've seen enough programs on the TV to know that the police only catch the ones who slip up. And so you plan. You make sure that every little thing is covered.

You're pleased with the way you planned for the babysitter. You knew you couldn't walk into the room while she was naked without her seeing you and screaming loudly. And so you came up with a plan. You'd once heard the babysitter suggest using a blindfold to the rugby player. You'd adapted her idea, knowing she was predisposed to it. And so, when she saw it listed as an instruction, she hadn't hesitated.

Your plan worked. You walked nonchalantly into the meeting room, knowing she would have followed your instructions to the letter. You were able to walk around the room, the babysitter assuming from under her blindfold that you were her rugby player. You were able to take a good look at the goods. She was stunningly beautiful, made even more so by her vulnerability.

The icing on the cake was how you fooled her into allowing you to touch her. By far, it had been the best part of your plan. You were particularly proud of that. On your smartphone, you had recorded the rugby player's voice from the webcam site. You caught a perfect little snippet of him saying, "Sshhh, Audri." And each time she'd spoken or looked doubtful, you'd played it from your phone. It had kept her calm, reinforcing the illusion that she was in the room with the rugby player.

You used the time to feel her all over. Fondle her breasts, squeeze her nipples and even finger her wet pussy. She was begging for it. And it had made you so damn hard. Close to bursting.

And so all your planning came to a sudden halt after you knocked her over and placed the knife to her throat.

You'd planned to take your time. But you rushed it again. In the heat of the moment, you rushed it.

What a waste.

Still, there are plenty more fish in the sea. You've already selected the next one. The one a lot like her.

And you've already booked the meeting room. You've got a deadline to meet.

You've come up with a plan. After all, you've been watching her for months. You know so much about her, how can you possibly fail?

"Ah, nice of you to finally join us, DI Price," said Da Silva, his sarcastic tone indicating the exact opposite. "Where the hell have you been?"

The briefing room was full to the brim, about thirty people: detectives, uniform and civilians. Heads swivelled round to stare at Jenny. Da Silva stood at the front, like a teacher addressing a class. Jenny caught Alan's eye, but he shrugged his shoulders, letting her know that he didn't have a clue what was going on. She had never seen Da Silva take front and centre before.

"I was just — "

"Just sit down," he commanded.

She looked around. The only seat available was next to Alan, right in the middle. She quickly made her way to it, people standing to make room for her to pass. Da Silva folded his arms melodramatically and waited for her to sit. She felt like a chastised schoolchild, and her face flushed red.

"As I was just saying, I am not happy at all . . . " Da Silva stared at Jenny as if everything was all her fault.

She wondered what on earth could have happened in the last hour to cause this uncustomary behaviour. She had been on the phone during most of the journey back from Watford, getting updates from the team. None of them had mentioned anything about Da Silva being on the warpath.

"One." Da Silva held up his index finger, emphasising the point he was about to make. "I spoke to the press earlier and one of the journalists knew the name of our prime suspect. Now they all do. I want to know who let that little gem of information slip." Da Silva looked around the room slowly, making it clear he believed someone on the team had done it.

He held up a second finger. "Two, the evidence on which we have arrested Mr Saxton is circumstantial at best. I've just sat down with the Chief Super and he ripped me a new arsehole over it. If we put what we currently have in front of the CPS, they will just laugh in our faces.

"And most importantly, number three. I do not believe that everyone here is giving the two hundred per cent I asked for when I first spoke to you all a couple of weeks ago. Carry on with this level of performance, and we'll slip further down the rankings on the Commissioner's dashboard. And, let me tell you, I will not have that. Not on my watch." He held up his third finger, even though he'd made the third point already.

Jenny had never heard Da Silva use foul language before. It didn't take a detective, even though there were plenty in the room, to understand that it was the second point that had riled him up so much. But she was surprised at his first point. She supposed it could have been someone on the team. But there were many other potential sources.

"I have already dealt with the first point. I've reminded the press of their obligations under the law. They cannot publish the identity of our suspect until I say so. The third point you will all deal with by upping your game with immediate effect. And I'd better see a difference. That leaves the second point. Let's discuss that now."

Da Silva clasped his hands and allowed silence to fill the room.

He turned his back on them and studied the wall-to-wall whiteboard. On it were written the bullet points from yesterday's briefing that Jenny had led and Fiona had written up. Added since were other new lines of enquiry, smiling photos of both victims, blow-ups of both bodies in situ, other shots from the crime scenes and copies of all three communiqués from the killer; the email inviting Anna Parker to her fake audition, the note to Audri Sahlberg asking her to come to Derek's fake office, and the instructions Audri followed when she arrived at the meeting room.

While his back was to them, people started looking at each other, shrugging and mouthing things like, "What the fuck?", "Where did he pop up from?" or, more simply, "Dickhead" and worse. Jenny sat still, still bristling from how discourteously Da Silva had treated her in front of her peers and juniors. No DCI had ever done that to her before.

"The video footage from the two Flexbase receptions," said Da Silva loudly, quieting the crowd, "Where are we with that, DC Jones?" He kept his back to them.

Jenny could see that he had read the first line of enquiry from the board.

"We received both video files from the Flexbase headquarters about an hour ago," said Fiona. "They've only got footage of the reception in both buildings. Neither had CCTV anywhere else. I've just started going through the footage."

"Is it just you going through the two video files?"

"Yes, guv."

"That's not enough. Get someone else to help you."

"Right, guv."

"While we're on the subject of CCTV, who's pulling together footage from the area around both Flexbase offices?"

"That'll be me, guv," said Karim. As Da Silva did not turn to face the new speaker, Karim added his name and rank.

"Well, DC Malik. What's your update?"

"Nothing for Watford except Watford Junction train station at the end of Clarendon Road, but that doesn't seem to be much use to us. Paddington Basin has some. We found footage of Anna Parker exiting the tube station, carrying her cello, but other than that we don't really know what we're looking for."

Da Silva whirled around theatrically. "You don't know what you're looking for?" He stared Karim down. "Someone help DC Malik here please. What should he be looking for?"

No one spoke. Da Silva looked around the room, the challenge in his eyes. "No one?" he asked the room, surprise in his tone. "I don't believe this. Call yourself a murder investigation team?"

One of the indexers, a middle-aged woman, sat at the front, tentatively raised her hand.

Da Silva said, "Go on."

"Search the CCTV footage for the prime suspect, Mr Saxton?"

"Correct. A gold star for you. DC Malik, did you hear that?"

"Yes, guv."

"Right, next. The fingerprints on the letter delivered to Audri. Who's on that?"

"Me, sir," said Alan.

Jenny was wound up now. She hated seeing her team treated like this, especially in front of the rest of the supporting staff, civilians and uniformed officers. She'd already heard enough snickers of derision to know this had gone far enough. She stood up, placed her hand briefly on Alan's shoulder to let him know not to say any more and shuffled her way to the front.

Da Silva stared at her incredulously.

"What do you think you're doing, DI Price?"

"Can I have a word in private, sir?" She spoke conversationally.

"Not right now."

"It's important, sir." Jenny held up her phone. "I've just received a text message with some new information that may change the direction of our whole investigation. But it's delicate. I need your personal input."

Da Silva looked at her suspiciously and then said to the room. "Okay, let's dismiss for now. You heard what I said. Two hundred per cent. Nothing less."

The room emptied.

"Let's go to my office, then."

Jenny had already walked off in the direction of his office. Da Silva caught up with her. She entered the room and immediately began lowering the blinds to block visibility from the floor; this was not something that anyone else should see.

Da Silva entered behind her and said, "What do you think you're doing, DI Price?"

"Saving you from yourself, that's what I'm doing. With respect, you were making a fool out of yourself out there, sir. It was becoming obvious to me and, most likely to every one of those officers, that your experience of leading a major investigation is . . . limited."

Da Silva stared at her impassively. She held his gaze, willing him to register that she was putting her neck on the line to help him. It was obvious he was weighing up his situation, deciding how to handle this, perhaps wondering how much he could trust her. He was hung up on rank; she knew that. Could he overcome the fact that she was a junior officer? Or would he revert to type, let his pride get in the way and throw her out on her ear for insubordination? She hadn't thought through the consequences of her actions. It slowly dawned on her that he could actually suspend her for this.

It was up to him now.

Da Silva slowly sat down. "But I have to lead from the front." He spoke quietly.

Jenny sat in the chair on the opposite side of his desk, perching sideways to avoid seeming confrontational.

"Since when? You've done all right these last two weeks."

"Not everyone would agree with you . . . "

He was right. He was the main subject of gossip at the water cooler.

Da Silva stared down at his hands, then looked up at her. "You know I've being relying on you these last two weeks."

The vulnerability in his eyes caught Jenny by surprise, but not as much as the admission. She had been sure that there was some nefarious ulterior motive to the way he had allowed Jenny to lead the team briefings and suspect interviews. She had thought him lazy. Or that he was giving her enough rope to hang herself. Something that benefited him to her detriment. But what she hadn't considered was that he was completely out of his depth. That he had relied on her.

"Only in the details, sir. The overall investigative strategy, keeping DCS McLintock at bay, handling our liaison with Bedfordshire and Hertfordshire, the media engagement. That's all been you. From the front."

"Some of it, but not the operational tactics, prioritising lines of enquiry, following the leads, interviewing the witnesses, all that stuff. I'm the SIO and I've not been close enough to any of it. You've done all that."

"Why did you leave it to me?" she asked.

"It was the right thing to do."

"Because . . ."

". . . Because the Met's Murder Investigation Manual is all process, policy and procedure. I've read it plenty of times. I've completed the training courses with flying colours. But without the experience of having actually been part of a murder investigation, it's hard to know which bit to apply when. You do."

Jenny was flattered. She had not expected that at all.

"What was your last role, sir?"

"I ran the kidnap unit in Scotland Yard."

"And did you personally negotiate any kidnappings?"

"No. I had a strong team. They all knew what to do when we had a case. I focused on making sure everyone had the correct training, the resource levels were right and all the other management activities were handled correctly."

"Right. The background strategy was your forte and you relied on your team to do their job."

"Yes."

"Which is what you've been doing for the last two weeks. What happened to make you change that today?"

He looked at Jenny and leaned forward. "This conversation is absolutely confidential, DI Price." He looked at Jenny's raised eyebrow and corrected himself. "Sorry, I mean Jenny."

Finally, a first name. Maybe there was hope. "Of course, sir."

"Somehow, word has got back to the Chief Super that I've been running things from a distance. Delegating a bit too much. This afternoon, the real reason McLintock tore me a new one was because of that. It was nothing to do with only having circumstantial evidence so far. Although, he isn't happy about that either, but he expects us to pull through on that now that we have Saxton in custody."

"And do you think that your approach in front of the troops earlier was the right one?"

"Clearly not, given this conversation." He chuckled. "I thought that it was time I showed a firm hand."

"So you thought giving that speech, belittling me and my team in front of everyone, and generally lording it up would generate the right level of respect for you as DCI?"

Da Silva didn't answer. He didn't need to.

"Okay, I have a few suggestions . . ."

For the next twenty minutes, Jenny and Da Silva spoke over his options. He allowed her to help him. He listened to her ideas. They agreed on a plan of action that would leverage the skills he had and utilise Jenny for the tactics in the field, building upon the approach he had taken naturally in the first two weeks. They agreed how to keep communication lines open between them so that he was always in the know. Established where he could safely learn on the job without exposing himself. In suspect interviews, they would make sure it was just the two of them. Each day, they would get together in his office and prioritise the lines of enquiry, which he could then assign to the team. He agreed to it all.

Jenny reminded herself that while she had also passed all the courses and been a senior member of murder investigation teams before, she'd never been the Senior Investigating Officer and had certainly never worked a double murder. She pointed out to Da Silva that there were other, far more experienced DCIs and DIs from whom he could take advice. But she only said it for effect. And he dismissed it anyway.

Back at his apartment, Brody cracked open a new, untraceable pay-as-you-go SIM card and placed it inside a spare mobile phone. He entered the destination phone number from memory. Then he keyed in the text message he'd thought up earlier.

DI Price. I have critical information on the Audri Sahlberg case that you need to know. I will only discuss with you personally. Tomorrow 10:00 a.m. Alone. Somewhere public. Let me know where. His finger hovered over the send button.

Brody had obtained DI Jenny Price's mobile number by phoning Holborn Police Station pretending to be DCI Jeffries from Watford police station. He had come by DCI Jeffries' name by first phoning Watford and asking who was in charge of the murder investigation on Clarendon Road. All facts he had overheard earlier, while parked outside the Saxton household.

He knew that when he pressed send on this text, there would be no going back. The law was binary: zero or one, right or wrong, black or white. Brody was a hacker, someone who operated very much in the area between the black and the white. As a white hat, he discovered and publicised weaknesses in systems that would otherwise be kept secret and exploited by black hats with low morals and malfeasant purposes. His deeds always had honourable intentions, but his methods were problematic. They were often the same ones used by the criminals. In his own way, he fought fire with fire. The only problem was that it was difficult for laypeople to see the difference. To see who was white and who was black. To them, they were all grey.

And despite this, here he was choosing to jump into bed with the police.

But what choice did he have?

Brody pressed the send key and waited.

Jenny sat at her desk, smiling to herself. Across the major incident room, through the glass half-walls of Da Silva's office, Bruce Nichols, the Office Manager, was making copious notes in his notepad as he took a long list of instructions from a very animated Detective Chief Inspector Raul Da Silva. Da Silva frequently pointed at his whiteboard, where each thread of the case was already listed in Jenny's handwriting — he hadn't complained this time when she'd taken marker pen to the whiteboard — to help make his points. Nichols was fourth in a line of officers that Da Silva had briefed since his chat with Jenny an hour before. The Press Officer, the Finance Manager and the HOLMES 2 Support Manager had all been summoned, consulted, briefed and dismissed.

Although she hadn't planned the confrontation with Da Silva earlier, or its surprising outcome, Jenny wondered at her own motivations. She could easily have stood back and allowed Da Silva to screw up. The way he was going, it wouldn't have taken long. It could still happen despite their off-the-record pact. And then there would be a vacancy for a new DCI. But she knew that she was still three or four years away from being in a position to even be considered for promotion. No, her motivation was more straightforward. The situation gave her an opportunity to shine. An experienced DCI would personally run all key lines of enquiry, with Jenny in his shadow. This way, she would lead — albeit not in name — and obtain investigative leadership experience far more quickly than she otherwise might. Da Silva had his fast-track career sorted. This could be her own mini version.

"Got you!" cried Fiona, from across the room. She turned around and waved Jenny to come over a big grin on her face. "Look at this," she said, pointing at her screen.

Black and white CCTV footage of the Flexbase reception in Paddington was paused on her computer screen. It was mounted high and took in all of the reception area, the desk on the left, the entrance doors in the centre and the waiting area to the right. The female receptionist sat behind the reception desk painting her nails. A time code in the bottom corner said, "16:09." Fiona resumed playback. Nothing happened for a moment and then the entrance doors rotated and a cycle courier walked in, carrying a large letter. He wore trainers, a shiny charcoal tracksuit and carried a backpack. His head was still covered in a black cycle helmet and facemask, the kind used by cyclists to filter carbon monoxide. He spoke to the receptionist, although nothing could be heard, as there was no audio. She nodded and he walked forwards towards the camera and then underneath, out of sight. Fiona stopped playback.

"Right ?" said Jenny, noncommittally.

"Now watch this." Fiona pulled up another CCTV feed. Jenny recognised this as the reception area from Watford, smaller and less grand than its cousin in Paddington. This time, a security guard sat behind the reception desk, doing a crossword in his newspaper. The time code showed, "19:13." Fiona pressed play. After a moment the guard looked up towards the entrance doors. He pressed a button and the doors opened. A cycle courier walked in, in exactly the same garb as the one from the Paddington footage. After a short conversation with the guard, he too was allowed to enter the building.

"It's the same guy in both, I'm sure of it." Fiona rewound, put both video feeds on the screen and allowed them to run simultaneously. It was the same man. He wore the same clothes and moved in the same way. "And in both cases, he's arrived not long before each victim. You can see them coming in later."

"That's great work, Fiona." Jenny was impressed with the

constable's initiative. "Have you got footage of the courier leaving?" She was thinking of the time code.

"That's the strange thing. There's no footage of him leaving at all. It's like he came in and never left."

"That is odd." Jenny studied the two feeds. "What do you think? Is that Derek Saxton under that mask and helmet?"

"It's hard to say. Could be, I suppose."

Jenny wasn't sure. Saxton was powerfully built and muscular. The dark tracksuit bottoms and jacket worn by the cyclist made it difficult to gauge his build.

"Can you work with O'Reilly to see if we can get a close-up of his face? We might at least be able to see his eyes or something."

"I've just emailed him the two MPGs and asked him for exactly that."

"Good. And can you contact the team on-site at Derek's house and office? Ask them to search for any cycling gear."

"Already done," beamed Fiona.

When Jenny returned to her desk, she noticed a missed call on her mobile phone. Then she remembered that she'd left it on silent since the team briefing three hours earlier. She pressed a button and saw that she had missed four calls, all from different people: April, Alan, Karim, and Harry.

Her sister would have phoned to confirm arrangements for the coming weekend. It was Kevin's birthday. Which reminded Jenny, she needed to buy a present for her nephew. Alan, who was at the morgue, would have called to give her an update on the formal identification of Anna Parker, whose mother had travelled up from Torquay for the grotesque formality. Karim, who was at a different morgue in Watford, would have been giving her an update on the Audri Sahlberg post-mortem. And Harry, who had been forensically analysing Derek Saxton's laptop and home computers, searching for evidence of the Anna Parker email invitation or the Audri Sahlberg letter and instruction note, was returning her call. She had left him a voicemail earlier, telling him to meet her the next morning in Canary Wharf, and accompany her during her visit to the Flexbase headquarters. Given that they were looking into the meeting room booking processes, she wanted the computer expert with her for when the techno babble started.

She saw that three of the four had left voicemails. And then she noticed that she had also received a text. It was from a number she didn't recognise. She read it and gasped.

DI Price. I have critical information on the Audri Sahlberg case that you need to know. I will only discuss with you personally. Tomorrow 10:00 a.m. Alone. Somewhere public. Let me know where.

What the hell was this? She looked at the time. It had arrived twenty minutes ago. She composed a response and pressed send. *Who is this? How did you get my number?*

A minute later the reply arrived. Insistent. *Tomorrow 10.00 a.m. It will be worth it.*

Instead of replying with another text, she dialled it. It rang and rang. No voicemail. Eventually, she gave up. She thought about where to meet and recalled that she was going to Docklands tomorrow morning. She knew somewhere.

Okay. Taylor St Baristas, Canary Wharf. This better be good. Or I'll have you for wasting police time.

The reply was almost immediate. *You won't regret this.*

Jenny wasn't so sure.

"Thanks for the lift Patrick, but I think I need to be on my own."

"I'm worried about you, Kimmy. On your own in the house."

"I'll be fine. I'm not good company right now, anyway. Why don't you go out with some of your friends?"

"I'd rather make sure you're okay."

"That's very sweet of you. But I'm fine. Honestly."

Kim pulled the door handle and the passenger door partially opened. The garish red leather seats creaked as she leaned over to kiss Patrick on the cheek. He turned his lips towards her, expecting more. She lowered her head and so he jerkily planted a peck on her forehead instead. Kim withdrew, unclipped her seatbelt and climbed out of the car.

"See you tomorrow?" he asked.

"I don't know. I've got a full day of rehearsals and then straight into the final ballet performance."

"The show must go on, eh?" He grinned amiably.

"Yeah, I guess."

His faced dropped as he realised from her harsh inflection that he'd said something wrong. But, as usual, he had no idea what. The show must go on. Just like life must go on. But not for her friend.

Not for Anna.

She shut the door and turned her back on him. He would watch her walk up the path; she knew that. When she turned her key in the lock and pushed the door ajar, she turned to him and waved.

He waved back and then screeched off up the road, the rising exhaust note of his white Porsche loud in the quiet backstreets of Charlton this late at night. She watched him slalom at speed through the parked cars on the narrow road, wondering why he always had to drive so fast.

The front door closed behind her. The house was quiet, unnaturally so. The faint yellow light from the streetlamp outside passed through the arched window above the front door and provided minimal illumination in the hallway. The near dark matched her mood and she wasn't inclined to change it. The light or her mood.

All day she'd been in the company of people: her fellow students, her teachers, and the dancers in this evening's penultimate ballet production. She'd found that only when dancing was she able to forget. No, not forget. Suspend belief about her best friend's death.

Kim dumped her coat and bag and opened the fridge in the kitchen, its glowing interior the only light in the room. There was no wine left, she had drunk it all last night. She spotted a bottle of beer and opened it. Taking a greedy swig, she drifted upstairs. The further she went, the darker it became. When she reached the first floor landing, she had no choice but to put on the light. The first thing she saw was the open door to Anna's room, the Jasmine plaque crooked on the door from her encounter with Jenny, the nice detective from yesterday who'd kept her company till late into the night.

Feeling drawn, Kim entered Anna's room. She turned on all the lights, then turned off the centre light as it was too bright.

On the bed, she saw Theo, Anna's enormous teddy bear that she had brought with her from her home in Torquay. She placed her already empty beer bottle on the bedside table, lay down on Anna's bed, and wrapped Theo's massive arms around her.

The tears came quickly, followed by wracking sobs. She let them. Eventually, as the sobs became less frequent, she allowed herself to drift off to sleep.

She awoke with a start, initially disoriented. Why was she in

Anna's room? Why was everything so silent? Where was Anna? And then it all came back in an angry rush. Adrenalin flowed freely. Her anger and frustration grew within her like a nuclear chain reaction. She couldn't contain it. She had to burst. The guttural scream she howled was a start. Jumping off the bed, she grabbed the empty beer bottle and threw it wildly, immediately searching for another projectile as it flew from her grip. She heard the satisfying smash of breaking glass but then the room dimmed unexpectedly.

Shocked back into herself, she turned around slowly. The bottle had hit one of the wall lights, exploded and smashed the glass cover to bits. The bulb inside, now exposed, had been blown apart as well. Shards of thick, green bottle glass interspersed with thin, multi-coloured glass from the bulb and light-shade lay strewn about the corner desk and floor. She was lucky the fuse box downstairs hadn't tripped.

Disgusted with herself, Kim turned on the main light and carefully picked up the broken shards. She made a pile of broken glass on Anna's desk. When the floor was clear, she stood up and picked at bits on the broken wall light, in an attempt to make sure all the loose pieces were removed.

One piece offered up some resistance. She realised it wasn't actually a piece of glass, but some kind of electrical component, with two thin wires streaming out the back of it. She was no electrical expert, but it didn't look like it belonged in the light. The only electrical component that she thought should be there was the screw hole for the bulb. She pulled at the strange component and more wire flowed out and then it caught.

What the hell was it?

What the hell, she decided. She yanked it. It came free in her hand, but the fuse box downstairs tripped at the same time. All the lights went out.

Damn.

She pulled her phone out of the pocket of her jeans, swapping it with the electrical component she had liberated from the light. Using the phone's torch as illumination, she carefully made her way to the ground floor and found the fusebox cupboard in the kitchen, where she flipped the tripped fuse upwards. Light came back on upstairs. She switched on all the lights downstairs.

Her phone rang in her hand, the vibration and the noise making her jump out of her skin.

She looked at the display. Patrick. Why was he ringing this late? Why was he ringing at all? They usually messaged each other, text conversations being their normal mode of communication when not face-to-face. She couldn't be bothered to talk to him. They'd talked enough earlier. He'd only ask her if she was all right. And she damn well wasn't and didn't want to lie.

She pressed the red button, dropping his call.

WEDNESDAY

CHAPTER 10

Facing a mirrored wall, Brody watched DI Jenny Price enter the busy café. Her eyes darted round the establishment. He took the opportunity to study her. A chic grey trouser suit, a purple blouse and black, practical shoes, had replaced yesterday's maroon outfit. She carried a raincoat over an arm. This morning, her hair was pinned up although some auburn locks had slipped free. He could see the line of her slender neck.

He watched her use her phone to make a call, looking around as she rang. The display on his phone lit up — he'd put it on silent — but he ignored it. When it stopped, he pressed send on the text he had prepared earlier.

Your cappuccino is getting cold, DI Price.

He watched her receive the text and scan the room suspiciously. Eventually, she caught his eye in the walled reflection and held it. Brody nodded obligingly. She acknowledged him and then coolly turned away and approached the counter. He let out a deep breath, not realising he'd been holding it. He watched her order and pay. She was given a numbered wooden block.

"You're not a cappuccino girl, then?" said Brody as she sat down opposite him, pushing the coffee he had bought her to one side.

"I've already had my breakfast."

"So you're Italian?"

"No, but I agree with Italian coffee etiquette. It makes sense."

"That explains your choice of this place. You know your coffee." Brody took a sip of his espresso. "And this is damn good coffee."

"It's Guatemalan."

"Yes, from the Huehuetenango region just North of Guatemala city."

"I'm impressed," she said, nodding, "that you can pronounce Huehuetenango."

Brody chuckled. The waitress arrived and placed Jenny's order in front of her. An espresso and a tall glass of tap water.

"Well DI Price, it seems we're both passionate about coffee," Brody commented. He watched her sip her drink and savour its flavour. He felt genuine admiration.

"Looks that way, Mr . . ."

"Taylor. Brody Taylor."

"So, Mr Taylor. You have information about Audri Sahlberg?"

"Please, call me Brody."

"And you can call me —"

He cut in. "— Jenny?"

"DI Price," she corrected him. "But I am intrigued how you seem to know so much about me and this case."

"There's a simple answer to that. I saw you at the Saxton house in Bushey yesterday."

"Where were you then?" She raised one eyebrow. "I didn't see you."

"I was at home," he lied.

"I don't understand."

"Why don't I show you?"

Brody whipped out his tablet PC and launched an Internet browser. He brought up the SWY site, logged in and selected *Au Pair Affair*. Of the seven camera feeds, he saw movement in Audri's bedroom. He selected it and it filled the screen. Men in white over-suits were systematically poking about the room.

"You're saying this is the Saxton house?"

"Yes. I think this is the girl's bedroom."

"Hold on a minute, that's Jason Edmonds," said Jenny, incredulously. And then, more calmly, "He's the crime scene manager. And that's his team. Is this live?"

"Yes. Although there's a couple of minutes time lag as the video travels over the web."

Brody minimised the feed and selected the master bedroom. Hilary Saxton lay on her bed talking on the phone. Brody turned up the volume. Jenny leaned in closer to hear over the background hubbub of the café.

"They won't let me see him," Hilary said. "He's been there all night. I don't know what's going on. Dad, why would the police suspect Derek? It makes no sense . . . "

Brody muted the volume.

"And you saw *me* on this yesterday?"

"Saw and heard. You were in the kitchen with Hilary Saxton and a posse of other police officers." He clicked out of the bedroom and brought up the kitchen. It was empty.

"What kind of website is this?"

Avoiding the whole pentest saga, Brody summarised what he knew about the site while giving her a tour of it, randomly selecting locations and feeds. He explained how you registered, paid for basic webcams and then paid more to access additional feeds and audio. And he finished with his belief that all the webcams were in the UK.

"Is it legal?" she asked.

"No idea. I guess it depends on whether the people in all these locations have given their permission to the site."

"Do the Saxtons have any idea that their house is being broadcast to all and sundry over the Internet?"

"I don't know. Most of the people on these webcams seem to be completely oblivious. But in the case of the Saxtons, I'd go as far as to say that they know the webcams are there. I saw Audri look up at one of the webcams yesterday morning. Knowingly, it seemed to me. But whether they're aware that these feeds are viewable by just anyone, you'll have to ask them."

"I will."

"Did you know that Derek Saxton was having an affair with the au pair?"

"Yes," she replied. Brody was dismayed. He'd thought that would be new information. She continued, "But how do *you* know this?"

"I've observed them fooling around under the wife's nose. Quick gropes here and there, that kind of thing." He didn't want to mention the bath scene that he and Leroy had watched.

"Interesting." She narrowed her eyes. "What's your role in all this, Mr . . . Brody? Why do you watch these feeds?"

It was the most difficult question and he'd planned for it.

"I do contract work for an IT security consultancy. I specialise in helping their clients protect their systems and networks from cyber threats." As he spoke, he realised that was the nearest he'd ever got to the truth when meeting a woman for the first time. It didn't even sound that bad. For once, he had avoided inventing a film industry related profession; film director, cameraman, movie producer, or even stuntman. But then, this was no date. He looked Jenny in the eye and, despite his instincts to the contrary, lied to her face. "One of the other security consultants is going out with someone who works in a call centre business. It seems she's being stalked. As a favour to him, I'm trying to find out the identity of her stalker."

"Go on."

"This is the call centre . . . " Brody selected one of the three call centre locations he'd found on the site. "Someone's been emailing her video footage of her talking on the phone, not always on official call centre business, if you know what I mean."

"I'm not sure I'm with you."

"They're both embarrassed because the recordings were from her side of their conversation. Talking dirty with her boyfriend."

"I see. Can't you just trace the email?"

"I've tried. It's from a Russian site that provides disposable email addresses, completely untraceable."

"Presumably, the email headers make it appear like it's from someone she knows?"

"I'm impressed. Again," he said.

"Don't be," she said. "We've had something similar happen on this case."

"That's interesting. Which anonymous email service was used?"

"I've no idea. And anyway, I can't talk about case details." She sipped her espresso. "What name was used on the fake email?"

"No one they know. Seems to be a made-up name." Brody was now inventing fake facts on the fly. He hadn't expected to go into this much detail.

"Do your friends know the video is broadcast on this website?"

"No, I haven't told them that yet. She thinks it's one of her co-workers who's got access to the CCTV system at work, which is what I thought initially. It's only when I traced the source of the video file she sent me that I discovered SecretlyWatchingYou.com."

It was a convoluted story. He should have gone for something simpler.

She wasn't finished. "Does the call centre company know they're being broadcast on this site?"

Brody continued improvising. "I haven't asked them. The girlfriend wants to keep it all hush-hush, so my approaching the employer won't help." He hoped she didn't ask who the company was. He didn't have an answer for that.

"So why were you watching the Saxtons if you're focused on this call centre location?"

At last, back on track.

"I wasn't particularly. I was just getting to know the site, looking around, when I saw you and half the Met. I figured you probably didn't know about the webcams and that you ought to."

"Well, that's very public spirited of you." She cocked her head to one side, studying him. Brody couldn't tell if she believed his story or not. Jenny seemed very sharp. He'd invented the friend-of-a-friend stalker story to appeal to her compassionate side. In his head it had sounded plausible, like most of his deceptions, and although he hated lying, he could hardly state the truth – *DI Price, I'm in a desperate race against another hacker to be first to crack the SWY site. All so that I can retain my online god-like-status among my fellow hackers around the world.*

Jenny said, "But I don't see how these webcams fit in. We've got the husband in custody. He orchestrated the whole thing."

"Derek Saxton."

Brody noticed that she hesitated before nodding her head in confirmation.

After a moment of silence, he asked, "Would you like another coffee?"

"No, one's enough, thanks." Jenny looked at her watch. "Anyway, I've got to be somewhere soon. I was expecting my colleague to turn up by now." She picked up her phone, tutted and said, "Two missed calls from him and a voicemail. I bet he's running late."

"Who?"

"My computer expert."

Jenny held up her hand while she listened to a garbled message on her phone. Her face dropped. "Damn, he's not coming."

"Was he going with you to the Flexbase headquarters?"

Jenny eyed him suspiciously. "How the hell would you know that?"

"I must have overheard someone mention Flexbase when I saw you in the kitchen." He watched her try to recall whether this was true. "And anyway, the news cameras have been outside the Flexbase building in Watford. That's where Audri's body was discovered, right?"

"And so you just put two and two together?"

"I guess. It makes sense. And you chose this coffee shop, right near their Docklands head office."

He wasn't sure she had bought it. "What did you need a computer expert for?"

"None of your business, why?"

"Well, I'm here. Maybe I could help."

"Definitely not, Mr Taylor."

He gave her his best smile and said, "I thought we had this sorted, DI Price. Call me Brody."

It was the second time in his life that he had spent the night in a police cell. The first had been fifteen years ago after a drunken night out in Bath, when he and one of his Sarries teammates ended up in a massive brawl with some local rugby fans in a nightclub. That time Derek had awoken with an almighty hangover. This time he found himself soberly facing up to the stark reality of his predicament.

Last time, the fight and his overnight internment had become front-page news. He'd earned the nickname *Mad-Dog Derek* because he had put one of the fans in hospital with both arms and three ribs broken. Derek wondered whether he'd be on the front of today's papers. He'd heard somewhere that any publicity is good publicity and his agency could certainly do with some. But to be in the headlines as a murder suspect? That was too much.

He had spent most of the night awake, lying on the hard surface of the cell's bunk, his thoughts oscillating between Hilary and Audri.

He couldn't believe the police had accused him of rape and murder. Him? At first he'd thought it was some kind of sick joke. But as it slowly sunk in that Audri — young, beautiful, carefree, wild Audri — was dead, rage threatened to blow through. And, for everyone's sake, especially his own, he needed to control his temper. But the horrific images of her last few hours coursing through his mind were overwhelming.

The letter was a problem. And it bothered him immensely. Who could possibly have written it? The whole idea of Audri coming to his office late at night virtually naked had been something they had chatted about a few weeks ago. But they'd never got round to it. She must have told someone about it — he certainly hadn't. But then that meant that she had talked to someone about their relationship. Her friend Ornetta, maybe? Audri hardly knew anyone in England.

And then his thoughts would sway towards self-preservation, thinking about his wife. What if it all came out about his dalliance with Audri? He would lose everything. His gorgeous baby daughter, his home, his whole damn life. And, yes, the wife he loved. What the hell had he been playing at? What a bloody fool. *Never shit on your own doorstep*; rule number one. And he'd broken it. In style.

His lawyer had given him assurances that Hilary wouldn't find out about the affair, but Derek wasn't convinced that his lawyer cut the mustard when it came to criminal law. He made a mental note to get a criminal specialist, whatever the cost. And anyway, he'd been arrested and detained. For murder. Surely that meant the police would follow every angle. Even the ones that led nowhere. Like his relationship with Audri. That policewoman, DI Price, didn't seem to care. In fact, he was convinced she would enjoy dropping him in the shit with his wife. Or perhaps the press.

No, he had to sort this out. And quickly.

He only had one card he could play. It would muddy what he'd achieved yesterday with the two medallists from London 2012. At least Arthur Aguda was signed up and on the books after their champagne lunch. No way out. But his evening meeting with Stacey Goodwin, the Paralympic rower, had only been an initial pitch, although it had gone extremely well. Boosted by her upcoming autobiography, she was sure to become his most lucrative client. If only she signed on the dotted line.

But now he would need to drag her into this sorry mess. It would be bad publicity for her. Definitely not the right way to begin their business relationship. And the result was bound to be her dropping him like the proverbial hot potato. And then there would be a knock-on effect. Prospective clients would choose other sports agencies. Existing clients wouldn't renew their contracts. If he couldn't be seen to be in control of his own life, how could he be expected to manage his clients' careers?

Despite the high cost, he had no choice.

Derek stood up and banged on the door.

"Guard," he shouted. "Guard!"

Was she completely mad?

Jenny had already asked herself that at least twenty times during the short walk from the coffee shop to the Flexbase headquarters. She decided that she must be, choosing to accept Brody Taylor's offer of assistance. Certifiable even.

His story about the Internet webcams in the Saxton home was interesting. Intriguing even. But was it relevant to the Audri Sahlberg case? That was the real question. They already had Saxton detained and he had no alibi. The invitation letter was clearly written by him. He had admitted to an affair with the second victim. Keeping that secret from his wife was a viable motive, although extreme.

But for each of these reasons, there were loose threads that didn't tie up. So far nothing linked Saxton back to Anna Parker, the cellist. His fingerprints weren't on the letter, the sheet of instructions or anywhere in either crime scene. After killing Audri, he could easily have taken the letter and the instruction note from the crime scene and disposed of them, but for some reason he hadn't. Jenny supposed he could have panicked and accidentally left the incriminating evidence behind, but there was no sign of any panic in either crime scene. Both murders were orchestrated with precision and seemed to have gone exactly to Saxton's twisted plans. Something didn't add up.

She would know for sure soon enough. The DNA profiles from the semen recovered from both victims had been sent to the labs on the highest priority, along with saliva swabs from Saxton. The results would come through later today. She had no doubt all three would match each other. Then the evidence against Saxton would no longer be circumstantial.

So where did these webcams fit in?

It made Jenny wonder if there was more to the case. There was certainly more to Brody Taylor. He was definitely holding something back; she could sense it, although she had no idea what. Everything he had shown and told her, despite being incredibly strange, was all very convincing. So why did she have the feeling she was being manipulated?

For better or worse, she had consciously decided to keep him close. Technically he was a witness and she had told him so. And that he needed to come to the station and give a formal statement, which he'd readily agreed to.

He was tall and well built, toned rather than muscly, and his piercing green eyes sparkled with mischief. His thick blond hair was fashionably swept back while short at the sides and his stubble was neatly trimmed. She hoped that the reason she'd consented to him tagging along to Flexbase wasn't because she found him attractive? She wanted it to be on professional grounds. To be about keeping him close, because he was a witness who had more to divulge. To be about the convenience of him being there with all his IT skills when Harry had let her down at such short notice, with his voicemail about his daughter being bullied at school. To be about something that had nothing to do with him as a man.

"You okay?" asked Brody, keeping pace alongside her.

"Yes, of course," she replied. "Actually, if you're going to attend this meeting, there's some background you need to know."

"Like what?"

"I need to know you'll keep this to yourself. This is to be treated as completely confidential." She halted suddenly and so did he, businessmen and women veering around them. They were on a pedestrian bridge over one of the locks. Boats were moored nearby. In every direction, huge skyscrapers reached for the clouds. She focused her gaze on him, emphasising the seriousness. He furrowed his brow but then nodded his agreement. They resumed their walk.

"Audri is the second victim. Another girl was killed on Friday."

"I heard something about a student being killed on the news on Monday. Somewhere in Central London wasn't it?"

"Yes, Paddington."

"Are you saying they're linked in some way?"

She nodded, hesitantly.

"But the media haven't discovered that, have they? They'd have a field day if they did."

"They will in time."

"Wow! So Derek Saxton is a . . ." He paused, seemingly unsure of his words, ". . . serial killer?"

"There's the rub. So far, we can't find any connection between Saxton and Anna Parker, the first victim."

"So what makes you think they're linked?"

"Same MO for both victims. They were lured to a meeting room under false pretences, disabled, tied up in the same way, brutally raped and then had their throats sliced from behind in one sweeping motion with the same weapon, a double-edged dagger."

"That's awful." He spoke quietly while shaking his head incredulously. "You deal with this kind of thing all the time?"

"No, thank God. And there's one more common factor. Flexbase."

"I don't get you."

"Both girls were killed in meeting rooms in two different Flexbase buildings, three days apart."

"Blimey. Why Flexbase?"

"That's what I'm here to find out this morning. The meeting rooms were booked in advance. I need to know if there's a digital trail that can be followed back to Saxton."

"Ah, I see. Now, DI Price, that is where I can help."

They arrived on the twentieth floor to find a second reception area awaiting them. This one had the Flexbase logo prominently displayed behind an ostentatious reception counter, a massive glass and steel structure with blue mood lighting built in. Sandwiched between the reception desk and the logo were two supermodel-style receptionists, one blonde and the other a redhead, both made-up and manicured to within an inch of perfection. To their left, floor-to-ceiling windows afforded breathtaking views of Canary Wharf and the other Docklands skyscrapers.

It was a massive contrast to the building's primary reception area on the ground floor, which served more as a functional security gatepost confirming that visitors were expected by one of the building's many tenants – most of which were well known financial services institutions – and then routed to the correct floor with a picture badge firmly pinned to their lapel.

The blonde receptionist welcomed Jenny and Brody with an over-the-top, toothy smile. Jenny gave her name. The receptionist confirmed that she had been expected and that Mr Dawson would be with her in a minute. She asked them to fill in the visitors' register, pointing at an electronic tablet resting on the counter.

Jenny took one look at the touchscreen device, decided it was far too complicated and came up with a new plan, "Brody, you said you wanted to help. Well, here you go. Hopefully, this computer won't be too much of a challenge for you."

He took a quick look and said dryly, "I think I can handle it." As he was keying, he leaned back towards Jenny. "Who's Dawson?"

Before Jenny could point out she had no idea, the receptionist answered helpfully, "David Dawson is the Chief Executive Officer of Flexbase."

"Didn't realise you were so important," said Brody.

A booming voice sounded behind them, "Any police investigation involving my company jumps to the top of my queue."

Jenny and Brody turned around and then looked up. Dawson was incredibly tall, at least six foot eight, and bulky, looking a lot like a contestant from *WrestleMania* squeezed into a business suit. Dawson held out a hand to Jenny. Her hand was engulfed in his. She expected to be squashed, but he shook it gently.

"Thanks for giving us your time," Jenny said, trying to sound assertive, despite inadvertently feeling like a small child. "This is my colleague, Brody Taylor."

Brody shook Dawson's hand, and said, "So I take it this isn't the first time you've been involved with the police, Mr Dawson?"

"Well . . . no," Dawson said slowly, eyes narrowing. "Although our previous experiences with the police have been limited to the occasional ram raid at one of our buildings, but nothing where anyone was hurt. Shall we go to my office?"

They followed him down a corridor. On one side, a glass partition revealed an office full of call centre staff, mostly women in their twenties. Dawson paused to allow them to take in the busy scene. Speaking like a brochure, he said, "This is the heart of our virtual receptionist service. Every Flexbase client in the UK has a unique switchboard number. Whenever their number rings, it flashes up on the next available operator's screen with an agreed greeting text specific to the customer. The operator can either take a message or pass them through to one of the customer's employees. For smaller businesses, it gives the illusion that they are much larger."

"What do you do out of normal business hours?" asked Brody.

"Our clients can either opt for voicemail or our offshore receptionist service."

"Does the same offshore service kick in when your lines become too busy? There's what . . . twenty operators there. How many Flexbase customers do you reckon share this service?"

Dawson resumed his journey down the corridor, answering as he walked, "We have forty-nine serviced office locations around the country, each with an average of twenty or thirty tenants."

"Yeah, but don't you offer the, what did you call it . . . virtual receptionist service? Yes, that's it. Don't you have loads of customers who aren't even tenants in your buildings who can take one of your switchboard numbers and use this service?"

"Yes, Mr Taylor. It's a popular service."

"How popular? Tens, hundreds, thousands? A lot more than the twenty in there can handle, that's for sure!"

Dawson changed the subject abruptly as he pushed open a wooden door, "Here's my office suite. Sarah, can you bring coffee through?"

With Dawson's back to them, Jenny mouthed to Brody, "Cut it out," emphasising with a brisk slice of her hand across her throat. He shrugged, as if to say, "Not my fault."

Despite her need to bring Brody to heel, Jenny was impressed with his quick analysis of the service. Clearly, the room they had just observed was mostly for show. A demonstration facility for new clients. Most of the incoming calls would be handled offshore, probably in India. But despite Brody seeing through the sham, she was perturbed by his style. She wondered what had riled him up so much. Perhaps it was a Napoleon complex brought on by the presence of the much taller Dawson. Not that Brody was short; he was just over six feet. Maybe he just wasn't used to looking up to anyone.

A few minutes later, seated on the opposite side of a massive antique walnut desk, the CEO stated, "The reason I wanted to meet you personally was to reinforce that the full resources of Flexbase are at your disposal to help you with this investigation. It's been a terrible few days. Obviously, we're deeply concerned about the way Flexbase has been dragged into this situation."

Brody made to speak, but Jenny set her hand to his knee briefly. He stayed silent.

"That's very good of you, Mr Dawson. And there are some people we'll need to talk to this morning. I think we need access to your Head of IT and Head of Security, or whoever controls the CCTV systems."

"Sure. Our Head of Security is Ray Stone. And our CIO is Magnus Peggler. I'll escort you up to them in a few minutes."

"Do you have any theories as to why Flexbase has, as you say, been 'dragged into this'?"

Dawson looked surprised by the question. "I've honestly no idea. Coincidence?"

"So you haven't started your own investigation then?"

"Well, yes, of course. But you'll need to talk to Ray Stone about that."

"I take it you are including your employees in the investigation?"

He squirmed in his chair. "Well yes, but just for elimination purposes. It's highly unlikely to be a Flexbase employee. We have a strict code of conduct."

Brody burst out laughing. Jenny stared him down, but he spoke anyway, "Listen to yourself, man! What murderer is going to care about your employee code of conduct?"

"Well, I never . . ."

"We need access to your records. Employees, customers. Past and present," stated Jenny.

"But that's commercially confidential information. And then there's the Data Protection Act."

Jenny retorted quickly. "What happened to the full resources of Flexbase being at our disposal, Mr Dawson?"

"If you can just assure me that Flexbase will be kept out of the media."

So that was what this was all about: protecting Flexbase's brand. Jenny replied, smiling inwardly, "That's something you'll have to discuss with my boss, DCI Da Silva. He's handling the media engagement strategy."

"The press haven't linked the two crimes yet?" questioned Dawson.

Brody answered, repeating Jenny's words from earlier, but managing to make it sound like he was making a threat. "They will."

Jenny gave Dawson Da Silva's direct line. They finished their coffee and Dawson told them he'd take them to Ray Stone, whose office was on the floor directly above.

As they walked, Dawson resumed his sales pitch. He explained that this was Flexbase's flagship centre. How they owned the whole building, leasing most floors to long term tenants in the traditional way, but reserving five floors for Flexbase's own use. Two of the five comprised their head office and three were serviced offices, rented to short-term customers just as in all their other buildings. The floor they were currently on was Flexbase's own office space and the one above housed their completely secure, highly resilient computer datacentre facility, hosting hundreds of racks of computers and communications equipment for themselves and many of their clients. Jenny zoned out after a few minutes, texting Da Silva as she went, warning him about Dawson's impending call.

They reached a secure door. Through its small glass window, Jenny could see steps leading upwards. As Dawson reached for his pass, Brody patted his pockets and apologised that he'd left his phone in Dawson's office. He ran back while Jenny and Dawson waited. Unfazed, Dawson began talking about his plans to expand the Flexbase business into the USA through the creation of a franchise model. Jenny listened politely, nodding in the right places. After a couple of minutes, Brody returned, sheepishly waving his phone in his hand.

After Dawson waved his security pass at a sensor and entered a code, they ascended a private flight of stairs. He explained this was the only way to access the floor above and that the public lift didn't have an exit to the floor. "In fact, the twenty-first buttons in the lifts are only there for show. If a lift was somehow forced to stop and the doors opened, you'd be facing a concrete wall."

The stairs opened into a hallway. There were two further doors, both security controlled. One was a man-sized vertical glass tube, some kind of double-security door, on the other side of which was a massive room full of racks of computer equipment. The other door off the hallway was located next to a glass window, similar to the glass partition with the call centre staff on the floor below. It gave the view of a CCTV control room, banks of monitors displayed at its rear. In front of the wall of screens was an operator with three further screens in front of him, his back to Jenny, Brody and Dawson. Inside the room, the door of to an internal office opened and a man stepped out. Spotting Dawson through the window, he waved and headed over to them.

Ray Stone was wiry and thin, with the build of a marathon

runner. His hair was close cropped and his navy suit was pinstriped. Sparkly jewelled cufflinks competed with his loud pink striped tie for attention. Dawson instructed Stone to provide full employee and customer details to the police. Jenny thanked them both and Dawson made his excuses, leaving them with Stone.

"Were the CCTV video files I had emailed over to you any use?" Stone asked Jenny.

"Yes, but there were only feeds from the reception area." She pointed to the bank of CCTV screens through the window. "You seem to have way more than just that on display there."

"Well, it depends on which building. Watford and Paddington are class three buildings, so the security measures are more relaxed. This one is class one and so we have cameras everywhere." He pointed to the corner above Jenny's head. Sure enough, a CCTV camera was looking down on them.

"On the video feeds, we spotted someone we're interested in. Do you have the original videos to hand? I've got a couple of questions."

"Sure," He gestured like a showman, "Come into my lair." Just as he was about to swipe his security pass at the sensor by the CCTV control room door, his attention was diverted by a swooshing sound behind them. They turned to see an internal door slide open from the computer room.

"That's Magnus Peggler, our Head of IT."

A man with unkempt black hair and wearing an open-necked plain white shirt stepped into the glass tube. He wore his security badge on a Flexbase-branded lanyard around his neck and carried a tablet computer, at which he busily swiped. The door behind him closed. And then, after a short pause, the external door slide open to allow him to exit and join them in the hallway.

"Nice mantrap," commented Brody.

"Yeah," agreed Stone. "It opens if you've got the right security credentials on your pass and corresponding six-digit code. Then there's the pressure pad on the floor. It weighs you to make sure you match the weight we've got stored against you in the computer. If the weight is out of range, it traps you in there and sets off the alarms. Stops theft and prevents tailgating."

"It doesn't drop you into a piranha tank below then," quipped Brody.

"No, that feature comes with the version above this one," retorted Stone. "But if Magnus here doesn't stop losing weight on his new fitness regime, I reckon it'll only be a couple of weeks before he goes under the weight tolerance built into the system."

"Actually Ray, there's a self-updating algorithm built into the system to avoid exactly that," said Peggler.

His voice was high-pitched. So much so that Brody raised his eyebrows at Jenny and smirked. She almost laughed herself, but instead introduced herself and Brody and told Peggler that they needed to ask him some questions. He glanced at his watch and told them he had exactly twenty minutes before his next meeting.

A few moments later, the four of them stood in the CCTV control room.

Stone introduced the CCTV operator. "Ron here is our *senior* eye-in-the-sky. He never misses a thing. We've installed the same CCTV system as the Bellagio in Las Vegas and Ron here used to work for them. We're lucky to have him."

Jenny wondered if Stone's emphasis of the word senior was meant to be some kind of an in-joke.

Ron nodded, embarrassed and, with one hand tapping on his black keyboard and the other guiding a black joystick, a garish gold band of multi-coloured gems on his ring finger incongruous against the room full of dark electronic equipment, began searching through video footage. Ron brought up the Paddington footage from Friday evening on the large screen at the centre of the room. Jenny guided him to the correct time point. They watched the cyclist enter the building, talk to the receptionist and head towards the lift. Ron rewound the footage and paused on the cyclist.

"This is our suspect," she told the group. "As you can see, he's used a cycling helmet, sunglasses and mask to cover most of his face. He arrives about forty minutes before the first victim. And then the same cyclist shows up at Watford on the Monday evening, again not long before the victim. Now that we're on the original footage, is there anything you can do to get us a better image? Maybe do something about the sunglasses — if we could see his eyes properly I'm sure it would help."

"Nothing we can do here that you can't do with the copy we gave you. It's an exact copy," explained Stone. "It's not like video tape that degrades the image with each copy made."

"What file format is it recorded in?" asked Brody.

Stone shrugged. "Standard video file format."

Peggler shook his head. "Single CIF resolution recorded at twelve-point-five frames per second using MPEG-4 compression."

Jenny made a mental note not to make assumptions based on Peggler's unusually high-pitched voice. Anyone who could put that much geek-speak into one sentence certainly knew his stuff.

"That explains the average image quality then," said Brody. "But even if you had four-CIF, there'd be little you could do about the sunglasses." He turned to Jenny. "It's not like in the movies where you'd see someone apply some magic colour filter correction gizmo and reveal what's behind the glasses."

"Fair enough." Jenny turned back to Stone. "What about the fact that the cyclist wasn't caught on camera when he left the building?"

Stone shrugged again. "Could be loads of reasons. Maybe he did but not dressed in the cyclist gear. Or maybe he stayed in the building all night."

"Perhaps. Although on both recordings, we've studied everyone who left after the cyclist arrives. We're pretty sure he doesn't leave. Are there any other exits?"

"I'd need to check. It's been a while since I've been to either of those offices."

Jenny wasn't sure whether Stone was being deliberately evasive or not. "Let me help you,' she said, "as I have been to both offices recently. Paddington has a fire exit at the back of the building. And Watford has a fire exit to the side. Both are accessible from the internal staircase."

"Well DI Price, it looks like you already had your answer."

Jenny glared at him. Brody spoke up. "What I think DI Price is asking is whether your building control systems track whether the door was opened."

"Well," said Stone, imitating cheerfulness. "Why didn't you just ask that in the first place?"

Sensing the growing tension, Ron spoke up, pointing to the main screen. "I've brought up the logs. You're right, external fire exits were opened afterwards. The Paddington one at 6:33 p.m. and the Watford one at 7.45 p.m."

"And does opening these doors set off any alarms?" asked Brody.

"Well, yes actually. We get an alert here. And so we would have phoned local security to make sure it was all good." Ron looked through some logs on his screen. "Yup, we followed the process. The tickets are here. Security reported everything was fine. False alarm."

Stone sounded relieved. "There you go; all is in order."

Jenny jotted the times in her notebook. This narrowed down the time periods for the squad to work on, especially on CCTV footage in the surrounding area. She also knew that the SOCO team had already swept both fire exits on the presumption that the killer had exited the building that way. Any fingerprints and trace evidence found there would become a priority.

"The meeting rooms. Can you confirm who booked them?"

Stone shrugged again. Jenny was becoming annoyed with him. Ron offered that he didn't have access to that system. They turned to face Peggler, who had been absently swiping away at his tablet in the background. Sensing their eyes on him, he looked up. "Yes?"

Jenny repeated the question. He confirmed he had the required access and began more finger swipes and typing on his tablet.

"What is that thing?" asked Brody. "It's not an iPad."

"No, I'd never use one of those. Useless in a corporate environment like this. No, this is a Dell Venue Pro. Full Windows PC environment but in tablet form. Best of both worlds, you see. And with proper integrated security. IPads and Androids are far too easy to hack."

"Really? I wouldn't know," said Brody.

A few minutes later, Peggler confirmed what Jenny already knew. That the Paddington room had been booked by someone called William Webber, using the account number from WMA. And Watford had been booked by Derek Saxton, using an account number from Colnbrook Services Ltd. Both were booked using the public website.

"According to the two companies, both reservations were made using fake email addresses," said Jenny.

"Let me guess . . ." said Brody. "The booking system just sends a confirmation out into the ether, not bothering to record or alert on the bounce email received back from their mail server."

Jenny remembered Fiona figuring this out on Monday. Brody was certainly quick to catch on.

"Er, well . . ." Peggler squirmed, his voice becoming even

squeakier. "I've already submitted an enhancement request into the vendor for that as a new feature."

"Do you record the IP address of the device used to make the booking?"

Jenny remembered Fiona also talking about the IP address as being important. She understood that if they had that, they might be able to pinpoint from where in the real world the booking originated.

"Not to my knowledge. But I can check with the booking system vendor."

"Can't you just see on there?" Brody pointed at Peggler's tablet PC.

"No. I can access the application, but the booking interface and reports are fairly basic. Certainly no IP address."

"But what about doing a query direct to the database? What is it, Oracle, SQL Server? Just because you can't see it on the reports doesn't mean it wasn't logged in the database."

"But going direct would invalidate our license. Don't worry, I'll contact the vendor."

Brody turned to Jenny, "If I had access, it would only take me two minutes."

"But you don't have access, Mr Taylor," retorted Peggler. "So no, it can't be done in two minutes."

"If you just give me your PC for a moment . . ."

"That would be unethical and against our security policy. I'll talk to the vendor later on today, okay?"

"No, not okay." Brody changed tack. "How about looking at the firewall logs for the times the bookings were made?"

Peggler nodded, hesitantly.

Brody continued. "I'm sure we could work out which sessions relate to the booking system and then get the IP address from there."

"Our firewalls are managed by a third party company. I can put a request in to them if the booking systems vendor doesn't store the IP address."

"Call yourself an IT Director?" said Brody, his frustration growing.

Stone jumped in. "There's no need for that tone, Mr Taylor." He turned to Jenny. "Please control your lapdog, DI Price."

Jenny placated them both. "I apologise for my colleague's persistence, but we are trying to make sure we follow up on every lead with as much urgency as possible." She handed them both her business card. "Mr Stone, please send over the employee and customer databases to this email address. Mr Peggler, I'll expect a call later with an update on the IP addresses used to make the bookings."

Jenny's phone buzzed. She checked the caller display. Da Silva. She excused herself and stepped away from the group.

"Sir?"

"Where are you? I need you back here." His voice sounded desperate.

"What's going on?"

"I've had to let Saxton go."

"What! Why?"

"First of all, his alibi turned up at the station earlier."

"Eh?" Jenny took a moment to process this. "He must have put someone up to it."

"But this is Stacey Goodwin."

"Who?"

"British Paralympic rower. Bronze medallist in the London games. She says that she met with him on Monday night in his real office. Right at the time of the murder."

"That's a bit convenient. Why didn't Saxton tell us this yesterday? Was he screwing her too?"

Brody, Stone and Peggler all looked up at this. She turned her back and listened to Da Silva's response.

"He says that he didn't want to involve her in his problems. That he's just about to sign her up as a new client. Apparently, she's written an autobiography and Saxton was going to be her agent. But dragging her into this might make her change her mind about him."

"I hope it bloody well has —"

"That's not all, DI Price — I mean, Jenny. We've just got the DNA comparisons back from the semen recovered from both victims. They're both from the same person."

"But that's what we expected. Evidential proof that both crimes were committed by Saxton."

"But neither are from Derek Saxton."

CHAPTER 11

"Mr Patel, this is Sarah McNeil from *Commercial Aviation News*. If you had been in your office to take my call, this is what you would have heard. Eight out of ten of the top aircraft catering companies are increasing the number of new contracts won every month while at the same time halving their customer acquisition costs. Mr Patel, are you looking for improvements in these two sales performance areas in your organisation within the next three months? Oh, wait a minute, this is your voicemail and you can't answer that. However, you can reach me directly with your answer anytime this afternoon." Sarah completed the message by adding her phone number and a cheery finish. She disconnected the call.

On the computer screen, she marked the task against Mr Patel's record complete and scheduled a follow-up call for a week's time. Another name automatically appeared in her cold-calling queue. She decided she needed a couple of minutes break and, with a deep sigh, removed her headset.

Enviously, she looked around the open-plan office. Most of her colleagues were engaged in animated telephone conversations with customers, some walking around freely; hand gestures amplifying their sales patter. If only she could find someone who would actually talk to her. So far this morning she'd hit eight voicemails, three secretaries in full gatekeeper mode either pretending to take a message or taking one and throwing it in the bin, and two abrupt disconnects after only getting a few words into her script.

Commercial Aviation News was one of a handful of magazines and industry websites that new sales staff at Maiden Media were assigned to in order to prove they had what it took to sell advertising space. If they could miraculously achieve their monthly targets three months in a row, then they would be promoted onto one of the company's more prestigious titles where the targets were higher but where there was plenty of run-rate business to make it less stressful, allowing you to focus on hunting high-impact clients.

Sarah was in month three with a week to go. She'd scraped through the first two months, but so far she was only at twelve per cent of April's target. If she didn't strike gold in the next few days, she would be in serious trouble.

Her phone rang. Surprised, she quickly threw her headset back on and pressed the button to accept the call. Perhaps it was Mr Patel actually returning her voicemail.

"Sarah McNeil, *Commercial Aviation News*," she greeted, over-exuberantly.

Before even hearing a voice, she realised that it couldn't be Mr Patel, because his name would have been automatically displayed on her computer screen. Instead it was a phone number she didn't recognise, although from the 01628 area code she knew the caller was from the local Maidenhead area.

"Ah, Miss McNeil, glad I've caught you. It's Janice Walker from Sunnyside Care Homes here."

"Is my Dad okay?"

"Yes, yes, of course," said Walker. "I'm from the finance team. I'm calling you about your account. It seems that you've not paid the last two months' invoices yet, despite our reminder letters."

Sarah's heart sank.

"Oh, I see."

She had been dreading this call. Avoiding it, just as her prospects seemed to avoid her calls. The final notice letter from Sunnyside had arrived on Monday, strongly demanding that she paid them the six thousand pounds she owed.

"Miss McNeil, many people confuse commercial care homes like Sunnyside with state or charity-funded homes. I must stress that we are a business and incur costs in the provision of our care service. Your account has now been escalated to me. When were you planning on paying the outstanding amount?"

"Oh, I'm so sorry about this. My brother was supposed to pay this month. Has he not done it?"

"We have no record of Mr McNeil having a son? He certainly doesn't visit."

There wouldn't be any record. Sarah had just invented him on the fly.

"No, he lives in Australia and so I didn't bother putting his details on the admission forms. But we have an agreement to take turns each month paying our father's bills."

"Miss McNeil, the account is two months behind. I presume that you are responsible for February's invoice. When can I expect payment to be made?"

"I'll bring a cheque when I come and visit my father after work today."

It would bounce, but she was running out of options.

"Thank you Miss McNeil. And I trust that you will chase your brother for his month's payment as well."

"Yes, of course. I'll email him now."

"Okay, I'll make a note on your account. If this is not resolved in the next week, I'm afraid that you will have to make alternative arrangements for your father's care."

The line went dead.

Alternative arrangements? There was no other choice, except Sarah becoming her Dad's full-time carer all over again, just as she had been for the last two years ever since he had been partially incapacitated by a stroke. Well, up until ten weeks ago when she had got the telesales job, convincing herself that if she could make it in sales, all the commission would cover the bills from the care home. She knew she could just about get by on the small basic salary provided. And so she had placed him into Sunnyside and got her life back.

Initially, she had felt guilty. But when she went to visit her father he was in much higher spirits than when he was stuck at home with her. There were lots of people around and, although her Dad could hardly speak and was wheelchair-bound, he seemed to respond to the environment positively. He'd even taken to playing chess again.

And for Sarah, returning to work had been fantastic. She worked hard; she had to. But it was more than that. She enjoyed the challenge of the job, the amiable competitiveness around the room, the banter that went with it, the highs and the lows. The first time she had rung the winner's bell in the centre of the office to announce she had made a sale had been glorious. The looks on her colleagues' faces showed either admiration or envy, depending on how they were doing. And she'd managed to ring it four times since, but not at all in the last two weeks. And now her picture was slowly being relegated towards the bottom of the month's sales leader board. If she were behind target and in the bottom five by the end of the month, her boss, Joe Ashley, would immediately fire her, along with the other four. It was a cutthroat environment, but for those who succeeded, there was good money to be made. And the buzz of it all was addictive.

She had even started to go out after work with some of her colleagues, usually exploring the haunts of Maidenhead, where their office was based, but on payday straying further afield to the more salubrious party towns of Windsor or Reading. She hadn't had any form of social life for two years and valued it greatly. She took it easy, not able to afford much, but it was enough to make her feel human again. Nothing romantic had happened yet, but she thought that one of the top performing sales guys was starting to take an interest. The odd look across the floor. Always seeming to time grabbing coffee from the machine whenever she did. The jovial chatter at the water cooler. If only she could hold onto her job long enough, maybe something romantic would happen.

Joe Ashley walked past her cubicle on the way back to his own. It was enough to spur her on. She needed to make this job work. More importantly, her Dad needed Sunnyside. Neither of them could return to that other life.

Sarah picked up the phone, took a breath and dialled the number of her next prospect.

Brody sat on edge in the passenger seat, his left hand gripping the door handle and his foot repeatedly stamping an imaginary brake in the footwell. Jenny flashed her lights and beeped her horn at cars that hogged the outside lane of the North Circular, undertaking them if they didn't move out of the way and ignoring the fifty miles per hour speed limit strongly indicated by the numerous signs and speed cameras. What made it worse for Brody was that she dutifully followed her satnav, clearly driving in unknown territory.

He looked at the length of time that the satnav calculated for their journey to the Saxton house in Bushey. Forty-five more minutes, which was ironic because the satnav had predicted fifty-five minutes at the beginning of their journey, well over half an hour ago. At this rate, it would take at least two hours.

Jenny swerved passed an articulated lorry. Brody closed his eyes.

After they had reached Green Lanes, the road narrowed to two lanes. Jenny was forced to slow down and Brody began to relax. Another ten minutes later, a mile from the junction with the A1, the traffic came to a standstill.

"Next time, Brody . . ." she began to say. It was clearly something that she had been mulling over for the last few miles. "Look, I'll be blunt. I know you're trying to help and everything but I can't have you, a civilian, winding up the witnesses and screwing up my investigation."

"I don't know what you mean," he said, knowing full well she was referring to his initial conversation with Dawson, the Flexbase CEO.

"The way you confronted David Dawson earlier. There was no need for that."

"He was trying to pull the wool over your eyes. There's no way that call centre was for real."

"Maybe so. But it had nothing to do with why we were there, so there was no need to rile him up over it."

"But if we just accept all that crap he came out with, then he'd think he could get away with telling you any old crap. By my thinking, at least this way he was more honest when it got to the real conversation."

"Who's the police officer here, Brody?" Jenny made a melodramatic show of looking around. It did nothing to calm Brody's nerves as her passenger. "Ah, it's me."

"Doesn't mean I'm wrong." He felt compelled to stand his ground, even though it was unimportant in the scheme of things. As a detective inspector Jenny was clearly used to things being done her way. He reminded himself that he needed to keep on her good side so that he could gain access to the Saxton home. A little concession might go a long way. "But I'll try to keep my gob shut next time, okay?"

She looked over at him briefly to judge his demeanour. He gave her his best smile.

"Thank you," she said.

The traffic began moving slowly. Jenny pulled off again.

He decided to change the subject. "What about Stone and Peggler? Do you think they were deliberately evasive?"

"I'm not sure. Stone should have volunteered the information about the fire exits before now. That's critical information to the investigation."

"And Peggler should access the database directly to see if the IP addresses are stored. All that talk about violating his software license was rubbish. I reckon he just doesn't know how to construct a SQL query and didn't want to be embarrassed."

"Well, we'll find out about the IP addresses later today, either way. I'm sure they're both just being protective about their company. Like Dawson."

"Yeah. It reminds me why I hate corporate organisations. Senior executives like those three make all their decisions based on which action best serves their career or protects their job. Completely self-serving."

Jenny's phone rang. She pressed a button on her steering wheel and answered via the hands-free.

"Hi guv, it's O'Reilly here."

"Hi Harry. Is everything ok with your daughter?"

"Yeah, all grand thanks. It was some kind of mix-up. When I got to the school, no one was expecting me! There's no bullying. No issues with my daughter, at all. Thank God."

"Well, that's good to hear."

Brody smiled to himself. No suspicions. He'd gotten away with it.

After he'd texted Jenny Price yesterday requesting their meeting, he'd gone one step further. He'd been unable to help himself really. He had just wanted to gather as much information as possible about her and the police investigation; get on the inside track before meeting her in person. So he'd used a caller ID spoofing service freely available on the deep web to hack into her mobile phone's voicemail. By spoofing Jenny's own mobile number, the voicemail service was tricked into believing that the call had come from the mobile phone itself and because, like ninety-nine per cent of people, Jenny also hadn't set up a pin to secure access to her voicemail, he was able to listen to her voicemails as if he was her.

Brody knew it was illegal, especially after all the public furore following the demise of the *News of the World* newspaper a few years before prompted by its journalists getting caught hacking into a missing teenager's mobile phone voicemail. But, as far as Brody was concerned, he wasn't doing anything harmful — not like those desperate journalists.

She'd had a few voicemails. But the one that had caught his attention was from a DS O'Reilly confirming that he would meet her at the Flexbase office in Docklands the following morning. Brody had quickly tracked down O'Reilly, and discovered that he was a Met Police computer specialist. And so he'd improvised, judging that if O'Reilly didn't show up Jenny might feel more inclined to accept Brody's offer of help with the case. And it had worked; she'd allowed him to tag along to the Flexbase meeting but now they were on their way to the Saxton house, his planned objective.

A bit more digging into O'Reilly's background and he had enough information to ensure O'Reilly bailed this morning at the last minute. Pretending to be from his daughter's school, Brody had phoned O'Reilly with a vague story about bullying involving his daughter and an urgent need for him to come to the school. It had been simple and effective, and no one had been harmed. A perfect social engineering hack.

"So I just wanted to say sorry for letting you down this morning. Do you want me to head over to Docklands now?"

"No, it's okay. I handled it on my own." She glanced at Brody, making sure he didn't say a thing.

"You handled it yourself?" Brody could hear the incredulity in O'Reilly's Irish voice.

"Yes. If the IP addresses are stored in the booking system database, we'll have them later today when the IT guy talks to the vendor."

Jenny looked at Brody again, this time for confirmation that she'd been accurate in her statement. He nodded encouragingly. She smiled.

"Ah, well that's grand." And then, as an afterthought, "Who'd have thought, eh?"

"Excuse me, DS O'Reilly. I am a member of the modern world, you know. I've even got a Facebook account."

"Sorry, I didn't mean to offend —"

"Anyway, can you head to the station? And when you get there, I'd like you to look into a website called www.SecretlyWatchingYou.com."

"Eh?"

"I've received information that it might have a bearing on the Audri Sahlberg murder in some way." She repeated the site address for him and told him to focus on a location within the site called *Au Pair Affair*.

"I don't understand."

"You will when you see it."

She ended the call.

Brody asked her, "Do you have a Facebook account?"

"Yes, my nephew set it up for me years ago." She pulled a sheepish expression. "But I've never logged back in and I've no idea what the password is."

They laughed together.

Ten minutes later they had joined the M1 and were heading north-west at speed towards Watford. Leveraging the reference to her nephew, Brody had engaged her in conversation about him. She had talked animatedly, opening up a little at first and then more freely as he showed interest. The frosty air of authority that she exuded as a police detective quickly disappeared. She was proud of Damien, her nephew, and his mother April, her sister, who had raised him on her own when his father had taken off a few months after Damien's birth. Evidently, Damien was an avid online gamer, but when Brody had unconsciously let a tut slip through his lips at the mention of Xbox being Damien's gaming platform of choice, Jenny had rounded on him.

"But you're a computer geek! You're obliged to like gaming."

"Actually, I'm not that much into gaming. But even if I was, I happen to know that there's a hierarchy of gaming platforms. And at the top is the traditional personal computer. How can an Xbox controller compete against a keyboard and mouse?"

"But PC games are mostly massive multiplayer online role playing games. Bor-ing!"

"Damien tell you this, did he?" Brody was intrigued by the zealousness Jenny was showing for the subject. He was sure there was more to this passion than just her nephew.

"Well, I suppose."

A silence formed in the car. A few minutes later, Jenny exited the motorway.

Brody recalled the phone call she had taken at the Flexbase office and asked her about it.

"Derek Saxton was released from custody earlier."

"I thought you said he orchestrated the whole thing?"

She gripped the steering wheel hard, her knuckles going white. "Well, it looks like we were wrong."

"How come? I thought you had evidence."

"Circumstantial at best. Turns out he has an alibi for the time of the murder. And the DNA found on both victims was from someone else altogether."

"That's not so good then."

"It's not. Which is why, Brody, I'm suddenly a lot more interested in your webcam theory than I was earlier. It's our only real lead."

"And so this is why we're going directly to the Saxtons' house?"

"You got it. Derek Saxton may not be the killer, but there's definitely something dodgy about those webcams. And I mean to find out what it is."

Kim's phone vibrated. She glanced down and saw on the screen that the message was from Patrick. Sometimes, his good-natured attentiveness was too much. She wanted to be left alone. She'd told him so earlier, but he was so persistent.

Despite herself, she swiped the message and read what he had to say.

It said, *Knock, knock :-)*

She jumped out of bed and looked out the window onto the street. Damn, his car was parked outside. He was here.

She opened the window and called, "Two minutes, Patrick," closing it immediately.

She tied her thick towelling dressing gown tight, ran into the bathroom and examined her reflection in the mirror. She was shocked to see how red and blotchy her eyes were from all the crying. She splashed water over her face, dried it and painted on some mascara and lipstick. It would have to do. What did he expect anyway? Her best friend had been murdered.

A minute later, she opened the front door and let him in.

"I had to check you were all right, Kimmy. I just had to. I've been worried sick."

"I'm fine." But she wasn't, and there was a catch in her voice.

He pulled her into his arms. She resisted briefly and then allowed herself to be hugged. It felt good. He kissed her on the top of the head. She resisted the urge to cry again.

"There, there."

A few minutes later, resigned to having company and feeling guilty for being so ungrateful, she asked him to make them both some tea. She felt the need to keep herself busy. Kim recalled that her flatmates were returning from Greece later on today and would probably take over the washing machine for the next few days. She went upstairs and filled her laundry basket with every item of clothing strewn across her floor. Back in the kitchen, she began loading the machine.

Patrick made idle chitchat as the tea brewed, talking about his university lecturers being unable to keep up with the fast pace of IT; about how he wasn't looking forward to returning to Imperial College after his placement with the television company's IT department; about how the recent *Star Trek* sequel had lost its way from Gene Roddenberry's humanist philosophies (who Gene Roddenberry was, Kim hadn't the faintest idea); about perhaps going for lunch somewhere nearby.

Kim had zoned out and was staring into space. She sensed that he was waiting for her to say something.

"Sorry?" she said, and resumed loading the washing machine.

"Lunch. I thought it might be good for you to get out of here for a bit." He waved his hands around. "There's this nice Thai café in Blackheath that does a fantastic lunch menu."

"I can't, Patrick." She checked the pockets of her dirty jeans for tissues.

"Come on Kimmy, it will do you good. Trust me. A bit of fresh air. It's even stopped raining."

Kim pulled something out of the pocket.

"What's that?" asked Patrick.

She looked at what was in her hand. It was the strange component from the wall light she had broken by accident last night. She had stuffed it into her pocket when the fuse box had tripped and forgotten all about it until now.

"I'm not sure." She explained about accidentally breaking the wall light and the odd device, although made up an excuse about tripping over rather than telling him the truth.

"Can I see it?"

Kim handed it over to him. He turned it over in his hands, studying it.

"I'm no electrician," he mused, "but isn't this the transformer that makes the light dimmable?"

"But there's no dimmer switch in Anna's room."

"Yeah, but if one was fitted it would work with the wall light."

"Oh, I didn't realise you had to have special lights for dimming."

"Yeah, I think that's all it is."

Patrick pressed the pedal on the rubbish bin and threw the device into it.

"Now, what about that Thai lunch?"

Jenny parked her car by the corner green opposite the Saxton house, exactly where Brody had been parked the morning before, although facing away from the house. Brody looked in the passenger wing-mirror. The towering Saxton household filled it completely, both sets of double-gates securely shut.

The journey had taken just under two hours, over double the satnav's original prediction back in Docklands.

As she opened the car door, Brody said, "Hold on a second, DI Price. I've got an idea."

She sat back in her seat and waited patiently as Brody fumbled in his satchel and withdrew his tablet PC.

"Why don't we take a peek at what's going on before going in?"

"Because the words 'police officer' and 'breaking the law' should never go in the same sentence, that's why."

"Which laws?"

"You don't get it, do you? That site of yours is probably breaking hundreds of privacy laws and you're perpetuating it."

"But it's in the public domain! How is browsing a public website breaking the law?" He continued to click through to the website.

Jenny folded her arms.

Brody persevered, "And it might be interesting. You might learn something about Derek's guilt."

"Or innocence," she countered. "And anyway, I'm not sure if anything I see on there could be used as evidence. Whenever we mount any covert surveillance operation we have to get all sorts of authorisations and permissions beforehand."

"But this isn't surveillance. It's a website displaying feeds from webcams that the Saxtons are completely aware of being mounted throughout their home."

Brody clicked through to the *Au Pair Affair* location. He could see movement on the kitchen-cam. Before Jenny could say anything else, he clicked on it, turning up the volume.

"I don't get it, Derek. There's got to be more to it. Why would they arrest *you*?"

On the screen, Hilary Saxton was pouring water from the kettle into two mugs. Derek sat cross-legged on the floor, holding Izzy's hands as she bounced excitedly up and down in an elastic harness suspended from the doorframe.

"Because there's some evidence they found at the scene which gave the impression that I had invited Anna to the office."

"But it wasn't even your office."

"I know. That's what I told the bloody police."

"So why does this *evidence* link to you?"

"I don't know the specific details."

Jenny growled, "He bloody well does. He's just trying to avoid his wife finding out about his affair with Audri."

"Well, there's definitely something fishy going on," said Hilary Saxton.

"Definitely," agreed Derek Saxton. "And anyway, some other girl was murdered the other day somewhere else. They think it was the same killer."

"Which brings me back to my original question. Why were *you* arrested? What aren't you telling me Derek?"

"Da-da!" exclaimed Izzy brightly. "Da-da!"

"Yes, it's your daddy, Izzy-Wizzy," said Saxton, in a silly voice. "Who's a clever girl?"

"Derek. Don't ignore me," instructed Hilary. "And don't call her Izzy-Wizzy."

Still sitting on the floor, Derek turned his attention to Hilary, leaving his daughter to her bouncing. "Listen to me, Hilary. I have no idea why they arrested me. But it's all over now."

"It's not over for Audri's mother," sighed Hilary Saxton. She handed her husband a mug of tea. "It's just beginning for her. I talked to her earlier. She hasn't seen Audri in over a year, no contact or anything. And now she's flying over to collect her dead body."

"That's terrible. She's not staying here, is she?"

"I did offer, but no, she doesn't want to. She's staying in a hotel in Watford. But she'll pop over to pick up some of Audri's things though." Hilary sat down next to her husband and cooed at their daughter. After a moment she remarked, "You know, she said she knew something terrible would happen the day she watched Audri leave Sweden on the ferry. Imagine if it was our Izzy."

Saxton reached his arm around his wife and pulled her to him. She leaned her head on his shoulder. They sat there quietly. Brody thought he could hear sobbing.

Brody looked up from the computer and caught Jenny's eye. Her brows were furrowed in confusion.

"We shouldn't be watching this," she said. "It's not right."

Brody put the PC into sleep mode.

"Let's give them a couple of minutes before we ring the bell," he suggested.

After a few moments, the silence in the car became uncomfortable. Brody broke the silence. "What evidence was Derek talking about?"

Jenny hesitated and then brought him up to speed, giving him the bare facts. Brody learned how Audri had received a hand-delivered typed letter in Derek's name, deceiving her into going to what she thought was his office to continue their affair. How she had followed the instructions and left the Saxton household by taxi in little more than an overcoat. How more instructions awaited her in the meeting room getting her to strip naked and effectively immobilise herself. How she had been brutally raped and killed. How Derek Saxton admitted to the affair and the sex games, but that he had an alibi for the evening. And how the DNA of the recovered semen did not match the DNA taken from Derek's cheek.

Brody tried to make sense of these events. It was all so alien to someone who lived mostly in cyberspace. Life and death were not concepts Brody ever thought too much about. As he listened to Jenny, he began to appreciate how disengaged he was from reality.

This was a life cut short of a beautiful, sexy young woman that he had only yesterday witnessed full of verve. It was difficult to comprehend.

Brody mentally pulled himself together and forced his analytical brain to take over. He asked about the first murder and received a similar set of bare facts. This time the victim had been another pretty young woman. She was called Anna Parker and was a nineteen year-old cellist in a music school. She too had been lured to a Flexbase meeting room — although in a different building — on false pretences, this time exploiting her lifelong dream to play in an orchestra. She had thought she was attending an important audition, but was raped and killed in the same way as Audri. DNA proved that the same perpetrator had committed both crimes.

"Can't you just match the DNA to some big brother police database?"

"He's not on file. Which means he's not been arrested before."

"What about a familial search?" Brody was aware that it was possible to use DNA to search for close biological relatives as the genetic data from family members has more in common.

Jenny raised her eyebrows in surprise. "Watch a lot of detective shows do you Brody? I'm impressed. We've kicked one off, but I'm not expecting a result. We only have 5% of the UK population in the database."

Brody thought about the two murders. The common factors. There was something they were missing. His brain was closing in on *something*; he could sense it, just out of reach. He needed to tease it out.

He went back to basics, hoping to find his way to the missing link. "So, your priority is to identify a connection between the two victims. Someone both of them knew . . ."

"Yes, go on."

"But there isn't anyone obvious." He stopped his line of thought and asked a specific question. "I take it you've not found a direct link between the first victim and Derek Saxton?"

"Correct."

"But it has to be someone who knew an awful lot of personal information about both victims in order to set up such convincing charades. Like a psychiatrist or counsellor or something?"

"We haven't come across anyone like that. Not yet anyway."

"A lecturer would know Anna's dreams. Did Audri go to school or University? Maybe a teacher working more than one school?"

"No."

Damn, this was difficult.

But then it occurred to him that, in a way, both girls had been *social engineered* to do something they wouldn't have done otherwise, just like he did all the time. Although in his case, he usually only tricked his targets into divulging information he could use for another purpose. But the principle was similar. Someone had used privileged information, in this case about both girls' individual hopes and dreams, to make them walk willingly into a situation where they would be alone with their killer. Like lambs to the slaughter. He needed to approach this as if it were one of his own social engineering attacks. How would he go about finding out if someone was having an affair that involved over-the-top sex games? Or find out about someone's personal ambition to play in an orchestra?

"You've checked out all the social media sites both girls used? Facebook, Pinterest, Instagram, that kind of thing?"

"Yes, we have. No obvious links between them."

"No, that's not what I mean. What about if they shared information about their hopes and dreams? You know, Anna's desire to play in an orchestra? Something that the killer could use to make the scam work."

"Yes, we've checked. And there's nothing like that so far. And anyway, Audri was hardly likely to talk about her sex games with an older man on Facebook."

"You'd be surprised what people put on Facebook."

"Perhaps, but no, we've found nothing."

Brody continued his line of thought. He was sure he was onto something.

And then it clicked into place. It was staring him in the face. There was something he would need to check, but —

"This is harassment, this is!" a booming voice shouted.

Brody looked up startled. Derek Saxton's face was leaning down to the driver side window. Jenny visibly jumped but recovered quickly, opening the door and stepping outside.

"We were just coming in, Mr Saxton," she said coolly. "We have a few more questions for you."

"Well, you can stick your questions where the sun don't shine. I've had enough of you lot." He turned and walked off in the direction of his now open gate.

"Are you sure you want to walk away, Mr Saxton?" shouted Brody, also climbing out of the car.

Saxton halted and looked back. "Who the fuck are you?"

"I'm just someone who spends far too much time on the Internet," Brody retorted. Saxton doubled-back a few steps and loomed over Brody. He was massive.

"What are you on about, mate?" Saxton's teeth were bared. Brody was suddenly convinced this was going to get ugly, but he stood his ground. The adrenaline coursed through his bloodstream. He could hear his own blood flowing inside his ears. Everything slowed down.

"Mr Saxton, we really do have some questions. Can we please come in and talk to you," persisted Jenny. "Calmly."

Saxton clenched his fists. He glared at Brody. His pupils were like pin-pricks. Brody knew he was about to be punched. It was like the school playground all over again. He thought he'd left that life way behind. Brody tensed his body.

"Yes, of course you can come in," said a female voice from further away. It was Hilary Saxton, standing by the open gate, her baby daughter in her arms.

Saxton pivoted around. "Hilary, no! I will not allow this. The police had me in a cell all fucking night and I do not have to put up with this shit."

As if Saxton hadn't spoken, Hilary asked, "Would you like tea, officers?"

They sat around the rustic kitchen table. Four steaming mugs of tea, a bowl of sugar and a matching jug containing milk were the only items on the wooden surface. Mr and Mrs Saxton sat on one side, Jenny and Brody on the other. Hilary Saxton had placed the baby in a playpen full of toys in the living room.

Surreptitiously, Jenny glanced up above Mrs Saxton's head in the direction of where she thought the webcam was, but could see nothing obvious. On the wall was a painting of fruit and just above it on the ceiling was a smoke detector.

"So what's the new information?" demanded Saxton. He had

calmed down a little since the confrontation outside.

Jenny had been impressed at the way Brody had stood his ground against the massive ex-rugby player. It had been touch and go. Jenny had seen far too many testosterone-fuelled fights in her time as a police officer and knew that Saxton had been moments away from decking Brody. Brody didn't strike her as the physical type, but then she hardly knew him. Perhaps she was making assumptions because he was a computer geek, although she had spotted Brody's hands jittering uncontrollably as he reached for his man bag from the car, a sure sign of someone unused to being exposed to physical violence.

She decided to approach the subject head-on. "Tell me about the webcams in your house, Mr Saxton."

"What've they got to do with anything?" asked Derek.

"Our nannycams?" queried Hilary Saxton.

"We don't have to discuss this. Our webcams have got absolutely nothing to do with anything." He gave a loud sigh and then said, "Just drink your tea and go."

"Derek . . ." cautioned his wife. "We've got nothing to hide. Think about poor Audri for a minute."

Derek ignored his wife. He looked from Jenny to Brody and back. He was clearly uncomfortable with the subject. He went on the offensive again.

"How the fuck do you know we've got webcams?"

"We'll come to that," said Jenny. "When did you have them installed?" She deliberately went for a simple question this time, one that would generate a straight answer and hopefully lead them in the right direction.

Hilary answered, "Just over a year ago, right after we got our first nanny. A few weeks after she started I began to worry about Izzy when I was at work. Mother's intuition or something. One of my regular customers at the florist told me about these nannycams you could get. So we did."

"Did the nanny know you installed them?"

"No. And thank God she didn't. That evil bitch was leaving Izzy crying her eyes out in her cot, without changing her nappy or anything, while she sunbathed out in the garden. She was smart enough not to listen to an iPod, because every time I came home from work she must have heard the car on the gravel and flew upstairs to deal with Izzy. But once I saw what she was up to on camera, I came home and caught her in the act, parking up the street and sneaking in quietly."

"How do you access the webcam feeds?" asked Brody.

"The installers gave us both access to a secure website, just for us," said Saxton.

"Would you mind showing it to me?" Brody grabbed his shoulder bag from the floor. "I've got my computer here . . ."

"Sure," said Hilary.

Saxton closed his eyes and gave an almost imperceptible shake of the head, as if resigning himself to what was happening.

Brody opened up his tablet, ensuring the keyboard was connected, making it look like a regular laptop. He said. "Actually, I'll need to connect to your Wi-Fi. Would you mind entering the passcode here?" He turned the computer round to face the Saxtons.

"I'll just get the card with the Wi-Fi password printed on it. It's by the router in the hallway."

Jenny thought she glimpsed a self-satisfied smirk on Brody's face, but it disappeared as quickly as it had appeared.

Hilary Saxton returned a moment later, handing Brody a card. He read out a series of numbers and letters as Hilary typed them in. Brody stood and walked around the table to be behind Hilary so that he could see the screen. Jenny stayed where she was. She wanted to be able to observe the Saxtons' reactions.

"Okay, can you bring up the website you use?" said Brody.

Hilary clicked and typed. Brody watched the screen. Jenny watched Saxton, who was visibly squirming.

Brody looked over to Jenny and said, "That's interesting. They're using a website called www.HomeWebCam.co.uk."

Jenny grasped that this was a different site than www.SecretlyWatchingYou.com that Brody had showed her earlier, but wasn't sure she understood the implications. She would ask Brody later.

"Derek, shall we use your logon?" asked Hilary.

"I can't remember the password," he replied. "Use yours."

"I'm not sure if I can remember mine. It's automatically entered when I log in from my own laptop." She looked up at the ceiling as if seeking inspiration. "Hold on, I think I know what it is."

Saxton dropped his head. Jenny was convinced there was

something else going on here. He was visibly fidgeting.

A moment later, Brody, pointing at the screen over Hilary Saxton's shoulder, said, "So you have three webcams in the house, do you? Let's see. The Kitchen." Brody turned around and waved at the wall behind him. "The baby's bedroom. And, last but not least, the living room." Standing behind the husband and wife and out of their line of sight, Brody raised his eyes theatrically to Jenny and silently mouthed the word, "Three?"

Jenny confirmed, "So every day, you go to work at the florists and log into this site from your laptop so that you can observe the nanny."

"Yes," she confirmed. "Derek can log in from his office but he also has a HomeWebCam app on his phone that allows him to observe from any—"

Saxton placed a hand on his wife's arm. "So what? I still don't see what this has to do with anything. I want you to leave." He stood up.

Jenny stood up as well, but she had no intention of leaving. Instead, she walked over to the wall where the camera must be. She studied every inch and then lifted the framed painting slightly. "Is the camera inside the frame, then?"

Derek turned around and answered smugly. "No. The camera needs a power source. It's in the smoke detector." Jenny looked upwards and studied the round device closely. She spotted a tiny grey bubble and guessed that was the lens. Impressive. Although she did feel a little stupid for suggesting the picture frame.

"It's wireless presumably?" asked Brody.

"Yeah, it connects to the Wi-Fi network within the house and broadcasts to a receiver in a dedicated computer upstairs in my study. We access the feeds on the network video PC remotely from this secure website."

"It all seems very professional, Mr Saxton," said Jenny.

"Derek had a specialist firm do the installation. They were very good."

Jenny sat back down, opposite Saxton. "Did Audri know about these webcams?"

Saxton held her gaze, his face impassive. His wife answered, "No, we never told the nannies. It would have defeated the point."

"Are you sure?" Jenny asked watching Saxton. Brody had said

earlier that he was sure that Audri knew about the cameras. The fact that he was letting his wife answer all the questions told her plenty.

"Of course we're sure," Hilary said, allowing some frustration to eek through into her voice.

"And it's just these three cameras in the house, is it?"

Again, Saxton said nothing, but this time looked down in defeat as his wife answered for them both. He'd worked out that Jenny and Brody knew there were more webcams and he was powerless to stop it coming out in front of his wife.

"Were you here the day the installers put in all the webcams, Mrs Saxton?"

She thought for a moment and then said, "No. Derek handled it. I remember being impressed when I came home, because there was no mess at all."

Jenny stayed silent. She hoped Brody would do the same. He had retreated to stand by the kitchen sink and, having zoned out of the conversation, was lost in his mobile phone, keying in something with both thumbs. Typical geek, a second to themselves and they have to play with their toys. But at least he was leaving her to drive the questioning.

Mrs Saxton looked at Jenny and then at her husband. She was making the mental leap from the line of Jenny's questioning. Not quite wanting to confront what was becoming obvious, she asked her husband, "Derek, what's going on?"

Derek opened his mouth, still ignoring his agitated wife. Instead, he spoke to Jenny. "When we were at the station, you agreed to some confidentialities. Why are you doing this now?"

"Because it may be relevant to the enquiry, Mr Saxton."

"What do you mean, confidentialities?" Mrs Saxton's voice wavered. And then, without warning, she stood up and slapped her husband across the face. Hard. "Bastard! You dirty pervert. You installed more than three cameras, didn't you?"

Saxton stood and faced his wife, stroking the red mark on his cheek. He towered above her, but her aggressive stance evened up the standoff.

Saxton backed down. "Hilary," he pleaded. "I'm so sorry."

"Sorry? *Sorry?*" she shouted incredulously. And then, in a slow voice, "How many Derek? How many cameras?"

He turned to Jenny with a look of malice and then back to his wife. "Seven."

"Show me," she demanded.

Brody placed his tablet PC back on the table and then stood back, out of Saxton's range. "I've logged Mrs Saxton off the HomeWebCam site. Why don't you log in under your credentials?"

Saxton didn't move. Hilary Saxton placed her hands on her hips. He gave up and leaned down to type in his account name and password. Hilary Saxton watched in horror as the site presented all seven feeds.

"Audri's bedroom! I knew it. How could you, Derek?"

He wisely stayed silent. Mrs Saxton then placed her hand over her mouth, which had dropped open. "Both bathrooms? And our bedroom! Why on earth . . ."

"There's nothing untoward, darling. It was impulsive. When the installers were here, I just thought that we might as well get totally secure."

"You don't expect me to believe that load of codswallop do you? You've been watching Audri in her bedroom. And the nannies before her. How could you? They're only young girls." She wrapped her arms around herself. "What kind of pervert are you?"

"I, I, I —" he stammered. "Darling, it's not like that. Anyway, no one else can see them."

"Ah," said Brody from behind. The Saxtons turned at his voice. "There's something you need to know."

CHAPTER 12

The door to Crooner42's apartment slammed shut behind him. He hurried passed the pinball machine while trying to unlock his smartphone. He miskeyed the passcode twice and had to stop and focus to get the right code. Once into the phone, he brought up the home automation app and clicked on the secret door icon. In front of him, the bookcase swung outwards.

As always, the bank of monitors displaying a selection of SWY locations greeted him.

"Hello world," he greeted the wall of webcam feeds, laughing to himself. Like many people when they learn computer programming, his first ever program had been coded to output the words, 'Hello World' to the computer's display. He had always remembered that day fondly — the newfound sense of achievement and purpose solidified in seeing those two words appear on the computer screen.

His good spirits were down to the fact that he had Fingal beaten. And he mustn't forget dear Matt_The_Hatter. Yes, him too. He sat down at the laptop. It was time to log into the CrackerHack forums and claim his victory. Publicly take Fingal's crown. After all, it had now been forty-eight hours since the SWY pwn challenge had been accepted. And so far, the site remained completely intact. Nothing had broken through his defences.

Another chuckle escaped his lips, as he navigated through to the correct forum.

Earlier this morning, just before he'd had to pop out, Crooner42 had deliberately posted aggressive taunts on the forum in an attempt to provoke a final response from Fingal. But the best he'd elicited were defensive statements from Doc_Doom on Fingal's behalf. Crooner42 decided that after he'd dealt with Fingal, he'd go after Doc_Doom. That guy was a royal pain in the arse. Assuming he was even male; it was impossible to tell. Online, so many people pretended to be something they weren't. After all, Crooner42 smiled to himself, he was an expert in that.

Crooner42 opened up another window and scanned the SWY logs one last time, just to make absolutely sure. He checked them for activity on the untraceable email address Fingal had used when registering on the SWY site. There was virtually no activity logged against the account, just a couple of logins earlier in the day and, as before, with the activity seemingly focused on the SWY location named *Au Pair Affair*. But, more importantly, his firewall logs showed that the unusual network activity from Fingal's botnet had stopped altogether.

Yes, Fingal had given up.

He flipped back to CrackerHack and scrolled and paged through the chat feed. He thought about how he would phrase his claim for victory. Should he be humble? No way! Should he be completely arrogant or just matter-of-fact? No matter what tone he chose, this was going to be a massive blow to Fingal's status in the hacking community. But Crooner42 wanted to milk it. He decided on utter and absolute arrogance.

He reached the bottom of the logs and suddenly spotted a post from Fingal himself. It was less than five minutes old. Shocked to finally see a communication, he skim read it but didn't quite take it in. He reread it slowly, not quite believing what he was seeing.

Fingal: Crooner, your site is pretty secure. But nowhere near secure enough. I will pwn SYW within 48 hours from now. If I fail, I will down tools and leave the hacking community for good. But when I win, I won't just take root and walk away. I will destroy the whole SWY site. It's an abomination. You have been warned. Do you accept?

Crooner42 held his head in his hands. This was terrible. He had been moments away from victory and now this.

Other posts had already appeared in response. He read them

quickly.

Mawrpheus: Yeah sure. You're just playing for time Fingal. You haven't got a hope.

Doc_Doom: Great words Fingal. An increase in the stakes, I like it! And as Crooner42 never set a time limit on the original challenge, your proposal is valid. 48 hours from now. That's 4:00 p.m. on Friday.

Random_Ness: What about Matt_The_Hatter? He needs to agree to the deadline.

Doc_Doom: Matt? You there?

The chat logs paused while everyone waited to see if Matt_The_Hatter was online and would respond. But what about *him*, Crooner42? It was *his* challenge. *His* rules. This was so damn frustrating. If only he'd set a bloody deadline at the beginning, he wouldn't be in this position.

What possible angle did Fingal have? He must have something up his sleeve to have raised the stakes like that. Publicly stating that he would withdraw from the hacking community altogether was the ultimate gamble. Crooner42 couldn't believe Fingal had put everything on the line. Crooner42's original objective had been to damage Fingal's credibility beyond repair, but, now that he thought it through, this was even better. Fingal dropping out of the hacking community altogether because of losing a get root challenge to Crooner42 was fantastic. His own status would immediately be elevated among the hacker gods.

Crooner42 tried to determine if there was any substance to Fingal's claim that the SWY wasn't secure enough. But he'd scanned all the logs and Fingal had come nowhere near breaking through. Perhaps Fingal's apparent inactivity had been because he'd been developing a brand new zero-day exploit that would work against SWY. But what were the odds of success? A hundred thousand to one at least, Crooner42 estimated. And to have perfected it inside forty-eight hours? That was pretty much impossible. No, this was a complete bluff. Fingal was buying time in the forlorn hope that he would somehow break through.

He decided to declare his presence and began typing.

Crooner42: Fingal, let me get this straight. You've failed so far and now you want to gamble your elite status for another 48 hours against SWY? This would mean No More Fingal on ANY hacker forum anywhere online. Agreed?

Fingal: Agreed. But it won't happen, Crooner. I'm taking SWY down.

Crooner42: Then we have a parlay.

Doc_Doom: Okay everyone, the challenge has been accepted. Let's put the word out folks! There's a helluva lot at stake here.

Matt_The_Hatter: Hey, you fucking idiots. I'm still in this challenge. I get the 48 hours too.

Doc_Doom: Ah, you are there Matt! Okay, agreed. And if you fail? Will you match Fingal's bet and drop out of the hacking community altogether?

Matt_The_Hatter: Fuck that for a game of soldiers! Fingal chose to make it personal with Crooner because he's desperate. I'm not desperate. I'm in this against Fingal. Not Crooner. I'm sticking to the original stakes.

Doc_Doom: Fair enough, Matt. Shame though, we could all have done with a break from your rants on these forums!

Mawrpheus: LOL!

Matt_The_Hatter: Fuck you, Doc.

Crooner42 was delighted with the improved challenge. It was more than he could have hoped for. But something niggled in the back of his mind. Was there some way Fingal could break in that Crooner42 hadn't considered?

He recalled Fingal's strange focus on *Au Pair Affair*. What was it about that particular location that was so fascinating for Fingal? Crooner42 looked up at the wall of screens. *Au Pair Affair* was on one screen to the bottom right. He grabbed the tablet PC he used to control the screens and brought up all the *Au Pair Affair* feeds. He saw movement in the kitchen-cam and popped it onto the large central screen.

The last time he had done this, he had observed police informing the owners of the house that their au pair had been killed. It had been morbidly fascinating to watch.

This time, there were four people in the kitchen. Two he recognised as the husband and wife, who were sitting at the kitchen table with their backs to him. A laptop sat between them on the table. He wasn't sure, but the other woman, who was sitting opposite the husband, might have been one of the police officers from the other day. The last man he hadn't seen before. He was standing behind the couple with his back to the webcam. Crooner42 could only make out the back of his head.

The husband and wife were gesturing animatedly. He turned up the volume.

"Oh, that's just fucking great, that is." It was the wife. Her tone was angry.

Crooner42 wondered what was going on.

The husband ran both his hands through his hair. "I can't believe this! How could this happen? I didn't mean for this. Oh my God. This is awful!"

The wife turned around to the other man. "So, anyone could have been watching?"

"Yup."

"Oh fuck. Oh fuck. Oh fuck." This was the husband again.

"How could you Derek? People have been watching us in the privacy of our own home! Doing private things, for God's sake. I feel so violated."

"I'm so sorry, I didn't mean for —"

"— How did this happen?" asked the wife, turning to the man who had his back to the camera.

"Right this minute, I've no idea."

The policewoman spoke, saying something that nearly made Crooner42's heart stop dead. "So you're saying, Mr Saxton, that you had no idea about SecretlyWatchingYou.com?"

Crooner42 couldn't believe it. The police had discovered SWY? How the hell had they done that? And they were discussing it in one of the broadcast locations? Crooner42 had always known that it was statistically possible for someone somewhere in the many locations he had feeding the site to stumble across SWY on the Internet and discover themselves, but the odds were so infinitesimally high that it was ridiculously unlikely. So how come the police had found it? And, more importantly, that they had figured out that the Saxton household was one of the locations feeding the site?

"Honestly, no," said Saxton. "Have we been hacked?"

"I don't know yet," said the other man still with his back to the camera. "Who installed the webcams in your house?"

"A firm called McCarthy Security Ltd. They're based in Slough."

"How did you find them?" asked the policewoman.

"I just searched the Internet."

"Did you check them out?"

"Yes, they had references and everything. I even went to their showroom. They're a legit firm. They mostly do corporate CCTV surveillance systems, but they said the home market is where they're focusing these days."

The other man commented. "Yeah, I'm not surprised. Now that we have cheap IP cameras and high bandwidth Wi-Fi networks and broadband, it's definitely a booming market."

"But how does any of this relate to Audri's death?" asked the policewoman.

"Yeah," echoed Saxton, turning to the man who was not visible.

"Well, I have a theory, but I need to check it out."

"Hold on a second," said Saxton. "You come into my house, spouting all this crap about my webcams, in front of my wife, and you've no idea if any of it's even related to Audri's murder? That's just fucking rich, that is."

"I'll tell you what's rich, Derek," shouted Mrs Saxton standing up. "You! Thinking I'm some kind of idiot."

"What?"

"You've been fucking her, haven't you?"

"Hilary, no," pleaded the husband. "Of course not."

Crooner42 saw the policewoman avert her eyes from the arguing couple.

"I knew it," Mrs Saxton railed. "I fucking knew it. I should have known better. You've never been able to keep your dick in your pants."

"No Hilary. It's not like that."

"Well, what *is* it like, then? Eh?" She lowered her voice and scathed, "You disgust me, Derek."

Mrs Saxton flew out of the kitchen. A few moments later, Crooner42 saw her appear on one of the other streams, her bedroom, where she flung herself onto the bed and heaved sobs into the pillow.

Back in the kitchen, Saxton stood up and addressed the two police officers: "There was no fucking need for any of this. You had nothing to gain from bringing this up in front of Hilary. You should have talked to me discretely. Now look what you've gone and done."

He stormed out, after his wife.

At the retreating Saxton, the policewoman said in a voice deliberately too low for Saxton to have heard, "I think you'll find you're the one who went and did it."

On the feed from the bedroom, Crooner42 saw Hilary fling a pillow at her husband, who had arrived in the doorway. Although the audio feed was still coming from the kitchen-cam, he still heard her hollering, "Get out!"

Back in the kitchen, the man sat down opposite his colleague, his back still to the camera.

She spoke first. "So, this theory of yours. . ."

"Yes?"

"You think the killer watched the goings-on in this house and used the information to lure her to her death, don't you?"

"Basically, yes. It fits what you said in the car earlier, DI Price. If it wasn't Derek, then how else could her killer have known so much about her to set up the trap?"

DI Price must be the lead detective on the murder case. The other man talked like an IT guy. He was most likely a police IT specialist assigned to the case. Crooner42 picked up the tablet controller. He'd seen enough. They may have found out about SWY, but they were hardly going to focus on it as a major line of enquiry.

"But if your theory is right, that means there must be a webcam at Anna Parker's place as well."

"That's what I want to check out."

The tablet controller dropped from Crooner42's hands, crashing to the floor. He ignored it. He was in shock. While he was aware of the two murders and the fact that both victims lived in locations that happened to be broadcast on SWY, he'd just assumed it was a macabre coincidence. He'd had no idea they were perpetrated by the same killer and that SWY might be a factor in how they were chosen.

But that led to a more chilling supposition. If a murderer really was using SWY to select his victims, then that meant one of his hundreds of thousands of customers was a serial killer. And SWY was his hunting ground.

Shit, what had he done?

And if all that were true, wouldn't the police focus all their energies on SWY itself? Maybe even bring in the National Cyber Crime Unit? The NCCU were the leading computer crime specialists in the UK with access to huge resources. They could pose a serious threat to him.

No, he was overestimating the police. Fingal was one of the world's elite hackers. If he couldn't break through SWY's defences then the police had no hope. But even so, Crooner42 felt uncomfortable being in the sights of the police.

"But you've looked around the site a lot. Haven't you seen Anna Parker's place?" asked DI Price on the kitchen-cam.

"I might have, unknowingly. I don't know what it looks like. I've not been there. I take it you have?"

"Yes."

"We could look through the locations on SWY now, he said pointing at the laptop, "and see if you recognise any."

DI Price held up her phone. "I really need to get back to the station. I've been away all morning and I've got loads of texts here from the team about both cases. Can we do this later?"

"Sure, if you like." Crooner42 could hear the disappointment in the man's voice.

"I guess we'll have to let ourselves out," joked the policewoman.

Crooner42 allowed a smile to slowly spread across his face. He realised they hadn't yet proved that the house where Anna Parker lived was one of the SWY locations. If they weren't able to find it on SWY, then they'd hit a dead-end and would no longer focus on SWY as a common factor between the cases. Then the police would leave his money-spinning site alone.

He knew how to handle it. He'd completely disable the *Student*

Heaven location on SWY. He'd remove any trace of the location where Anna Parker had lived from the site.

He reached for his tablet computer.

Brody cursed under his breath. Two young mothers, overloaded with prams and babies, sat chatting in his usual seating area. Annoyingly, his favourite high-backed chair in the window recess was actually free, but he could hardly position himself in the middle of their group, breaking up their gossip. The coffee lounge was very busy. Just as he was resigning himself to ordering a takeaway coffee instead, he noticed someone waving at him from one of the expansive three-seater sofas . He looked over and saw it was Leroy, with Danny beside him. And an empty space next to him.

He joined his flatmate and his boyfriend. Their table was littered with their half-consumed cappuccinos and cakes. After swapping greetings and pleasantries, Brody became aware of someone standing behind him. He turned to see Stefan, the head barista.

"Ah, Mr Brody, so glad to see you. I was just asking Mr Leroy where you been lately."

Leroy chuckled, "Yeah, and I told Stefan that you've been busy playing handcuff games with a sexy policewoman."

"He's always joking is Mr Leroy. Always joking. What can I get you Mr Brody? Let me guess . . ."

Brody allowed Stefan to play out their customary guessing game. He still felt bad for his behaviour two days ago. As usual, Stefan guessed correctly: a single espresso. Realising how famished he was, Brody requested a toasted ciabatta with Parma ham and sun-dried tomatoes. Stefan skipped away with the order.

"So, how was it?" asked Leroy, sitting forward eagerly. "I was just telling Danny about your dodgy voyeur site, the dead babysitter and the foxy police detective you've just conned your way into meeting."

"There are easier ways to get dates, Brody," chimed in Danny, with a big, beefy smile.

"Really?" responded Leroy, with a knowing wink. "And you think following me into every night club in Key West counts as subtle?"

"I think you'll find that you're the one who did all the stalking," retorted Danny.

"It wasn't a date," stated Brody bluntly. "I was working."

"Working?" Leroy's question was filled with convivial incredulity. "Since when have you ever had to hold down a job like us mere mortals?"

Normally, Brody enjoyed nothing more than bantering with Leroy and Danny. But he was itching to get going with his new inside track into SWY. He fished his tablet PC out of his bag, opened it up and powered it on.

"See," he said, pointing at his computer. "I'm still working."

Leroy sensed the seriousness in Brody's reply, looked at his partner and shrugged.

Ever since Jenny — he couldn't think of her as DI Price, despite her initial insistence on professional formality — had dropped him off at Holborn tube station earlier, he had been dying to explore his newfound knowledge. The journey back had not elicited much more information. She had spent a lot of it on the phone but with earphones plugged in so that he could only catch her side of her conversations, most of which were her asking questions about the progress on the cases, hearing the responses, and asking more. It amazed him the level of detail that the police had to wade through when processing a murder case. Never mind two.

But the cases were none of his business. His objective had been to learn how the webcams at the Saxton household were routed through to SWY. While it turned out to be far more convoluted than he'd thought, at least he'd made some progress.

"You didn't answer my question, Brody," persevered Leroy. "How was it?"

"Interesting," said Brody, noncommittally. His tablet had woken from sleep mode and connected to his private Wi-Fi network successfully. As always, he rerouted his traffic via TOR and two proxy servers. Once he was safe, he brought up the HomeWebCam site that the Saxtons had been using to remotely view their webcams.

Brody had been pleased with the subtle way that he'd got both Hilary and Derek Saxton to login, on *Brody's* computer, to *their* accounts on the HomeWebCam site. Before he'd turned the tablet around for them to login to the site, he'd switched on a keystroke logger. Both their passwords were now neatly stored on his tablet PC in plain text. Brody looked up Derek's password and logged into the HWC site using his credentials. As far as the HomeWebCam administrators were concerned, Derek Saxton had just logged in.

Leroy explained to Danny, "When he's like this it's easier to get blood out of a stone. Watch this . . ."

Brody had three or four theories as to how SWY received the feeds from the Saxton household.

". . . Look!" exclaimed Leroy. Through his peripheral vision Brody was vaguely aware of Leroy pointing at something. "That kid has just nicked Stefan's tip from that table. Can you fucking believe it, Brody?"

Brody clicked through to Derek's account settings within the HomeWebCam site. As he thought, a specific IP address and port number were listed against 'webcam server' alongside space for his username and password details. Brody surmised it was the public IP address of his broadband router and that port forwarding would be configured on the router to send all traffic on the named port through to the PC located within the Saxton household. Acting as a local network video server, it consolidated and stored the high-bandwidth video traffic and was the point of contact from external sources such as the HomeWebCam site.

Leroy added, "Bloody hell! Now he's reaching over the counter and helping himself to the money in Stefan's till. Shouldn't we do something, Brody?"

Having met Derek Saxton, Brody surmised that configuring port forwarding on a router was way beyond the ex-rugby player's capabilities. Which meant that the CCTV installation firm he had mentioned had probably done it as part of the service they provided. Which probably meant they'd made life easier for themselves in regard to helpdesk support. He fired up the remote desktop application built into Microsoft Windows and pointed it at the same IP address, but over port 3389. He waited, not really sure if this would work.

Leroy reared back in his chair and sucked air through his teeth as if in pain. "Jesus-fucking-Christ, Stefan's only slammed the till on the thief's fingers. Look Brody!"

It worked. Up popped a Microsoft Windows login screen, but from the screen of the network video recorder PC in the Saxton household fifteen miles away. The remote desktop application, which Brody knew from common knowledge defaulted to port 3389, allowed him to interact with the PC as if he was right in front of it. Brody reused the username and password details he'd already conned out of Derek Saxton. The mouse pointer icon turned to an hourglass for a second . . .

"I reckon we'd better phone the hospital," said Danny, reaching for his phone. "And the police. This is going to get ugly. Brody, what do you reckon?"

. . . He was in. The PC was running Windows 7. He quickly navigated around, looking for the master webcam program so that he could understand how it was all set up.

"I give up," said Leroy. "See, he's so single minded when he's like this."

Brody found the webcam server application. It was set up for all seven cameras. There were no others. There were settings for everything: how many minutes to maintain recordings on the PC; full motion or drop the frame rate down to a more manageable number to save disk space; audio configuration; motion activation; and a myriad of lower level settings.

Stefan returned, placing Brody's toasted sandwich, espresso and glass of tap water down beside him.

"Don't worry, Stefan. It's not you," said Leroy. "He's plugged into cyberspace like in *The Matrix*. He has no idea you're even there, mate."

Stefan shrugged and left.

With this additional information, Brody was now down to only two working theories as to how the webcam feeds made it through to SWY. The first, and more likely, was that the SWY website was also connecting into the server in the Saxton household using the same port and security credentials as HomeWebCam. Which meant, unbeknownst to the Saxtons, their webcam server was being accessed remotely by two completely different websites. The legitimate one they knew about, HomeWebCam, and another that they had been completely unaware of, SecretlyWatchingYou.

There was one way to confirm and it looked as though the CCTV installers were making it easy for him once more. Microsoft Network Monitor had been installed on the network video PC in the Saxton household. He guessed that the CCTV installers had done this so that they could quickly debug any issues remotely should the Saxtons ever call their helpdesk with a problem. Using the Network Monitor, Brody was able to study the network traffic in and out of the webcam server at packet level, the lowest level of detail.

"Shall we head off then?" asked Danny.

After scanning the network logs on the remote PC, Brody discarded his theory that SWY was directly accessing the webcam server in the Saxton household. The only access to the Saxtons' PC was from the HomeWebCam site itself. Which meant that Brody was now down to one last working theory, one that would be much harder for Brody to progress from here. This theory was that SWY was obtaining its webcam feeds indirectly from the HomeWebCam website. Which led to the obvious question: were the HomeWebCam site administrators oblivious to this access by SWY or were they in on it?

Brody sighed. This challenge truly was impossible. He still hadn't tracked down a back door route into SWY.

"May as well," agreed Leroy. "One last attempt at communication. Right, here goes. Brody, we're off. See you later, mate."

Brody looked up, noticing his friends were gathering their belongings. "You off?" he asked.

"Oh, for fuck's sake."

"What?" asked Brody.

Sarah's phone rang. Number withheld.

She hoped it wasn't that finance lady from the Sunnyside again. But then Sarah remembered that when she'd phoned earlier, the care home's phone number in nearby Burnham Beeches had popped up on her screen.

Hesitantly, Sarah answered it. "Sarah McNeil, *Commercial Aviation News.*"

"Ah, Miss McNeil. I wonder if you can help me."

"Yes?"

"I've been given your name by John over at the CAA. He told me that *Commercial Aviation News* is the best business-to-business magazine in the UK for aviation."

John must have been someone she had cold-called at the Civil Aviation Authority, although she didn't recall any meaningful conversations with the CAA. Still, it was nice that someone had listened and word of mouth still worked in this day and age.

"Yes, we have a monthly readership of over one hundred and twenty-three thousand professionals right across the broader UK aviation industry. How can I help you, Mr . . .?"

"Oh yes, sorry I didn't introduce myself. My name is Francis Delacroix. I'm the Marketing Director for FCS Software. In the USA, we've developed an advanced flight control computer system that's now in use in many American commercial airports. We're looking to launch with a bang in the UK over the next four weeks."

Sarah could all but see pound signs going off like fireworks all around her. She took a breath and tried to stay calm. Finally, she had struck gold.

"You've come to the right place, Mr Delacroix. Through our magazine, Internet presence and our annual exhibition – which is in four weeks I might add – we should be able to help you build awareness with virtually everyone in the UK aviation industry."

"That sounds fantastic. Well, I'm looking to do eight-page advertorials, exhibit at your event and place some standard adverts, print and online, for an initial run of about six months. Are you the right person to assist me?"

"Why yes, I am Mr Delacroix!" Sarah's sales training kicked in. "Do you have a budget in mind?"

"Well, yes of course. Good question. Glad to see I'm dealing with a professional," he laughed. "We need a high impact product launch, so our marketing budget is well over \$200,000. I haven't decided how to break that down yet, but I'd really like to discuss this with you in person."

Two hundred thousand dollars. Sarah quickly calculated the exchange rate. He was going to spend around £120,000. Her monthly target was only £5,000. This was a life-changing deal. She would be *numero uno* on the leader board overnight and stay there for at least six months.

But she was an internal sales representative.

"Well," she hesitated, "I usually do all my business over the phone . . ."

"Oh, that's disappointing. Well, I'm told there's also the CAA's own industry magazine, but —"

"— No, don't worry. Yes, of course we can meet."

"That's great. Let's see. I fly into Heathrow tomorrow and I've got some meetings in the afternoon. Would you be able to meet me at our offices in Windsor in the morning? Say, 11:00 a.m.?"

Windsor was only about twenty minutes' drive from her home. Thank God he hadn't said Edinburgh or somewhere far away. But her job was to find and close deals over the phone. She wasn't like the more experienced external sales people working the more prestigious titles who met with customers face-to-face all the time, wining and dining them. If she mentioned this to Joe Ashley, he would take control of the opportunity himself, *and* all the commission. No, she would do this herself. She would book a half-day's annual leave for tomorrow, claiming something had come up with her Dad. That way, she could land this opportunity singlehanded, prove herself and make sure all the kudos and, more importantly, the unimaginable amounts of commission, stayed with her.

"Yes, I can do 11:00 a.m. Can you let me have an address and phone number, please?"

Jenny pushed open the door of the major incident room's adjoining meeting room and felt the tension immediately. Da Silva and the core officers from the murder investigation team — DS Coombs, DC Malik, DC Jones, Jason Edmonds from SOCO, the pathologist Dr Gorski and DS Schuster, the press officer — all sat rigidly around the long table.

"Ah, good timing, DI Price," said a relieved Da Silva from the top of the table.

What the hell was going on? The next briefing was supposed to have been in an hour from now. What had happened to the pact Da Silva had made with her yesterday? They had agreed that they would plan the team briefing sessions together and pre-assign actions, then jointly host the briefings. All in a collaborative effort to help Da Silva gain credibility with the team.

Alan caught her eye and nodded knowingly to the speakerphone in the centre of the table. She saw that its three LED lights were green, indicating it was on.

"DI Price as well, eh?" sniggered a deep voice from the speakerphone. Jenny recognised DCS McLintock's West Country accent. "Raul, you may as well call me back from the middle of the incident room. You seem to have pretty much squashed the whole enquiry team into that alcove."

Da Silva's face flushed at the insult. Jenny guessed that McLintock had called a one-to-one briefing with Da Silva at short notice and, rather than risk exposing his inexperience to the Chief Super, Da Silva had invited the core investigation team in to ensure the briefing went well. Especially after having had to let go their prime suspect, Derek Saxton. McLintock would have seen through it in seconds, but it was probably the best call Da Silva could have taken in Jenny's absence. Jenny sat in the remaining empty seat next to Da Silva.

Da Silva leaned forward to respond, but Jenny jumped in. "Sir, I'm sure DCI Da Silva just wanted to make sure you had the absolute latest on the two cases, direct from all the lead officers."

Alan, Karim and Fiona all turned as one to gape at her, surprised that she had risen to Da Silva's defence. Jenny hadn't informed them about her little agreement with Da Silva.

"Well now," said McLintock, with an amused tone. "You really are all singing from the same hymn sheet today. I'm impressed." He clearly wasn't. Jenny assumed McLintock had been trying to catch Da Silva out. Station gossip said McLintock had had it in for Da Silva from day one because he'd had been forced to accept Da Silva as the new DCI over a personal friend he'd lined up.

Da Silva attempted to reassert some control. "DI Price, we have almost finished the briefing and the DCS supports the current investigative strategies we've outlined. And we have all the resources we need. However, in these last few minutes it would be good if you could update us all on the new line of enquiry you've been chasing down."

He had worded it well, not giving away that he had no idea what she'd been up to for the last few hours. Other than a brief text saying she was going to the Saxtons' house, Jenny hadn't had a chance to give Da Silva any explanations for her absence.

"Sure, but I'm not sure it's going to come to anything."

"We eliminate *every* line of enquiry, DI Price," stated McLintock's voice. "That's our job."

"Yes, I know that, *sir.*" Jenny felt the hairs bristle on her neck at his insinuating tone. It seemed as though he had locked his sights on her now that she'd been seen to side with Da Silva. "While at the Flexbase offices this morning, a witness came forward with new evidence that the Saxtons have had private webcams installed in most rooms in their house. However, unbeknown to Mr and Mrs Saxton, it seems that their webcams have been hacked into and have been broadcasting everything going on within their home to an Internet site available to Joe Public."

"That's all very interesting," said McLintock, "but I fail to see how this has anything to do with the murder of Audri Sahlberg, never mind Anna Parker."

"And I agree, sir. I've spent the morning successfully *eliminating* this new line of enquiry."

She noticed Alan suck air through his teeth at her catty response. Even Da Silva nodded once with a brief smile before catching himself.

"Yes, yes, I'm just coming," said McLintock, his voice muffled. He was obviously talking to someone else. His voice became clear again and Jenny realised he had completely missed her rejoinder, which was probably a good thing. "Right, I've got to go see the Commissioner. Keep at it everyone. Obviously, we're out of the critical first forty-eight hours for Anna Parker, but the second victim is still fresh. Chase down every lead and I'm confident we will apprehend this sadistic killer. And no more fuck-ups like Saxton."

The line went dead. Karim reached over and pressed the button to end the call.

"Are you completely barking mad, Jenny?" said Jason Edmonds. "Even in SOCO we know his nickname is Tick-Tock. And why. He's a walking time bomb with a fuse shorter than the match used to light it." He shook his head. "My advice? Don't ever be the match."

"Yeah, Jen, be careful," continued Alan. "I've seen Tick-Tock blow a few times. It's not pretty. I've seen bloody good senior officers reduced to quivering jelly."

Jenny was surprised at her colleagues. She was fully aware of McLintock's reputation, but in the two years she'd been based at Holborn, she'd seen no evidence of it personally. She'd only heard the stories third-hand. And anyway, why should she pander to yet another self-aggrandising senior officer? As long as she did her job well she knew she could get away with some attitude. In fact, as a female officer, fronting up some attitude was a necessity. As long as it was based on good police work.

"Come on you lot. Let's focus on the case and not Tick-Tock."

"Please! Can you all refer to the Chief Super with the respect he deserves," said Da Silva.

For a second, Jenny wasn't sure if Da Silva was making a joke or ordering them to use McLintock's rank and proper surname. She turned to look at him and spotted a small smirk. Well, well. Perhaps there was hope for Da Silva after all.

"So, what are these investigative priorities you've all agreed with DCS McLintock?" she asked.

"Top of the list is Flexbase," offered Fiona. "It's the thing that links the two crimes, other than the same MO. Whoever killed them has to know their meeting room booking processes intimately. We're running down every Flexbase employee, every tenant and all their employees, and even every visitor to either office in the last six months."

Jenny agreed. It was the highest priority.

"I'm still running with trying to work out if there is any link between the two victims other than the crime scene," said Karim.

"And I'm after supporting both these strands," said Harry, the computer expert. "For Fiona I'm automating some background checks of all the employees. We received the employee list from Flexbase about half an hour ago."

So, the Flexbase CEO had already delivered on his promise to her earlier.

"Are the files limited to *current* employees?" asked Jenny.

"They are," replied Harry, and then seeing where she was going added, "I'll ask yer man for ex-employees for the last two years."

"What about tenants? When I was at Flexbase earlier, their CEO, David Dawson, said he'd have that info sent over as well."

"It's coming. I received the email with the employee file from a . . ." Harry studied his Blackberry. ". . . Magnus Peggler. Yer man says here that the tenant file will follow later."

"Yes, I met Peggler. He's their IT Director. You said you were supporting both strands. What about Karim's?"

"I'm after doing a pile of social media analysis to see if there's anything in common between the two victims."

"Anything so far?"

"Just the one hit. On both their Facebook profiles, they've both *liked* the same nightclub in London, called Ice, so it is."

"That's fantastic, Harry. A real lead."

Harry beamed at her praise.

"Yes, I've picked that one up," said Alan. "I'm off over there when we're done here."

"My guess, for what it's worth," said Fiona, "is that they've both 'liked' it on Facebook in order to get on the club's guest list. These days, nightclubs do online guest lists with cheaper entry but in return they get access to your Facebook profile and free advertising to all your friends. The kids all lap it up."

"Blimey, what a downer, Fiona,' said Karim. "Our first decent lead and you're pissing all over it already."

"Just bringing you old fogeys up-to-date with the modern world," retorted Fiona, looking round at each of her colleagues. "And anyway, it's still worth checking it out. Just because they 'liked' it to get in on the cheap doesn't mean they weren't there at the same time. They might have met each other. Or been chatted up by the same guy. Anything."

"Okay," said Jenny. "Let's also come at the nightclub angle from the other direction. Karim, make sure you check with Anna and Audri's friends about Ice. Have you tracked down Audri's friend, what's her name?"

He looked at his notebook. "Ornetta Stavoli. I'm seeing her later today. I'll ask her then."

"Good."

"I'll talk to Kim Chang, Anna's friend, about it," said Jenny. She turned to the Crime Scene Manager. "What's the latest from the crime scenes, Jason?"

"Well, we can definitely pin down the same perpetrator to both crime scenes - the same fingerprints, DNA and trace evidence all show up at both meeting rooms, but nothing on our databases. We're still eliminating employees though, just to make sure."

Da Silva asked, "What about the cleaning services company?"

They all stopped and stared at him. Seeing their dubious looks, he explained himself. "Well, most office firms outsource the cleaning to some specialist company. I'm thinking they won't be on the employee list for you to eliminate. You never know, the same cleaner could have been to both sets of offices and cleaned both meeting rooms, leaving the same fingerprints, DNA and trace evidence."

"That's actually a bloody good point, sir," said Jenny. And then realising she had sounded a little condescending added, "It really is. You got that, Karim?"

"Yeah, okay." His displeasure at his mounting workload was patent, but he wrote his action down.

She turned to Dr Gorski. "And pathology?"

Jenny leaned forward to listen attentively to ensure she understood Gorski through his thick accent. "Nothing that you do not know already. It is same dagger used on both victims. Slicing motion from right to left across throat is cause of death in both cases. Both were raped. Analysis of semen recovered from both victims indicates it is same killer, but we will wait for labs to confirm."

"So everything points to the same perpetrator. We are still proceeding as a linked series?" she asked Da Silva, who nodded.

"Have the press got wind of this yet?" She looked at DS Schuster, the press officer. Jenny had only met him two or three times. As before, he was sharply dressed in a plain black suit with a white shirt and plain grey tie. It was as if he wanted to give the press the image that everything he said was absolutely straight. No colour was being added.

"Not yet, but they will. And in the next few hours, in my opinion. My recommendation is that we announce it first. That way we can maintain some control."

"I agree," said Jenny.

"And so do I," said Da Silva, "but DCS McLintock doesn't. He wants us to announce it at the same time we make an arrest. And, as he said, an arrest that sticks, this time."

Jenny looked at her watch. "The odds on us making an arrest in the next few hours are pretty slim. We've got some good leads to trace down, but I just don't see it happening."

"The boss is the boss, Jen," stated Alan helpfully.

"What about this SecretlyWatchingYou website, DI Price?" asked Harry. "Are you sure there's nothing in it? I took a quick look when you told me about it on the phone earlier. It's hosted in Russia. If all those locations on there are like the Saxtons and are being broadcast without their permission then, for the life of me, it must be breaking hundreds of invasion of privacy laws."

"What does all that add up to?" asked Alan.

"In layman's terms," said Harry, "it means its the Devil's website."

Jenny spoke. "There is an outlandish theory I'm going to check out later to do with SWY."

"SWY?" asked Da Silva.

"Sorry, sir. Short for SecretlyWatchingYou.com."

"Since when do you talk like a geek, Jen?" asked Alan. He turned to Harry. "Sorry, Harry. No offence, mate."

"You've gone and got yourself some outside help," accused Fiona, with a smirk. "Harry not good enough for you anymore?" And then, putting two and two together added, "So, who's this witness who came forward about SWY?"

"All right, all right. The witness is called Brody."

"Brody who?"

"Brody Taylor. The point is that the website might be being used by the killer to stalk the victims, gathering the information he needs to trick them into going to a Flexbase office."

There was complete silence while everyone processed this.

Harry broke the silence. "I hope your theory is wrong. From what I saw, the site is a fortress and there's not even a cat in hell's chance of the Russian police helping us."

"So what you said to Tick-Tock earlier was a complete lie," pointed out Alan, shaking his head at her foolhardiness.

"Not really, Al. It's such an outlandish idea the odds on it being for real are pretty slim."

"How are you going to test this theory?" asked Edmonds.

"I'll check whether Anna Parker's place is on . . . the site." She had been about to say SWY again but quickly changed tack.

"With *Brody*," said Fiona, in the voice of a teenage girl talking about some hunky boy.

Bloody hell; was she that easy to read?

"Yes, Fiona. With a key witness who is able to help us with this line of enquiry."

Jenny's phone vibrated in her handbag. Normally she wouldn't answer her phone during a meeting, but she needed a way to distract everyone from the weird turn it had taken. She looked at the caller ID and saw that it was a mobile phone number, but not one she had programmed in.

"DI Price," she answered. And immediately kicked herself. What if it was Brody?

A female voice spoke through tears. "Jenny?"

Jenny sat up and the room hushed.

"Yes?" Jenny suddenly recognised the voice. "Kim, is that you?"

"There's something strange going on here, Jenny," Kim said through sobs.

"What do you mean?"

"Well, I broke a light in Anna's room. By accident, mind . . . "

Where the hell was she going with this? Jenny waited patiently. Her colleagues stayed silent, cognisant of Jenny's serious tone.

"Anyway, this electronic bit came out of it. Patrick said it's just the dimmer bit of the light, but that can't be right, can it?"

Jenny had no idea what Kim was burbling on about. "Sorry Kim, I'm not following you."

"Well, I took it out of the bin and had a proper look at it."

"What is it?"

"Jenny, I think it's some kind of camera. I think someone's being spying on Anna."

Jenny felt the whole world tip on its axis.

CHAPTER 13

Brody abruptly stood up from his desk, clenched his fists and stomped away from his computer. He paced three circuits of his living room before throwing himself onto the leather sofa and burying his face in the cushion, which muffled his bellowed groan of despair.

"Did you say something?" asked a cheerful Leroy, leaning his head out of the kitchen. Leroy held a half-full glass of red wine in his hand and was wearing an apron displaying the image of a white, muscly naked man sporting a massive, erect penis. Against a soundtrack of loud drum and bass blasting from the kitchen speakers, he and Danny were concocting a romantic meal for themselves to dine in on later. They had already set the table for two in the seldom-used dining room, lighting candles and laying down enough cutlery for four courses.

"No," said Brody, the pillow failing to stifle his exasperation.

"What's wrong, mate? This one got you beat?"

"Go away, Leroy." At that very moment, Brody wanted his apartment back to himself. He wanted peace and quiet. Room to think. To strategise.

"Uh, excuse me," retorted Leroy. "But aren't you the one who should be *going away*? You do remember offering us the flat to ourselves for the night to celebrate our fifth anniversary, don't you? You promised you'd be missing in action tonight."

"Did I?" But Brody knew full well that he'd offered them this as an anniversary present to them both. He'd just forgotten all about it in the midst of the SWY hackathon.

"You know you did, mate."

"Yeah, I'm sorry. I do remember," he said, sitting upright.

"Why don't you work some more magic on that hot police lady tonight?"

Brody glared at his best friend. Leroy retreated into the kitchen.

A beep sounded from Brody's tablet PC. He sat back in his chair. It was a message from Doc_Doom inviting him to a private chat room for a catch up. Brody clicked on the link.

Doc_Doom: Hate to state the obvious, but you're running out of time. You making progress, Fingal?

Fingal: Hi Doc. I thought I was, but it turns out my whole strategy was flawed.

Doc_Doom: Anything I can do?

Brody thought for a moment. He hadn't accepted anyone's offer of help since he was a kid. Everything he'd ever done in his life, online or in real life, he'd done on his own. But then he'd never failed to overcome an obstacle before. He found himself not quite accepting, but going a step further than he'd ever expected.

Fingal: Actually, I'd appreciate walking you through things so far. Perhaps another perspective will help.

Doc_Doom: Well, if I can help, it would be a real pleasure, especially for someone of your ilk.

Fingal: Enough with the flattery.

Doc_Doom: LOL. Okay, where shall we start?

Fingal: Right here goes. As we discussed last night, the site is exceptionally well defended. No frontal assault I can come up with gains any traction and I can't find any zero-day exploits on the deep web that will work with the site's configuration . . .

Brody added the ellipses and pressed enter as a form of online chat pause, just in case Doc_Doom wanted to jump in with anything. He did.

Doc_Doom: Yeah, you mentioned you'd found a back door.

Fingal: Ah. Yes, I did, didn't I? Well, turns out there is a back door, but I was looking for it in the wrong place.

Doc_Doom: ?

Fingal: From what I can tell, the webcams are all physically located in the UK. My back door was to find one of these webcam locations and track the route that the webcam feeds take back into the SWY site, in the hope it was less well defended.

Doc_Doom: Wouldn't that be hard to do from over there in Australia ;-)

They were back to that old chestnut: Doc_Doom trying to get Brody to admit he was physically in the UK. He could bluff as usual. Or should he consider trying the truth for a change? But trusting someone in cyberspace whom you've never met in person was a difficult step to take. Brody recalled his argument with Leroy just two days ago about the quality of online friendships over real world ones. Although Brody had defended his cyber-friendships strongly, in the face of making a leap of faith, he did accept that Leroy had a point. Without being able to physically look someone in the eye, trust was much harder to achieve online. You really did have no idea who was on the keyboard at the other end of the chat. He and Doc_Doom had been online friends for three years now. Maybe it was finally time for him to take another step and break his own rules.

He hesitated before typing.

Fingal: Okay, okay. I'm trusting you here, Doc. I can trust you, can't I?

Doc_Doom: Of course Fingal. I would have thought you'd have figured that out by now.

Fingal: Fine. And yes, you've been right all along. I am in the UK, not Oz.

Doc_Doom: I knew we were both English.

Fingal: I didn't say I was bloody English!

Doc_Doom: LOL

Well, it was done now. He had crossed a line he never thought he would. And, surprisingly, it actually felt good.

He decided to get them back on track.

Fingal: So I tracked down one of the webcam locations to an address in the real world . . .

Doc_Doom: Blimey. That's impressive. How'd you do that if you couldn't hack into the site?

Fingal: Trade secret :-)

Doc_Doom: Okay, smart arse! Did you go there?

Fingal: Yes. Figured out the webcams all send their video streams wirelessly to a network video recorder PC on the same local wireless network. The PC is accessed by a website called HomeWebCam.com. The owners of these webcams log into it remotely to view their webcam feeds.

Doc_Doom: Sounds logical. Let me see . . . so you thought SWY was also logging into the same network video PC and stealing a copy of the webcam streams and then publishing them without the knowledge of the owners?

Brody was impressed at how rapidly Doc_Doom figured that out.

Fingal: You got it in one. But . . .

Doc_Doom: SWY isn't getting the feeds this way?

Fingal: Yup.

Doc_Doom: How can you be sure?

Fingal: I hacked into the concentrator PC itself and looked at every packet going in and out of its network interface.

Doc_Doom: Okay, that'll do it! Hmm, that only leaves one other explanation: SWY must be getting its video feeds directly from HomeWebCam.

Fingal: Agreed, it's the only other source.

Doc_Doom: Do you think HWC is in on this?

Fingal: Not sure. I've been searching for a link between the two sites for the last few hours. Short of hacking in, which I'm pretty sure I could do given a day or so, all I've found out so far is that HWC is hosted in Delaware in the USA and SWY is hosted somewhere in Russia.

Doc_Doom: That doesn't mean they're not run by the same people behind the scenes. If I'd set up an illegal site like SWY, I'd host it in Eastern Europe.

Fingal: Agreed. But HWC seems to be completely above board. It's got helpdesk phone numbers, the lot. Whois records even point to the same people listed on the about pages on their website.

Doc_Doom: Have you talked to them?

Fingal: You mean phone their helpdesk and say, "Hi, just wondered if you realised some of your webcam feeds are being rebroadcast on a dodgy website called SecretlyWatchingYou?"

Doc_Doom: I see your point. But anyway, what if you phoned the guys at

the top? I'm looking at their website now. Their CTO is called Dwight
Chambers. Give me a minute and I'll track down his mobile number for you.
    Fingal: *How're you doing that?*
    Doc_Doom: *Trade secret ;-)*
    Fingal: *Touché!*

Brody really would be impressed if Doc_Doom could pull that off. Brody had already done a preliminary background check of the HWC owners, including Dwight Chambers, the Chief Technology Officer. The best he'd managed to get so far was his email address. However, Brody hadn't got serious yet.

Brody's laptop beeped with another instant message. It was from Doc_Doom. He shook his head in disbelief. It contained an American mobile phone number for Dwight Chambers followed by a smiley face. How the hell had Doc_Doom done that, and in less than a minute? It reminded Brody that perhaps he didn't know every trick in the book. Brody thanked him.

Brody checked his watch. It would be morning in the USA. He inserted an unused pay-as-you-go SIM into his phone and dialled the number.

The phone was answered immediately.

"Dwight here."

Brody thought swiftly. "Hello Mr Chambers. This is DCI Frank Burnside with the Met Police in London." Brody had automatically recalled the name of a well-known character from an old police British TV series called *The Bill*.

"Yes?"

"We're investigating a site called SecretlyWatchingYou.com. Have you heard of it?"

"Nope."

"Are you sure?"

"Of course I'm sure." Suspicion oozed over the line.

"Mr Chambers, do you offer any content sharing services to partners for video feeds on your HomeWebCam site."

"Of course not. Our customers expect a fully secure and private service. Why on earth would we share their content? It would completely ruin our credibility."

"Well sir, that may be so. But we have reason to believe that video feeds from your webcam sites are being rebroadcast on their site."

"That's impossible! What's the site again?"

"SecretlyWatchingYou.com." Brody could hear the CTO type on his keyboard. Brody assumed he was online, looking at the SWY site.

"I see it." There was a pause while Chambers looked around and whistled. "What a strange site. Is it legal?"

"No. It's breaking every invasion of privacy law here in the UK."

"So you think that some of these video streams are sourced from HWC cameras?" Brody liked that Chambers also shortened his own site's name for convenience.

"Exactly."

"Well, theoretically speaking, the only way that could be achieved is if this SecretlyWatchingYou site was also accessing the HWC server based in the same location as the webcams, forcing the PC to send its feeds to two places."

"We've checked that, Mr Chambers. It isn't, yet the feeds are on both sites."

"That's impossible."

"Can I ask you to check your network and firewall logs, please?"

"You think this site is somehow getting its feeds from us? That's ludicrous!"

"We're just trying to eliminate all possibilities, sir."

"Fine. I'll check it out, but it will take a while. Can I get back to you?"

"That would be great. Can you ring me on this number? Look for any activity to the IP addresses for SecretlyWatchingYou. Do you want me to give them to you?"

"Mr Burnside, I'm the CTO of a publicly listed company. I think I can handle looking up an IP address."

Chambers put the phone down.

Before he had time to bask in his own glory for his intuitive improvisation, Brody's phone rang. He picked it up, thinking Dwight Chambers had been far too quick, but it was silent. Then he realised it was his other phone ringing.

He saw Jenny Price's name on the cheap handset's screen and answered it without hesitation.

"Brody, I think you're right about the site being used by the killer to stalk his victims," she stated.

"How come? You didn't seem that convinced earlier."

"Yeah, well that was before I discovered that the first victim I told you about had a webcam in her bedroom that she didn't know about."

Brody thought for a second. That would mean a second location. This was perfect. If he was able to visit this second location, he could determine if it was set up the same as the Saxton household and whether its video streams were also being sent to HWC. *And* SWY.

"Okay, how can I help?"

"Can you come over to Charlton? Now?"

"Sure." Brody smiled to himself. "What's the address?"

A few minutes later, Brody grabbed his jacket and shouted out to Leroy and Danny that he was off out.

"Really?" asked Leroy, poking his head out again. Seeing Brody grab his jacket and car keys, he said, "Aw thanks, Brody. You're a real mate. You really are."

You can't believe how smart you are. Your new plan is just perfect. You've executed it to precision. The wheels are all set in motion.

This time you're scheduling it for the morning, not after work. When the building will be full of people and it will all be going on right under their noses. Just the thought of it makes it even more exciting. It will be like having a workplace romance. Albeit a very brief one. You've always wanted one of those.

You feel a stirring down below and smile.

The police have no idea. You've heard them on the TV and radio, you've seen them on the webcams, you've even seen them in real life. They're so far from getting anywhere near the truth that you're feeling invincible. You'll be able to carry this on for ages. You've got three more lined up after tomorrow.

You wonder about your next choices. They're all good ones; you've studied them for months on the webcams. You even know how you'll go about luring each of them. You've even booked the meeting rooms in advance. But you've spotted the policewoman now. You wonder if there might be a way to have her join in the party. She is like *her* more so than all the others.

You'll need to give it some thought.

You need to come up with a plan.

* * *

Jenny handed Brody a transparent evidence bag. As he examined its contents, he was conscious of Harry O'Reilly studying him intently.

Brody had arrived at the address in Charlton a few minutes before, delighted that his Smart Car had come into its own once again, allowing him to squeeze into the smallest of parking spaces in the congested Victorian terraced road. Jenny had ushered him into the house, up the stairs to Anna Parker's room and introduced him to O'Reilly, the police's own IT specialist, and Kim Chang, the victim's housemate and grieving best friend. She was now downstairs making some tea.

Brody focused on the evidence bag. It contained the remnants of a wall light. Shards of opaque white glass and bits of pink plastic from its housing littered the bottom of the bag, leaving the light's main unit exposed. At its base, he could see what looked like a small black hole, the size of a ballpoint pen tip. He held it up and caught light reflecting from it and realised it wasn't a hole but an incredibly small concave lens. Coloured wires, exposed from the light having been broken ran from below the bulb holder into the light's housing at its rear.

"This is really smart stuff," he commented. He held the bag so that Jenny could see. "See these wires? My guess is that they run from the lens to the main controller. It must have a wireless transmitter within it to send the video feed to a nearby PC."

"I take it you don't just walk into a Dixons store and buy this kind of gear, then?" asked Jenny.

"No. But there are loads of specialist spy gadget shops on the Internet that stock this stuff. You know, voice recording pens you leave behind in a meeting room, miniature GPS tracking devices, semen detection kits, that kind of thing."

"Semen detection kits? You're joking!"

Brody shook his head. "The biggest market for spy gadgets is people who think their partners are cheating on them."

"Sounds typical," sighed Jenny. "Any chance it's government issued?"

From the way Jenny had placed her hand on O'Reilly's arm as she asked the question, Brody inferred that this was something he had proposed before Brody's arrival. Brody turned towards O'Reilly, who shrugged defensively.

"I've never seen the like of it."

Brody could easily have replied that he hadn't either, but chose not to. His expertise was why Jenny had called him and admitting that he was winging it would undermine his credentials in her eyes and pass the role of Jenny's technology advisor back to O'Reilly. He offered a confident but condescending tone, aiming his reply at O'Reilly, "What, you think MI5 or MI6 would be surveilling a house full of female students?"

"You never know with —"

Jenny cut O'Reilly off. "So, do you recognise this room at all, Brody?"

Brody looked around Anna Parker's room. It felt strange to be in a young woman's bedroom with all her private belongings on show. He wondered if his uneasiness was because of being in a girl's bedroom in her absence or because everything he saw in the room spoke of a life lived to the full by a girl who was now abruptly dead. There were musical items everywhere: instruments in every corner, sheet music on the desk, an old-fashioned record player and posters of bands on the walls. He saw clothes discarded across a chair, as if the outfits had failed to offer the right look for her last outing, and glitzy shoes piled up under a desk. But all of it was made impersonal by the yellow numbered crime scene markers, something he'd only ever seen before on TV.

"I'm not a hundred per cent sure . . . I think so . . . maybe," he said. And then, with greater confidence, "How about if I sit down and scan through SWY now that I've seen Anna's room? If it's on there, then we'll see a still image at least."

"Even though the webcam is banjaxed?" asked O'Reilly sardonically, pointing at the broken camera in the evidence bag.

"The site's configured with static images to tempt you. Once you click on one, the video stream is displayed. Of course, the feed will now be dead, but the static image might still be there. And anyway, if we find it we'll also see the other webcams that are bound to be all over this house."

"What?"

The three of them turned around to see Kim standing in the doorway, holding a tray with mugs of tea, a look of bewilderment on her face.

Brody spoke to Jenny. "You haven't told her, have you?"

"Told me what?" demanded Kim. The mugs on the tray began to rattle.

Jenny threw daggers with her eyes at Brody and then walked over to Kim. "Here, let me take that."

Fifteen minutes later, Brody and Harry O'Reilly begrudgingly sat beside each other at the dining table in the living room, both pairs of eyes on Brody's computer screen as they scanned through all two hundred locations on SWY looking for images of the house they were in. Three empty mugs and one full of lukewarm tea, Kim's, had been set down on the wooden table top amongst its many scratches and heat rings.

Kim had gone deathly pale when Jenny had explained their suspicions that there were other webcams hidden in the house.

"You mean there could be one in my bedroom?"

"It's possible, yes," confirmed Jenny.

"But I don't have any wall lights in my room."

"They could be hidden anywhere," Brody said. "In the other house, one was in the smoke alarm on the ceiling."

"What other house?"

Jenny raised her eyes upwards as if seeking divine intervention. Brody realised he had said too much again.

"Anna's death might be linked to another case we're working. I can't go into it right now." Jenny then changed the subject. "Why don't we go see if we can find one in your room?"

They left the room, leaving Brody and O'Reilly to scan through the SWY site.

"So how are you after knowing Jenny — I mean DI Price?" asked O'Reilly after a couple of minutes, still staring at the screen as Brody clicked into each webcam location.

"I don't. We met this morning."

"So you're telling me you just came forward after seeing her on the SWY webcams in the Saxton house? Like some kind of good Samaritan?" It was more of an accusation than a question.

"Uh, yes." Brody turned to O'Reilly and, with a straight face, stated, "I felt it was my civic duty."

"Hold on now. So, when I conveniently didn't show up this

morning, you were after *helping* her out at Flexbase."

"Yes."

This was unexpected. Techie or not, O'Reilly was still a copper. Did he suspect something?

"What do you do for a living, Brody?"

"I'm an independent security consultant."

"What kind?"

"I help organisations understand if their security measures are strong enough to keep out the bad guys."

"So you're after being a penetration tester?"

"That's one of the services I provide, yes."

"Now, what's an *independent security consultant* doing hanging out on SecretlyWatchingYou?"

He was persistent, that was for sure. Brody didn't know if he actually suspected Brody of something or whether it was professional jealousy because Jenny had called Brody in. Brody decided on a new tack.

"You've had a good look at it, haven't you?"

O'Reilly shifted in his seat. "Looked? I have, but only this morning when Jenny told me about the site."

"But you've seen enough to know that it's a voyeur's wet dream, right?"

"It is that."

"Well, there you go. I'm an independent security consultant *and* a part-time voyeur."

O'Reilly screwed his face up. "You're telling me that you pay money to this site for your personal entertainment?"

"Yup. Doesn't cost that much. There's a couple of locations on here with some really fit women, Harry. Sometimes they even get naked and, if you're lucky . . . well, you can guess. You should try it out. You never know, you might enjoy it."

O'Reilly folded his arms and leaned towards the screen.

"There —" O'Reilly pointed at the screen.

Brody clicked on the static image. It filled the screen. It was a girl's bedroom but not Anna's. They studied it closely anyway.

Jenny and Kim returned from upstairs.

"Is this one of your housemate's bedrooms?" Brody asked Kim. Kim hadn't been able to show them all of her housemates' rooms as they were padlocked.

She leaned over and then shook her head. "No, I don't recognise that at all."

Brody exited back to the location list. He carried on scanning through. "Any luck finding a webcam?"

"Not sure. There's a mirror fixed to the wall that might have one hidden in it. And then there's a double plug that is mounted unusually high on one wall. But it's hard to tell for sure."

Brody sat back from the computer, perplexed. "Well, that's all the locations on SWY looked at and no sign of this place."

O'Reilly stood up and, unable to hide his triumph, crowed, "Ah well, Brody, it looks like your theory's fierce wrong, so it is."

"It was a possibility."

"Well, it was worth following up on," Jenny said. She turned to Kim and said, "I'm sorry to have worried you unduly. Looks like the webcam thing is a red herring."

"Thank God." Kim was visibly relieved.

"I'd better phone Da Silva and bring him up to speed," Jenny said to O'Reilly. She headed for the hallway.

"That's it?" asked Brody, incredulously. "That's the extent of your investigation into these webcams?"

Jenny halted.

"Well, what else would you be having us do?" O'Reilly countered. "We're after looking through SWY and Anna Parker's room is not there. Sure, that there wall light might not even be a camera. There's no proof yet that the glass yoke is actually a lens."

"Let me get this straight." Brody's voice became unexpectedly loud. "You're a Met Police computer expert and you think that's the end of it?"

"Well now, what else is there?"

"Bloody hell, O'Reilly. Do you actually know anything about technology? Or is your job limited to running forensic analyses on PCs recovered from crime scenes?"

O'Reilly bristled and Brody realised he'd hit a nerve. Perhaps the police techie really was only used to safely analysing data found on computer hard disks. The police had very strict processes to image-copy hard disk data from suspect computers so that all their investigative work was done on copies, which helped them avoid changes being made to the original, stored separately as evidence. It was a skilled job with specialised tools but if that's all O'Reilly did every day, he'd be next to useless on this case.

"Come on boys," said Jenny. "Play nicely."

Brody glanced at his watch. "Jenny, give me five minutes before you make that phone call. Let's make sure first, okay?"

"Uh, sure."

Unimpressed, O'Reilly folded his arms and pushed out his bottom lip.

Brody fired up a command console on his tablet PC. He ran a command to display the IP address he'd been given when he'd connected his computer to the wireless network in the house earlier. Next to it, as expected, was the IP address of the router within the house. He opened up an Internet browser and typed in the router's IP address. Up popped a login box asking for a username and a password. He entered 'Admin' into the username field.

"You're logging into the broadband router," said O'Reilly. "But how're you after knowing the password?"

Brody ignored him. He walked out of the living room, into the hallway and headed for the small table just inside the front door. On it, he'd noticed earlier, perched the home's broadband router, a small white box with a plastic aerial sticking out the back. He picked it up, careful not to disconnect the lead that went into it from the telephone point, studied its base and memorised the serial number. O'Reilly had followed him into the hallway but had to jump out of the way as he stomped back into the kitchen.

Back at his keyboard, he entered the serial number into the password field and was immediately given access to the router's configuration settings.

O'Reilly said, "Okay. What's the story now?" He was genuinely interested, clearly having no idea what Brody was trying to achieve.

Brody worked through the menus to the command which listed every device that had connected via Wi-Fi to the router and been given an IP address so that it could communicate on the network within the house. Many were showing as disconnected. He assumed most of these were the laptops and smartphones of the other students in the house.

Of the remaining ones, he settled on the one that had been active on the network the longest. He ran a ping command against it. It immediately replied, meaning it was definitely active. It could be anything — a phone, an iPad, a laptop or even the Sky satellite box he could see under the television — but he figured that if there really was a PC receiving webcam streams, as in the Saxton house earlier, it would have been active on the network longer than the other devices.

Brody brought up the Windows Remote Desktop application on his own PC and told it to connect to the target IP address over port 3389. His logic was that if there really were webcams in this house, the PC they connected to would be configured in the same way as in the Saxton house, especially if it had been installed by the same company. And if that were true, then it would also have remote desktop control to enable remote support by the webcam installers. But if he pointed at the IP address of some other device, then an error message would be displayed.

On his computer's display, a second Windows screen appeared. It was in locked mode with a username called WPike. He was now remotely connecting to a PC located somewhere within the house, using his own tablet PC's keyboard and mouse to control it from afar.

Brody caught Kim's eye. "Any of your housemates called W Pike?"

Kim shook her head.

"Do you know anyone called Pike?"

"No, I . . . hold on a second." There was a note of recognition in her voice. "I have an idea. Give me a minute." She ran out of the room. Brody heard her footsteps climbing the stairs two at a time.

Jenny and O'Reilly were standing behind Brody, looking over his shoulder at his screen.

"Now then, how were you after knowing to use an RDC?" O'Reilly asked.

Ah, so O'Reilly did know something about what Brody had just done, referring to the Remote Desktop Client by its acronym. Brody ignored him again, clicked on the 'switch user' button and typed in 'Administrator' in the username field. Leaning slightly forward so that Jenny and O'Reilly couldn't see his fingers on the keyboard he quickly typed in a password and pressed enter. The mouse pointer turned into an hourglass. This was the moment of truth.

"How do you know the password?" O'Reilly asked, oozing suspicion.

"I don't," Brody lied. "I'm guessing. Come on Harry, what's the most common password people set for the Windows administrator account?"

"Well now . . . I suppose it's *password*. Or it's left empty."

"Exactly."

Brody didn't want to have to explain himself to O'Reilly. Telling the truth would require him to own up to hacking into the webcam concentrator PC located in the Saxtons' house earlier today. That time he had been privy to Derek Saxton's username and password and had broken in effortlessly. But this time he had no idea who 'W Pike' was. But what Brody did know was that every Windows PC had an Administrator account that gave full control over the PC. Saxton had told him that the company that had installed the webcams in his house had also provided the PC. Brody's theory was that if the same company had installed webcams in this house, then they would probably have supplied a PC set up with the same Administrator account password. The webcam installation company would have done this for ease of support across all of their installations, to save having to maintain records of every administrator password in every location around the country. Earlier, while remotely logged into the Saxtons' PC as Derek Saxton, Brody had, as a matter of course, installed and run a freely available password cracking program called *John the Ripper*. It employed dictionary and brute force-based attacks to crack every password on the machine. From this he had found out that the password for the Administrator account on the Saxtons' PC was 'McCarthy123', which was what he had really just typed in a second ago.

The hourglass disappeared. The password was accepted.

"There you go, you were right first time, Harry."

O'Reilly commented, "*Password*? That was lucky."

"Yeah, I was born lucky."

"So where is this PC you're remotely controlling?" Jenny asked, looking around the living room.

"I don't know. Definitely somewhere in the house as it's on the local network. But I have an idea as to how we can find it without tearing the house apart."

"I had a feeling you might," O'Reilly muttered. He clearly didn't like being shown up.

Via the remote desktop program, Brody brought up a web

browser on the remote PC. He pointed it to the BBC news website and clicked on live news. As it began streaming, he clicked on the icon that controlled sound on the remote PC and set it maximum. The news began playing. Ironically, it was a story about the Audri Sahlberg case. The footage switched from the news anchor to a serious looking journalist outside the Flexbase headquarters.

...Police have now linked the brutal murders of music student Anna Parker and babysitter Audri Sahlberg. Both crimes were committed in offices owned by a building services company called Flexbase. Although they were carried out in two different Flexbase locations, one in Docklands and another in Watford, both victims were killed in meeting rooms within the Flexbase owned buildings...

"Shit," Jenny blurted, "Tick-Tock will go mad."

"Who's Tick-Tock?" Brody asked.

"The Chief Super," explained O'Reilly. "DCS McLintock."

Brody muted the sound on his own computer.

"Brody, I need to hear this," Jenny demanded.

Brody leaned his head to one side and made a show of listening. "I think you still can."

The news item was muted on Brody's PC but could still be heard faintly. The source was coming from outside the living room.

At that moment, Kim came bounding back down the stairs. "I've figured out who W Pike is," she said breathlessly, handing the policewoman some papers. "This is the rental contract we each signed with the letting agent. The letting agent is in Charlton High Street, just around the corner, but look at the name of the actual owner of the house."

Price scanned the document and looked up. "Walter Pike. And there's an address in Dartford."

"That's about nine miles away," stated O'Reilly.

"Let me get this straight, Brody," said Price. "You think there's a computer hidden somewhere in this house that belongs to the owner?"

"Looks like it." He pointed at the doorway. "You can hear it faintly somewhere in the hallway, playing the BBC live news feed."

As one, they left the room in search of the PC.

Unbeknownst to Jenny, Brody, O'Reilly and Kim, Crooner42 was observing them via the webcam feeds still coming into SWY from the *Student Heaven* location. Although he had disabled the location from the website earlier today, Crooner42 still had his own private access to the video streams, prompted by overhearing the conversation on the *Au Pair Affair* feed earlier. He had monitored the two techies, Brody and O'Reilly, trawl through SWY and fail to find anything. At that point, he had thought, rather smugly, that would be the end of it. The Irishman hadn't even been convinced that the light fitting the girl had broken was even a webcam.

But then the other techie had smartly traced the concentrator PC on the house network, and they were now physically searching for it. Crooner42 wasn't overly concerned about its discovery. All it would prove was that there were webcams in the house connecting to HWC.

But this Brody character was interesting. He was smart and resourceful, and he knew what he was doing.

"It's coming from a padlocked cupboard under the stairs." O'Reilly's voice was picked up by the webcam in the living room. Crooner42 couldn't see them and there was no webcam in the hallway he could switch to.

"We've never had access to that cupboard." Kim's voice now, slightly fainter. Crooner42 increased the volume on his computer. "The agents told us that the owner kept some private things in there."

"Well, we'll see about that." The policewoman's voice. "I don't suppose you or the other students have any tools lying around?"

"Uh, no."

"Harry, let's go see if we can find something. I'll take the kitchen. You look in the car, see what you can find."

Crooner42 heard a faint buzzing sound. He saw Brody, still in the living room, remove a mobile phone from his pocket and study it. He quickly walked over to the door, peered into the hallway and then gently pushed the door shut.

He doesn't want his colleagues to overhear him.

He answered the phone and spoke quietly, while heading to the window, the farthest point in the room from the hallway.

"This is DCI Frank Burnside."

What the hell was this? Crooner42 knew the man's name was Brody – he'd heard the policewoman introduce him to the others earlier. And thinking about it, wasn't DCI Burnside the name of a dirty copper from some old television series he'd seen reruns of?

"Ah, Mr Chambers, thanks for getting back to me. Did you get a chance to check the HomeWebCam firewall logs?"

What the . . . HomeWebCam? And in a sudden moment of clarity, Crooner42 knew what Brody was up to. He listened intently, seeking confirmation of his suspicions.

Brody was obviously surprised by the response. "What, no traffic at all?" A pause and then the clincher. "Are you *sure* you checked the right IP destination address? SecretlyWatchingYou.com . . . Oh, okay . . . That's so strange . . . Okay, thanks for checking."

Brody disconnected the call just as the door to the living room opened.

Crooner42 was dumbfounded. Could this Brody actually be . . .

"Well now, who was that?" asked O'Reilly, staring at the mobile phone in Brody's hands.

"My sister's mother's son. What's it to you?" Brody's tone was deliberately confrontational.

O'Reilly hesitated, unsure. He dropped his challenge. "We're after finding the PC. It's a Dell laptop, about four years old."

"Well done, Harry. You should get a gold star."

"Feck off, Brody."

The two women walked in. "So are there cameras here or not?" demanded the policewoman.

"We could all squeeze into the cupboard under the stairs to do this but as I'm already controlling the PC remotely, shall we just take a look at it from here?"

Seeing a nod from Jenny, Brody sat down in front of his own computer. The others all crowded around him. His fingers moved across the trackpad, clicking occasionally. He narrated his actions.

"This is the webcam server app that controls the webcam configurations. It defines how much footage should be stored on the computer, frame rates, audio and so on. See?"

"Yes, okay. But are there more cameras?" pressed the girl.

Brody clicked and her sharp intake of breath was answer enough. Simultaneously, they all turned around to stare at the hidden webcam in the living room, high above them on the wall opposite the room's entrance. Crooner42 felt disconcerted – it was almost as if the four of them were looking straight at him.

"I thought that was some sort of electrical junction box," said

Kim.

"It's made to look like one, for sure," said O'Reilly, walking towards it. He grabbed a chair, positioned it underneath and then his face filled the camera feed. Crooner42 could see acne scars on his cheeks. "Ah, yes, there's a lens here, in the centre." So close to the microphone, O'Reilly's voice boomed in Crooner42's speakers. "From down there you might assume it's the screwhead holding the cover of the box on."

"And because you think it's a junction box, you don't think to question the electrical wires going to it from the ceiling." This was Brody's voice, although Crooner42 couldn't see anything other than the hair on the back of O'Reilly's head, as he had turned around to face the others.

O'Reilly jumped down from the chair, allowing Crooner42 to see the whole room again.

"Is there one in my room?" The girl spoke hesitantly.

"I'm afraid so. Here it is," said Brody.

She looked over his shoulder and slowly shook her head. Slowly wrapping her arms around herself, she lowered her head. "Yuck, I feel so dirty. Disgusted. All these people watching me in my own room? That's sick." She fled from the room, clearly distressed.

Crooner42 checked the other webcams to see where she showed up. He heard a door bang and presumed by her absence in any of the feeds that she'd locked herself in the downstairs toilet, the only room in the house other than the hallway without a webcam.

The others all looked at each other helplessly.

After a minute's silence, the policewoman asked a question. "But I still don't get it. We've got webcams all over this place, just like in the Saxton house. But none of them are on SWY. I thought that was the common link, Brody?"

"I can't explain that," said Brody. Crooner42 smiled. His act of disabling the *Student Heaven* location on SWY had really paid off. "But the configuration is exactly the same as the Saxton house. That's too much of a coincidence. And the HomeWebCam site is linking to the webcam concentrator PC at both houses. It's exactly the same in every way. Except for not being on SWY."

"Maybe the location has been removed from SWY?" suggested O'Reilly.

"Why?" asked the policewoman.

"To stop you linking the two crimes, DI Price," offered Brody noncommittally. And then he leant forward with more assertion, "To stop you investigating SecretlyWatchingYou."

Crooner42 felt a chill down his spine.

"But how would the people behind SWY know to do that?"

Brody turned his head towards the webcam, his stare burning all the way through. Price and O'Reilly also turned.

"They're watching us!" gasped Price.

Brody nodded, maintaining his stare.

"Right then, I'm powering off the PC under the stairs. That'll stop 'em, for sure, and anyway, we need it as evidence," said O'Reilly, already striding purposely towards the hallway.

"Good idea, Harry," said Price. "I'll go see if I can help Kim."

Brody was left alone. He put his arms behind his head and leaned back in his chair away from his PC, still staring straight into the webcam.

Crooner42 felt the hairs rise on the back of his neck. *Brody, Brody. Are you who I think you are?*

Crooner42 knew he wasn't a police officer; that was certain. His behaviour and the technical one-upmanship between him and O'Reilly confirmed that. And then there was the conversation between them earlier; hadn't O'Reilly asked him something about why he'd came forward? Yes, Brody had said something about having met DI Price for the first time that morning. In fact, Brody had said that he was an independent security consultant — no, better than that, he'd said he was a *penetration tester*.

It had to be. It was the only thing that made sense.

And there was that secret conversation on the phone where he pretended to be a police officer. He was trying to find a link between HomeWebCam and SecretlyWatchingYou. But he hadn't mentioned HWC to O'Reilly or Price at the time, even though he clearly knew all about it. Which meant he was already one step ahead and was withholding information for his own purposes.

Crooner42 was now certain what that purpose was. Brody was trying to find out how the webcam feeds found their way into SWY. He was looking for a back door, the clever bastard. And there was only one reason why Brody would be doing that.

Crooner42 held Brody's stare and spoke in a low, menacing tone, even though Brody couldn't hear him. "Hello, Fingal."

CHAPTER 14

"Thanks for all your help today, Brody."

Jenny pulled up outside Charlton Station; her foot on the brake, ready to move off as soon as Brody exited the car. About half an hour ago she had phoned Alan back at base and asked him to meet her at Walter Pike's address. Pulling in Pike, the landlord of the student house and, far more significantly, the owner of the understairs PC that controlled the webcams, was now the most promising lead in the case.

Instead of opening the door, Brody, his head nodding as if settling his mind on something, turned towards her, an ear-to-ear grin plastered on his face. It occurred fleetingly to Jenny that this was probably the first natural smile she had seen him give, as if everything before now was some kind of act.

"You know, I've enjoyed doing this far more than I thought I would."

She suppressed her frustration at his delayed exit. "You sound surprised?"

"I guess I am. Look, I was wondering . . . maybe I could help you some more?"

"We'll take it from here, Brody. Look, I've got to go . . ."

"If you ever want to talk all the technical stuff through, I'd be happy to help."

"Thanks, Brody." Jenny dropped into neutral, took her foot off the clutch and slowly engaged the handbrake, deliberately not pressing the release button so that, as she pulled it up, each ratchet clicked noisily. "I've got your number."

"Yeah, okay." His tone was flat.

"Don't forget, we need you to come into the station tomorrow or the next day to make a formal statement."

"Yes, you do. I mean, I do." Brody opened the door and stepped out, suddenly brighter.

Jenny pushed the clutch back in, felt for the bite on the Audi's first gear and released the handbrake, ready to shoot off the second the door shut. She wanted to get to Dartford ahead of Alan.

But Brody leaned back in and said, "Perhaps we could do that tonight? Over drinks?"

Jenny was taken aback. Her head was in work mode and so she hadn't seen that coming. What signs had she been giving off that he would suddenly go there? He was attractive; she could appreciate that. He was smart. And he liked good coffee.

Suddenly, the car lurched forward two feet and stalled. Her foot had slipped from the clutch. Brody, who had been half in the car, was caught in the ribs by the doorframe and was knocked to his knees. His face fell flat on the passenger seat. Behind him, the heavy passenger door slammed shut due to the car's abrupt forward movement, and smashed onto Brody's rear.

"Argh!"

"Oh God, I'm so sorry. Are you all right?" Jenny scrabbled to unhook her seatbelt so that she could help him.

He raised his head up off the seat and used his body to push the door back. His knees were on the pavement. She looked him over, concern etched on her face, but he was laughing.

"If only I'd known the protocol when asking you out for a drink was to kneel down . . ."

"I am so sorry. Are you okay?"

"Nothing broken, Jenny. I'm still on my knees though . . ."

Jenny was trapped. She was desperate to get to Dartford. A thousand thoughts flew through her head. She couldn't delay anymore. Perhaps the quickest thing was to . . . And anyway, he wasn't a material witness so there was no real conflict of interest. If she kept him close, he might still be of use to the case. Harry was obviously an amateur by comparison.

But all day she'd had a feeling that something else was at play, as if Brody had an ulterior motive. Perhaps his asking her out was what she had sensed? She wasn't sure. But right now, right this minute; all she could see was an earnest, honest, hopeful expression.

What the hell. "I'll give you a ring later if I'm free at a reasonable time." It was an acceptance of sorts, but one that at least gave her a way out if she decided to change her mind. Hopefully, it was enough for now.

"Perfect." He stood up awkwardly, manfully masking the pain that the lurching car had caused him. "I'll see you later, then."

He waved her off. She glanced in the rear view mirror and saw him tentatively make his way towards the train station entrance, one hand holding his side.

A frustrating hour later — for what should have been a twenty-minute journey — Jenny exited a roundabout towards Dartford town centre, her window wipers now on full. Her phone rang. She glanced at the display and saw it was Alan. Damn, he was there already.

"Are you near?" he asked through the Audi's speakerphone.

"Sat nav says four minutes."

"Okay. In that case, I'll let you see this for yourself."

"See what?"

"You'll see."

"Al, come on, this is serious."

"You'll understand."

This wasn't like Alan. She kept the line open as she drove down Dartford Road. The satnav forced her to turn left and announced that she had reached her destination. She pulled to a halt and scanned her surroundings, but even with the window wipers on full speed it was becoming hard to see clearly. She could make out a run of office buildings rather than the residential road she had been anticipating. Up ahead and under a golf umbrella she spotted Alan waving to her, while holding his phone to his ear. His voice came through her car speakers.

"Over here, Jen."

"What is it?" She pulled up next to him.

She disconnected the call and jumped out of the car, moving in close to Alan under his umbrella. She repeated her question to his face. "What is it, Al?"

He indicated behind them and then rotated them both around

within the confines of the umbrella's shelter.

She took it all in at once. The number '15' was mounted in large modern looking aluminium lettering on the front wall. They were definitely outside the address Kim Chang had found on her rental contract for Walter Pike. But behind the wall was a six-storey, purpose-built office building. Above the entrance was a large sign. Despite the incessant rain, she easily recognised the logo and her brain did a double take.

Flexbase.

"Anything from the computer yet, Harry?"

Harry O'Reilly was on his knees, fiddling with some wires under his desk. Only his backside was visible. Jenny heard a thump and an Irish expletive as he banged his head on the underside of his desk. Above him lay five or six computers, most with their covers off, exposing their hi-tech innards. Wires and other leads meandered all over the messy desk and down the back. Many components were in evidence bags, but she could also see empty bags and envelopes. She wondered at the computer specialist's ability to properly maintain chain of custody for evidence.

Harry backed out from under his desk, rubbing his scalp. He recognised Jenny and smiled weakly. "Nothing we don't already know, Jenny."

"Which one is it?" Jenny indicated the clutter on his desk.

"Ah don't worry yourself, it's not one of those. It's properly logged into the evidence room downstairs. I've been after taking a mirror image of its disk and I've been analysing that instead."

"Anything with Walter Pike's real address?"

"Not so far. I'm thinking the PC's been used for nothing other than receiving the webcam feeds. The cache is empty. There's no browser history, no cookies, no passwords, nothing."

"Okay, thanks."

Harry nodded and crawled back under his desk. She left him to it. A few seconds later she heard another bump and another expletive. She shook her head.

Her journey back from the Dartford Flexbase office building had been frustrating. Although she still hoped it was the breakthrough they so sorely needed, she had arrived there after the building's day-staff had finished, leaving behind a hapless security guard who could offer no real help. Her frustration had been compounded by the traffic travelling at a snail's pace most of the way back to Holborn, slowed down by more showers. It was certainly April in London.

The rest of the enquiry team were out working through the backlog of outstanding leads on the two cases. Her attempts to track down Walter Pike had so far come up short. The land registry for the house rented by the students had his name on it, but no other address. The letting agents were shut and not returning calls or emails. In desperation, she'd left a detailed voicemail for David Dawson of Flexbase, given the unexpected connection between Walter Pike and Flexbase. She'd also reminded him that he owed her the tenant database.

Having exhausted her immediate priorities, Jenny was catching up on admin, including the paperwork piling up on her desk, and the digital tasks assigned to her on HOLMES2, typing up notes and statements with index fingers taking turns, one letter at a time. All the while she resisted the urge to dump it all on Verity, who would selflessly bail her out, as usual.

She found herself smiling about Brody's proposition earlier, stalling the car and smashing the poor man's ribs. She'd been taken aback, unused to civilians coming on to her, especially when she was in work mode. She'd only agreed to the date to get rid of him. At least that was what she'd been telling herself all day since. But there was something about him. She found him attractive, that was for sure, especially those sparkling green eyes. He wasn't a copper: a definite plus. And although he was a techie like Harry, he didn't seem particularly geeky. Perhaps she *would* meet him later. Maybe she'd text to confirm.

Decision half-made, she quelled all thoughts about Brody and got back to attacking her massive workload.

"You got a minute, DI Price?"

Frowning at the abruptness of his tone, Jenny looked up at Da Silva. "I suppose."

"My office, now." He strode off.

She looked back at her computer screen and clicked on the button to save her work. An error message appeared and her heart sank. She'd pressed the wrong button, cancelling her work rather than saving it and had just wasted the last hour. Disgusted with herself, she stopped at Verity's desk and, swallowing her pride, begged her indulgence.

"Dearie me," said a sympathetic Verity, "You shouldn't be bothering yourself with all that. Just you leave it with me. Go on now, dear, off you go."

Jenny effusively thanked the kindly indexer and stomped over to Da Silva's office. Sat behind his desk as if he was Lord of the Manor, Da Silva indicated with a regal wave of his hand to close the door.

"Sir?" Jenny pushed the door shut with her heel.

"I'm in the middle of updating the Decision Logs on HOLMES. I just want to make sure I've got everything straight. We wouldn't want a murder review to catch us out later."

Jenny lamented inwardly at his use of inclusive words like 'we' and 'us'. He knew full well that it was his responsibility as SIO of a murder case to define and note the key strategic and tactical decisions made on the investigation and record them, along with their rationale, in Decision Logs. As SIO, only he would be questioned on the decisions by any future murder review team, not her. And that was only likely if a case dragged on for over a month with no real progress. It wasn't surprising Da Silva, like her, was now playing catch-up given the velocity of these two cases, but treating it like passing a test was certainly not the way to approach it.

"How can I help, *sir*?" She was becoming irritated. Didn't he realise that she was carrying her own massive workload? Babysitting Da Silva through leading his first murder investigation was starting to become tiresome, despite the exposure she was gaining from it personally.

"I just want to make sure I've got the logic behind every line of enquiry. Let's start with DS Coombs. He's gone to check out some nightclub in Soho, right?"

"Yes, it's called Ice. Other than Flexbase and the killer's MO, it's the only link we've found between the two victims."

Da Silva made notes on his pad. He was certainly focused on getting this right. He looked up. "Victim selection?"

"Yes, what if the killer knew them or at least saw them at the club?"

"Doesn't that conflict with this webcam website idea? That's also about victim selection?"

"Yes. It's one or the other. Or some other connection between the victims we haven't uncovered yet."

"Can't we just talk to whoever owns this website?"

"Unfortunately not. O'Reilly says it's located in Russia. No contact details. Probably because what it does is totally illegal. He's put in a request with the local Internet service provider, but he's not hopeful of a response in his own lifetime."

"What about following the money? People are paying to view these webcams."

"O'Reilly's on it. He's even called in support from National Cyber Crime Unit."

"Good. But aren't we dealing with some other website with a load of webcams? Where does that fit in?"

"It seems that Derek Saxton and the landlord of the house where Anna Parker lived both signed up to using one called HomeWebCam.com, which seems to be a legitimate service, except that —"

"— their webcam feeds have somehow made it onto the Russian site."

"You've got it. NCCU are now on that as well."

"Okay, what about Flexbase?"

"We know the killer is intimate with their meeting room booking processes. He's got to be a tenant or employee."

"Or ex-tenant. Or ex-employee."

Jenny nodded. Da Silva may be inexperienced, but he wasn't clueless. She needed to remember that.

"So that's why the landlord is a person of interest."

"Yeah, Walter Pike. He's Anna Parker's landlord. We think he installed the webcams in the house. And the address he used on the tenancy agreement was for a Flexbase office. All told, that's a pretty complete set of connections."

"But what about Audri Sahlberg? Does Pike link to her?"

"Not as far as we can tell. But when we pull him in we'll see."

As they talked, Da Silva filled up pages of his notepad. Now that they had the employee database from Flexbase, Fiona was working on cross-referencing names between them and with any known criminals. They were still waiting on the tenant database. Karim had interviewed Audri Sahlberg's only friend, Ornetta Stavoli, but nothing of note had come from it. Harry was examining the computer retrieved from Anna Parker's home, the one that captured the webcam streams. They had released video footage of the cyclist entering the Flexbase receptions to the media. Members of the team were trawling through Facebook and the other social media sites, searching for any kind of correlation between the victims. Later that would be extended to the Flexbase employees. Da Silva's earlier idea about a cleaning company common to both locations had already been eliminated.

After about fifteen minutes their discussion came to a natural end. Jenny stayed silent as Da Silva flicked back through his notes, checking to see if he'd missed anything. God knows how he'd summarise that lot into a HOLMES compliant Decision Log.

He shook his head. "Lot of angles to cover here."

"Yeah." It was probably the understatement of the day. Every avenue created numerous leads, each of which needed following up and led to more. Like most investigations, the amount of work grew exponentially.

Her phone rang. It was a Central London number. Da Silva nodded his assent even though she was going to answer it anyway.

"DI Price," she stated.

"David Dawson returning your call, DI Price."

Jenny recognised the posh accent of the incredibly tall Flexbase CEO she had met that morning with Brody.

"Thanks for getting back to me, Mr Dawson. I do hope you've got the tenant database because I'm sitting here with my DCI discussing court order applications."

Da Silva furrowed his brow. He had no idea what she was referring to.

"There's no need for that, DI Price. I told you we would assist the police any way we can." He sighed. "What I called to say was that I've got a present for you . . ."

She waited him out. He was trying to assert control by making her reel in the information.

Another sigh at her refusal to play his game. "In your inbox is the full tenant database."

"Thank you."

"That's not the present, DI Price . . ."

Bloody hell, he was persistent. "Fine, what is it?"

"I did listen to your voicemail earlier. If you search through the database I've sent you, you'll find the home address that we have on file for a certain customer of our virtual receptionist service."

It took her a moment to make the mental leap. Walter Pike. At last.

"You're welcome, DI Price," said Dawson sourly when she hadn't responded. She tried to offer her thanks, but he had already hung up.

Heading towards her desk, with Da Silva on her tail, Jenny shouted urgently for Harry. The office stopped what they were doing to stare at her, aware that something had broken on the case.

A loud thump sounded from under Harry's desk followed by a weak, "Feck."

"Harry, get your arse over here." She reached her desk and her PC. "Now."

The long escalator slowly but persistently carried Brody up to ground level from the depths of Angel tube station. Rubbing his side, he wondered if he'd cracked a rib or two. He was tempted to lift his shirt up to check for bruising.

Wincing, he speculated if Jenny Price was worth all this pain. He hadn't really planned to ask her on a date. It had popped out of his mouth, surprising him almost as much as it seemed to surprise her. Was he completely mad? He was deliberately courting the company of a member of the police service. Not that he was a criminal, mind. It was just that he knew full well that some of his actions in the course of his work strayed very much outside the boundaries of the law.

From the moment he'd first seen Jenny on the webcams he'd been intrigued. But when she'd sat down opposite him in the coffee shop that morning he'd been captivated; not just by her natural beauty, which was probably enough in itself for most men, but also by her coolness, her assertiveness and her unwavering focus on getting the job done. The combination of qualities was intoxicating.

The exclusive Internet dating site Brody frequented offered unlimited introductions to many women. Many of them were attractive. Some of them had powerful occupations. A few were intelligent and witty. But the unnatural situation of blind dating meant that both parties were constantly attempting to present themselves positively, while at the same time weighing up the other.

Rarely did Brody agree to a second date. He wondered if the unusual backdrop of tagging along with Jenny while she carried out her profession — and he secretly carried out his — allowed him to encounter the real Jenny Price, unencumbered with the artificiality of dating? He liked what he saw and was impressed with the way she conducted herself. Then he reminded himself that today had not been a date. For Jenny, it had been her job. At best he had been some kind of witness. Tonight would be the dreaded date, assuming she actually phoned. Perhaps the usual dating pressures would come to the fore, but he hoped not. Hopefully, they'd already built enough of a foundation to ride through the usual pitfalls.

Brody exited the station into a dank evening and turned right towards Upper Street. He must have missed a heavy rainstorm while he'd been travelling on the Underground. Shiny pavements and wet black roads reflected the streetlights and headlamps from passing traffic. Fast-running impromptu streams flowed alongside pavement gutters, searching for drains. Pedestrians held on to folded umbrellas, ready to raise them at the slightest hint that the heavens would open again.

Five minutes later, Brody reached the front door of his flat. His thoughts during the walk from the Underground station had slowly become darker, matching the downcast weather. His inability to make any serious progress on hacking SWY was becoming seriously frustrating. He'd publicly thrown down the gauntlet earlier today with his poker-style 'all-in' challenge that he would pwn SWY within forty-eight hours. He'd typed the challenge onto the CrackerHack forum message boards via his mobile phone while standing in Saxton's kitchen, just as it was starting to dawn on Mrs Saxton that more than three webcams had been fitted in her home.

At that moment, he'd been absolutely convinced that he was about to uncover the back door into SWY; unearthing the route the source webcam feeds took to get to the site. If he'd realised at the time that their route was somehow completely masked, he would never have been so bold. His hopes had been raised again when Jenny had invited him to visit a second SWY location at the students' house. But all he'd actually proved was that it was a mirror configuration of the Saxton webcam setup. The backdoor route into SWY still eluded him.

It made no sense at all. And now everything was at stake and he was running out of time.

Brody pushed the key into the lock on his front door and, just as he was about to turn it, suddenly recalled his promise to Leroy earlier. Damn, he was supposed to be giving Leroy and Danny free rein on the flat tonight, so that they could celebrate their anniversary. But it was wet and cold out here and he needed access to his equipment. He had work to do. He glanced over his shoulder and saw from the bright lights across the road that Bruno's coffee house was still open. Okay, he'd given them the hour or two that Bruno's remained open. Then he'd have no choice but to disturb them. After all, he was hardly going to spend the night in the cramped confines of his Smart car, parked outside his own flat just to give Leroy and Danny some privacy.

Despite the lateness of the evening, the coffee shop still had a few customers. Perhaps the warm, dry environment had been an unplanned refuge from the earlier showers. A smiling Stefan trotted over to him. Brody didn't know whether to be impressed or saddened that Stefan was still working, this late into the night.

"Ah, Mr Brody, Mr Brody. Is raining dogs and cats, no?"

"Yes Stefan, it's wet out there."

Brody's favourite seat by the window was free and, as usual, Stefan attempted to predict Brody's order. But Brody couldn't remember coming in so late and so this was uncharted territory for them both. Apologetically, Brody corrected Stefan's normally correct guess of a late-evening single espresso with an out-of-character request for herbal tea. He left Stefan to choose the flavour.

As Brody opened his laptop case, he felt a waft of cool air from the front door as two or three customers left. As the door was about to seal shut it opened again, sending another chilly draught his way. As someone trudged in, leaving wet footprints trailing behind, he wondered if he should sacrifice his seat by the window with its optimal Wi-Fi reception and move into the warmth. He was fairly sure he could still pick up his private Wi-Fi signal further back in the coffee house.

Stefan returned, placing a steaming sepia-coloured beverage on the table.

"Is Liquorice tea, Mr Brody. You like?"

Brody had no idea. "I'm sure it'll be lovely, thanks Stefan."

"Is good for making feel better."

"That's just what I need." Brody lifted the cup to his lips, compelled by Stefan's hovering presence to sample the liquid. He sipped a little and then loudly slurped lots of air over the hot liquid to avoid scalding his tongue. "Jesus, that's . . ." He had been about to swear but caught himself in time. " . . . That's very nice, Stefan." And with the temperature having dropped to a palatable level, he realised he rather liked the mellow aniseed aftertaste.

Satisfied, Stefan left him to it.

Brody had work to do. He didn't believe what Dwight Chambers, the CTO of HomeWebCam, had told him over the phone at Kim Chang's house earlier; that there was no trace of traffic between HomeWebCam and SecretlyWatchingYou. Brody figured Chambers was either covering up his company's failings from preventing the leak of data from his website or that Chambers was somehow involved in SWY. He had to find out, one way or another. And the only logical step was to break into HomeWebCam and track the feeds from there.

Brody logged on to his tablet PC and connected to his private, securely encrypted Wi-Fi network.

"Which property?" asked Walter Pike, stroking his chin. "I can't remember every place in my portfolio."

They were in Interview Room 4 in Holborn Station. Pike sat on the other side of the metal desk from Jenny and Da Silva. Jenny knew he was playing for time, trying to figure out their line of questioning. She and Da Silva had just finished going through the interview preliminaries, pointing out his right to a solicitor, which he resolutely declined. Da Silva thanked him for coming down to the station at short notice, not that Jenny or DC Jones had given him any choice when they had met him on the drive of his imposing family home, just as he was returning home from work. When Jenny explained they needed to discuss some issues related to his tenants he had immediately offered to come to Holborn rather than invite the two policewomen into his home. He claimed that he didn't want to bother his wife with his work.

"Troughton Road in Charlton," Jenny stated lightly, holding his eye, steadfastly maintaining a friendly manner.

She knew that Pike was well into his sixties, but the only

giveaway was the lines leading away from his eyes. His thick head of hair was artfully spiked in the style of a twenty-something. And even though it was silvery, the colour looked as if it was a deliberate fashion choice rather than a result of ageing. Under a brown suit, he wore a white t-shirt. Jenny was reminded of Don Johnson in the 1980s show, *Miami Vice*, but the signature shoulder pads were missing. Not that Pike needed them: he obviously spent plenty of time at the gym.

"Okay, I know it. Yeah, it's one of mine. So what's got you lot out of bed then? Bins left out on the street? Neighbours complaining because there's nowhere left to park? Whatever's going on you'll need to take it up with the tenants. I'm only the landlord."

"Who are the current tenants, Mr Pike?"

"Just a bunch of students. Massive profits in students, you know." He balanced his chair onto its rear legs, leaning back dangerously. "You take a Victorian two up, two down, stick in a few partition walls, convert the dining room into another bedroom, and *voilà*, you've got six bedrooms. Stick an advert in the local Uni and suddenly you've got six new tenants. Everyone thinks students are hard up, but you add up the rent for six rooms in what was previously just a three-bedroom house and suddenly you've got a lucrative income. From students, no less."

"Female students, I notice."

"Yeah, well, simple business decision. Much less damage from bints."

That was a term that Jenny hadn't heard in a very long time. Pike may have modernised his image, but his attitudes were clearly stuck in the 1970s. She tried not to let her distaste show.

"Tell me about any extras you've had installed in the house."

"Extras?" Pike remained balanced on the rear legs. "What are you on about, girl?"

"DI Price, Mr Pike," corrected Da Silva. "You do not address a police officer as *girl*."

Jenny bristled with indignation, noting how Da Silva rose to her defence.

"No offence."

"The house that you let to these six students . . . Are they fully aware of everything inside?"

"I'm not with you . . ." He stopped himself and then, with a broad condescending smile, " . . . DI Price."

"Let me ask it another way. Is there anything in the house that the tenants should be aware of but are not?"

Pike remained balanced back on his legs. His silence lasted a beat too long before he said, "No."

Jenny changed tack and, in a petty bout of revenge, asked sweetly, "Are you a silver surfer, Mr Pike?" She'd heard the term on a radio phone-in show all about mature Internet users, never expecting to employ the phrase herself.

Da Silva turned in his head in surprise at her uncharitably-phrased question. Pike squinted his nose, trying to work out what she meant.

"Do you surf the Internet, Mr Pike? After all, not everyone from your generation is *au fait* with computers."

His eyes narrowed to slits. She wasn't sure whether it was because he'd taken offence or because he saw where she was going with her questioning.

"Yes, I browse the Internet, *girl.*"

She ignored his jibe. "And what do you use it for? Let's see, now. Do you read online magazines? Do you perhaps do Internet banking? Or maybe you even shop online? Is that it, Mr Pike? Or could it be that you watch porn?" She turned to Da Silva and, speaking as if Pike wasn't in the room, said, "You know, I think this could all be porn-related. That's probably where someone like him started with the Internet. Like a kid in a sweetie shop. Not like the old days when you had to buy a magazine in the newsagents from the top shelf. Now it's always on tap, with full motion video, no censorship or anything. But no, that wasn't enough for our dear Mr Pike was it?" She turned back to him and repeated, "Was it?"

His chair thumped back onto all four legs. "I think I want a lawyer after all."

An hour after Pike's lawyer had arrived, Jenny and Da Silva brought the interview to a close.

He had capitulated under the weight of evidence, but only in regard to the webcams and the computer they had in evidence with his fingerprints all over it, both physical and digital. He'd had the webcams installed two years ago. This was the second batch of female students from Trinity Laban that he'd secretly spied on while they went about their day-to-day lives at the house in Charlton.

Under pressure, he also admitted to having installed webcams in four other rental locations around the country, two in other parts of London, one in Leicester and the last in Southampton. All rented out to groups of female students. But there were only four locations, a mere drop in the ocean compared to the hundreds on SWY. He claimed not to know anything about SecretlyWatchingYou; all of his activities had been contained to his personal account on the HomeWebCam site, which gave him access to the webcams in the four locations.

On the surface, his situation was a complete mirror of Derek Saxton's: just another voyeur getting off on secretly watching young women. But there were two main differences. Saxton had installed webcams in the home in which he personally lived, whereas Pike had clearly broken numerous privacy laws. Jenny wasn't specifically certain which laws had been broken and had tasked Karim with researching them. It didn't stop her arresting him though.

The second difference was that Pike was linked to Flexbase. He claimed that he only used their remote office service to provide a legitimate business address for his mail and a professional receptionist service for his business phone line, nothing more. He claimed never to have booked a meeting room in any Flexbase office. They would check.

"Look, I've been upfront about the webcams. What more is there? I don't understand what's got you lot all riled up. Surely, they're not that big a deal."

Jenny raised her eyebrows, not buying it, but he held her gaze, confusion etched all over his face.

"Murder," she stated.

"Murder?" Incredulity infused his tone. "Fuck off!" And then, after turning to his lawyer, frowning and pointing his thumb towards Jenny and Da Silva, as if to say, "can you believe this?" Pike finally realised Jenny was serious. "Who?"

"One of your tenants."

"In Broughton Road?"

She nodded.

"Which one?"

"Why don't you tell us?"

"Well, it's one of two. Either Kim or Anna. God, I hope it's not Kim."

"Why not the other three?"

"They're on holiday, obviously." He looked at Jenny as if she was stupid and added some clarification, "Abroad."

He obviously watched them a lot. Far more than she had anticipated. "Why not Kim?"

"She's gorgeous." As if that's all the explanation necessary.

"Okay. Why Anna?"

His lawyer put a hand on his arm, but he shrugged it off. "Anna's a right tart. She might look like a good shag, but that's where it stops. She —"

"Mr Pike," interrupted his solicitor, firmly. "I advise you not to say anymore. You are under caution."

"I'm trying to help, for fuck's sake. It's not as if *I* murdered them . . ." Pike's voice trailed off as he looked from Jenny to Da Silva to his solicitor, while it slowly dawned on him that's exactly what they all thought.

His face turned ashen. Finally, he looked his age.

CHAPTER 15

Towards the rear of Bruno's coffee shop, Crooner42 observed the man he knew online as Fingal. Or 'Brody', as he seemed to go by in the real world. Crooner42 wondered about that. There was usually some linkage between an online handle and its owner's real-world name. Although considering his own circumstances, he immediately discarded the thought. Crooner42 had nothing to do with his own name. It was a nickname he'd earned as a teenager after singing 'It Had to Be You' in a passable impersonation of Frank Sinatra during a school concert. The addition of '42' in his online moniker was to make it unique. And even then, the number had meaning because it was the answer to the ultimate question, at least as far as *The Hitchhiker's Guide to the Galaxy*, one of his favourite books as a teenager, was concerned.

Once Crooner42 had deduced that Fingal and Brody were one and the same, he had bolted from his flat in Docklands and gunned it towards Charlton, throwing his car around the darkening London streets. He felt like a bullet powering through a rifle as he accelerated through the southbound Blackwall Tunnel, appreciating the sound of the vehicle's exhaust note rebounding loudly off the tunnel walls, and burst out onto the three-lane A102, braking hard for each speed trap before accelerating again. He exited onto the Woolwich Road but slowed to a crawl as the rush hour traffic clogged the single-lane main road. Even so, he arrived at Troughton Road in under twenty minutes, just in time to spot Fingal and the policewoman getting into a silver Audi A3 outside the student house. Cheekily, he flashed his headlights to let them out and followed behind. After a couple of minutes, they pulled up outside Charlton Station and Brody exited the car. Crooner42 looked around and nabbed an empty space, even though it was clearly signposted that parking required display of a valid resident permit. He just hoped his car wasn't towed away when he returned later.

On foot, he followed Fingal, who had plugged earphones in and seemed oblivious to all around him, down onto the platform. Crooner42 kept him in sight but maintained enough distance to avoid being spotted during the overground train ride into London Cannon Street, the short distance to Bank Underground Station, the Northern Line to Angel and finally, a walk along Upper Street. Fingal had stopped outside an apartment block and placed his key in the external front door lock and then paused, looking round. Crooner42, who was in the doorway on the other side of the road, thought Fingal had somehow clocked him. But instead, he seemed to have become aware of the coffee shop opposite and had decided upon a nightcap.

A few minutes later, Crooner42 had slunk into the coffee shop, straight past Fingal who was ensconced by the front windows with his head in his computer. Taking a seat at the rear, he ordered an Americano from the foreign-sounding waiter, who just about held back a tut at the choice, and sank back in the leather sofa, staring at his nemesis.

When Crooner42 had originally concocted his plan to discredit Fingal using SWY, he had never thought it would work out this well. In its best outcome, his plan did little more than dent Fingal's reputation on CrackerHack and every other deep web hacker forum. By failing so publicly to crack SWY, Fingal would be proven fallible. He would no longer be a god walking amongst mortals. His elite status would be tarnished forevermore. And at the same time, Crooner42 would be elevated to the higher echelons. And there was nothing more important to a hacker than reputation.

But now, here was Fingal in the flesh and in the palm of Crooner42's hands. It had never occurred to Crooner42 that Fingal would track down the real-world webcam locations. He had assumed that Fingal would do what every other hacker would do — what Crooner42 himself would probably have done — and throw everything he had at an online frontal assault. Begrudgingly, he was impressed with Fingal's initiative in seeking a back door route into SWY via the source of the webcam feeds.

It had also never occurred to Crooner42 that both he and Fingal were located in the same country, let alone the same city. It was almost impossible to tell from the chat rooms where anybody was from, other than by deduction from word-spellings, idioms and turns of phrase. But this was difficult to do; so many hackers were from China or Eastern Europe where English was a second language. And those with English as their mother tongue often disguised themselves behind geek-speak and the chatroom etiquette of acronyms and abbreviations. So was it a coincidence that Fingal was also British? A bit, he supposed. But it wasn't that unlikely. After all, the UK was consistently one of the top ten hacking countries in the world. And anyway, it was to Crooner42's fortune that they were both from the same country, for it had enabled Fingal to attempt his back door plan, which had led to this very moment, where both hackers were physically in the same place at the same time.

Crooner42 realised he had nearly everything he needed to wreak absolute destruction on Fingal. He had his real-world name: Brody. It wouldn't take long to get a surname. Or was Brody the surname? Ah well, he'd know soon enough. He had his address: Upper Street. It wouldn't take a minute to check the building number from where Fingal had paused, his key in the lock.

Yes, this would be retribution on a biblical scale, way beyond a mere dent in Fingal's hacker status.

With a stupid giggle, he whipped out his own laptop and got to work.

He scanned the wireless networks within range. There was an unencrypted network called 'BrunoCoffee' obviously provided by the coffee shop for its customers. He couldn't see Fingal using that one. He fired up Kismet, his Wi-Fi hacking tool of choice. Like a dog tracking a scent, he let it sniff the air for a minute. It revealed a hidden Wi-Fi network, one that did not broadcast its name. But Kismet saw through such a simple precaution and immediately exposed its name: 'F!NG@L'. Crooner42 almost laughed out loud, but just about managed to catch himself just in time.

Any lingering doubts over whether this real-world Brody and the virtual-world Fingal being one and the same were instantly vanquished.

Crooner42 reasoned that Fingal sat at the front of the coffee shop in order to pick up the strongest signal of his own private Wi-Fi network, the name of which he'd hidden from being broadcast so that your average coffee shop patron wouldn't spot it. But even here, at the back of the coffee shop, the signal was strong enough to work with. And Crooner42 was hardly your average customer.

Fingal's Wi-Fi network was protected with WPA2 encryption, the strongest method of securing a wireless network. He would have expected nothing less of Fingal. Crooner42 rubbed his hands together. This was going to be fun.

Via Kismet, he placed his network card into 'promiscuous' mode. Normally, when a computer is connected to a network, its network card examines each frame of data that it receives and automatically discards every frame not addressed to it. By going into promiscuous mode, all traffic is received, regardless of its destination. Crooner42 once explained promiscuous mode to someone using the analogy of a postman making multiple photocopies of a letter addressed to you and dropping one in every letterbox in your street before finally dropping the original through your letterbox. Because you received the original, you've no idea that everyone else has also received a copy of your mail.

A WPA2 network encrypts all data using a 256-bit key, broadcasting clear data as gibberish. Only because both ends of the network — the Wi-Fi router in Fingal's apartment across the road and the network card in Fingal's laptop — both shared the same key, were they able to decrypt the broadcast gobbledegook back into meaningful data. So, although Crooner42 was now recording every frame of data being passed between Fingal's laptop and his Wi-Fi router, it was completely meaningless.

He needed the key. And the key was nothing more than a password.

Because Fingal had already connected his PC to his Wi-Fi network before Crooner42 had arrived at Bruno's, the authentication of Fingal's computer onto the 'F!NG@L' network had already occurred. Fingal's computer had validated that it was allowed onto the network by sending a copy of the key over the network for validation. And, of course, even then the key itself was encrypted.

Crooner42 needed Brody to re-authenticate his PC to his Wi-Fi network. If he did that, then Crooner42 would record the frames, albeit encrypted, containing the password. The easiest way would be for Crooner42 to walk over to Fingal and pull the plug and battery out of Fingal's PC. After rebooting the computer, it would then be forced to re-authenticate and Crooner42 could record the frames containing the encrypted password within them. But obviously that would expose Crooner42 to Fingal and that was the last thing he wanted right now.

But there was a sneakier and simpler way to achieve exactly the same outcome. From the data he had captured already, Crooner42 knew the network card address of Fingal's PC and the name of the Wi-Fi network. Using Kismet, he crafted a forged frame of data and broadcasted it onto the Wi-Fi network. The frame of data was an instruction to Fingal's computer to de-authenticate from the Wi-Fi network. Once received, the network card would blindly carry out the instruction, assuming it had been sent by the Wi-Fi router, never knowing that it had actually originated from Crooner42's computer, and then it would automatically re-authenticate, sending the password as encrypted data.

Crooner42 pressed send.

He studied Fingal just to make sure he didn't notice. Even though the de-authentication and re-authentication happened within a microsecond and was impossible for Fingal to notice, Crooner42 was still momentarily concerned. Fingal was an elite hacker after all. Maybe he had set up some kind of alarm on his computer to alert for de-authentication requests? No, Crooner42 realised his imagination was running away with itself. No one would do that.

Fingal remained hunched over his PC, with his back to Crooner42. He absently reached for the beverage next to his laptop. He drained it and returned his attention to whatever it was he was doing. Presumably trying — and failing, Crooner42 chuckled to himself — to find a link between HomeWebCam and SWY.

Crooner42 scanned the data captured in Kismet. He was looking for a sequence of four packets, a four-way handshake that occurred in WPA2 authentication between Fingal's computer and the Wi-Fi router. Within the four packets lay the encrypted password.

After a few minutes, he found them.

Crooner42 almost jumped for joy, but then remembered where he was and held himself together.

He connected to the Internet, via his own mobile phone rather than any of the Wi-Fi networks — after all, you couldn't be too safe — and brought up a site called CloudCracker. It was an online password cracking service that, for a small fee, would compare the encrypted password to the millions of words in its numerous dictionaries.

In the morning, Crooner42 would have the cleartext password for Fingal's private Wi-Fi network. Then all hell would break loose.

"I'm so sorry Mr Brody, but is closing time."

Crooner42 looked over to see the waiter standing by Fingal, his hands spread out in front of him emphasising that there was nothing he could do. Fingal was reading something on his phone. He looked up at the waiter, smiling.

"That's okay, Stefan. I was just leaving anyway." Fingal waved his phone and cheerfully announced, "I've got a date."

"Wonderful, wonderful," Stefan commented exuberantly and moved on to warn the next customer about closing time. Crooner42 caught Stefan's eye and gave him the thumbs up to acknowledge that he'd also heard the message. The waiter smiled and nodded.

Not wanting to draw any attention from Fingal, Crooner42 waited for him to pack up first. He did so quickly and without so much as a backward glance, rushed out of the coffee shop.

"Good luck, Mr Brody," Stefan called out as the door swung shut.

Crooner42 watched Fingal cross the road. The hazard lights on one of those impossibly small Smart cars flashed. Crooner42 watched incredulously as Fingal climbed into the driver's seat of the garishly coloured orange and black vehicle. The car pulled out into the traffic and shot off.

Crooner42 finished his coffee, packed up his computer and left Bruno's. He needed to return to Charlton Station and recover his own car, a much more fitting set of wheels for one of the worlds finest hackers.

Brody knocked on the unremarkable black double doors set into the plain brick wall. He peeked at Jenny Price beside him. She stood passively, her arms loosely folded, looking up at the dark sky as if working out whether it would rain again. He found her nonchalance disconcerting. Where were the questions voicing her worries about where he was taking her? How could she remain so calm standing outside this unmarked door in this Soho backstreet? All he'd said earlier when he picked her up from Holborn Station was that he'd take her to a bar, deliberately not providing any further elaboration. He knew from his own experience and from the numerous first dates he'd escorted to this strange black door that their hackles were automatically raised, a sudden irrational fear that Brody was some kind of psychopath drawing them into his secret lair. His dates' palpable relief when they saw what was inside never failed in breaking the ice.

The door opened inwards.

"I absolutely love speakeasies," Jenny announced breezily, and cruised confidently into the establishment, by-passing the massive bouncer standing in the dark entrance area.

Brody's astonishment rooted his feet to the spot.

"Welcome, Mr Brody," said the bouncer.

"Uh . . . oh, hi," stammered Brody.

Damn, she knew all about speakeasies. That explained her calm demeanour. She'd taken him at his word about going to a bar and as they'd approached the nondescript door in the long stretch of redbrick wall, she had put two and two together and worked out he was taking her to a speakeasy, a hidden bar that could not be seen by passers-by. Originally created in the United States during the Prohibition era as secret places to illegally consume liquor, they were now in revival as ultra-chic bars for those Brits in the know. In the three years Brody had been a member of Bromptons this was the first time one of his guests had already been familiar with the speakeasy concept.

He entered, allowing the bouncer to close the door behind him.

"You've been to a speakeasy before then?" he asked Jenny lightly, trying to keep the disappointment out of his tone.

"I was taken to a couple in New York. It hadn't occurred to me that there were any in London."

He led her through the blackout curtains into the main bar area. The subdued lighting just about reached the exposed brick walls. Mellow jazz played at the same noise level as the hubbub emanating from the club's guests, all secreted away in cosy booths.

They seated themselves on two leather and chrome stools, facing a massive mirrored wall, supporting numerous floating glass shelves that displayed a wide-ranging assortment of spirits. The barman offered them a cocktail menu, but Jenny declined, ordering herself a gin and tonic. Brody requested the same, but specified Hendrick's, saying to Jenny, "If we're only going to be having the one, let's make it a good one."

"Good thinking."

They chatted about other speakeasy experiences, which led to comparing holiday destinations. She spoke passionately about hiring a red convertible Ford Mustang and driving through the desert to Las Vegas, which, probably because it was the polar opposite, made her recall Brody's tiny car, prompting a second round of merciless ribbing, the first having happened when he'd picked her up earlier.

She'd exited Holborn Station and saw him leaning on his two-tone black and orange Fortwo coupe waiting for her. Failing to stifle a peal of laughter, she declared, "I'm not getting in that! What if someone saw me?"

He'd feigned a hurt expression and patted his car as if to protect it from her unkind words. "Come on, jump in."

"Seriously, I've got a proper car just around the corner."

"Tell you what. I'll drop you back here after."

She pondered for a moment and, failing to find a flaw in the plan, climbed in. "Like I said in my text, Brody. Just the one drink. After the day I've had, I've earned one nice drink."

"One *nice* drink? Hmm, let me see. Yes, I know a good place."

Ten minutes later he had pulled up outside Bromptons, with its innocuous black double doors.

Jenny placed her glass back on the counter, empty save the cucumber garnish. "That was fantastic. I really needed that after today."

"The case?"

She sighed. "Yeah."

"Did you track down the landlord?"

Jenny hesitated, unsure whether to discuss work. Brody sipped at his drink, still half-full.

"Yeah, he's in custody now."

"For murder?"

"No, not yet. We're still gathering facts. He's denying it, but there's an awful lot of circumstantial evidence. But for now we've got him under the sexual offences act for voyeurism and the human rights act for right to privacy. Unlike in the States, it turns out the UK doesn't have a specific law covering invasion of privacy."

"Do *you* think he killed them?"

Jenny considered his question. She picked up the glass and, remembering it was empty, placed it back down.

"Would you like another?" asked Brody. "You said it's been a tough day."

"I'd love one, I really would. But I need to be able to drive later."

"I can give you a lift home," and then, to reduce any implication, he teased, "If you can bear to be seen in my car."

Leaning on the bar with her elbow, she turned to face him. "It's no fun drinking on my own."

"You know, that's why God invented black cabs."

"Which has one additional benefit . . ."

"Oh yeah, what's that?"

She flashed a smile. "I don't have to be seen in your toy car."

A few minutes later, two fresh gin and tonics were placed in front of them. They chatted amiably and after a while the conversation returned to the murder cases.

"No, I don't think Walter Pike is the meeting room killer," said Jenny, loosening up. "Even though he installed that perverted webcam system *and* he's a customer of Flexbase."

"Flexbase, really? In what way?"

"He uses their remote office service. You know, the one you took umbrage to with David Dawson this morning."

"So this Pike knows all about their meeting room booking processes?"

"He says that he knows that you can rent meeting rooms but that he's never had to. We're checking with Flexbase."

"That won't prove Pike doesn't know his way around the booking system. After all, the rooms were all booked in fake names using fake email addresses."

"Yeah, I know."

They were both silent for a few moments, thinking through the implications.

Brody then spoke a thought that had been bothering him. "You know, I'm convinced that Flexbase are holding back. There's got to be a way to link the meeting room booking back to an originating IP address. Any decent web application developer worth his salt would store that little titbit inside the database. At the very least for debugging purposes."

"You're losing me here, Brody." Jenny smiled and added, "Could be the gin though." Her glass was empty again. Brody ordered another round.

"All I'm saying is that I reckon the IP address associated with the booking is stored in the database used by the application. That IT guy, what was his name?"

"Peggler. Magnus Peggler."

"Yeah him. He was flannelling us with all that talk of needing to go to the vendor who wrote the booking system. Any decent IT guy could just go natively into the database and take a look."

"Really? Right, I'll put some proper pressure on them tomorrow. Thanks, Brody."

"Actually, I thought of something else. I took a look at the Flexbase public website earlier and went through the meeting room booking system."

"Go on."

"Well, by default when you set up a new account, any booking would require a credit card to complete the booking. But Peggler said that the booking was linked to an existing corporate account. Which means that the booking is just added to the company's bill, rather than asking you to provide your credit card details."

"I'm not sure I follow."

"Well, when I created a new personal account on their site, I couldn't see a way to link it to a corporate account. Which means that it needs to be done behind the scenes by someone in Flexbase. Or, if the system is designed well, by the administrator of the corporate account."

Brody could see the frown on her face in the mirror as she tried to process this.

"That means that the killer knew how to get an individual account linked to a corporate account to avoid leaving a credit card trail," he continued. "It would need to have been carried out in advance of making the actual booking. There should be an audit trail on the system."

"That's brilliant, Brody. I really appreciate this. But can you do me a favour?"

"Yes?"

"Can you repeat these ideas tomorrow? I'm three G and Ts in and so I'm not convinced I'll be able to remember all of it."

They laughed together. He agreed to help. He was happy to, despite it taking time away from his primary objective of hacking SecretlyWatchingYou. Helping Jenny Price on her two murder cases at least made him feel like he was making some kind of progress. But he knew he was just fooling himself. He was happy to help as an excuse to spend more time with her. He found her presence intoxicating – and not just because he was also three G and Ts in. He appreciated the self-assured way she conducted herself. He guessed much of it came from being a police officer, putting herself in dangerous situations and relying on her wits and training to handle it. In work mode, she was intense, focussed and, well, bossy. But socially she was more feminine, relaxed and likeable. And in both modes she was strikingly beautiful.

"One for the road?" he asked.

She hummed and hawed and then said, "Yes, but let's do something different."

Jenny called the barman over, requested the cocktail menu and scanned it. She turned to him. "We established you're a fellow coffee lover first thing this morning, didn't we?"

Brody had no idea where she was going with this. The last thing he wanted was a coffee, this late at night. But he shrugged warily.

She ordered two espresso martinis. A few minutes later, two long-stemmed cocktail glasses containing a dark ochre liquid with a cream top appeared. Brody was in unchartered territory. He watched Jenny sip hers and give an appreciating nod to the barman. Brody tasted his, taking time to savour the unexpectedly pleasant combination of coffee and alcohol, made cold by the ice in the cocktail shaker.

"Kahlua, vodka and espresso," Jenny explained.

Greedily, he took a larger sip. "So simple."

"Nice moustache," she said, leaning over to wipe the cream off his upper lip with the tip of her index finger. She studied her finger and then, self-consciously catching herself, demurely wiped it on a napkin.

"You should see yours."

"No!" She looked straight ahead into the mirror. And then, realising he had tricked her, playfully struck him on the arm.

They sipped their cocktails companionably.

"I don't believe you're a pervert," Jenny stated with a mischievous grin.

"Huh?"

"Harry. He thinks you're some kind of voyeur."

"Who's Harry?"

"Harry O'Reilly. Our Irish computer geek that you met earlier today."

"Oh, course, how could I forget Harry? With his incredibly gifted technical mind, his decades of programming experience and his uncanny ability to make gadgets do the most unlikely things. You know, with the massive rise of cybercrime in the world, I feel invulnerable at the thought of Harry out there keeping me safe online."

Jenny punched him lightly in the arm again. "Don't be mean."

"Well, he couldn't even spot the webcam in the light fitting! And don't get me going on his knowledge of networking —"

"Don't change the subject, Brody. We were talking about Harry's opinion that you're a voyeur."

"Whatever gave him that idea?"

"Apparently, you. You told him you were one."

"Yeah, you're right. I did."

"Well, are you?"

"What do you think?"

"Why else would you have been looking at SecretlyWatchingYou?"

"I told you this morning. I was helping out a friend whose girlfriend is being stalked on there."

"But that's not really true, is it Brody?"

Brody shifted in his seat. Suddenly he felt like a mouse trapped between a cat's paws, unsure whether he was a plaything or a victim. And it was so typical. Just when he'd started to relax. What was he thinking, asking a policewoman out on a date? What an idiot.

He played for time. "Why'd you say that?"

"Because," she was no longer smiling, "When you found out about the two murdered girls and one of the common links being SecretlyWatchingYou, you didn't show any concern for your friend's girlfriend. She could be the killer's next victim."

"I doubt it. She's not exactly good-looking."

"But if the stalker knows who she is in the real world — after all, you said he was sending her these videos — then so could the killer."

She was tying him up in knots. "Okay, okay, stop, will you?"

Jenny turned to face him, waiting.

He admitted. "Fair cop. You've caught me red-handed. There is no stalker."

"Or woman in a call centre who talks dirty."

"Well, there's bound to be a woman somewhere who . . ." He saw her stern expression. "No, there is no girlfriend."

"So, why?"

"Why, what?"

"Why were you watching the Saxtons on SecretlyWatchingYou when you saw me?"

"Maybe I told Harry the truth. Maybe I am a voyeur."

"I don't believe that."

"Well, what do you believe, Jenny?"

She paused and slowly sipped her drink.

"You could be the killer."

Brody was taken aback. He hadn't seen that coming. In a flash, he understood her angle. "Oh, I get it. I'm one of those serial killers who wants to toy with the police. I commit the crime and then find a way to involve myself in the police investigation, just to prove how smart I am."

"And how stupid the police are, yes. It's been done before."

"So is this why you came for a drink with me? To see if I'm the killer?"

"One of the reasons, yes."

Brody held his arms out in front of him as if ready for her to handcuff him. "Well, you've got me officer. You saw through my little charade far too quickly. You'd better take me into custody before I hurt someone else. After all, that's what I subconsciously want."

"Prove to me you're not."

"Not what?" But he knew where this was going. Now he felt like he'd just been checked in a chess game.

"Not the killer."

"Isn't it you who has to prove my guilt? I shouldn't have to prove my innocence."

"Humour me, Brody. Here I am having a drink with someone I hardly know, something I rarely do. I'm asking myself whether I can trust this person. This person who rocked up out of nowhere this morning with a convoluted story that's since been proven untrue. But a person who has privileged information that is pertinent to the investigation. Which indicates you're the killer, a pervert or something else. Which is it, Brody?"

His alarm bells were going off now. He was such a fool to have gone anywhere near the police. Leroy was right. His ego had got in the way again, thinking he could use the police investigation to further his own ends. Brody studied her face. Underneath her intense stare, he thought he could see something. Was it hope? There was only one way out of this. He needed to tell the truth.

He inhaled deeply and breathed out slowly. "I saw you."

"What's that supposed to mean?" She was angry now.

"When I saw you on SWY, I just had to meet you. You were so . . ."

Her eyes bored deeply into him.

He continued, almost whispering. "I *am* an IT security consultant – that bit's true. But it wasn't work that brought SecretlyWatchingYou to my attention. It was my flatmate, Leroy. Initially, we were just fooling around on it, having a laugh, trying to work out if the people in the webcams knew they were being watched. But I began to become suspicious about the site and started looking into it. It's obviously completely dodgy. And then, when I saw you and the other police, it was obvious you didn't know anything about it. I had no idea if it would have anything to do with your case. And, to be fair, we still don't for sure. But by telling you about it . . ." He realised he was almost pleading. He paused and then finished brusquely. "I got to meet you."

Jenny processed what he had said.

She laid a hand on his arm. "And there's nothing else?" She had a catch in her voice.

Brody knew with complete certainty that he needed to tell her the rest. What he had said so far was mostly true and he could tell she wanted to believe him. But it was only half of it. He needed to tell her about his objective of hacking into SWY. That he had used her investigation as a means to further his own ends, to find an unprotected back door into the site. But he was a hacker and she was a policewoman. Even though he was a white hat, he knew that to achieve his own ethical objectives he often strayed just outside the law, the one thing that she was programmed to uphold. If he told her the complete truth, he would lose her before they'd even had a chance. He knew that instinctively.

He took her hand. "No Jenny. This is just about you."

Her smile broke his heart.

She whispered, "Well, that's all right then," and reached an arm around his neck and lightly pulled him towards her. He offered no resistance. They kissed, deeply, hungrily and, for him, bittersweetly. Whether it was the gin or his guilt at holding back from admitting the whole truth he wasn't sure. Some time later she pulled back, a mischievous grin on her face.

"Harry was right then."

"Eh?"

"You are a voyeur."

THURSDAY

CHAPTER 16

She sensed the early morning daylight streaming through the window but kept her eyes shut, not quite ready to face the day and all its implications. Tentatively, she stretched a foot towards the other side of her bed, expecting to meet warm resistance. But her foot kept going. She reached out with her hand and felt only cold linen. She opened her eyes and silently swore. The other half of the bed was empty.

Jenny Price felt the humiliation rising up from her stomach.

Strewn across the floor lay all the evidence she needed — a trail of clothes from their rushed disrobing, hands having fumbled with each other's zips, buttons, clasps and buckles as cumbersomely entwined, they backed their way from the front door, down the hallway and into the bedroom, finally naked and falling onto her bed — but the crime was more apparent from the evidence that was missing: his clothes. She grabbed her pink dressing robe from the back of her door to cover up her naked body and stormed out of the room. A quick scout around her flat confirmed her fears. Brody had taken off.

In the bathroom, she brushed her teeth, preventatively popped some Paracetamol to shore up her defences against the hangover she knew loomed on the horizon, and avoided looking in the mirror. She didn't want to see the face of the stupid girl who had allowed herself to be duped once again. When would she ever learn? Why couldn't she just treat a one night stand as something to be enjoyed in and of itself? Why did she always want sex to mean something more? This was the modern world, why on earth couldn't she play by its insouciant rules?

She splashed cold water over her face, flung open the bathroom door and walked straight into Brody.

"Whoa," he said, backing up, holding onto a cardboard tray containing takeaway coffees and croissants.

"I . . ." Jenny gathered herself. "I thought you'd left."

"I didn't want to wake you." He held up the tray of goodies. "I left the door on the latch and went foraging for provisions. Looks like you've got some half-decent coffee places round here. Cappuccino Okay?"

"That would be lovely. The kitchen's just down there." Now she really did want to look in the mirror. Jenny backed into the bathroom. "I'll be with you in a mo."

Her reflection required some repair work but first she let go a stream of silently mouthed curses at herself for doubting him. Relieved, she took a quick shower and gave herself a light application of mascara, eye shadow and eyeliner. She wondered back into the kitchen, in her pink robe. Her hair was brushed back, still wet.

Brody had laid out breakfast on the kitchen table. He'd even transferred the coffee from paper cups into china ones from her cupboard. He was leaning on the sink, back to the window, hands in his pockets.

"Hi," she said.

"Hi," he replied. How could one word be so laden with meaning?

They stood looking at each other. She began to feel a little awkward.

He removed a hand from his pocket, smiled and reached out to her. She took his hand and allowed herself to be reeled in. He kissed her and she no longer felt awkward. She responded by reaching her arms up behind his shoulders. With his other hand, he pulled her closer. She could feel his hardness.

"Well hello," she quipped, pressing her body forward.

He backed her towards the kitchen table and lifted her onto its surface, tugging the robe from her shoulders. She shrugged out of it and then unzipped his flies while he reached behind her to push the breakfast towards the safety of the other side of the table. She could feel her heart booming.

"Time out," she declared.

He stopped, confused. She extricated herself from the table and said, "Don't move a muscle. I'll be right back."

Jenny skipped out of the kitchen, suddenly conscious of his eyes on her naked rear, darted into her bedroom, reached into her sideboard drawer, found what she needed and scurried back into the kitchen. Understanding dawned across his face when she waved the condom packet at him, more as a distraction from her full frontal nakedness. She manoeuvred herself back into the exact same position as when she had left.

"Right, continue."

Moments later, she guided him into her and lay back on the table, arching her back to heighten the intensity. Gently, he stroked her flat stomach, her small breasts, and her neck. His thrusts started to take on more vigour and she wrapped her legs around him, pulling him in closer. The table began to move jerkily across the limestone tiles and she could hear the cups, saucers and plates sliding about on its surface. She hoped they didn't fall and crash to the floor, but the nearer she came to climax; the less she cared about the damned crockery. And when the inevitable crash occurred, she commanded him not to stop. By the time they had finished, all of the crockery lay smashed on the floor amid puddles of steaming coffee and soggy croissants.

"I think," said Jenny, panting into Brody's ear, "this gives new meaning to having someone for breakfast."

"Or," he lifted his head from nuzzling her neck to look her in the eye and, deadpan, said, "laying the table."

A few minutes later, Jenny swept up the broken crockery and croissants while Brody mopped up the spill. They agreed it was probably better if they ventured out for a replacement breakfast. But then Jenny remembered that they'd both left their cars in Central London and suggested that they grab a bite on the way to Richmond Underground station.

Twenty minutes later, they were sitting in Taylor St Baristas just outside the station. Jenny put her foot down over paying; pointing out with a smirk that Brody had already bought breakfast that morning.

As Jenny munched on a *pain au chocolat*, her phone rang, bringing the real world back into focus with its shrill tone. She sighed, seeing from the caller display that it was Fiona. Rapidly, Fiona explained that she had been in the station since 5:00 a.m. to get a head start on cross-referencing the employee and tenant data supplied by Flexbase, which made Jenny feel guilty. A few names had popped up on the police database, but there was nothing particularly promising. It did, however, suggest that there was one company that rented office space in both the Paddington and Watford Flexbase offices, which was why Fiona had phoned: to let Jenny know that she was just heading out to follow up on it. Jenny wished her luck, knowing in her gut that it was a weak lead; like most of the lines of enquiry they were currently pursuing.

"There must be something we're overlooking," Jenny said to Brody, as she put the phone down.

"Sounds like you're covering every angle to me."

"We've got so many links, so many connections between the two crimes. But nothing that's getting us anywhere."

"Is that how it works? You find all the common points of reference between the two victims to lead you to a common perpetrator?"

"One of the ways, especially with stranger killings. But sometimes there are just too many commonalities."

"And even if there isn't, the theory of six degrees of separation says everyone is connected anyway."

Jenny had heard of the theory. That everyone in the world is six or fewer steps away, by way of introduction, to everyone else in the world. It was a comforting notion that made the world seem a smaller place.

"True, but we're looking for someone with a direct connection to both victims. Find them and usually we find our answer."

"But that assumes the killer knew the girls beforehand. What if SWY really is playing a part in this? Then you're two degrees away, with the site acting as one of the degrees."

It made sense. If the killer really was selecting his victims from watching webcam feeds, then he was already two steps away.

"Well, let's assume it's true for a minute. Surely that means that the killer is registered in the site's database?"

"Agreed, but you've got at least three major hurdles to overcome. One, the site is hosted in Russia. No one is going to give you access, even though you're police. In fact, *especially* because you're police. Two, the personal information people provide when they register is minimal and, in most cases, probably fake. For example, when I signed up to it, I created a completely fake email address. There's no way you'd be able to track me down from the data in that database."

"But what about payment? If the killer is addicted to watching the webcam streams, he'll have paid the upgrade fees to gain access to the premium webcams and the audio. Surely we can trace the money. It's electronic after all."

"It's not that difficult to remain completely anonymous online, even when you're buying stuff and especially if you're not shipping anything physical. Like paying to watch webcams for instance."

"But credit cards have to be registered to a real-world address."

Brody shook his head. "There's pre-pay gift cards you can buy without giving your address, where you top up the balance and then buy stuff as if they were a credit card. Or you can use digital cash. Same thing."

"That's depressing. And three?"

"Three what?"

"You said there were three major problems with using the site's database. You've only mentioned two."

"Oh right," he smiled. "Three is about the people behind SecretlyWatchingYou. Whoever the site admins are, they know full well they're breaking tons of privacy laws all over the world. Which is why the site has some of the best security defences I've ever seen, much better than your average online bank. And given the laws they're breaking, they're hardly going to come forward and help the police by giving them access to their customer database."

"Do you think these site admins are in the UK?"

"I've had a quick look, but there's no way to tell for sure. It's not like they've left their contact details."

"But the webcams are physically in the UK aren't they?"

"Definitely some of them. Maybe all. No way to tell for sure."

"Maybe the people behind HomeWebCam can tell us?"

"You're assuming every webcam on HomeWebCam is also on SecretlyWatchingYou. And vice versa."

"They're not?"

"Again, I don't know for sure. I'm pretty sure SecretlyWatchingYou is somehow getting its feeds from

HomeWebCam. It's the only logical explanation."

"Which makes it even more important to talk to the people behind HomeWebCam." Jenny then had a worrying thought. "Unless they're in cahoots with each other."

Brody thought for a moment and admitted, "You know, I hadn't thought of that. HomeWebCam very much trades a legit business, located in the USA and with its servers in the USA. SWY is located in Russia. Doesn't mean they're not working together. And I imagine SWY makes a ton more money. All that said, I think it's unlikely. But you're right, it's well worth checking out."

Jenny wasn't sure if he meant for the police to check out or for himself. Either way she was pleased to have thought of something herself.

"Now that I think about it," he said, "You do actually have another connection between the victims."

"Oh yeah?"

"McCarthy Security Ltd. The company who physically installed the cameras? Saxton mentioned them yesterday and Hilary Saxton even mentioned how good a job they'd done. I bet Pike used the same firm to install his webcams."

Now he said it, Jenny remembered the name. This was promising. She made an effort to contain her excitement. "Why do you think that?"

"Both installations were professionally fitted. No exposed power line wires or anything. And, more importantly . . . Do you remember the PCs in the two homes that the webcams connect to wirelessly?" She nodded, so he continued. "They're set up exactly the same as each other, which means the same installation company must be behind both."

"Where does HomeWebCam fit in then?"

"HomeWebCam just provides the website for people to gain secure remote access to their webcams over the Internet. And if you look at their site, everything's in the USA. The webcams can be bought from anywhere. Loads of spy gadget shops in London or online sell them."

"That's brilliant, Brody, thanks." She wanted to kiss him.

"It's better than that."

"What do you mean?"

"Well, so far one of the common factors between your victims is that their home locations were on SWY, both of which were installed by the same company, so . . ."

Jenny had made the mental leap. "So maybe McCarthy Security installed *all* of the webcams being broadcast on SecretlyWatchingYou. Maybe that's how they get chosen for the site. And if that's true, we might be able to get a list of every location, contact the webcam owners and prevent anyone else from being targeted."

Brody leaned back, folding his arms: a job well done.

Jenny knew they were onto something at last. Something tangible. "I could kiss you."

"Go on then."

She did.

"You won't believe what I'm up to today, Dad!" She didn't wait for an answer. "I've got a business meeting with this big shot from some American company. He's flying in this morning to meet me. Me!"

Sarah McNeil allowed herself the embellishment. She knew full well that Francis Delacroix was fitting her in between his flight landing and some business meetings in the afternoon. But she wanted to make her father proud, just like the old days when he'd been thrilled at every achievement she'd made, no matter how big or small. Whether it was six-year-old Sarah winning the primary school egg-and-spoon race or twenty-two-year-old Sarah graduating from the University of Reading, James McNeil had lived every moment and been there to support and cheer her on.

Sarah continued pushing the wheelchair along the pathway, which wound its way between perfectly maintained lawns and colourful flowerbeds laid out in flowing swoops, all in front of the imposing Georgian building that housed the horrendously expensive Sunnyside care home.

She leaned forward to see if there was a flicker on her Dad's face at her news. But his blank expression steadfastly remained in place as if he hadn't heard a word she'd said. The doctors had told her that he was still able to hear and understand, but that he'd retreated further into himself following his last stroke. Only the sight of a chessboard seemed to evoke any reaction from him. The fact that he could still play — very slowly with only his right hand clumsily moving pieces — and win told her that some part of her father was still alive inside. She just couldn't reconcile why her presence couldn't animate him like the black and white squares and chess pieces. The doctors had talked to her about logical versus emotional centres of the brain. But they didn't actually know for sure what was wrong. All she could do was hope that somewhere deep inside he was still cheering her on.

The meeting with Mr Delacroix was at 11:00 a.m., in just over two hours. She'd dressed in her sharp two-piece black suit, cream silk blouse and pointed high heels. She loved the way the open collars of her blouse wrapped over her suit, with its ability to draw men's gazes down towards her substantial cleavage. Today she was going to use every asset at her disposal to secure the majority of FCS Software's advertising budget. She meant business.

The day before, Joe Ashley had agreed to her having the following morning off, but only after she'd laid it on thick about it being her father's birthday and that the care home were laying on a party for him. Sarah knew that the minute anyone in the team talked personally about themselves, especially if they mentioned nurseries, childminders, hospitals or, as she had, care homes for the elderly, Ashley's inter-personal skills no longer functioned and he would immediately extricate himself from the conversation, agreeing to almost anything in the process. All he ever wanted to discuss was the number of calls made, deals booked and performance against quota. He'd still pointed out sharply that taking time off work when at only twelve per cent of the month's revenue target with only a week to go was plain stupid. But if her father's birthday was more important than her job well, maybe she needed to rethink her career.

Sarah grinned to herself. If Ashley only knew what she was up to today. She looked around, taking in the grandiose surroundings. Her smile widened. The commission on this deal alone would keep her father in Sunnyside for at least a year. It would be wonderful for him. He could play chess to his heart's content and she would be free to continue building a new life for herself.

Sarah looked at her watch. She had two hours. From here, she needed to allow three-quarters-of-an-hour for the drive to Windsor. Time to go.

She turned the wheelchair around and rapidly pushed her father back towards the house. She would arrive very early: it was better to be safe than sorry. It wouldn't do to be late for the most important meeting of her life.

Brody opened the front door of his flat and listened.

It was quiet; the kind of silence that only comes from the apartment being totally empty. He checked his watch: it was just before nine. Leroy and Danny were most likely still enjoying breakfast together. As part of their anniversary celebrations, Danny had booked them a table at The Breakfast Club, a small, deliberately shabby café just a short walk from Brody's apartment. There they would eat American-style pancakes in honour of their first morning together in Key West five years before.

Brody hoped that Leroy and Danny would spend the whole day together or, more specifically, that Leroy wouldn't return to the apartment and bug him. He seriously needed to finish off the reconnaissance of HomeWebCam that he'd begun in Bruno's last night before he'd hooked up with Jenny. He was sure that HomeWebCam would provide the key he could use to unlock the back door into SWY. But to find the key he needed to come up with a decent attack vector and, for that, he needed no distractions, especially Leroy-sized ones. As a West End stage actor, Leroy's life was usually nocturnal with productions most evenings, followed by a social life that began after each show and carried on into the small hours. It meant that Leroy usually slept in until mid-afternoon, freeing Brody to work undisturbed for most of each day. But Danny's stay this week, centred on the couple's anniversary celebrations, had altered the pattern. The fact that they were breakfasting this early in the day meant that Leroy would be awake for the rest of it, grumpy and antagonistic from lack of sleep.

Unfortunately, Danny wasn't going to save him. Brody recollected overhearing Danny explaining how manic his schedule was with its back-to-back candidate interviews. As a headhunter in the telecoms industry, Danny's reputation with his clients came down to his skills in sifting through numerous candidates for an open position and only ever putting forward the very few who nailed the brief. Much to Leroy's chagrin, Danny never mixed business with pleasure and so Brody resigned himself to the door bursting open any moment.

He showered and changed, forcing himself to think about how he'd approach his attack on HomeWebCam. But he couldn't. His every thought was of Jenny Price. Of their amazing night together. Of her stroking the cream from his lips; the moment when he'd became sure that their evening together would continue through the night. Of her straddling him on her bed, naked and in control except for the moment when she came, pleasure and confusion etched across her fine features. Of their lustful breakfast antics in the kitchen. Of their kiss in Taylor St Baristas, the taste of coffee on their lips.

When he'd left without waking her first thing that morning, he'd briefly considered allowing the door to quietly close behind him, leaving the lightly snoring — a wonderful sound that had made him chuckle with affection — sleeping beauty to her life of law and order, untainted by his half-truths and white lies. Walking away was what he had done in nearly every other similar situation. But this time something felt different. It was the first time he hadn't been a cinematographer, stuntman, or second unit film director. He'd been Brody Taylor, independent IT security consultant, by far the nearest he'd ever come to the truth of his ignoble profession. And it had changed things.

Working alongside her on the murder cases provided a completely different perspective. She was authoritative and professional, calm and in control, focused and intense. All qualities he admired and very different from the version of her that had gone out for drinks with him. That Jenny Price was sharp and witty, relaxed and uninhibited, charming and funny. It made him understand that these contradictory sets of character traits were just snapshots. He'd seen enough to know that he didn't yet have the full picture, but, for the first time in a long time, enough to know he wanted to. And, as the door to her flat began to close, he'd reached in and flipped the latch, enabling him to return.

Now Brody sat at his desk in front of his computer and the bank of three widescreen monitors and shook his head, a physical attempt at clearing the thoughts of Jenny from his head. On his smartphone, he brought up the Sonos app, upped the volume to high and selected the soundtrack from *1492: The Conquest of Paradise*. The film about Columbus's discovery of America may have been a box-office failure, but Vangelis's electronic music synthesised into an orchestral chorus with strong haunting melodies provided the perfect backdrop to help Brody maintain focus while hacking HomeWebCam. He rested his fingers on the keyboard, took a deep breath, waited for the opening melody to kick in, and began.

Twenty minutes later, he completed his reconnaissance of the publicly available information about HWC. Unlike SWY, HWC was a classic bricks and mortar company, with its headquarters in Silicon Valley. It employed 150 people and turned over $12 million a year. It had satellite sales offices elsewhere in the States but no presence in Europe or Asia. The company was a wholly-owned subsidiary of a multinational called Agincourt Plc, based in Boston. HWC had its own dedicated 24-hour help desk for customers of its remote webcam viewing service. All of its systems were hosted in a datacentre somewhere in the USA. The CEO was called Ken Toomey. Dwight Chambers, whom Brody had talked to yesterday, was their Chief Technical Officer and reported into their Chief Operations Officer. There were also Chiefs of Marketing, HR, Strategy, Legal, and IT. With so many chiefs on board, Brody wondered who did all the work.

The HomeWebCam.com domain name was registered to Dwight Chambers and even listed his home address in Redwood City. As far as Brody was concerned, that was a schoolboy error for someone who was supposed to be the company's lead technologist. A quick search of LinkedIn gave Brody a list of over one hundred employees, their roles and some insight into their relationships with each other.

Brody gave the parent company a cursory once-over as well. Agincourt had offices everywhere, even here in London. It provided its clients with an impressive portfolio of security services. From security guards for buildings to armed escorts, from installing access control and CCTV security systems to alarm receiving and monitoring facilities, from electronic tagging of offenders to prisoner escorting and from managing ATMs to secure transporting of cash in high security vehicles. Brody suspected the acquisition of Internet-focused HWC eighteen months before had been more about enhancing the attractiveness of Agincourt's shares on the stock markets.

Brody knew what he needed to achieve today. First he needed to hack into HWC's internal network in San Francisco and find a way to view their firewall logs. He was convinced HWC was relaying their webcam feeds over to SWY, despite Chambers' protestations to the contrary. Whether HWC was doing this knowingly wasn't his concern. Once he analysed the logs, he'd be able to identify the route being taken and reuse those security credentials to gain access to SWY. If the password was encrypted, he would use brute force techniques to decrypt it. And from there, he'd finally be able to sneak inside SWY without detection.

But his challenge right now was time. Or, more accurately, the time difference. San Francisco was over five thousand miles away and eight hours behind Greenwich Mean Time, which mean it was just after one in the morning there. The implications of this were that there would be few people awake whom he could entice to help him. But as he thought it through, he realised that he might be able to make the time difference work in his favour. A plan began to form.

Ten more minutes of preparation and he had enough to begin.

He took a deep breath and rang the HWC help desk number.

Manuel Cortez felt his eyes glazing over again.

He forced himself to stand and walk around the empty control centre. If he could get his blood flowing then the tiredness would lift. He hated being idle. Waiting. If only the phone would ring: that would get him busy. Years of experience had taught him that being busy made getting through to morning without nodding off a breeze.

Cortez also knew from years of experience that he should have got some shut-eye earlier, before coming to work. But that would have meant missing Daniela's swimming trials. And thank God in Heaven that he'd gone. He had been so proud to witness his dedicated eight-year daughter win her two hundred-yard breaststroke race by a clear three body lengths. If she continued to improve at this rate, Cortez was convinced she would go far in the sport; perhaps even make it into the USA Olympic team in time for Tokyo 2020. But for that to even have a chance of happening, he needed to keep his daughter in her expensive private school. And that meant he would have to keep working as many shifts as he could. Without the overtime and the extra thirty per cent shift allowance, Daniela had no hope.

Sheesh, it was *too* quiet tonight.

He glanced at the large central display screen just to make sure everything really was okay. The traffic light icons were green across the board. No customers queuing for support. No network links down. No servers down. No backlog of cases from the day shift. Yup; it was going to be a slow night.

Only twice in his three years as a help desk support engineer had he gone through the night shift with zero customer issues to occupy him. Maybe tonight would be the third. Although the majority of its clientele were in the States and Canada, necessitating a full ten-man day-team, HomeWebCam also had thousands of clients all around the globe, hence the minimal overnight cover of one engineer, which Cortez and two other multi-lingual engineers took turns to handle.

Cortez loved talking to people from other countries. The English with their wonderful accents straight off the television were his favourites, although he found the broad accents of their Scottish and Irish neighbours almost impossible to comprehend. Occasionally he got to speak Spanish and French, the languages gifted to him by his Mexican mother and his French-Canadian father, and one of the main reasons he had got this job. In the last three years, he'd also used the downtime to master German and was now making an attempt at Mandarin. Maybe one day he'd even visit some of these exotic locations. But with every spare cent going towards Daniela's schooling . . .

The phone rang.

Thank God in Heaven for that.

He sat back down at his desk and donned the headphone and mic. He saw from the display that the call was coming from a blocked number.

"Hi. You're through to the HomeWebCam customer support line. This is Manuel Cortez, how may I help you?"

Although the official script required him to immediately ask for name and customer account details before allowing them to describe their problem, Cortez felt that offering a more open and confident introduction usually helped diffuse the customer's frustration with whatever technical problem they needed help with. And anyway, on the night shift, there was no one else around to stop him applying his own personal style.

"Cortez, you say?" The accent was Texan, spoken loudly and deeply. "This here is Ken Toomey. Does that name mean anything to ya?"

He sat bolt upright in his chair. Toomey was the CEO of HomeWebCam. He felt a rush of adrenalin course through him.

"Yes Mr Toomey. How can I help you, sir?"

Cortez had never spoken to Ken Toomey before. The nearest he'd come was standing at the back of the hall watching him present to the workforce at the annual all-hands meeting. Although charming in public, Toomey's propensity to fly off the handle was often the subject of gossip around the water cooler. There were legendary stories of people being fired for the most minor of things. Apparently, he'd gone through at least six secretaries in the last two years.

"How many people on shift tonight, Cortez?"

"Just me sir."

"Uh, okay. Well, how busy are you, son?"

Cortez had no idea how to answer. Telling the truth was a risk. But before he could offer an answer, Toomey continued.

"You see, I got me this problem with my work laptop, Cortez. Now I know you're supposed to be there helping all our customers but I say what use is a help desk if it can't help its own employees as well, never mind its CEO. Do you see what I mean, son?"

"Uh, yes, I see, sir." At least he thought he did. The company did have a two-man internal IT team that normally dealt with employee issues, although they were strictly nine to five.

"Good, 'cause I've got to present to the damn board tomorrow and I'm still up putting the final touches to this damn presentation and the damn computer has just frozen completely. If I power the damn thing off I'll damn well lose hours of work and I sure as hell don't even want to think about that."

"What's the problem, sir?"

"I told you, it's frozen! There's a strange message on the screen. Damned if I know what it means."

"What does it say, sir?"

"I've taken a photo of it with my phone. Let me email it over to you. What's your email address, son?"

Cortez told him and waited for the email to arrive. He was pretty good at fixing webcam issues for customers over the phone, after all that's what he'd been trained to do, but when it came to general computer issues, he was probably no better than the next guy. He hoped it was something obvious.

"You got it yet, son?"

"No, I — there it is." Cortez quickly opened the email. There was no text, just an attached JPG. He double-clicked the picture file. It took a few seconds more than normal, but then finally displayed an image. In the picture, Cortez could see a laptop screen, but it was hard to make out the details. He tried enlarging it, but the picture's focus was off. He couldn't make out any details. He felt beads of sweat forming on his forehead. His hand shook as he moved the mouse.

"Uh, Mr Toomey. Would it be possible to take the picture again? The one you sent is —"

"Well that was quick! You're a miracle worker; it's started working now. Thanks, son. What was your name again?"

Cortez hadn't done a thing, but if Toomey wanted to infer that he had, that was okay with him. "Cortez, sir. Manuel Cortez."

"Well Manuel Cortez, you're an absolute credit to the company. While I'm at the board meeting tomorrow, I'm going to put you forward for a special bonus. Thanks, son."

The line clicked dead.

Cortez removed the headset and leaned right back in his chair, taking deep breaths to calm himself down. After a few minutes, he started to think more clearly.

A bonus? He couldn't believe it. He wondered how much it would be. Perhaps it would be enough to fund Daniela's next semester. What luck.

He decided he deserved a coffee break. Using his security pass, he let himself out of the control room and wandered down the corridor to the staff kitchen, whistling to himself. At the vending machine, he purchased a sweet black coffee. After a moment's hesitation, he treated himself to a Hershey bar.

He seated himself at the one of the many tables and slowly savoured the coffee and chocolate, absently staring through the large window across the lake at the other glass fronted office blocks, each one proudly displaying the logo of a well-known IT company. He wondered how many of them had twenty-four-hour help desks. Maybe one day he might move on from HomeWebCam; join a company with a larger help-desk; one with a night shift of more than one lonely soul.

He felt his eyelids droop again and quickly pulled himself together. It was time to return to the control centre.

Glancing at the main display screen, Cortez froze. It was no longer all green. In fact, the network traffic lights were all flashing red.

He ran to his computer, wondering what the hell was going on.

Just as he fired up the network monitoring application, his phone rang.

"Yes?" He was so panicked that he forgot his personalised introduction, never mind the one on the script. He was about to add some clarification when a voice spoke.

"Is that the HomeWebCam service desk?" The voice was demanding but rushed.

"Uh yes, who's this?"

"This is Mike Baker. I'm the Service Desk Manager over at Agincourt, here in Boston. Who's this?"

Cortez knew Agincourt was HomeWebCam's parent company, but he'd never talked to anyone from there before.

"This is Manuel Cortez."

"Manuel, are you seeing any network problems?"

"Uh, yes. I was just starting to diagnose what's going on." It was only a slight fib.

"Damn." Then the phone was muffled as Baker spoke to someone else, presumably putting his hand over the microphone. But Cortez could still make out what Baker was saying. "HWC's being attacked, as well. They're every-fucking-where." And then the muffling was gone and Baker was talking to him again. "Manuel, let me explain. We've got to move double-quick. The whole of Agincourt is under a coordinated DDOS cyberattack. I've just had Homeland Security on the phone. It's some kind of Al Qaeda hacking cell pissed off with us for our security work in Afghanistan supporting the Army. How are your firewalls holding up?"

Cortez clicked into his network map. Both firewalls were red, but nothing on the inside of the network was compromised. At least, not yet. The firewalls were doing their job. Beads of sweat appeared on his forehead again, and he felt faint. Too much sugar in the coffee and chocolate.

"Yeah, I think the firewalls are handling it okay."

"That's good. We've had breaches over here. Our website's down. Our CRM system is down. Our ERP system is down. We're in bad shape. Are you sure your firewalls are okay? How can you tell?"

"I'm looking at the network monitor. They're red, but they're still up."

"You can't rely on that, Manuel. That's just SNMP traps; they're never going to give you the full story. I need you to log into the firewalls manually and check the logs."

Cortez did as he was told. He hadn't been anywhere near the firewalls for months, but he vaguely remembered how to do it. After a couple of missteps, which he quietly kept to himself, he was in. The administrator password was the same as the other systems he was more used to managing.

He scanned the logs. There were thousands of alerts.

"They're okay. They're handling it okay. They've recognised it's an attack and are blocking it okay." Cortez couldn't help but keep the pride out of his voice. Perhaps HomeWebCam's systems were stronger than those of its parent company. "We're using an intrusion deception system combined with deep packet inspection firewalls, what about you?"

"Nah, nothing so glamorous here. I've been saying for ages that we need to upgrade our defences with DPI and IPS. I bet they'll fucking listen now." And then Baker's voice was muffled again as he talked to someone else. "What do you mean, stopped? Show me?" There was a long pause.

And then in front of Cortez's eyes, the network monitor icons turned from red to amber and then to green. Even the main display returned to green.

Baker was back. "The attack seems to have stopped over here. What about you, Manuel?"

"Yeah, it's stopped." Cortez was smiling from ear to ear, pleased as punch that his defences had held up better than Agincourt's. After getting the credit from Toomey a few minutes earlier, the last thing he needed was to have to phone around saying all their systems were compromised. Where would his bonus be then?

"Well, you're lucky Manuel. Listen, we've got a load of clean-up and recovery work ahead of us. I'll leave you to it. But when we come up for air, I'll give you another ring. Looks like we need to get hold of whatever firewalls you've got. Good work."

The line clicked dead.

Cortez leaned back in his chair again and allowed his body to calm down. What a strange night. But he'd survived his fiery CEO and a terrorist attack. Not a bad night's work, even if he did say so himself.

And no damage done. Now that really was impressive.

He allowed his thoughts to return to the bonus that Toomey had mentioned. Maybe he'd also be able to buy Daniella that professional low-drag racing swimsuit. She'd be even faster.

In the meantime, he decided to treat himself to another Hershey Bar. The sugar would help him stay awake.

Brody almost felt sorry for Manuel Cortez. He'd been far too easy to dupe. Just like every help-desk support engineer in the industry, he *so* wanted to help.

After a brief search, Brody had found a couple of video interviews of Toomey on the Internet from around the time he'd sold his company to Agincourt. He had a deep Texan drawl that reminded Brody of John Wayne. During the call, Brody, wearing his wireless headphone mic, had stood up, hunched his shoulders and compressed his neck to make it easier to channel the American icon's distinctive voice as the basis for his impersonation of Toomey. Despite feeling foolish, especially when Brody caught himself pacing the room with Wayne's off-balance swagger, it had gone well.

Cortez had immediately dropped all protocols when he'd heard his CEO's voice. The story about a frozen computer was a good one, especially the idea of taking a photo of it; Brody would use that again. It was believable enough, especially these days with everyone having camera-phones. But its real purpose was to disarm Cortez into opening an attachment in an email, something he was trained not to do.

It had been safe to assume that Cortez would be familiar with email phishing. The scam involved mass fake emails pretending to be from a trusted source and designed to trick people into doing something foolhardy; either opening an attached file, which would install a deadly payload on their computer, or visiting a fake website masquerading as a legitimate one, but that ultimately persuaded victims into divulging personal details, enabling the phisher to steal entire identities. The crime's close cousin, spear-phishing, involved carefully targeted singular emails using readily available online information.

Brody had only one chance with the HomeWebCam help desk and he didn't have the time necessary to craft a legitimate-looking email, which Cortez may well have spotted and deleted.

Instead, Brody decided to combine spear-phishing with his favourite social engineering technique of 'hacking the human'. The phone call from 'Toomey' had predisposed Cortez to receiving the email and not looking too closely at its headers. Brody had gone for simplicity and speed, and had only changed the display name and reply address to match Ken Toomey's. However, the actual address he'd sent it from had nothing to do with Toomey. Fortunately, Cortez hadn't noticed in his fervent desire to help his CEO and keep his job.

And then there was the attachment. Again, because of the phone call, Cortez was all set up to believe it was a real JPG. But in reality it was a malware program. When Cortez had double-clicked what he thought was a picture file, it had installed its payload, the freely available remote access tool, Poison Ivy, customised to Brody's specifications. Once installed, it had 'called home' over the Internet. In this case, 'home' was one of Brody's untraceable proxies acting as a command and control server, to which Brody had also connected into anonymously.

The last step of the malware's installation was to open the computer's standard image viewer and display the photo Brody had embedded within the installation of Poison Ivy. When Cortez had seen exactly what he'd expected to see after double-clicking, a photo of someone else's computer screen, he'd had no idea that he'd unwittingly installed malware. Brody had deliberately blurred the picture he'd snapped of one of his own laptops, not wanting to leave any clues. Once the Poison Ivy payload had successfully been installed and called home, Brody had rapidly brought the phone call to an end.

Brody was particularly proud of the second phase of the hack.

With Poison Ivy installed, Brody now had full, remote access to Cortez's computer. But he still did not know the correct credentials to gain access to the firewalls. So, Brody had done something he'd never done before: he'd used his private botnet of servers hidden all over the world to launch a distributed denial of service attack against HomeWebCam. He was definitely straying into black hat territory doing this, which was disconcerting. But he'd deliberately constrained it to be noticeable rather than damaging. A real DDOS attack was designed to overload a network, overpowering the servers completely, so much so that they'd crash. Brody had only wanted to set off the alarms.

Coupling the DDOS attack with another fake phone call, this time from 'Mike Baker', the Service Desk Manager from Agincourt – at least according to LinkedIn – had been risky but necessary. Brody had gambled that Cortez had not met or talked with Baker previously. He'd noticed that they weren't connected to each other on LinkedIn. Convincing Cortez that Agincourt was also under attack, he'd been able to talk the engineer into logging into the firewalls. In the background, Poison Ivy's keystroke-logging feature recorded the account names and passwords that Cortez had used to gain administrator access.

And now Brody had all the access he needed.

Via Poison Ivy, Brody ran a series of background commands on Cortez's computer and connected to each firewall in turn. He spent time browsing the logs, analysing the flow of data in and out of HomeWebCam. He was searching for any reference to SWY or any of its native IP addresses.

After some time, Brody concluded that the webcam feeds were not actually flowing in from the network video recorders in every webcam location around the world managed by HomeWebCam, which had been his initial working premise. As this finally became clear, Brody bashed his forehead with the heel of his hand, berating himself because he should have worked this out without hacking into HomeWebCam; breaking God knows how many laws in the process. With the benefit of hindsight, he now realised he could have analysed the outbound network traffic passing through the router at Derek Saxton's house — after all, he had full access. Yesterday, he'd even traced the traffic on the Saxtons' home network, but because he'd been so focused on looking for packets going to SWY, he hadn't considered what did or didn't flow through to HomeWebCam. Had he looked more broadly, the

Saxton network traces would have shown him that the webcam feeds only left the Saxton local network for HWC whenever Derek or Hilary were logged into HomeWebCam, viewing the video footage. It was a classic case of his assumptions getting in the way of the data.

Sometimes he was such a fool.

It did make him wonder about the purpose of HomeWebCam. After all, it was technically possible to connect to network video recorder PCs directly. After some head-scratching and further research, Brody concluded that the site's function was to centralise and simplify the way its customers gained remote access to the network video recorders located in their own homes and offices. Without the full HomeWebCam service, their customers would be required to figure out how to reconfigure their routers to remotely access their network video recorders from the Internet as well as set up the security on them. HomeWebCam did all this for them and provided a full twenty-four-hour help desk.

Moreover, Brody realised, there was the recurring revenue. Rather than just make a one-time sale of webcams and a network video recorder, HomeWebCam was able to charge monthly for its on-going service, a far more profitable arrangement.

But all this clarity left Brody completely stumped. Dwight Chambers had been right: SWY wasn't gaining access to the video feeds through HomeWebCam. And he knew from his work yesterday that SWY was not connecting directly into the network video recorder PC in the Saxton house.

How the hell was SWY gaining access to the video feeds?

He buried his face in his hands. It made no sense. Crooner42 had thought of everything. Brody only had twenty-four hours left. At this rate, he would never pwn SecretlyWatchingYou.com by tomorrow.

And then, inevitably, as if his day couldn't get any worse, Brody heard the key turn in the front door of his flat. The door opened and Leroy ambled in.

"Hello, darling," he greeted cheerfully.

"Fuck off Leroy. I'm not in the mood."

CHAPTER 17

DC Fiona Jones pressed the button on the empty reception desk and waited. Presumably somewhere behind the secured inner doors a bell had gone off, announcing their presence.

Jenny had parked her car in the only visitor space outside the single storey, converted factory building. It was one of many similar buildings in the Slough Trading Estate; a sprawling industrial business park situated just west of London, built around its own power station – two mammoth brick chimneys visible for miles around. The only indication they'd chosen the right building was a small plaque just outside the front doors announcing the company's name, McCarthy Security Ltd.

Jenny studied the bare reception area. There was a complete absence of marketing; nothing to verify the sign outside was still valid. There were just two posters, both framed, one on fire alarm procedures and the other on health and safety laws. Three uncomfortable looking oval chairs were lined up against the back wall, under a television showing a muted BBC News channel. On the plain wooden reception desk sat a signing-in book. Jenny flicked through its blank sheets and commented, "I don't think they get many visitors."

"You'd think there'd be some CCTV cameras, given what they do," said Fiona.

"Maybe there's a load of secret cameras watching us right now," suggested Jenny, suddenly self-conscious.

"Where?" asked Fiona, lifting the picture frames containing the posters and bending down to look underneath. "There's nothing here."

Jenny recalled the Saxtons' kitchen. "I bet that smoke alarm on the ceiling is one."

"That's clever. Okay then, what about the exit sign above the front door?"

Jenny turned to look up at the illuminated sign. "Probably."

At the swoosh of the inner door opening behind them, both officers turned around.

"Just the two?" said a hugely overweight man, a smile on his face. He gave the two women a lascivious onceover, his smile broadening in appreciation.

"You were expecting more than two of us?" demanded Jenny, bristling at his blatant leer.

"No. I mean the number of secret cameras monitoring this area. You've only spotted two of them."

"How many are there then?" asked Fiona looking around.

"Plenty, including that one hidden in the carpet tile pointed up your skirt."

Fiona jumped backwards with a screech.

The man leaned back and guffawed loudly, his enormous belly rippling in rhythm with his laughter. "Hah, just joking. But you should have seen your face. From that reaction, I'm guessing you're not wearing any knickers. If only I'd known, I would have put a camera there."

"Oi, mate." Fiona's voice was caustic. "You can go —"

Jenny cut in, loudly. "Mr McCarthy?"

"*Oui, c'est moi.*" His Essex accent masked any hint of French. He showed no shame in his poor pronunciation.

Jenny flashed her warrant card. It had the desired effect.

"Fuck me, I'm well gutted. If I'd known you were the filth, I'd have . . . " He folded his arms across the expanse of belly. "Hah, I'd have done nothing different." His tone turned hostile. "What do you lot want?"

"We need to ask you some questions. About two webcam installations done by your company."

"Why, what's happened to attract the attention of the police? A camera fallen on someone's head or something?"

"No, it's a bit more serious than that, Mr McCarthy. This is about the murders of two young women."

"I don't understand."

"Well, if you did," said Fiona, still bristling from his earlier comment, "then that might make our conversation a damn sight more interesting."

"Is there somewhere we can talk properly?" Jenny glared at Fiona while speaking to McCarthy, emphasising what she said next: "We really need your help."

Fiona glanced at her feet: a muted apology.

"Uh, sure," said McCarthy; more amiable now that Jenny had played the damsel in distress card. Her experience of chauvinistic men — and she had no doubt from his sexist comments that McCarthy was a relic from an earlier age — was that it worked both ways; they could be downright rude, but they were usually the first to jump to a woman's rescue. "Come through to my office."

They followed McCarthy through the inner security door and into a short corridor. On one side was a massive window overlooking a room with tall benches, piled high with computer equipment. Two male employees, one with short dark hair, the other with blond hair in a ponytail, stopped working at the sight of the two police officers trailing behind their boss.

McCarthy stopped to offer some commentary. "This is our staging area. We preconfigure all our installations here before fitting them at our clients' premises. Just leaves the creative job of running all the wiring on site."

"Are your clients mostly residential?"

"Nah, that's just a sideline we've developed in the last few years, although it's turning out to be highly profitable. We face lots of competition for the major commercial contracts, so a nice run-rate of consumer IP webcam business is certainly helpful."

McCarthy opened the door at the end of the corridor. They followed him through, passing a kitchenette and a storeroom.

"Businesses don't use IP webcams then?" asked Fiona.

"Some do, especially if they're spying on their staff. But our core business is traditional CCTV installations. From builders wanting to secure their yards to councils installing city-centre control room systems, we do the lot. The best camera systems aren't hidden; they're on full show. If you see a camera is watching you, you're less likely to do anything dodgy. They're preventative."

He opened the door on the left and they entered a more traditional office area. Office workers, chairs, desks, phones, computers, filing cabinets and waste paper bins filled the large expanse. Windows looked out onto a staff car park, with one bright red Maserati standing proud amid its more prosaic neighbours.

"Welcome to my harem," proclaimed McCarthy, his arms open as if surveying his life's work.

Only then did Jenny realise that the seven or eight employees she could see were all women. In fact, they were all stunning-looking women. The two nearest looked up as they entered and threw their eyes up at McCarthy's line, obviously having heard it many times before.

"From order taking to invoicing and collection, my beauties here manage it all like a well-lubricated machine."

They followed him into a large glass-walled inner office, from where, Jenny surmised, McCarthy spent all day ogling his workforce. She felt nauseous at the thought of having to work for such a lech.

As they sat at the small meeting table in the corner, McCarthy offered them tea or coffee. Fiona chose tea. Jenny declined, requesting a glass of water instead. She still had a dull ache at the back of her head, no doubt dehydration caused by last night's unexpected excesses with Brody.

McCarthy stepped out and relayed the order to the nearest employee, presumably his secretary, referring to her as Sheila.

He joined them at the table, squeezing his huge behind into the small chair. "So how can I help?"

Jenny brought him up to speed with the facts he needed to know. Two victims having being raped and killed, both lured to their deaths under false pretences. Other than the MOs of the two crimes, the only common factors were that both women came from homes that had webcam systems installed by McCarthy's company.

"Surely that's just a coincidence?" Jenny noted that he asked the question more out of interest than defence.

"Perhaps, but there's another factor." Jenny nodded to Fiona, handing her the metaphorical baton, enabling Jenny to avoid the more technological aspects of the case.

"What's your relationship with HomeWebCam.com?" asked

Fiona.

"We're their only authorised implementation partner in the UK. Why, what's this got to do with anything?"

"So you do the installation and as part of it you link up the onsite network video recorder PC to HomeWebCam's remote access service?"

McCarthy was unable to hide his surprise. It was hard to tell whether it was because he was impressed with Fiona's technical accuracy or taken aback at a woman talking technology.

"Yes. We configure them to HomeWebCam's standard specifications, set it all up for the customer and train them how to log into the web service. And the best bit is that HomeWebCam covers the help desk support. If there's an onsite issue they'll call us back in. For a fee of course."

Sheila arrived with their drinks. As she placed them on the table, it occurred to Jenny that the girl presented herself in the way a porn star might play the part of a secretary, at least at the beginning of a scene when clothes were still involved: see-through cream blouse open to the cleavage, dark coloured bra, bright red lipstick, large glasses, long dark hair tied on top, short tight skirt and bare legs, all perched on top of impossibly high heels. Jenny wondered how McCarthy recruited these women and whether or not they were willing participants in his fantasy.

Fiona continued, "Have you heard of a site called SecretlyWatchingYou.com?"

"No. Should I?"

Fiona explained how some of the feeds from HomeWebCam were somehow also appearing on SecretlyWatchingYou. As she explained, McCarthy reached over to his desk and grabbed an iPad. He slowly entered the web address, stubby fingers making multiple mistakes on the tablet's glass surface, each one eliciting a light curse.

Fiona continued her explanations as he explored the site. She wheeled her chair around to his side and directed him to *Au Pair Affair*. As he studied the static images that previewed the location, he started shaking his head in disbelief. Fiona explained how the static images became live webcam footage once you were a paid-up customer. Jenny added their theory that the killer was using the site to observe his intended victims and utilise the private information he'd gleaned to lure them to the site of their murder.

He hollered through the glass window. "Sheila! Get Derek and Dave in here. Now!"

He turned to them. "This site is fucking unbelievable. Are you saying that every HomeWebCam site is on here?"

"We're not sure yet," said Jenny. "We know for sure that's the Saxtons' home. We think the other one was on there up until recently, but now that we've taken away the network video recorder PC you can't see it on the site. We haven't tracked down any other locations yet."

"Are these feeds from all over the world or just the UK?"

"Again, we're not sure yet."

"HomeWebCam must be supplying these feeds. It's the only thing that makes sense. Whether they're doing so knowingly is the question."

Jenny recalled Brody making the exact same statement this morning in the coffee shop.

The two men they'd seen in the staging room earlier entered the office. The dark haired one was introduced as Derek. The blond one was Dave. McCarthy brought them up to speed and asked them if they recognised any of the locations on SecretlyWatchingYou. As Derek and Dave hunched over the iPad, fingers and thumbs driving in and out of different locations, McCarthy explained. "These two cretins do most of the installs, at least the ones in the South East of the country. They might recognise some of the locations."

After a few minutes, they had identified three locations, in addition to the Saxtons'. McCarthy moved behind his desk and brought up details of the customers.

"I can't believe HomeWebCam would be this dumb. I'll phone Ken Toomey later, as soon as it's morning in the States. He's their CEO. He'll make sure this gets stopped."

"Don't worry," said Fiona, "He'll be getting a visit from his local police department."

It was one of the lines of enquiry they'd brainstormed that morning when the team had first got together. Da Silva, always keen to be the public face of what was becoming a high-profile case, had taken the action to contact San Francisco Police Department and request their support locally. Jenny suspected that Da Silva believed international exposure would be beneficial to his career. She had assigned herself and Fiona the more important lead of visiting the webcam installation company, which was starting to look like it would pay off, despite having to deal with the sleazeball who owned it.

The printer in the corner juddered to life. McCarthy reached over, grabbed the sheet of paper it produced and handed it to Fiona, explaining that it listed the addresses of the three locations identified by Derek and Dave.

"Lads," he addressed his two male employees, "Drop everything. I want you to sit yourselves in front of a proper PC each, register and pay — on expenses of course — for full access to this SecretlyWatchingYou site and have a proper look through it. See if there are any more locations that we've installed. Now."

Muttering their consent, the two men left the room.

"Thanks Mr McCarthy," said Jenny, "that's a good start. But there's more."

"What do you mean?"

"One of the other working theories we have, and the other reason for coming here, is that the common factor between the two murders is your business, not HomeWebCam. SecretlyWatchingYou might be getting its feeds through something you or one of your employees is doing."

"That's fucking outrageous!"

"Where were you last Friday between 4:00 p.m. and 8:00 p.m?" Jenny asked, pointedly.

Fiona added, "And the same times on Monday evening?"

"You're taking the piss."

"Do we look like we're joking?" Jenny retorted.

"Sheila," McCarthy called to his secretary with a sudden note of confidence. She opened the door and peered in. "Where was I last Friday night? And Monday?"

Without hesitation, Sheila spoke. Her accent was pure Essex, through and through. "Awe Nicky, I can't believe you even need to ask, my love. You was wiv me, remember? We had dinner at The Tramshed in Shoreditch on Friday. And on Monday, we saw *Billy Elliot* at The Palace in Victoria."

"Thanks Sheila: that will be all." Sheila pulled the door shut as she left them to it.

Jenny refused to allow her brain to imagine McCarthy and Sheila together. How the hell did a mid-twenties porn star-come-secretary end up with a forty-year-old lump of lard like McCarthy? And before the question had even fully formed, the answer was already there, embodied by the red Maserati parked outside.

Money.

"Anything else, ladies?" McCarthy's hostility was back.

Jenny bit her tongue and said what needed to be said. She needed his assistance first and foremost. "Sorry, Mr McCarthy, but you must understand, we had to ask. With two unsolved murders, we can't leave any stone unturned." Privately, Jenny resolved to verify Sheila's story later. Just in case it was a prearranged alibi.

McCarthy was somewhat mollified. 'Okay, I guess. But I can't believe that my firm, or anyone in it has anything to do with this."

"I'm sure that's true. But, we do need to eliminate everyone from our enquiries. I know it's a lot to ask, but we need a full list of all your staff and all your customers."

"But that's —"

"Just your IP webcam customers," clarified Fiona.

McCarthy grumbled, but didn't argue. Despite his Victorian ideals, McCarthy seemed inclined to help. Jenny decided to give him the benefit of the doubt.

They would crosscheck the employees against all known offender databases and then interview them one by one, verifying alibis. What action they took on the customer database was something she would need to discuss with Da Silva, but she had a proposal for him, one that might at least prevent another murder. For if anything was certain in Jenny's mind, the killer was not yet done.

Just over an hour later, McCarthy escorted them back through his office complex. Fiona held a USB stick full of data.

Returning to the reception area, Fiona asked the question that was also on Jenny's mind. "Out of interest, just how many hidden cameras *are* here?"

"Hah," his enthusiasm had returned during their subsequent conversations, as the focus shifted away from him as a suspect. "How many do you think? DC Jones, you first."

Fiona studied the room for a good thirty seconds, her fingers counting as she studied the room. "I'm going for three or four. The smoke alarm and the exit sign for sure. Then maybe the picture frame and the plant."

"And you, DI Price?"

"I'll add the little design holes in the reception desk to Fiona's list."

"Not bad. Six; all correct. The record for the most correct spots is eight."

"So how many are there?"

"Twenty-eight." He failed to conceal his pride. "We use the room to demonstrate to potential customers the creative ways we're able to hide these webcams. If you want, I can pop back to my office and grab my iPad, log into HomeWebCam and shown you them all."

"Next time, eh?" said Jenny, fully intending to delegate any follow-up activity that required spending further time in McCarthy's smutty presence. Unless one of his female employees lodged a sexual harassment complaint against McCarthy, then she'd personally come down and arrest the dinosaur.

Leroy placed a takeaway cup of coffee in front of Brody. It was from Bruno's, across the road.

"Blimey darling, cheer up. It may never happen, eh?"

"Told you Leroy, I'm not in the mood."

"Not in the mood? You're in the worst mood I've seen you in for ages. What's up?"

Brody was beaten, that's what was up. Crooner42 had wiped the floor with him. Fingal would probably never recover from this. His online persona wasn't just going to be taken down a peg or two; Crooner42 would ensure he was completely discredited in every deep web hacking community. Fingal's crown was going to be usurped by nothing more than a lowly script kiddie – as far as Brody knew, Crooner42 was not even a fully-fledged hacker.

And what was worse, Brody had no idea how he'd done it. SecretlyWatchingYou really was one of the most secure websites he'd ever come up against, resisting every exploit ever discovered. And that was Brody's problem, every *known* exploit. Anything known could be defended against. The only way Brody could win now was to deploy an *unknown* exploit, a zero day, an attack known to Brody but unknown to everyone else. No site could guard against an ambush from an unknown vector. But this line of thinking was only hypothetical. Brody had trawled through every hacker forum on the Internet and the deep web, even using an online translator on some of the obscure Russian communities, and had not found a single zero day mentioned that might work against SWY's configuration. He was even prepared to pay for one, that's how low he was willing to stoop to win. Although, as the thought passed through his mind, so did the typical going rate, which was usually in the hundreds of thousands of US dollars. Brody wasn't sure his reputation was worth that much.

So far, Brody had wasted two whole days trying to figure out how the video feeds arrived into SecretlyWatchingYou, convinced that this would expose the weakest point in the site's defences. And while that theory still held water, he'd only found the beginning of the trail. The video feeds were accessed and controlled from HomeWebCam but the trail went cold there. He felt like a tracker dog whose quarry had jumped in a fast-flowing stream to mask its scent. Maybe he should have used the last two days to try and develop a completely new zero day? But he knew from experience how hit and miss that was. The odds on uncovering a vector that might form the basis of a zero day exploit in under two days were almost nil, unless you were plain lucky.

Crooner42 was clearly much smarter than Brody or anyone else on CrackerHack had given him credit for. And, in the eyes of the hacking community, his victory over Fingal and Matt_The_Hatter would send his kudos through the roof.

"I'm completely stumped, Leroy."

"What, on this webcam site?"

"Yes."

"So what's the big deal? I thought you were just doing a favour for a mate, that's what you said the other day."

"Yeah, well, there's a bit more to it than that."

"Like what?"

"You wouldn't understand."

Leroy sat on the armchair, making a show that he was here to stay. "Normally, I'd agree with you and then I'd change the subject to something far more interesting and important," he beamed, "you know, like me. But as you did Danny and me a huge favour last night by giving us some privacy to celebrate our anniversary, I'm going to try and show an interest for once. So explain it to Uncle Leroy. What's the big deal?"

Brody tried his best to explain. Leroy tried his best to understand.

Despite himself, Brody began to feel a little better from talking it through.

"So this is all about you protecting your elite online status as Fingal? It's not about winning or losing?"

"Well . . . maybe a bit of both."

"So hackers are just like politicians on TV?"

"Eh? Not sure I follow you."

"The only currency you have is your popularity and status with the general public. Lose it and you become ostracised, fading into obscurity, wondering what to do with yourself. No longer listened to. No longer consulted. No fans. No letters from your constituents."

"You can't possibly compare hackers and politicians."

"I haven't finished. And with you being an *elite* hacker, you're like one of the ministers in the cabinet. And so this is like you being forced to resign from the cabinet. It doesn't mean you can never make it back in. It just means you have to do your time in exile, while the world forgets. And then eventually you can show up again."

Brody chuckled at the comparison. Surprisingly, it wasn't that far off the truth.

"Hah, a smile. I see my work here is done!"

Brody laughed and sat back in his chair, feeling some tension dissipate.

"So, how was your special night with Danny?"

"It was fantastic. I bought some oysters from Borough Market. Wanted to make sure we got some bedroom action going later, if you know what I mean."

Brody made a show of covering his ears with his hands. "Too much info, Leroy."

"Well, it worked. And with you out all night, well, let me tell you—"

"Leroy, stop. Please."

"That reminds me. Where'd you end up? You didn't come home."

"Nowhere." Brody allowed his voice to rise in pitch at the end, as if asking a question.

Leroy stared at him intently. "You never?"

"Never what?" Brody felt his cheeks flush.

"Bloody Nora. The policewoman. I knew it! I told Danny you were off chasing some policewoman you'd seen on a webcam."

"Her name's Jenny, if you must know."

"You little Casanova, you. Looks like you've got some new moves since our old Uni days. Well, at least it makes a change from women on that dating site. What did you tell her you did for a living?"

"Actually, I didn't stray that far from the truth."

"Really? So you told her you're a computer hacker?"

"No, of course not. She's a copper, Leroy. I told her I was an IT security consultant."

"Phah. You never learn." Leroy peered closely at Brody. "Ooh, you like this Jenny, eh? You can't stop smiling at the thought of her. Will you see her again?"

Was he that easy to read?

At that moment, Brody's phoned beeped with a message. He read it and, true to form, was unable to stop a massive grin spreading over his face.

He held up his phone. "Looks like it. She's just texted me."

"Well, I never. My best mate Brody, in a relationship that's lasting longer than one night. What's the text say?"

"Don't worry, it's not romantic. She's thanking me for my insights on the murder case."

"What? You've been helping to track down a killer? Do tell!"

Brody brought Leroy up to speed with what he knew about the two cases, Leroy's hands covering his mouth in horror.

"That's so exciting!"

"Yes, it is. But the reality is, two young girls have been killed. Makes it all very sobering."

"Finally discovering some meaning to what you do, eh Brody?"

"What's that supposed to mean?"

"Tell me, when was the last time you applied your hacking skills to actually help someone?"

Brody folded his arms.

"Come on Brody, answer the question. I'm being serious, here."

"On Monday then. When I helped Atlas Brands avoid a massive law suit from their number one competitor, which they would have lost."

"Brody, listen to yourself, will you?" Leroy placed a hand on

Brody's knee, an intimate gesture to remind Brody that Leroy was his friend and was trying only to help. "When was the last time you helped a human being, not some faceless corporation?"

Brody fought the urge to pull away, to withdraw. He knew where Leroy was going. It was yet another version of their recurring argument over Brody prioritising virtual relationships over real-world ones. Usually they just agreed to disagree. But this time, as Leroy held his gaze, Brody realised maybe there was something in what Leroy was trying to say. Brody lowered his eyes.

"You've got so much to offer the world, Brody," Leroy continued gently, "You've got all these skills and enough money not to have to work for a living. You could make such a difference, you know. You shouldn't waste all your talent competing with people who are little more than ones and zeros."

Brody chewed his lip. Leroy was calling into question Brody's whole lifestyle. *His whole existence.* Brody would normally lash out in defence. But this time there was something in what Leroy was saying. Only yesterday, he'd stood in Anna Parker's bedroom and felt very uncomfortable. Her personal belongings lay strewn about, awaiting her return. But he'd realised she never would. And Kim Chang, her grieving best friend, putting on a brave face, but those dark rings under her eyes gave away the hours of crying. He recalled Hilary Saxton discovering her husband had been cheating, right under her nose; their lives now ruined. And then there was Jenny Price. Their night together. And now, her simple thank-you text.

In just one day, he'd witnessed more raw emotion than every other day in the last year put together. It had changed something in him.

And despite generally being completely insufferable, here was Leroy, his best friend for so many years trying to reach out to him. To help him understand that there was a different way to live his life. To give it some meaning. To stop him hiding from meatspace with all its wonderful, and terrible, happenings. To prioritise his existence in the real world over his status in the virtual.

Maybe he should just give up on trying to pwn SWY. For once in his life, maybe he should accept that being the best — no, being seen to be the best — wasn't actually necessary. After all, whom was he trying to impress? Crooner42, Matt_The_Hatter, Doc_Doom, Random_Ness, Mawrpheus, and all those other faceless forum idiots. Who the hell were these people anyway? He'd never met them, that was for sure. And if he somehow bumped into them in real life, he doubted whether he'd enjoy their company much anyway.

Brody, whose eyes had closed as he lost himself in these thoughts, was only peripherally aware that Leroy had quietly withdrawn to his room, leaving him to process it all.

This line of thinking was far too hard. He knew then and there, that he was at one of those life-changing moments. The implications were massive. He hated Leroy for forcing him to think about it all.

It was time to make a decision.

But not that decision. Restructuring and re-prioritising his whole lifestyle necessitated plenty more contemplation. He'd think about all that stuff another day.

Brody decided to focus on something else. Anything else.

His thoughts turned to Jenny and the murder cases. There *was* something he could do to help her again, he realised.

As he turned towards his computer, Brody noticed the takeaway coffee cup Leroy had bought for him. He grabbed it and raised it in the direction of Leroy's room, silently toasting his best friend.

She was early, far too early.

The massive digital clock on the wall said 10:35 a.m. Surely she would look too eager.

"Can I help you?" asked one of the two glamorous receptionists. The visitor who had been in front squeezed back past her and made his way to the waiting area behind the queue. Sarah stepped forward, and stood beside a sharp-suited man, with gold cufflinks and a handkerchief protruding from his top pocket, being attended to by the other receptionist.

"Yes, I'm here to meet Francis Delacroix," she announced.

"Which company, please?"

"FCS Software."

The receptionist moved the mouse on her computer screen, clicking and dragging. Her brow furrowed. "Delacroix? Sorry, I can't find him listed under FCS."

Just as Sarah was about to spell out his name, the second receptionist interrupted her handling of her visitor and spoke across the desk to her colleague, "Mr Delacroix is in meeting room 612. He phoned down earlier and left a message saying to call him when his guests arrived."

Guests? More than one? Sarah was suddenly concerned that, despite what he'd said on the phone yesterday, he'd organised meetings with other aviation industry magazine titles. She knew full well there were three others in the UK that might meet his needs. Damn. Competition would undoubtedly drive down her price.

The receptionist turned her attention back to Sarah with a smile. "Please can you sign in?"

Sarah filled in her details in the visitor's book. The receptionist turned it around and, following the serrated edges, cleanly ripped out the piece of paper and placed it in a plastic holder with a clip. She handed it over to Sarah.

"I'll just phone through now, Ms McNeil."

Sarah glanced nervously at the clock again. "Actually, I'm a bit early for my meeting. I'll wait over there for a bit. Then you can phone through, if that's okay?"

The receptionist shrugged and looked beyond Sarah to the person waiting behind. She'd been dismissed.

Sarah perched on the edge of one of the two leather sofas. It was far too deep to sit back in and maintain a professional demeanour. Then she wondered if perhaps she should stand like the other three visitors, all quietly waiting for their hosts to arrive.

She realised that the building was much bigger than it had looked from the street outside, where only two glass revolving doors and an opaque window made up its frontage. Beyond the reception desk, flanked on either side by turnstiles barring access to unescorted guests, she could see a large open atrium that reached right up to a glass ceiling. Glass lifts on either side of the atrium silently ascended and descended between the building's five levels. On each, an open landing provided access to numerous offices and meeting rooms.

The time passed slowly for Sarah, causing her to become more and more nervous about meeting Mr Delacroix. Eventually, the clock told her there were ten minutes to go. That was far more respectable. Not too early. Not too eager.

Sarah stood and caught the eye of the receptionist that had dealt with her. She mimed making a phone call and the receptionist nodded her understanding and picked up her phone. After a short conversation, the receptionist called over, "Mr Delacroix said he'll be down to meet you in a couple of minutes."

Sarah remained standing, took a deep breath and waited.

"What a dinosaur," stated Fiona, indicating left as she approached the roundabout for the M4 motorway, which would take them back into Central London.

"I know. I thought his type went out with the ark," Jenny replied. "And his receptionist, Sheila. Can you believe that?"

"I guess it takes all sorts."

"Well, at least we've finally had a break in the case." Jenny held up the USB stick containing McCarthy Security's customers.

Hopefully, it contained the addresses of all the UK locations being covertly broadcast by SecretlyWatchingYou. She'd come up with an approach that might work and had already walked Da Silva through it on the phone while Fiona slowly navigated her Volvo out of Slough, through heavy traffic. Da Silva was already putting in manpower requests to support her suggestion.

When they got back to Holborn, they would put together a central team of officers who would log into SecretlyWatchingYou, cycling through the hundreds of locations on the site. It galled her that public money would be spent by officers registering for upgraded access to the premium video feeds on the site, but they needed to gain access to *all* of the cameras. They would then send police officers to every address on the USB stick around the country, over a thousand of them. It would require liaison with nearly every force in England and Wales. And maybe even Scotland, depending on the addresses. Da Silva's voice had failed to hide his excitement at having to coordinate resources from so many forces, an activity Jenny suspected he saw as something that would raise his profile even further.

Then, as each address was visited by local forces, the central team would observe all of the webcams on SecretlyWatchingYou to see if they could spot uniformed officers on any of the cameras. If none were spotted, they could eliminate the address. But if seen, they would inform the webcam owners about the fact that their webcams had been hacked by SecretyWatchingYou and leave it to them to decide if they wanted to turn off their cameras. She knew it would cause an uproar, with so many people around the country discovering that their private lives had been broadcast all over the Internet, but it was a necessary step to cut off the killer's food supply. It may not help them catch him, but at least they might prevent further deaths.

As Fiona accelerated the Volvo up the slip road to join the M4, Jenny's phone rang. She looked at the caller display and saw Brody's name. He was probably just ringing her back following the text she had sent him from McCarthy's earlier. It had just been a simple thank-you as his idea about the webcam installers had worked out so well. But it had also been an excuse to stay in touch after their night together. And — she felt the red rising in her cheeks at the thought of it — their breakfast.

"Aren't you going to answer it?" asked Fiona, turning briefly to study her.

Jenny clicked the 'decline' button. "Nah, it's only my Mum."

"Why are you blushing, then?" enquired Fiona, with a smirk.

Her phone buzzed again. A text this time. Glad of the distraction, she clicked on it.

Her heart jumped into her mouth.

Brody stared at his phone on the desk next to his computer. It had full signal. Why didn't she ring him back?

He stood up and paced around the room, circling his desk so that he could quickly grab the phone when it rang. She would ring. She had to.

Was there something else he could do? Someone else he could call?

No, just give her one more minute.

Like a caged lion, he paced around the mobile phone, then picked it up and re-checked the text he'd sent, just to make sure it was strong enough.

Ring me URGENTLY. Discovered location of killer's next murder. Happening RIGHT NOW. Brody.

After his talk with Leroy earlier, when he'd finally thrown in the towel on trying to pwn SWY, he'd turned his attention to helping Jenny with her case. At least he'd be trying to help someone, a real person, just as Leroy had suggested.

Brody had decided to find out for himself if the Flexbase meeting room booking system stored the IP address of whoever connected to their site when they booked a meeting room. Brody hadn't been at all convinced when Magnus Peggler, the Flexbase IT Director, had said they needed to ask the vendor of the system to access that information. It just didn't make sense, when all he had to do was access the application's back-end database with a few SQL queries. Any techie with half a brain could do that. If the police knew the IP address that the killer used when booking the meeting room, then they would obtain a court order and force the Internet Service Provider to divulge the real world location of the IP address's owner.

Brody obtained access to Flexbase's internal systems via the back door Trojan he'd installed the previous day, when he'd visited their head office with Jenny. It had been an impromptu action. Even now, he wasn't sure why he'd done it. At the time, he hadn't been sure if Flexbase somehow played into the whole SWY setup and so, to be on the safe side, he'd taken the opportunity to give himself easy future access should he ever need it.

At least that was what Brody told himself.

But part of him knew that he'd done it because he *could*. Like a sweet-toothed kleptomaniac stealing a cake when the baker's back is turned, Brody had installed his remote access Trojan on David Dawson's laptop. As Jenny and Brody followed Dawson to seek out Ray Stone, Brody had made up an excuse that he'd left his phone in the CEO's office and ran back for it. In the privacy of Dawson's office, he'd jumped onto Dawson's computer and navigated its browser to one of Brody's compromised websites. It had immediately installed a special payload on Dawson's computer, ready for whenever Brody chose to use it. Brody had closed down the browser and rushed back to Jenny and Dawson, waving his phone at them.

Through this back door, Brody had full control of Dawson's laptop, its owner completely unaware it had been enslaved and was being accessed remotely. Dawson was CEO of the company and so he had decent security access. Even so, it didn't take Brody long to elevate to administrator level and grant himself access to all other servers on the Flexbase network.

He poked around, trying to stumble across the meeting room booking system from within. What he discovered provided far more information than he could have expected.

The building control system was web-based and soon he found himself looking at status dashboards for the Docklands building. By floor, he could see air conditioning, temperature, as well as how many people were present, based on entry and exit through the building's security system. He was able to patch into its CCTV system. He found the cameras above the reception, noticing the redheaded super-model receptionist. The blonde one was absent. He found cameras monitoring the secure datacentre room on the floor above, neat rows of computer racks. He clicked through to the dashboards for the datacentre and saw real-time graphs displaying the flow of electricity, battery charges within the uninterruptible power supply should the external power supply drop, and even the status of oxygen levels within the room. The datacentre employed a hypoxic fire suppression system that lowered the amount of oxygen in the room to below the amount required for combustion to take place, but high enough to breathe safely.

Brody was intrigued; he'd never hacked into a building control system before. Most of them were proprietary systems, and not usually connected to the IP network, making it almost impossible to gain access remotely. But Flexbase had installed the most ultra modern systems in order to show off their prowess. If only they knew that by doing so, they had opened themselves up to attack. It was a good job he wasn't a black hat or performing a pentest; he'd have a field day.

Eventually, he discovered the back-end database server used by the meeting room booking system and gave himself full access.

He ran some initial sizing queries and, discovering that it wasn't that huge, downloaded a complete copy of the database so that, offline, he could safely analyse it to his heart's content. It didn't take long for him to find the database table with the core booking records. He scanned the columns and clenched his fist in triumph. There was indeed a column in the table that stored IP addresses.

Filtering the records based on the dates of the murders and the locations of Paddington and Watford, Brody rapidly homed in on the meeting room bookings made by the killer. The IP addresses used for both bookings were the same. Excited, Brody quickly cut-n-pasted the address into a reverse IP lookup website to see if it could shed any light on the real world location.

To his initial surprise, a specific address in the town of Newbury in Berkshire was listed.

Newbury? Wasn't there something about Newbury?

After a moment, Brody remembered what it was and smiled grimly at the screen. The murderer was either dead lucky or dead smart. The address was for Vodafone, the massive mobile phone company, with headquarters located in Newbury. Which meant that the murderer had accessed the meeting room booking website via his mobile phone. Brody couldn't take it any further himself without access to Vodafone's systems. However, the police could work with Vodafone to obtain the mobile phone number mapped to the IP address at the time the booking system was accessed.

If they were lucky, the phone number would come with a name and address of the account owner. However, if it was a pay-as-you-go number, there would likely be no details. Brody was pretty sure it would be pay-as-you-go. No one would be that stupid. Especially someone intent on committing murder.

Brody ran a query using the IP address as the search key to see if the murderer had made any more bookings. He was shocked at the results when he saw hundreds of records. But then he realised that many Flexbase customers must access the system from mobile devices connected in via the Vodafone network.

Brody was about to stop there but, staring at the raw records of the Watford meeting room booking on his screen, he noticed something. Following the train of thought, he quickly brought up the Paddington booking and saw the same pattern. In both cases, the murderer had booked more than one room in the building. Brody recalled Jenny explaining this yesterday.

Brody reckoned that it would be unusual for multiple meeting rooms to be booked at the same time by the same person. And with that in mind, he constructed a query against the database that searched all Flexbase offices for meeting room bookings with a similar pattern. He narrowed it down to the last six months. After a few refinements, the query returned the two bookings he knew about, as they naturally fitted the pattern.

But there were also four others.

Brody stared at his screen, initially not believing the breakthrough he'd achieved. He checked the IP address used to make the bookings and saw that it was the same. He'd found four more of the murderer's bookings. Four they knew nothing about.

And then he spotted the date and time of the first booking. It was for today in a Flexbase office in Windsor. He looked at his watch with a sinking feeling. Shit, the reservation had begun fifty minutes ago.

Immediately he'd phoned Jenny, but had got no answer. He'd left a voicemail and then rapidly typed out his text to her.

The other three reservations were for dates over the next few weeks, in different Flexbase offices all over the country.

Still pacing around the desk, Brody willed his phone to ring.

When it did, it made him jump. He grabbed at it, clumsily knocking it flying off his desk. But his adrenalin was flowing now and he managed to grab it before it hit the hardwood floor.

"Jenny, he's struck again."

CHAPTER 18

"Miss McNeil?"

Sarah had been surprised to hear her name come from the man's lips.

She'd been playing the guessing game as internal staff came down to greet their guests. It was a busy reception with a constant stream of visitors. Each time a man exited the lifts behind reception and made his way through the turnstiles, she'd predicted whether or not he was Francis Delacroix. So far, she'd been wrong twice. Both times the person had called out someone else's name and escorted them back through security. Sarah was expecting a middle-aged gentleman, overweight from too many client lunches, and wearing a sharp suit without a tie, his shirt collar open — after all, she knew he was American.

She had completely discounted the man who was greeting her now, with his dark beard and moustache. He wore black jeans, black boots, a plain black sweatshirt, a black cap and large dark sunglasses. The only colour was the flash of gold in the prominent Adidas logo embroidered on his cap.

"Oh, I'm sorry. Yes I'm Sarah McNeil."

Hesitantly, she held out her hand.

"Francis sent me down to collect you. He's stuck on a conference call with the States." With a slight smirk, he stared at her outstretched hand. As if making an important decision, he finally reached out his own and they shook hands lightly. She couldn't help but notice his sweaty palms and she did her best not to wipe her own hand after he turned his back and headed towards the security turnstiles.

Rather than go through the staff turnstile, he waved a security pass at the receptionist and stood by the glass door. The receptionist pressed a button and it swung backwards, allowing them both through.

The lift opened silently at the press of a button. Inside he pressed 'six', the top floor. The doors glided to a close.

Sarah stood slightly behind the man. She was disconcerted by his casual appearance and complete lack of graces. He hadn't introduced himself and offered no small talk. He hadn't even looked her in the eye, although it was hard to tell behind those dark sunglasses. And anyway, why the hell was he wearing them indoors?

Sarah collected herself. In her mind, she rehearsed her opening chitchat, reminding herself to politely ask about Mr Delacroix's flight. She tapped the leather satchel hanging from her shoulder. Inside were the last six issues of *Commercial Aviation News*. She would walk Mr Delacroix through them. She straightened her skirt and made sure her blouse was tucked in.

The doors opened and, without a word, the man stepped out and turned left. Sarah followed. Half-height sections of clear glass between the building's structural pillars acted as a continuous wall, preventing anyone plummeting six floors to certain death. She glanced into the open space of the atrium and was abruptly reminded that she was uncomfortable with heights. She immediately adjusted the line of her walk so that she was within touching distance of the grey wall on her left, which made its way right around the perimeter of the atrium, regularly interrupted with numbered oak doors.

At Room 613, the man stopped, opened it and indicated she should enter.

"I'll go get Mr Delacroix."

Sarah entered the meeting room and looked back to see the strange man close the door behind her. She was alone.

An oak meeting table with eight black leather and chrome chairs took up most of the space. A large window looked out onto the town. At this height, she had a wonderful view of Windsor Castle. She wondered if the Queen was in residence. Sarah had once toured the castle on a school trip and recalled that the Queen often held Easter Court during March and April. She spotted a Union Jack flying above the castle, but then couldn't remember whether its presence meant the Queen was there or not.

Admonishing herself for not keeping her mind focused on her meeting, Sarah turned her back on the view.

She placed her satchel on one of the chairs and then noticed tea and coffee flasks, cups and saucers, bottles of water and upside-down glasses laid out neatly on a side table. There were even biscuits, which made her realise she'd skipped breakfast. She wondered whether she should pour herself a drink, but decided it was probably more professional to wait for her host. But maybe, if she was quick, she could sneak just one biscuit? Their presence had set her stomach off. She was starving. She even felt an ominous rumble and then began worrying that it would be audible during her meeting. Damn, what a basic mistake to have made.

The door opened.

Sarah turned to greet Francis Delacroix, only to find that it was the same man again, still wearing his cap and sunglasses. She did her best to mask her disappointment. He walked around the table towards her.

"Mr Delacroix said he'll only be another five minutes." With one hand he indicated the beverages, the other remained behind his back. "Would you like a cuppa while you're waiting?"

"Uh, yes thanks."

The man made to move past her, but she said, "It's okay, I can make it." If he left, then with five minutes' wait she could munch through a few biscuits and stop her stomach from gurgling.

She turned her back on him and took a cup, trying to decide between tea or coffee. She reached for the coffee flask.

"You stupid fucking bitch."

Sarah froze, her arm still outstretched, trying to process what she'd heard. His voice was deathly in intent. Before she could stop herself, she felt her chin begin to tremble and her legs weaken.

"You come here dressed like that?" He was right behind her, breathily whispering into her ear. "You're begging for it again. You always do, you fucking whore."

Sarah realised she'd made a dreadful mistake.

Instinct took over; fight definitely overcoming her flight

response. Slowly, as if she hadn't heard anything, she gripped the coffee flask. She lifted it, feeling the weight, pretending to pour, as if she hadn't heard him speak.

"This time," he breathed into her ear, "You're going to beg."

Without warning, Sarah pivoted on the spot, swinging the coffee flask with all her might at the man's head. But he was ready, as if he had sensed her intentions, and skipped back a step. Sarah's momentum carried her all the way round, the flask crashing into the meeting room wall and dropping from her hands. Before it had even hit the floor, Sarah spotted the hand the man had kept hidden behind his back. It thrust towards her. Clasped within it was a large dagger. With crushing force, he smashed her on the side of the head with its weighty handle.

Sarah lost consciousness before she hit the floor.

"You've just had a visitor come in for Francis Delacroix. Where is she?" demanded Jenny breathlessly, Fiona right behind her. She scanned the visitors in the waiting area behind, but they were all men. Her eyes darted to the clock on the wall. Damn, they were too late.

The Flexbase receptionist arched an eyebrow at her colleague as if Jenny wasn't there. The other receptionist, clearly the more senior, shrugged.

"I'm a police officer." Jenny hunted urgently through her pockets for her ID, switching to the senior receptionist. "She's in danger. Tell me, where she is?"

"I'll have to get the building manager down," replied the receptionist, picking up the phone.

"There's no time for that!" shouted Fiona. She reached over the counter and grabbed the visitor signing-in book. She quickly looked at the most recently logged visitors. "She's here. Her name's Sarah McNeil. Look, signed in for F Delacroix from FCS. Only twenty-five minutes ago!"

"Tell me where FCS is?" commanded Jenny.

Dumbfounded, the receptionist remained silent. But her junior colleague stammered, "R-room 520. On the f-fifth floor."

Jenny jumped over the security barrier and ran for the lifts. She heard Fiona right behind her.

Jenny pressed the button.

And waited.

Impatiently, Fiona stared at her superior. "Fuck it," she said suddenly. "I'll see you up there." She sprinted off across the middle of the atrium, heading towards a large staircase.

The lift arrived. The doors slowly slid open. Just as Jenny was about to press the fifth button, she saw the junior receptionist running towards her.

"Room 520 is FCS's offices. But they're in 612. It's a meeting room on the sixth floor."

Jenny nodded her thanks and pressed 'six'. The doors closed.

As the lift climbed the wall, Jenny looked through its circular glass into the open area of the atrium. She could see that Fiona had made it to the stairs and was taking them two steps at a time. Fruitlessly, she tried waving to catch her attention, but Fiona's head was down. Jenny reached into her jacket pocket for her mobile to call her colleague, but it was empty. Damn, she'd left it in Fiona's car.

The lift dinged its arrival on the sixth floor. Jenny ran out, translated from the sign immediately ahead that her direction was left. She ran along the corridor. 601, 602, 603 . . .

Fleetingly she considered shouting to Fiona across the atrium that it was the sixth floor, not the fifth. But that might alert the killer. The thought made her quiver in fear as she flew past 609. She shook her head, forcing the negative thoughts out of her mind. She had been trained for this.

612.

Jenny halted, breathing heavily. She couldn't see anything through the opaque glass walls of the meeting room. She listened and, not hearing anything, decided on the only logical course of action.

She threw open the door and burst in.

The room was completely empty.

Sarah's eyes flickered open as consciousness slowly returned.

She tried to take stock of where she was.

A castle filled her vision. Was she dreaming? She sometimes had a recurring nightmare of being trapped in a tower and being rescued by her prince, only for the moat to sprout flames and the drawbridge burn before he could cross over on his white steed, trapping her forever more. Usually she awoke at that point, consciousness calming her that it had all been a dream. But now, even though she knew she was awake, the castle was still there.

She felt something slide up her back. Suddenly she felt cool air conditioning on the exposed skin of her back, reaching all the way down to her knees. And then it all came rushing back.

Sarah screamed.

But her mouth was gagged completely. She only managed a muffled sound.

She lay face down on the meeting room table. She could feel stickiness on her cheek and lifted her head. A pool of blood lay on the table. The side of her head felt numb. She realised she was the source of the blood and panicked. Trying to rise, she discovered her hands were bound together. Still, she pushed her body up by her wrists. She could feel the floor through her feet. Her high heels were gone.

"Stay still, whore."

The whisper was right in her ear.

Sarah froze, trying to judge the situation. The window with the castle view provided some reflection. The Union Jack was spluttering in the light wind. Dark clouds formed in the distance. She could just about make out his silhouette. He stood behind her, between her legs, leaning over to whisper. Seeing a glint in the window, her heart leapt into her mouth, as she made out what appeared to be a massive dagger in his right hand. Her clothes had been sliced open at the rear, trails of skirt and blouse having fallen to the table, only held in place because she lay on them.

To emphasise his command, her attacker placed the knife under her windpipe. She could feel the cold steel edge pierce her skin.

Tears formed. Saliva dribbled from her lips.

She felt him fumble behind her. His left hand brushing her naked skin. And, with burning clarity, she understood that he was opening his flies.

She screamed again, the sound caught in her mouth by the cloth gag.

Jenny stared aghast at the empty meeting room.

She was shaking with adrenalin. She had the right room, didn't she?

The receptionist had said 612. Jenny stepped out of the room and checked the number outside. Yes, 612. She looked over the balcony, but it was too far to shout to the reception and be heard.

Thinking quickly, she ran back in the room and grabbed the phone in the middle of the desk. She dialled '0', praying that it would ring on reception downstairs.

It was answered straight away. She recognised the voice of the senior receptionist.

"There's no one in 612," she panted. "Are you sure you've got the right room for Francis Delacroix?"

"Give me a second."

Jenny waited, forcing herself not to shout obscenities down the phone.

"Well, that's odd. He's got all five meeting rooms on that side of the building booked. From 611 to 615."

Jenny wanted to bash her head with her hand in disgust. *Of course*. He'd booked more than one so he wouldn't be overheard or interrupted. Just like in Paddington and Watford. He was in one of the neighbouring rooms.

She dropped the line and stepped out of the room. Left or right. She chose right. There was only one room to cover in that direction. Outside 611, she paused to listen. Again nothing.

Jenny threw open the door and rushed in. The door slammed against the wall. The room was empty.

Quickly, she stepped back out and made her way to 613.

Taking a deep breath, she threw open the door again. Just as she was about to rush in, a figure, all in black, rushed at her and knocked her back. Flailing, she staggered backwards. The man flew after her and pushed her hard once more, sending her sprawling. She tried to turn but crashed her side into the glass half-wall. Her momentum tipped her upper body over the railing and into the open space of the atrium. She grabbed the railing, but her assailant gave her one final push and she felt herself topple over.

Even from this height, Jenny could see the solid marble floor of the building far below. People in the atrium seating area were looking up and pointing at her to each other, their mouths open in shock. Jenny felt gravity take hold and began to plummet.

* * *

You are filled with righteous fury. How dare anyone interrupt you in the middle of it? Especially another woman!

You shoved her out of the room with all the force you could muster.

You surprised her as she opened the door. But that was because you were ready. You'd heard the bang of the door in the next room. You guessed you were about to be interrupted by someone. But you were surprised when it was female.

You watch in silent fascination as she cartwheels over the side, her legs flying overhead. Her body begins to fall.

Going . . . Going . . .

— but at the last moment, her hand reaches out and grabs the railing on top of the glass wall. Her body pivots and you see her hips smash into the concrete floor, jutting out beneath the glass wall. She screams in pain but grips even tighter, despite the momentum her legs have developed in the open space of the corridor beneath threatening to pull her hand away.

She hangs by one hand, taking deep breaths. You can hear screams from insects down below.

You peer over, ready to prise her hand from the railing and finish it. Insects are pointing up at you both, screaming. You focus on her.

"You fucking whore," you snarl, unable to stop yourself. You want her to pay for interrupting. You stare at her stricken face.

Unexpectedly, you recognise her. You immediately suppress the implications of that. You can deal with all that later. But there is one implication you can't get past. You will miss out on this one. What a shame.

You whisper gently. "Why did it have to be you? Such a waste."

Her face shows confusion as she hangs on.

Reluctantly, you grab her hand and begin to lift a finger.

"No, please don't," she begs.

Yes, she begs, just like they all do. Eventually.

And then her expression changes. A calmness falls over her. She stares at him intently, almost as if she can see through his dark sunglasses.

"What do you mean, such a waste?" she asks you, almost inquisitively, as if the situation were just a normal conversation over tea.

You stop lifting her fingers. Just for a moment.

"You would have been good. That's the shame of it. Far better than that whore in there." You nod your head backwards at the meeting room behind you.

"Then let me go," she says, steadily.

And for just a second you think about letting her go. Maybe you could line her up another time.

"The building is surrounded by police. Don't make it worse for yourself."

And you realise that the whore is just tricking you. Playing for time. Playing for her life.

You resume prising her fingers from the railing. As her grip begins to slide you say to her, "Goodbye, Detective Inspector Jenny Price."

And despite the imminent fall to her death, her face contorts in shock at the sound of her name. Her fingers lose their grip completely. You stand back and watch her body drop from view through the glass wall.

Such a shame.

She really would have been perfect.

You hear screams from below. They bring you to your senses.

You run for it.

After fifteen minutes, Brody gave up pacing the room, waiting for Jenny to let him know what had happened. He decided to head over the road to Bruno's. He grabbed his tablet PC and wallet and slammed the front door shut behind him, only then recalling with a wince that Leroy had disappeared back to bed. For once he deserved his morning lie-in. If it hadn't been for Leroy's earlier counsel advising Brody to apply his skills to helping real people, he wouldn't have discovered the killer's latest meeting room booking. He just hoped Jenny had made it in time to save whoever had been lured to their death.

When Jenny had finally returned his call Brody had hurriedly explained *what* he'd found, neatly avoiding the *how* of it. Shocked but then suddenly very hopeful, she quickly pointed out that there might still be time to save the victim. In the two previous instances, the killer had reserved the meeting room an hour before the victim's scheduled meeting time. She asked which Flexbase building it was so that she could contact the local force to storm the place. When he told her it was in Windsor, she swore loudly. They were only a few miles away but had just joined the M4 heading back towards London. Brody jumped on Google maps and instructed her to exit at the very next junction. There was a back way through the village of Datchet, skirting alongside both banks of the Thames straight into Windsor from the east. While on the phone, Jenny frantically relayed directions to her colleague, who was driving. When they finally screeched to a halt outside the building, she curtly thanked him and hung up.

And that was the last he'd heard.

"Ah, good timing Mr Brody, you're usual seat has just become free. Please sit down."

Stefan's toothy grin barely broke through Brody's daze. Numbly he sat down. The waiting was killing him. He looked at his watch. It was now twenty minutes. Why hadn't she phoned him back?

"Okay, let me see. Late morning. Too late for cappuccino. Too early for espresso. Maybe a macchiato?" Eliciting no response, not even a subtle shake of the head, Stefan looked confused.

Brody hadn't heard a word. On autopilot, he sat in his chair and opened his computer, just for something to do. At least Jenny hadn't asked him the obvious question about how he'd come by the information about the killer's meeting room reservation. But he knew it would come. He'd need to come up with a good story.

"Maybe Mr Brody would like . . ." Stefan couldn't hold back a chuckle, " . . . a large white chocolate mocha with a double caramel shot?"

Brody nodded absently, causing the barista to be taken aback. He stomped off, muttering to himself.

Brody connected to his private Wi-Fi network.

He had loads of open windows from his hacking session into Flexbase. He began closing them down, one by one. After a few minutes, he was presented with his web browser displaying the kitchen webcam feed from the Saxton household via SWY. Brody stopped what he was doing and studied Hilary Saxton, who sat at the kitchen table alone, staring into space. Scrunched tissues lay strewn about the table, evidence of her grief. Surely she couldn't have forgotten that nearly every room in her house was still being broadcast over the Internet, including the kitchen? She really must be in a state.

Maybe he could help.

And as the thought flew through his mind, he realised that his earlier conversation with Leroy was still working its way through his subconscious. Here he was, for the second time in one day, choosing to apply his skills to help a real person.

Brody still had remote access to the network video PC in the Saxton house. It sat there; permanently capturing the Wi-Fi webcam feeds from all over the house, sending them through the Internet to HomeWebCam. And somehow, from there, they were making their way over to SWY. But, if Brody remotely shut down the network video PC, the webcams would no longer broadcast over the Internet at all.

And Hilary Saxton would at least have some privacy.

Brody remotely logged into the Saxton PC. He quickly hit the 'shutdown' command. Brody waited for his remote control session to drop. Without power, the PC could no longer be connected. After a minute, the session dropped.

Brody switched back to his SecretlyWatchingYou view of Hilary Saxton still sat at her kitchen table. She grabbed a fresh tissue and blew her nose. Brody recalled that there was a time lag of a couple of minutes as the video streams made their way over the Internet, via the SWY servers and back to viewers like him. The feed would soon go black.

He waited.

Stefan returned, placing a massive mug down on the table next to Brody. It was full of frothy milk with sprinkles of chocolate on the top in the shape of a lightning bolt.

"What the hell is that?" asked Brody, incredulously.

"Is what you ordered, Mr Brody," laughed Stefan, good-naturedly. "Is large white chocolate mocha with a double caramel shot. Lovely, no?"

"I ordered that?" Brody looked around at the other patrons to see if anyone else wanted to claim it.

Stefan shrugged.

"Ah, what the hell. Thanks Stefan. You read me right again."

Stefan tittered like a child and left him to it.

Brody sat back holding the coffee in both hands. He took a sip. Despite being far too sweet, it wasn't that bad. He turned to the front window and began to watch life go by on Upper Street outside.

After a good ten minutes, Brody placed the empty mug on the table.

His PC had gone into power-saving mode, the screen darkening. He moved the mouse pointer and the windows returned.

The browser window displaying the Saxton's household in SWY was still there. Hilary Saxton had laid her head down on the table and was frozen in position. Odd. Maybe when the network video PC had shut down, the last image had remained static in SWY's feed.

He moved the mouse to shut down the window.

Just as he was about to close it, Hilary Saxton stood up and walked out of the kitchen.

Brody's jaw dropped. That was impossible. The network video PC in their house was powered off. Yet SWY was still broadcasting the Saxton household.

The shock soon receded as his logical brain took over; attempting to rewire everything it had thought about how the webcam feeds made their way through to SecretlyWatchingYou.

Brody thumped his palm against his forehead. What an idiot he'd been.

He knew how it was done. Maybe, he would crack SecretlyWatchingYou after all.

Further back in the coffee shop, Crooner42 watched Fingal fold up his computer, leave some money on the table and rush out. He crossed the road, jumping back briefly to avoid a cyclist speeding up between the stationary cars. On the opposite pavement, Fingal fished out some keys and let himself through his front door.

When Crooner42 had approached the coffee shop a few minutes earlier, he'd spotted Fingal through the front window, sitting in the same seat as the previous evening. He almost walked past to ensure he wasn't spotted, but Fingal was staring into the middle distance, completely lost in thought, clutching a massive mug. He took a calculated risk and entered, walking right past the hacker, relying on his peripheral vision to see if Fingal noticed him. Not a flicker.

Most of the tables had been occupied, but he'd found one near the back.

After a few minutes, his order taken by the waiter and Fingal having left, Crooner42 powered up his laptop.

He connected to the 'F!NG@L' Wi-Fi network and waited for the prompt to enter the WPA2 password.

When he'd woken this morning, an email from CloudCracker had been waiting in his inbox containing the clear-text password for Fingal's private Wi-Fi network. It was 'St@ffa1772'. At first Crooner42 had no idea if 'staffa' was even a real word. Intrigued, he ran a quick Internet search and discovered that Staffa was the name of an uninhabited island in Scotland's Inner Hebrides discovered in 1772. But more importantly, it was the location of a massive sea cavern, known as Fingal's Cave.

Crooner42 pondered Fingal's behaviour, linking the Wi-Fi password to the actual name of the network. In cyberspace, Fingal was impossible to trace, with multiple layers of security masking his true identity and real-world location. But here in meatspace, his defences were fairly simplistic. He supposed, like most hackers, that Fingal never expected to be tracked down in the real world and didn't give the same level of focus to his physical security. Crooner42 thought about himself and realised the same was true for him. He resolved to increase his security measures. Just in case.

Crooner42 entered the password. He was connected immediately.

He fired up Nmap and began mapping the network.

The waiter brought over his order, an Americano and a blueberry muffin.

From the inside of Fingal's private network, his defences were minimal. It didn't take long for Crooner42 to gain access to the two Linux servers Fingal had running. After a few minutes, Crooner42 determined that 'Brody', the name he'd heard him being called yesterday, was Fingal's forename. He knew that because he now also had his surname.

"Gotcha, Brody Taylor." he sneered.

After ten more minutes, Crooner42 had Brody Taylor's complete identity. Name, date and place of birth, passport number, national insurance number, bank account numbers, credit card details, mother's maiden name. Everything.

Crooner42 sat back and savoured the moment.

He now had the personal details of one of the world's elite hackers. It was what he would do with this information that was important.

An idea started to form in his mind.

Oh, revenge was sweet indeed.

"Are you sure you're feeling well enough to talk, Sarah?" concern was etched all over the face of the policewoman who had just introduced herself as DC Fiona Jones.

"What, now?" Sarah McNeil sat forward in the hospital bed. "Can't we talk later?" She swung her legs out from underneath the bed cover. She had to get back to the office. "I really can't stay here all day . . ."

Pain shot through her head. She placed a hand on it, feeling a massive bandage. Suddenly she felt faint.

"Oh, that's not good. Perhaps I will stay here for a little bit longer."

DC Jones helped her lie back down and pulled the covers over her. Sarah waited for the wooziness to pass.

"The doctor says you've got serious concussion. You'll need to take it easy for a bit. Definitely a few days off work."

Involuntarily, Sarah's eyes welled up. "But I can't . . . I mean I can't afford not to work."

She had to pay the Sunnyside Care Home bills.

"Surely your work will cover any time off?"

Sarah shook her head and then screwed her eyes shut at the stabbing pain. When it receded to a dull ache, she opened them again, wiping away the tears that had formed from a combination of hurt and frustration.

"What do you do?" asked the policewoman.

"I sell advertising space for a magazine."

"Which magazine?"

"It's called *Commercial Aviation News*. It's owned by Maiden Media."

"Are you based in Windsor?"

"No, Maidenhead."

"Is that why you went Windsor earlier? To sell advertising space?"

"Yes, I had an important meeting. But before I got to meet my client, that creep attacked me."

Sarah felt nauseous at the memory. She hadn't meant to think about that. She wanted to blot it out. Move forward, quickly.

"Are you sure you're okay to talk about this, Sarah?"

But despite her misgivings, she knew she needed to understand what had happened earlier. "Who was that man?" she implored. "What was he doing there?"

"That's what we're trying to find out." Sarah had the feeling that the detective knew more. "Who were you supposed to be meeting?"

"Francis Delacroix from a company called FCS Software."

"Had you met him before? Do you know what he looks like?"

"No. And I probably never will now." It wasn't fair. The most important meeting of her short sales career ruined by that creep. "If he takes his business to one of the other magazines because of what happened, I'll . . ."

"Sarah, what if I told you that Francis Delacroix doesn't exist?"

"What do you mean?" She might be concussed but she certainly wasn't stupid. "Of course he exists, I talked to him on the phone only yesterday."

"Okay, let's back up. Why were you meeting Delacroix?"

"To discuss his marketing plans for FCS Software. They're launching a new flight control system to the UK airport market and need lots of advertising space. He was flying in from the States this morning and we agreed to meet at their office in Windsor."

"How did you first get in touch with Mr Delacroix?"

She thought back to the day before. "He phoned me at work."

"And who suggested meeting at Windsor?"

"Well," she hesitated, starting to feel uncomfortable. "He did."

"And who set the time?"

Sarah spoke more quietly. "He did."

"And let's say you'd been late for the meeting, how would you have contacted him?"

"I'd have phoned him . . ." Realisation dawned on her. She gasped, "He was number withheld."

"We checked FCS Software. They do exist in that building in Windsor. But they're nothing to do with the aviation industry. They're a four-man company that develops games for mobile phones."

Sarah felt as if an abyss were swallowing her up. "Oh God. Oh God."

Tears streamed freely down her face. That meant there never was a deal. It had been some kind of trick. Deep down, she'd known it had been too good to be true. When was she ever that lucky? But if it wasn't true, then she had absolutely no hope of making her target. She'd gambled everything on that deal. At the end of the month, Ashley would fire her, just like all the others.

She buried her face in her hands and whispered, "I'm so sorry, Dad."

"At least you survived," said DC Jones. Sarah looked up at the unexpected sharpness in her tone.

"Well, yes. He was interrupted before he . . ." She shuddered. She'd told herself she wasn't going to think about what had happened. Or what very nearly happened. But she couldn't help herself. "God, it was so awful. He was just about to rape me, wasn't he?"

"Yes, he was." Jones nodded. "Perhaps worse."

Worse? Her job was as good as lost. Sunnyside would kick her Dad out at the end of the month. And all because of that creep.

"What the hell could be worse?" The question popped out of her mouth without realising.

The detective eyeballed her. "He was going to kill you, Sarah. He's already killed two women that we know of."

That was too much. No way. Not her. Who would want to kill her? She didn't understand.

"Fortunately for you," the policewoman continued, "He was interrupted before he could finish what he'd started."

Yes, she remembered. She'd been facedown on the table when she'd heard a bang in the next room. Despite the knife pressing on her throat she'd screamed out, but the gag had muzzled her. But he'd heard the noise too. Someone was checking the rooms. He stepped away from her. She heard him zip up his flies as he moved to the door. She didn't dare look back when the door flew open. She heard a commotion behind her and then, after a minute, it all went quiet. The room was empty and the door had swung shut. She'd tentatively slid off the table, blood trickling down from the open wound on her head, retreated to the corner of the room, and crouched into a ball, clutching her sliced open clothes to her body as best she could.

"Who saved me?"

Behind them, the door to the hospital room pushed open. Sarah realised it had been ajar for some time. Someone had been listening.

"That was me, Sarah," said the woman who entered. "Detective Inspector Jenny Price."

"What I want to know," said Karim Malik, sipping at his pint of soda and lime, "is how this Brody fella knew all about Windsor earlier today. Bit fucking suspicious if you ask me."

"Yeah, Jen," added Alan Coombs, "Are you sure he's not mixed up in it all somehow?"

Jenny leaned back into her tall stool, took a sip of her gin and tonic and studied her two interrogators. Both were stood with one elbow resting on a high wooden pub table. Half empty glasses on sodden beer mats covered the round surface. Empty stools awaited the return of Fiona Jones and Harry O'Reilly, who were at The Dolphin's busy bar, ordering the next round.

"I'm sure there's a good explanation. But don't worry, I'll get to the bottom of it tomorrow."

Jenny sincerely hoped there *was* a good explanation. When Brody had informed her about the Windsor meeting room reservation, she'd taken what he said on face value, prioritising the need to act rather than waste time determining his sources.

And thank God she had. They'd saved Sarah McNeil's life today.

"How do you know him anyway?" asked Alan. He downed the rest of his bitter while she spoke.

"He's a witness. He came forward yesterday about the SWY website. If it weren't for that, we'd have no idea how the killer was selecting his victims."

"O'Reilly reckons he's some kind of computer hacker," said Karim.

"Don't listen to Harry," cautioned Jenny. "He's pissed off because Brody showed him up yesterday by finding all the webcams hidden all over Anna Parker's house."

"Yeah, serious case of geek envy," laughed Fiona, returning with a tray of drinks. "Eh, Harry?"

Harry, who was right behind her, carrying bags of crisps and nuts, retorted, "Yer man is as dodgy as hell. Now Jenny, you need to be careful." He dumped the spoils on the centre of the table.

"Thanks, Harry. I'll take it under advisement." Jenny reached for the dry-roasted peanuts before someone else took them. "But let's face facts here. Without Brody's help today, Sarah McNeil would have been victim number three."

"To Brody," said Alan, lifting his fresh pint in a toast.

"To Brody," they choroused, raising their glasses. All except Harry, who mumbled something else that Jenny didn't quite catch.

She knew she was being defensive over Brody. She refused to believe that the man she'd just shared a passionate night with was somehow mixed up in this. She wondered if she was allowing her feelings to get in the way of being objective about him. They probably were, but even so, there was no evidence to support Harry's concerns. Brody was some kind of techie IT security consultant and was just better at technology than her own supposed expert. Brody had found SWY in the first place, spotted the police on it and used his initiative to let them know, meeting Jenny in the process. He'd uncovered the webcams at Anna Parker's place when Harry had given up. He'd come up with the idea of tracking down the company who'd installed the webcams, and that had been a masterstroke. Da Silva was even now back at Holborn Station, coordinating with almost every police force in the country, organising a visit to every address they'd got from McCarthy so they could determine if it was on SWY. And to top it all, Brody had then somehow come up with the Windsor meeting room booking, just in time.

Jenny snuck a glance at her phone under the table. Her last conversation with Brody had been a text exchange shortly after leaving the hospital. She'd let him know that his timely information had saved the life of a woman. He'd replied with a smiley and asked whether they'd caught the killer. Following her response that he'd unfortunately escaped, Brody cryptically texted back that he might be onto something that could lead to uncovering his identity. But since then, there'd only been radio silence, despite her repeated requests to know more.

"Tell us what happened at Windsor again, Jenny," demanded Karim. "It's just too fucking good."

"Fiona can tell it, she was there. She's the hero here."

"To Detective Constable Jones," said Alan, raising his glass again.

"Fiona!" they echoed.

"I only did what anyone would have done," said Fiona.

"Get on with it," insisted Karim.

"Alright, alright. So we pull up outside the Flexbase office and rush in. Madam here," Fiona nodded towards Jenny, "does a proper Carter-from-*The Sweeney* move and slide-jumps over the bonnet of the car, beating me into the Flexbase building. The two receptionists behind the desk are far more interested in looking pretty than actually helping anyone."

"Yeah," continued Jenny. "Fiona grabs the signing-in book, spots the name we're looking for and demands to know where he is."

"Only one of the stupid cows tell us the fifth floor for FCS Software and off we fly. Only, there's no lift. So I spot the stairs, thinking they'll be quicker."

"Whereas I wait for the lift. And just as the doors shut, the other receptionist shouts me a room number on the sixth floor. Only I can't get Fiona's attention to let her know."

"Well, not surprising really. You try running up five flights of stairs at full speed."

Everyone laughed.

Harry interrupted their flow. "Hold on now. Why didn't Brody just tell you the room number?"

"Assuming he knew it, you mean?" Jenny considered it for a second. "I'm not sure. Once he explained the situation, we were all panicking a bit. We were already on the M4 heading back when he phoned, so he used Google Maps and directed us over the phone to the Flexbase office in Windsor."

"Harry," Alan gently elbowed Harry in the side. "Let them tell their story."

"Okay, so I'm on the top floor," continued Jenny. "I rush into each meeting room. Two of them are empty before I barge into the one he's in."

Harry leaned forward. Alan held his pint halfway to his mouth. Karim left his hand inside his bag of crisps, not daring to make a sound and interrupt the story.

"And I think he must have heard me because he was ready. Just as I ran in, he charged at me, sending me flying backwards over the railing. Thank God I was able to reach out and catch it. That atrium is massive and the drop would have killed me for sure."

Jenny tried to sound upbeat, but couldn't help rubbing her right hip, which was bruised and sore. She hadn't anticipated the killer rushing out and catching her off-balance, knocking her flying over the railing and into six floors of open space. At that moment she had believed she was about to die, but instinct had kicked in and she had reached out, somehow catching the metal railing on top of the sixth floor glass wall. Her shoulder was almost wrenched out of its socket, but she held on. In all her life, Jenny had never come so near to death.

She took a gulp of her gin and tonic, forcing the memory away.

Fiona stepped in. "Yeah, so there's me running round the fifth floor trying to find FCS Software, cursing Jenny. I was thinking the lift couldn't take that long, surely. And then, all of a sudden, I see a pair of legs come flying down from the floor above. Jenny's."

"How'd you know they were Jenny's?" asked Karim, with a smirk.

"I'm a police officer, you dick. I'm trained to observe."

Everyone laughed good-naturedly.

"So, I rush over to these dangling legs, climb up onto the wall and wrap my arms around them."

Jenny remembered the feeling of Fiona's arms wrapping around her thighs. She hadn't known it was Fiona then, of course, but it had calmed her enough to believe she might survive. And with that confidence, she had engaged the killer in conversation. She had also tried her best to memorise his face, but he had concealed it so well there was little of use. His sunglasses and black Adidas cap covered the most of his features and he also wore a fake beard and moustache. He'd taken no chances. He didn't want to be recognised, which told her something about him.

"And then he prised my fingers off, and I fell. If it weren't for Fiona's quick thinking . . ."

"So suddenly, these legs become heavy and start to fall. So I push back with everything I've got, so that we fall onto the fifth floor corridor together . . . except that Jenny ends up crashing her shoulders on the wall of glass. That must've hurt."

"It did, but nothing like the atrium floor five floors below would have."

Karim began clapping and soon they were all giving Fiona a round of applause. Many of the pub's other patrons looked their way. Seeing nothing of interest, they resumed their conversations.

Alan began to repeat his previous toast. Fiona interrupted and changed it. "To catching this fucker."

They raised their glasses in unison. "To catching this fucker."

Jenny hoped they would. They were certainly making progress. It had been a busy day since her near-death experience.

This time, the murderer had entered the building disguised as a pizza deliveryman, pretending to have an order for one of tenants. He had been allowed through security without having to sign in. The huge boxes that comprised his disguise had been found in the room next door, pizzas intact. He had exited through the underground car park, CCTV picking him casually walking down the road, cap pulled even lower. On the sixth floor, the crime scene teams had picked up plenty of trace evidence that matched him to the other two locations. He'd booked the meeting rooms the week before, which was very interesting. Although he had only contacted Sarah McNeil, the intended victim, the day before, he'd clearly planned a meeting there long in advance. The question was, had he always intended Sarah to be his next victim?

As before, he lured his target with an invented story that exploited personal knowledge about the victim. This time, it related to Sarah's desire to make her sales target and sign a big deal. And so he'd presented her with an opportunity that was too good to resist. What was different was that he'd used a ploy based on her career, which indicated that the webcams were located at her place of work rather than her home. A quick crosscheck found Maiden Media's business address on the list of webcam installations carried out by McCarthy Security for HomeWebCam. Sarah's home address wasn't listed. The killer had phoned her, which was a step up from the email and hand-delivered note that he'd used for Anna and Audri.

A visit by Karim and Harry to Maiden Media's offices confirmed the webcams. Sarah's boss, Joe Ashley, took great delight in confirming he'd been responsible for their installation. Ashley had smugly pointed out that, because of the webcams, he was fully aware Sarah was attending a customer meeting while pretending to have the morning off as annual leave to look after her ill father. He thought she had shown great initiative and was disappointed to hear that the whole opportunity with FCS turned out to be a sham. Although, he pointed out, as a result, he'd probably have to fire her. As far as Jenny was concerned, Joe Ashley was no different to Derek Saxton or Walter Pike, although perhaps his objectives were less seedy. Ashley was using HomeWebCam to secretly spy on his sales staff to ensure they were productive. His self-satisfied smile had been wiped off his face when Harry showed him his office being broadcast publicly on SecretlyWatchingYou.

Thanks to Jenny and Sarah McNeil surviving their encounter, they now had better physical descriptions of the perpetrator. Although he'd masked his facial features, his thin and wiry build and average height had been noted. When pressed, both settled on his age being in the mid-thirties. His accent was London: not posh though. Although Sarah reminded them he'd put on an American drawl on the phone the day before.

Alan brought up the subject that had most bothered Jenny about her confrontation with the killer. "Didn't you say earlier that he called you by your name?"

"Yes, he did. Rank and name."

"Do you think he was somehow expecting you, Jenny?" asked Fiona.

"No. Just before he spoke, I saw him raise his eyebrows in surprise as he recognised me."

"It is weird, though," said Karim.

It was. Although what was weirder was the apologetic way he'd spoken to her as he prised her fingers from the railing.

You would have been good. That's the shame of it. Far better than that whore in there.

His words had chilled her to the bone. It implied that she'd already made it to his list of potential targets. It was the only part she hadn't told anyone.

"Maybe he's someone you've put away before," suggested Alan.

There were murmurs of agreement.

"My shout,' he declared. "Same again everyone?"

"Not me," said Jenny. "I need to head off."

"Are you okay, Jen?" asked Alan. "After what you've been through today, you could do with getting shit-faced."

"I'm all right Al, honestly."

But she wasn't being completely honest. She'd surreptitiously read a text on her phone.

It was from Brody.

CHAPTER 19

Through his rear view mirror, Brody observed Jenny park up directly behind him and open her door. He jumped out of his car and threw on his leather jacket. She was wrapping a cream, woollen scarf around her neck and tucking it under her long, black raincoat. He reached into his pockets and pulled on his leather gloves.

Brody indicated the surroundings of the residential street and shrugged. "This wasn't how I imagined our second date."

The icebreaker worked and Jenny laughed. "Me neither." She opened the driver's door, reached in and pulled out two small takeaway coffees. She handed him one. "It's only Starbucks, but it was all that was open this time of night. Flat white okay?"

"Fantastic. Thanks."

This morning they had lain in each other arms as intimate as two people could be. Now, only an arm's length away, she seemed unreachable. He didn't know how to cross the chasm of awkwardness. The steam from their coffees rose into the cold night air.

Jenny rested on the bonnet of her Audi. She cut to the chase. "Why here, Brody? And why specifically *outside*? How does coming back here help us catch the killer?"

Behind Brody, across the road, loomed the massive Saxton residence, secure behind its gates. Lights illuminated some of the rooms. He'd observed movement earlier when Hilary Saxton closed the living room curtains.

"What if I told you that I could get whoever's behind SWY to come here in person?"

"Then I'd say thank you and arrest the bastard."

"And you could interrogate them, gain access to SWY's member database and track down the killer."

"Sounds too good to be true. Can you do this?"

"I think so."

"How?"

He needed to answer this delicately, skirting around issues like him having hacked into the Saxtons' network. While he'd waited for Jenny to drive up from London, he'd prepared a logical explanation.

"I was checking out the SWY site earlier today and saw Hilary Saxton. Despite us telling them about it, her husband still hadn't turned off the network video PC and the feed from their house was still being broadcast. She was just sitting there, crying. It made me feel like an intruder, watching her like that."

That part was true.

Jenny sipped her coffee, waiting for him to continue.

"It didn't seem right to me. So I decided to drive up here and help her turn the damned thing off . . ."

Jenny's eyes narrowed a little.

" . . . But she didn't answer the door when I rang the bell. I knew she was in because I could see her on the webcam feed on my tablet PC. She just ignored it. And then I remembered that I had access to their home's Wi-Fi network. Remember when we were here yesterday? We connected my tablet PC to their Wi-Fi network."

She nodded, slowly. He wasn't sure if she was buying his story. He ploughed on regardless.

"So this evening I reconnected to their network from out here, found the network video PC and turned it off remotely."

He'd only changed the order of events. Surely the fact that he turned it off from his flat back in north London and then drove up here didn't matter in the grand scheme of things?

She drained her coffee.

"Okay, so let's say all that is true, Brody." She held her hand up to stop him attempting to defend himself. "What does any of it have to do with arresting the people behind SWY?"

Brody fished out his tablet computer.

"By turning off the network video PC, the logical conclusion is that the video feeds that make their way to SecretlyWatchingYou via HomeWebCam would suddenly stop. Yes?"

"Makes sense to me. You said this morning that SecretlyWatchingYou is hacking into HomeWebCam to steal the feeds."

"Well, it turns out I was completely wrong about that."

Jenny raised one eyebrow. Surprise or scepticism? He wasn't sure.

"Take a look."

He crossed over and, choosing the sturdier wing of the car, sat next to her. He brought up SecretlyWatchingYou and selected the *Au Pair Affair* location. All seven video feeds were still running. He scanned the thumbnail feeds and spotted Hilary Saxton in the daughter's bedroom. He clicked in and the scene filled the screen. She lay on a single bed reading a picture book to her daughter.

"And Thomas saw Percy steaming ahead of him. He tried to catch him up but he was pulling too many coaches —"

Brody muted the sound.

"Do you see?" he asked.

She turned to him, a look of exasperation. "So what? The network PC video whatchamacallit has turned itself back on."

"It hasn't. It's still powered off."

"Okay . . . Look Brody, all this techie stuff is way beyond me. Make it simple, will you?"

Brody had always loved Sherlock Holmes. One of his favourite quotes was, "... when you have eliminated the impossible, whatever remains, however improbable, must be the truth". He had always hoped that one day he would be able to personally apply this impeccable logic to a real-world situation. And that moment earlier in the day, when he'd noticed Hilary Saxton on SWY long after he'd remotely powered off the PC in the Saxton household, had afforded him his first ever 'Sherlock Holmes moment'. His brain, suddenly cleared of all his previous assumptions, rapidly rewired itself.

The majority of IP network traffic is sent from one point to another point. One sender and one receiver. Called unicasting, it's the backbone of most Internet communications. Brody had assumed that the IP webcams were configured to send their data to a single point: the receiver in the network video PC.

This was where he'd been wrong. They were not *unicasting*; they were *multicasting*. He'd never considered, until earlier, that the webcams would be configured to multicast their feeds over the Saxton's local area network. Obviously, the streams were picked up by the network video PC installed by McCarthy's business. But it wasn't the only PC receiving the streams.

Brody tried to keep it simple. "The webcams broadcast their video streams on the home's Wi-Fi network. It turns out there is more than one network video PC receiving their broadcasts."

"Why would the Saxtons have more than one of those?"

"They don't. The second one was added afterwards without their knowledge."

"Hold on a second. Let me understand this." Jenny squinted her eyes shut. "There's a second network video PC in the Saxton house?"

"No. Not inside the house. Outside."

Jenny looked all around. "Where? It would need a power source."

On the drive over to Bushey, Brody had stopped by Spymaster on Portman Square, a shop that supplied surveillance and anti-surveillance equipment. He'd rented a cellular activity monitor. Although it was primarily used to check for unauthorised use of mobile phones in prisons, hospitals, exam halls and offices, it also had a Wi-Fi mode. Using it to prove his new theory, he had traced the Wi-Fi signals to the boot of a car parked outside.

Brody pointed at the cheap, dull grey SEAT Toledo parked opposite them.

"Inside that car is a laptop powered by car batteries. It's connected to the Saxton's Wi-Fi network. See that antenna on the rear parcel shelf?" Jenny nodded. "It's directional, allowing it to easily pick up their signal even though its good fifty yards from the Wi-Fi router in the house."

"But car batteries don't last forever."

"Exactly. Every now and again they need to be recharged or replaced. Someone must come here on a regular basis to sort them out."

"That's crazy."

Which is exactly why Brody had never considered it in the first place.

Whatever remains, however improbable, must be the truth.

Brody felt like kicking himself. Yesterday, when they'd disabled Walter Pike's network video PC, the webcam streams from Anna and Kim's home had not continued to be broadcast on SWY. He and O'Reilly had manually searched through every location on SWY before it had been turned off. They had not found them because Crooner42 had already stopped displaying them on the site, despite his shadow PC still being active. As to why Crooner42 had done this, Brody could only speculate. The most likely scenario was that he'd noticed the police involvement at two of the webcam locations and so, by deactivating the feeds from the first, had made them doubt whether SWY was a factor. But this had also prevented Brody from deducing that the two sites, HWC and SWY, had different network video PC sources. He knew now that if he drove over to Anna and Kim's house or the office address for Sarah McNeil, he would find a shadow PC hidden nearby.

"Are you saying that every location on SWY has a car parked outside like this?"

"Most, I would think. Certainly all the private locations. Where there's public access maybe they're plugged into the mains supply somewhere in a secret place where the laptop can't be disturbed. Whoever's behind this needs access to them in case anything goes wrong. Computers break down all the time. If they were stored inside the premises, then how could they gain access to fix any issues?"

"But SYW has hundreds of locations. It would cost a fortune."

"Not compared to the amount of money the site's making. And anyway, that car is worth no more than a few hundred quid."

Jenny stepped out from between their cars to get a better look. "Right, I'm doing a PNC check on the number plate."

She pulled her mobile phone out of her coat pocket and made a phone call. After a short wait, she had an address.

She sighed. "It sounds suspect. The car is registered to John Smith at an address in Stratford. 6E Appleton Avenue."

"Give me a moment." On his tablet computer, Brody searched for the address on Google Maps. He switched to Street View, found the number six and zoomed in. He handed her the tablet.

"Do you see what I see?"

It was a large terraced Victorian house that had been converted into flats: four of them, numbered 6A to 6D.

"There is no 6E." She looked closer. "And there's only one letterbox for all four flats. So any post for number 6 gets delivered. The DVLA would probably be none the wiser."

"Sounds like too clever a scam to have only used it once," Brody suggested.

Jenny nodded her understanding and made another call. "Can you find out how many vehicles are registered to 6E Appleton Avenue, E20 9RP?"

She waited. After a minute she had the answer, thanked whomever she'd called and disconnected. "There are over a hundred cars registered to that address. All cheap and old. Just like that one."

"Very clever." Brody nodded in admiration. "They couldn't afford to use stolen cars. Your lot are bound to stumble across them. But this way, they're registered to what looks like a legitimate address. They're not reported stolen. And no way to trace whoever really owns them."

"Unless . . . I'll get someone round to Appleton Avenue anyway. The people who live in the flats must have spotted all the post piling up for the non-existent flat. Or someone there is collecting it all for him." She made another call and gave instructions.

"What's next?" he asked.

"I need to get a forensic team up here to take a look at that car."

"But that will take ages. And even if they find fingerprints or DNA, what then?"

"There's the computer . . ."

"Yes there is," he smiled, "isn't there."

She narrowed her eyes, unsure where he was going. "We'll need them to break into the car to gain access to it."

"Well, it seems like someone's on your side."

"What do you mean?"

"Have you noticed the driver's side window?" he asked, faking innocence.

Jenny walked over to the car. The window had been smashed in. A brick lay in the passenger seat. She bent down, examined the interior by eye and then peered over its roof at him.

"Brody, please tell me you didn't do this."

"It was like that when I got here, honest officer." He held up his gloved hands and grinned from ear to ear to let her know that he was lying through his teeth. "But as the car was accessible, I thought I might as well take a look inside."

"Brody . . ." she warned.

"Here, let me show you."

Brody joined her by the driver's side of the car. He reached inside the broken window underneath the dashboard and popped the boot. They walked around to the back of the car.

Brody had already seen the contents earlier. Jenny's reaction was similar to his own. "Fucking hell!"

Inside the boot, a large milk crate contained two rows of car batteries all connected together. To the right was a laptop computer on its side. It was connected to the run of batteries. Another wire ran from the laptop back through the rear seats to the directional Wi-Fi antenna.

"Quite impressive, eh?" said Brody.

"How long would this last?"

"I reckon that lot would do a whole month. Maybe two. The power draw on that model is pretty low, especially with the screen closed."

"So let me get this straight. This laptop receives all the feeds from the webcams across the road." Brody nodded. "So how does it broadcast them up to SWY?"

"It's so simple." He caught her affronted look and changed tack. "What I mean is that it's impressive in its simplicity. It sends the feeds back over the Saxton's own Wi-Fi network, through their broadband router, onto the Internet and up to SWY. It works completely independently from the network video recorder PC inside the house that connects to HomeWebCam."

"Please tell me you haven't touched the laptop, Brody."

He'd wanted to. It had been difficult not to. It probably contained the back door into SWY he'd searched for all week. But his motivation to pwn SecretlyWatchingYou was completely at odds with his motivation to help Jenny.

"Of course I haven't. I called you, didn't I?"

And anyway, helping Jenny might lead to him still pwning SecretlyWatchingYou.

"Now for my promise."

Brody reached a gloved hand into the boot and quickly pulled out the power supply and Wi-Fi antenna cables from the back of the laptop.

"What are you doing?" shrieked Jenny. "That's evidence."

"I'm getting the person behind SWY to come here in person, just like I said I would."

Understanding dawned on her face.

"Without power or access to the Wi-Fi network, the feeds will stop being broadcast."

He reached into his pocket, withdrew his tablet PC again and took off his gloves. He brought back up the *Au Pair Affair* location on SWY. Jenny leaned in to him to see, placing one hand on his wrist. It was the first time they'd touched. He could feel the electricity.

After a minute, on the screen, all seven video streams had blacked out.

As the front door slammed shut behind him, Crooner42 pressed a button on his key fob. Across the living room, the bookcase began to silently swing open. One day, he decided, he would upgrade the home automation system to play an excerpt of the *Thunderbirds* theme tune. Or maybe *Batman* would be more appropriate. The bookcase always reminded him of Tracy Island and Wayne Manor, completely innocuous on the surface, but with the click of a button swinging open to reveal the camouflaged hi-tech control centre behind. Okay, he didn't quite have a Thunderbird 2 or a Batmobile, but he did have a massive bank of monitors from which he controlled SecretlyWatchingYou.

He grabbed a coke from the wine fridge and sat in his reclining leather chair at the centre of his secret room. As the bookcase automatically swung itself shut, he picked up the tablet computer he always left on the side table and checked the site's status.

All locations were online and broadcasting. Well, all except *Student Heaven*, which had been one of the most popular locations for SWY customers. It had also been his own personal favourite, but it had been necessary to disable it once the police had taken an interest following the death of Anna Parker, one of the students who had lived in the house. He'd watched the police, aided by none other than Fingal, discover the webcams secreted within the house. They would only be able to link the webcams to HomeWebCam. And even if they did realise that the same webcams streams used to be broadcast on SWY, they would naturally determine that the feeds arrived there via HomeWebCam. It was the only obvious explanation once the network video recorder PC within the house was discovered.

No one would ever figure out his shadow network of network video recorder laptops, hidden in plain site outside each of the webcam locations. Which reminded him: he needed to pop down to Charlton tomorrow and remove the car that had been parked down the road from *Student Heaven* for the last few years.

It was quite timely, as it turned out, because he had recently identified a new webcam location in Brighton to add to the SecretlyWatchingYou site. His original plan had been to pop across the river to Deptford that evening, buy a new car at auction and then drive it to the south coast the next day. But with the vehicle in Charlton no longer required there, he would redeploy it to Brighton instead.

The location in Brighton was a tricky one. He knew he'd need to be patient waiting for a parking spot, free of yellow lines, to appear on the residential back street perpendicular to the main road where his target location lay. If he could get a decent line of sight, then it would work. And the gay massage parlour that offered services way beyond what was written on the price list displayed outside would become a new source of revenue on SWY. While it was not to his personal taste, their hidden webcam streams were bound to become a hit with a fair proportion of his voyeuristic customers; after all, SWY didn't discriminate.

Crooner42 checked the customer count and nearly choked on his coke. He almost had to pinch himself at the numbers. It was a brand new record, well over six thousand viewers active concurrently. He checked the total number of paid registrations and saw that it had increased by nearly a thousand new registrations since he'd last checked the day before. At this rate, he'd have over one hundred thousand paying customers by the end of the week.

Satisfied that SWY was in good shape, he moved on to his next task, the one he had been savouring the thought of all day.

Crooner42 sat at his desk, using a proper computer with a keyboard, rather than the tablet PC he used to control SWY. He rubbed his hands together in anticipation and, tunnelling through VPN server and TOR, logged into the CrackerHack forums, confident that his IP address could not be traced. He navigated to the discussion area entitled 'Vorovskoy Mir's Cyber Most Wanted'. The third name on the list was labelled 'Fingal' and the reward for information leading to his capture was $1 million in bitcoins; no questions asked. Crooner42 had no idea what Fingal had done to upset the Russian Mafia so badly, but nor did he care. This was revenge. Soon enough, instead of a silhouette, Fingal's real face would be displayed with the word 'ELIMINATED' across it, just like the four losers at the bottom of the list.

Crooner42 clicked on a button to submit a tip. On the form that was presented, he entered the identity information he had uncovered for Brody Taylor earlier that day. His Upper Street address, his passport number; everything he had found. Crooner42 also entered his own bitcoin wallet address, the only linkage back to himself and even then it was almost impossible to trace. Although Crooner42 would have happily offered up Fingal's identity for free, if the Russian Mafia wanted to pay him for the information, who was he to object?

Just as he was about to press the submit button, an alert sounded on his tablet PC.

He picked it up and quickly navigated to the issue. It was the *Au Pair Affair* location. According to the error message, the shadow PC had gone offline. He brought it up on the centre screen on the bank of screens opposite. Sure enough, the video streams were completely black.

He ran through the usual recovery processes. He sent a reboot command via the pay-as-you-go mobile phone connected to the computer at the location. He gave it a minute but nothing happened. He tried remotely connecting via the broadband router in the Saxtons' house. Again, no joy. He started to resign himself to a physical site visit.

It wasn't that concerning, just an inconvenience. Every now and then, a location would go offline and require in-person recovery. Most often it was a fault with the laptop or the batteries. One time, he'd arrived to discover the car had been stolen. He wondered what the thieves had made of the boot full of batteries and the laptop.

He looked up the address of the *Au Pair Affair* location on the system. It was in Bushey in Hertfordshire. He recalled the location. It was a well-to-do residential street with his car parked on the cul-de-sac opposite the massive detached house.

He temporarily disabled it from the SecretlyWatchingYou site. That way his customers would no longer see *Au Pair Affair* listed and wouldn't then complain about a series of black screens. But the problem would need to be dealt with swiftly.

It was looking like he would need to visit Bushey.

Crooner42 returned his attention to the Most Wanted list. All the identity data he'd filled in about Fingal was still there. He took a deep breath and, with a flourish, clicked the submit button.

As the taxi disappeared down the road, Derek Saxton fished his keys out of his pocket. They spilled out of his hands and dropped to the ground. He bent down to pick them up but lost his balance, falling forward and crashing into the front gate outside his home.

"Oops-a-daisy," he slurred to himself. He grabbed hold of the gate and slowly pulled himself up, only just remembering to grab the keys.

This time, he concentrated harder. He pressed the remote control button on the key fob. The electric gate obligingly slid to one side. Tentatively, he made his way across his driveway, careful to put one foot in front of the other.

He reached the porch, assiduously selected the right key and attempted to push it into the Yale lock of the grand double door. It took him three attempts to pinpoint it correctly, but even then it wouldn't go in more than halfway. Confused, he examined his keys. He'd correctly chosen the shiny silver one. The others were all brass or mortice keys. He tried again.

It slowly dawned on him what was going on and anger coursed through his veins.

"Hilary," he shouted, banging on the door, "Fucking let me in."

No answer. He shouted and thumped it again, this time with even more force.

"What do you want, Derek?"

Her calm voice came from behind him. He whirled around, but no one was there. His momentum continued and he staggered out of the porch and onto the granite paving stones of the drive, only just maintaining his balance.

"You're drunk." Her voice was coming from above, oozing disgust. The upstairs hall window was open. She stood there regally, clutching a sleeping Izzy to her bosom.

"You changed the locks." It came out as an accusation rather than the question he had intended.

"What did you expect?"

"Let me in, Hilary." It took every ounce of effort not to shout. He didn't want to wake Izzy. In fact, he didn't want Izzy to see him like this. "We need to talk."

"About what?"

"About us? You, me, Izzy."

"Us?" her voice was high-pitched, incredulous. "You ruined *us* when you fucked the babysitter."

"But . . ." He didn't have an answer.

He had done that. But he hadn't meant for it to turn out like this.

It wasn't really his fault. Not all of it anyway. He had tried to resist the temptress, who had constantly paraded around the house half-naked, leading him on, teasing him. And always when Hilary was out. But what hope did he have? He was a red-blooded man, not a stone cold statue.

"It was your stupid idea to get a live-in au pair. Now I know why."

"No. It's not like that, darling," he pleaded. "I was thinking of you—"

She hissed at him, "I'm not your darling." Izzy stirred in her arms and Hilary rocked her gently. When she spoke again, she was calmer. "Not being able to keep your dick in your pants I can almost understand. You've never stopped pining for your damn rugby days; beer with the lads, women throwing themselves at your feet. I should know. I was one of them."

"Hilary—"

She held out a hand to silence him. "But you know what I can't get past, Derek?"

He had no idea. If it wasn't sleeping with Audri then what the hell was it?

"I thought I knew you, Derek, I really did. But it turns out that you're a disgusting, dirty old man. You repulse me."

The damned webcams.

Her words cut him in two, but she wasn't finished. "You're not fit to be a father to Izzy. Now go away."

She reached out her free hand and began pulling the window

shut.

"I'm so sorry, darling. It was just a whim. A spur of the moment thing. I didn't mean to hurt you."

She stopped and railed at him, disgust dripping from every word. "You put one of those things in our bedroom, Derek. Our private space. And not content with that, you put one in our bathroom. But worst of all, you put one in the au pairs' bedroom. They were young women, Derek. Just like Izzy will become one day. *Young women.*"

"But—"

"And to top it all off," her voice rose as she hurled her accusations at him, "you turn our home into some kind of online Big Brother house, except on TV the contestants know the cameras are there. They *know.*" She took a sharp breath, stifling a sob. "We had no fucking idea. Me. Izzy. Audri. It's a violation, Derek. You violated us all for your deviant perversions."

"But I didn't know, how could I?" he shouted her down, angry now. "I'm a victim too, you know."

"There's only one proper victim in all this, Derek. And it's certainly not you. It's not even Izzy or me. We've had a lucky escape. No Derek, the only victim here is Audri. First you fuck her and then you kill her."

"I didn't kill her!"

Hilary was about to retort but bit her tongue. Instead, she shook her head in despair and closed the window shut.

"Please Hilary," he wailed, falling helplessly to the ground. "Please."

And before he knew what was happening, he was curled up on his stone patio, crying like a baby.

"Do you think we should do something?" asked Brody.

"Only if he gets violent," advised Jenny.

They had observed the whole sorry scene play out from inside Brody's Smart car parked in the cul-de-sac opposite their house. Both of them had lowered their windows to eavesdrop on the exchange between husband and wife. Saxton was lying on the ground, convulsions racking his body. It was uncomfortable to watch. Jenny glanced at the upstairs hallway window, but Hilary Saxton had disappeared from view.

After a few minutes, Saxton slowly pulled himself to his feet and took a long look at the home he was no longer welcome in. Eventually, he shrugged, zipped up his jacket, buried his hands into his pockets and left by the open gate, turning right towards Bushey village, meandering drunkenly down the street.

"Who needs SecretlyWatchingYou when you've got front row seats?" joked Brody.

Jenny offered a short grunt of agreement. She had little sympathy for Derek Saxton. She recalled his interview at the station a few days before and his complete lack of remorse over his extra-marital behaviour. It wasn't her job to judge or take sides, but in this instance she'd very much enjoyed observing Saxton face the consequences of his actions. Although she felt sympathy for his wife and baby daughter.

She kept an eye on Saxton as he staggered past Karim Malik's parked-up Vauxhall Astra, oblivious of the two officers sat within its dark interior. She could just about make out Alan Coombs' profile in the passenger seat, despite the yellow glare reflecting on the passenger window from a nearby lamppost. Further up the street in the other direction Fiona Jones and Harry O'Reilly sat in Jenny's own Audi A3, although she couldn't really see them as they were parked in a much darker spot.

When deciding on the stakeout, she had first phoned Da Silva to sell him the idea and obtain approval for the overtime. At first, he hadn't been pleased with her interruption. He was still at Holborn with other members of the investigation team, up to their necks coordinating the following morning's multi-force exercise to have local police officers show up at every address on the list of IP webcam installations provided by McCarthy. He had brightened when she informed him about the hundreds of cars registered at the fake address in Stratford, each containing the shadow PCs that made SWY work. For each address they found broadcast on SWY, then additional evidence would be provided by seeking out and seizing the car parked nearby. Delighted, he had eagerly approved the overtime without even checking with DCS McLintock.

Her team had been much less thrilled. They had still been in The Dolphin when she phoned, many more sheets to the wind than when she had left them. Well, except for Karim, who never drank. He had driven them up to Bushey for the stakeout, after collecting three walkie-talkies from the station. When they arrived an hour later, soft drinks and kebabs in hand, she introduced them all to Brody, only remembering that Harry had met him the day before when he deliberately snubbed Brody's outstretched hand. She quickly organised the three vehicles so that they covered all entrances and exits to the area and each had an unobstructed view of the grey SEAT Toledo.

It was going to be a long night. But probably much longer for Alan, Fiona and Harry, whose hangovers would no doubt kick-in halfway through. Thinking about her team made her recall the concerns they had voiced in the pub earlier.

"Something's bothering me, Brody."

"I thought something was up." He turned to look at her. She kept her eyes on the SEAT. "What is it?"

She folded her arms. "How did you figure out the booking in Windsor earlier?"

"Does it matter?" When she didn't reply, he answered his own question. "Obviously it does."

He gave the impression that he was disappointed that he had to explain himself. She turned to face him, needing to see if he would lie right to her face. Harry was convinced he was some kind of computer hacker and must have hacked his way into Flexbase to find out the information.

There was an almost imperceptible pause before he spoke.

"I had help, but I promised not to give up his name. He'd lose his job."

"Go on."

"When we met Magnus Peggler at Flexbase yesterday, he said that he needed to talk to the vendor of the meeting room booking system in order to find out if IP addresses were stored in the database."

That was true. She remembered that.

"I got the feeling that he was going to take his time over that so I thought I'd see if I could help. I tracked down the vendor. There was a press release from them on the Internet from a few years back announcing Flexbase as a new customer. It turns out I know someone who works in their support department who owed me a favour. He logged into their system remotely. I know it's a bit naughty, but he downloaded their booking database and emailed it to me so I could check myself."

It sounded a bit far-fetched to her, but Brody's face was totally earnest.

"Anyway, IP data is stored with each booking. It was the same IP address for both previous bookings. So I ran a search for any other bookings and up popped the one today at Windsor. That's when I phoned you."

"What about this IP address, you never mentioned that before? We could be tracking that down as we speak."

He thumped his forehead with the heel of his hand. "In all the chaos, I completely forgot about that. I'm so sorry. I'll email it to you now." He reached for his tablet computer. "The IP address links back to Vodafone, which means the booking system was accessed via a smart phone. But if you contact them with the information I send you now, they should be able to give you the actual mobile phone number. Hopefully, it'll come with a real-world address. But somehow I doubt it." His fingers flew across the screen.

Jenny didn't know what to think. His story was all completely plausible. And if he was lying, he was an absolute master. There was not a flicker. But there was just something in the back of her mind that didn't feel right. She couldn't put her finger on it. Could she trust him?

She wanted to. She really wanted to.

She needed to.

"I was nearly killed today." She surprised herself with the revelation. Even more surprisingly, she felt tears build up. Her body began to shake. She tried taking a gulp of air.

"Huh?" Brody stopped swiping his fingers on the tablet's glass surface, turned to scrutinise her and, seeing her distress, dropped the computer to the footwell and reached his arms around her. She allowed herself to be pulled towards him. To be comforted. She began to cry hot tears into his chest.

Objectively, she understood it was delayed shock. She'd been so busy since the encounter that she hadn't allowed herself to absorb it properly. As a police officer, she'd dealt with her fair share of violent situations, facing up to plenty of overly-aggressive drunks and junkies, a handful of knife-wielding criminals and had once donned protective gear to confront massive crowds of rioters, all overwhelmed with bloodlust. But nothing had ever come close to today's near-death experience.

She was overwhelmed with emotions, unsure how to handle them. She allowed the tears to flow. Brody held her tight, despite the awkwardness of his small car. He kissed the back of her head gently.

Slowly she began to retell the events of earlier. And unlike in the version in the pub earlier, which had been full of bravado, she tried to relate the feelings she had experienced. Her adrenalin-fuelled charge into each meeting room; her unnerving flight out into the openness of the atrium, six floors up; her instinctive grab for the glass railing; the humiliation of begging for him not to prise her fingers away; her sheer relief when she'd felt arms grab her legs beneath as she held on one-handed; her utter bewilderment as the killer spoke her name; and the physical pain she had endured as she landed on the fifth floor.

"He said your name?" Brody asked.

"More than that, he almost apologised for having to push me off. It was as if he had already fixated on me as a future victim and he was gutted he was going to miss out."

You would have been good. That's the shame of it. Far better than that whore in there.

She shuddered into his chest at the recollection.

"Maybe that's how he sees all women. As objects for his weird fantasy."

"But he knew *my* name."

"Yeah, from SecretlyWatchingYou, surely. The same way I found out your name."

"You think? It felt like something more. But I hope you're right."

"Me too."

You are angry.

You can hardly contain it. You want to lash out. You want to cry out loud how unfair it all is.

But you contain yourself. You know that if you react spontaneously, if you go on a rampage through the streets slashing at women at random, you will be caught and imprisoned. Like *her.*

You don't want to be caught.

You log back into SecretlyWatchingYou and look around. It calms you, spying on them all.

You find the locations where your next three choices are. You'll need to choose one of them.

But then you remember all your planning was focused around Flexbase. You know that avenue is closed to you now. They nearly caught you today. Why couldn't they have come just ten minutes later? At least you'd have been finished by then; finished with the telesales whore.

It had been going so well. Everything had gone to plan, just like it always did. You were throbbing with anticipation. And just as you were about to slide it in, your knife at her throat, you'd heard the noise next door. Fortunately, you took control of yourself and got ready for an interruption. You barged her so hard, she tipped over the balcony.

But when you looked over and saw it was the policewoman, you were shocked to the core. That was no coincidence.

And it really was such a shame that you had to let her go, literally. You smile to yourself at your little joke. It calms you. And yet you are sad. She was the most like *her* so far. And you had been working on a plan for the policewoman, only for it all to go to waste. She was dead now. What a shame.

You're going to need to adapt. You know that. Adapting is what will make you succeed.

You cannot use Flexbase anymore. Whatever trick the policewoman used to find you was repeatable. You'll need to find somewhere new. Come up with new locations to lure them to.

At least you've still got SecretlyWatchingYou, and an endless supply of women within its many locations. You'll continue to learn all about them and use that knowledge to trick them into meeting you somewhere else. It doesn't have to be a Flexbase building. There are plenty of other places. It was just so damn convenient. You knew your way around the systems so well. You were untraceable.

And then you chide yourself. Of course you weren't. The policewoman tracked your room down, didn't she?

FRIDAY

CHAPTER 20

Crooner42 dropped the car into second and turned off Bushey High Street.

The drive up had taken much longer than he'd anticipated. He'd thought heading out of London against the morning rush-hour traffic would have been far quicker, but the North Circular had caught him out. It had been heavily congested, as city-bound traffic skirted round London's inner ring road in both directions before turning inwards once again. On his return trip, he would take the A41 into the centre of town, and then follow it once more as it guided him alongside the Thames towards Docklands. He would save at least thirty minutes that way.

He needed to save as much time as possible; he had a busy day ahead. Once he dumped his car back at his flat, he would take a taxi across the river to Charlton and pick up the car outside what used to be called *Student Heaven* on SWY. From there, he would drive it to its new destination in Brighton. Once the shadow PC was set up outside the gay massage parlour, he would take the train back to London. With any luck, he would be back home for the evening.

He turned left into the road where the Saxton house was located. It had been over a month since he'd last been here to switch the batteries in the boot of the car. He wasn't actually scheduled to come here again for at least another six weeks, so the signal dropping completely was concerning. He just hoped the car hadn't been stolen.

He drove slowly along the road. Further down where the road curved, he could make out the Saxton residence, the imposing house protected by massive security gates. Opposite was the cul-de-sac where he'd parked the SEAT Toledo.

He indicated right. As he approached the junction, he glimpsed a flash of something bright orange. Metallic orange and black.

It couldn't be.

It wasn't possible.

He quickly flipped off the indicator and continued straight on, deliberately maintaining his meandering speed. As he passed the junction, he stole a long look up the dead end road. Yes, just as he'd thought. A two-tone, garish orange and black Smart Fortwo coupe. And inside he could make out the outlines of two passengers.

With his heart pounding, he drove on slowly, confident that he hadn't caught their attention. His indicator had been turned off before they would have seen the car appear and so, to them, he would have looked just like any other car driving down the residential road.

It was Fingal. It had to be. He recognised the distinctive car from the other night in Upper Street, when he'd watched him bound out of Bruno's coffee shop.

Crooner42's mind began processing the implications.

Somehow, Fingal had discovered the car containing the shadow PC. It was no coincidence that it had stopped broadcasting. Fingal had done that. And the reason was to draw him out. The fact that he was there waiting in person meant that he didn't know who he was. That was something.

Crooner42 checked his rear view mirror, searching for Fingal's car. He could see a silver car behind him, but there was nothing behind that. Certainly not the ridiculous Smart car.

All this week, Fingal had been searching for a way into SWY. He'd never given up. On Monday and Tuesday he'd been doing a classic frontal assault. Crooner42 remembered all the unusual network activity that signified his attempts to break in. As expected, his defences had held. And then on Wednesday morning, when he'd thought Fingal had given up, he'd bounced back with his forty-eight hour challenge, risking his whole reputation.

At the same time, there was all the police activity at two SWY locations, *Student Heaven* and this one, *Au Pair Affair*. Crooner42 remembered identifying Fingal at *Student Heaven* but now, as he thought back, there had been another man, a techie, at the Saxtons' house on Wednesday morning. It was obvious to him now he had also been Fingal. He'd been the one guiding the police all along. Perhaps Fingal was some kind of IT police detective pretending to be a hacker. Damn, that was concerning. But it explained why they were waiting there, trying to capture him in person. Rather than —

— And then it hit him. Backdoor. He'd provided Fingal a viable backdoor.

The PC in the boot, assuming it was still in the boot of the Toledo, had direct access to SecretlyWatchingYou. It tunnelled straight through all of his firewalls and his intrusion prevention system right into the heart of the site. He'd set it up like that because it was a trusted source and because he needed to limit the amount of latency when streaming the video feeds. On the PC were the login credentials that Fingal could use to break into the site. In fact, it was the same set of credentials on every shadow PC in the boots of cars stranded all over the country. He realised now that he'd made a huge mistake.

But it was only a mistake if Fingal followed up on it quickly enough. Right now he was sat in his stupid little car waiting for Crooner42 to show up and fix the shadow PC. But once he realised Crooner42 wasn't coming, it wouldn't take someone as smart as Fingal long — and yes, he had to admit, he was definitely a smart cookie to have figured out his network of shadow PCs — to figure out the backdoor contained in the shadow PC. But, even then, it would still take Fingal a good few hours to crack the hash-password on the PC.

Crooner42 still had time to sort this out.

He had to get back to his apartment in Docklands. Once there he would lock down the *Au Pair Affair* location completely and change the password on the account used by the shadow PCs. He'd need to write a script to remotely connect to each of them, one by one, and change their passwords to match. But once done, the backdoor would be blocked.

And Fingal would fail. His forty-eight hours would pass and Crooner42 would be declared the winner on CrackerHack. His status would go through the roof while Fingal would disappear forever. And all that was unrelated to whatever the Russian Mafia would do with information Crooner42 had provided them about Fingal's real-world identity.

Fingal had come close to beating him; he had to admit that. But not close enough.

He turned left and put his foot on the accelerator.

Kim awoke in Patrick's plush double bed. As she yawned, she could feel dried tear tracks pulling at the skin on her face.

She hadn't expected to fall back asleep when Patrick left for work early this morning. But without him around, she'd felt able to cry again. And she'd cried herself back to sleep, lucidly dreaming about attending her best friend's funeral in a few days. It was so final. So permanent. Even in her dream, she'd felt tears bubbling up again. Deep down she knew that she needed to find a way to say goodbye to Anna. Maybe travelling down to Torquay and standing at Anna's graveside beside her grieving family was the best way to do it.

Kim threw back the covers and headed for the en-suite bathroom.

A few minutes later, scalding hot water showered over her. She raised her face to meet the cascade.

If she were being forced to find a way to live without Anna, then maybe she should step up and deal with the other issue in her life. Her feelings about Patrick.

Finally, Kim was admitting to herself that their relationship wasn't quite right. There was one fundamental flaw. She didn't love him.

That he loved her, there was no doubt, which made the situation worse. But it was the way he loved her that was the problem. It was as if his love for her suppressed any individuality he might have had. Everything they did together was all about her. He obliged her in everything. He agreed with everything she said and did. He shared her interests. As far as she could tell, he had no interests of his own. If it weren't for his work, then he'd have nothing in his life that didn't revolve around her. She recalled Anna describing him as 'fawny'.

It really was amazing how much they had in common. She'd always felt that. And initially it had been a wonderful thing. From that first time she'd met him, when he'd sung her favourite song at the karaoke restaurant, only for him to explain it was his favourite song as well. That he was so into ballet, admitting it even before he found out she was a dancer. That he enjoyed shopping. For clothes, even. The soppy romcoms he chose were always ones she wanted to watch, almost as if he'd read her mind. That he even read sonnets to her in bed.

Where was his love of football? Or action movies? Or rock bands? Or anything manly?

She dried herself off and changed back into her clothes from yesterday. Leggings, blouse and dance shoes.

Even during sex it was all about her. He was so damn attentive to her needs. So gentle and caring. Why couldn't he just fuck her once in a while?

She wanted him to be a little bit selfish. Stand up for himself occasionally. Push back when her needs conflicted with his. To actually want something for himself. To have a fucking opinion that didn't echo hers for God's sake.

She grabbed her bag and, as she headed for the front door, she halted in the middle of the open plan apartment, studying it with fresh eyes.

It really was impressive. Shiny parquet flooring, leather sofas, framed art-house movie posters, stone busts for ornaments, glass tables and an amazing view over the Thames. There was a veneer of masculinity. A pinball machine, an arcade machine and a pool table. But for all his money, it was clear to her now that this bachelor pad was someone else's design. Definitely not Patrick's. He would need to have had opinions to put together this get-up.

Maybe she should leave him a note? She dismissed the thought as soon as it had formed. That was too cruel.

She would break up with him to his face. It would be the only way she would get through to him.

She wondered whether his passivity would last through a break-up scene? She hoped not. Maybe he would display some spark. Some fight. But even if he did, it would be too late.

She opened the front door and jumped back in horror. Someone was standing right there, hand raised, about to press the bell.

"At least you haven't got a knife this time, Kim?" said a smiling DI Jenny Price.

"Oh Jenny, thank God. You scared the life out of me."

She remembered back to Monday evening when they had

confronted each other either side of the door to Anna's room. She still had a bruise on her forearm where Jenny had smashed the door onto her arm, causing her to drop the knife she had been wielding, thinking the killer was inside.

Standing behind Jenny, she noticed the techie guy who had found all the webcams in her house.

"What are you two doing here?"

"It's a long story, Kim. Can we come in?"

"I was just leaving," said Kim.

Kim looked flustered. She was thinner than when Jenny had seen her just two days ago.

Jenny stood her ground in the doorway. Kim gave in. "Sure, come in."

They walked into an impressive apartment. It was a bachelor pad right out of a magazine. Not a floral design or soft furnishing in sight. All cream and dark-brown. And lots of large boys toys. Absently, Jenny wondered if she'd be any good at the Asteroids arcade machine.

"What's going on, Jenny? Why are you here? What's Patrick got to do with anything?"

Three very good questions, thought Jenny.

Earlier that morning, still staking out the SEAT Toledo after a long, uncomfortable night in Brody's car, her walkie-talkie had crackled again.

"Got a white 911 heading our way. Single occupant." It had been Alan giving the commentary. "Okay, he's indicating right. This could be our guy." A pause and then, "Sorry, another false alarm. Indicator's stopped. He's carrying straight on."

At that moment, Jenny saw the Porsche slowly cruise by the mouth of the cul-de-sac and recognised the car immediately. It had been striking when she had first seen it, parked outside of Kim's house on Monday, sparkling white on the outside, ostentatious red leather on the inside. She remembered being frustrated that she'd had to park further down the road and walk back through the pouring rain, yet its owner had fluked a parking space right outside just when he needed one.

"Run the number plate, Alan," she ordered back into the radio. "Fiona, you're facing the right way. Follow the Porsche, but don't let him know you're on to him."

She waited, watching Fiona drive off in her silver A3.

Brody asked her, "What's with the Porsche?"

"I've seen it before, or one very much like it. And in my book, coincidences rarely happen."

"Whose is it?"

"If his first name is Patrick, then we have our man."

Brody went to ask for more, but the radio crackled again.

"Okay, so it's registered to a Patrick Harper. Address is in Docklands."

Jenny clenched her fist in triumph. Brody fired up the car and pulled out.

"Alan, you and Karim wait here in case Fiona loses him and he comes back. Give it half-an-hour. If nothing happens, then get crime scene out here and process that vehicle. It's evidence."

Jenny saw Brody had plugged Harper's Docklands address into his satnav. After a few minutes, they reached the roundabout for the A41. Instead of following the road signs and turning right towards London, for some reason the satnav indicated they should drive straight on. He followed it blindly.

"Have you entered the address properly? London's that way," stated Jenny.

"So is all the commuter traffic heading into town. This satnav has a live link to the Internet and takes account of all that." He pressed some buttons on the screen and an overview of its intended route came up. It was taking them up the A1, around the north section of the M25, and back into London via the M11. "Although it's a longer route, it's mostly motorway. I reckon it will save us a good three quarters on an hour."

She rang Fiona. Harry answered. "Which direction has Harper taken?"

"He's on the A41 heading south. We're two cars behind him."

"Okay, stay with him. We're heading to his address, but we're taking a quicker route."

Despite its diminutive size, Brody's Smart car was much faster than she'd expected. He threw it around the back roads heading towards the A1 and, once on the multi-lane carriageways, he sat nicely in the outside lane. Only once, as the M11 approached the North Circular, did traffic clog up. She wondered if she should upgrade the satnav in her car.

"So whose this Patrick Harper then?" Brody asked, as he sped past a white van.

"You remember Kim Chang?"

"The friend of the first victim?"

"He's her boyfriend. I met him on Monday. I did wonder about the car at the time, especially when Kim told me he was a student. I thought he must have rich parents, but she explained that he was running an online business, something to do with advertising. Click . . ."

"Click-throughs."

"Yeah, something like that."

"Well, it looks like his lucrative online business is SecretlyWatchingYou. It's certainly making him enough money to buy a car like that."

Brody coughed abruptly, the small car juddering slightly. "Why would Harper broadcast his girlfriend on SWY?"

"Maybe he gets off on others watching."

As the final destination came into view, a dockside warehouse converted into apartments, Jenny phoned Fiona. "Where is he now?"

"Traffic's been awful. We're only just passing Lord's Cricket Ground. Looks like he's heading home."

They were still a good thirty minutes away.

"Okay, we'll be there waiting when he arrives. Make sure you follow in right behind him as he enters the building. I don't want him to see us and do a runner. After spending the night cooped up in this matchbox toy, I'm not sure my legs could take it."

She ignored Brody's affronted look.

On Jenny's suggestion, Brody parked his car around the corner, out of sight, and they tailgated in through the secured front door when another resident exited for work. Harper's apartment was a luxury penthouse. They took the lift to the top floor. Jenny had anticipated waiting for him right outside his front door. As they stood in the hallway, Brody suggested pressing the bell, just in case. And as Jenny had raised her finger to the button, the door had opened, making her jump.

Quickly, Jenny considered the best way to answer Kim's question about why they were there.

"We're here to ask him some questions about his online business."

"Is this related to Anna?"

"It might be, yes."

"Oh."

"Nice flat," said Brody, looking around.

"What?" Kim was unsettled. "Yes, I suppose." She sat herself down at the glass dining table, a round sheet of glass resting on what looked like a tree stump. Jenny joined her.

"Are you okay, Kim?"

Brody left them to it and began nosing around the flat, poking his head into each room. She watched him pull a device out of his canvas man bag, some kind of handheld scanner.

"Yes. No. I'm all over the place since Anna was . . . since Anna died." She wrapped her arms around herself. Jenny could see tears beginning to form. She grabbed a tissue from the box on the table and handed it to her. Kim wiped her eyes and blew her nose. "Her Mum came round yesterday. She was ice cold as she poked through her things. Not a flicker of emotion. I know they didn't get on but come on, it's her daughter."

"Maybe shutting off her emotions is her way of grieving."

As they talked, she could see Brody at the bookcase on the far wall, selecting books, examining them and placing them back on the shelf. He dropped the scanner back in his satchel, pulled out his tablet PC and began swiping his fingers on its surface.

Jenny tried to swing the conversation with Kim towards Patrick.

"How long has Patrick lived here?"

"He told me he moved in here about a month before we met. We've been together just over a year now."

Brody piped up from the other side of the room, his eyes fixed on his computer. "Just the one bedroom?"

Kim turned to answer him. "Yeah, over there."

Jenny wished he'd leave the conversation to her. She was the professional here.

"Do you know the name of his online business? The website?" asked Jenny.

Kim furrowed her brows and shrugged. "Sorry, I never thought to ask."

Brody walked over to the hallway door, looked at his watch and interjected. "He's still a good twenty minutes away and, I don't know about you Jenny, but I'm famished. I'm going to pop down to that coffee shop we passed on the way in and grab some provisions. You want anything?"

Jenny was irked at Brody's interruptions. Perhaps it would be better if he were out of the way. "Just a cappuccino for me. Kim, you want anything?"

She shook her head.

"Okay, back soon."

Jenny heard the front door shut behind him.

She chatted with Kim. The conversation was less an interview and more akin to two friends catching up. Kim even asked after her nephew, surprising Jenny who'd forgotten she had shared some personal details when they'd talked the other evening. About ten minutes later, Jenny heard a faint thump through the walls and looked at Kim questioningly.

"Must be the neighbours."

There had been two other doors on the top landing. Jenny let it pass.

Her phone rang. It was Fiona.

"He's just passed Tower Bridge, heading east. Definitely heading your way. Satnav says eleven minutes."

"Okay, thanks. See you soon."

Kim asked. "Did Brody mean Patrick earlier? When he said someone was on the way here?"

"Yes."

"What's he done, Jenny?"

Jenny didn't want to lie. Yet at this stage she didn't have any direct evidence of anything. Alan and Karim would be treating the SEAT Toledo as a crime scene by now. Hopefully, there would be prints and DNA in it that tied back to Patrick. And then they would need to forensically examine the PC in the boot of the car. Maybe the techies would find something on there that tied back to SWY. It was all very hopeful, but at this stage she had nothing concrete. And anyway, she couldn't risk Kim warning him.

"I can't say until I speak with him. I'm sorry Kim."

Kim seemed to accept it.

Her phone rang again. It was Da Silva's number. There was no way she could give him an update in front of Kim. She let it go to voicemail.

After another ten minutes, her phone beeped with a text from Fiona. "Harper's on the way up."

Inside the lift, Patrick Harper, known on the CrackerHack forums as Crooner42, pressed the button for the sixth floor.

As it rose, he studied his reflection in the mirrored interior walls, marvelling that if he stood to one side and looked towards the corners, he could see his profile just as others would see him, the mirrors double-reflecting at ninety-degrees to each other and affording him this rare glimpse of himself. He could even see the same reflection repeated behind, smaller each time, disappearing off to infinity. Perhaps he ought to change his round glasses for something more stylish. He'd take a look through *GQ* later.

SecretlyWatchingYou had given Patrick all the trappings of wealth. The clothes, the grooming, the sports car, the penthouse apartment, and, in a different way, the girlfriend. His reflected profile displayed some of those trappings but, now that he could see himself as others saw him, he could still make out the geeky kid hidden within. The child who had been mercilessly bullied at his inner-city school for always having his head in a book, or for always being in front of a computer. The teenager who had been sent to juvenile detention centre not once, but twice. At thirteen he had set fire to the school sports centre after having blocked both exits and trapped all his tormentors within, although they had been saved from burning to death by the heroics of their physics teacher. After eight months of unbelievably worse torture from vicious youth detention centre kids who made the school bullies look like pussycats, he had been relieved to be returned to society, only to find that his parents refused to take him back, fearful for the lives of his two younger siblings.

Four sets of foster parents later, Patrick's second incarceration took place a year after he'd settled down and began to enjoy life for the first time, having finally been adopted by the Smith family. This time, a certain computer hacker called Fingal, who had been hired by the online gambling sites to crack down on cheaters, had ruined his life. Not only had Fingal exposed a hacker called Zyr0ss as being behind an impressively sophisticated poker bot scam, but he had somehow led the police to his home, where his unsuspecting adoptive parents had duly washed their hands of sixteen-year old Patrick Smith. After another eighteen months of unrelenting torment in a different youth detention centre, he was free again, never to make it out of state care homes, only restricted to accessing computers at the local library.

When Patrick turned eighteen, he dropped his adoptive surname and had it legally changed back to Harper, his birth name, vowing to one-day wreak revenge on Fingal. It had taken him much longer than planned. He'd needed to build up his credibility in the hacking circles from scratch once more, unable to use his old handle Zyr0ss, its reputation having been destroyed by Fingal's scalp. That's when Crooner42 had been born, and a couple of other backup handles just in case. And here he was, moments away from ruining Fingal's online credibility, exactly what Fingal had done to him five years ago. He licked his lips in anticipation.

The lift doors slid open.

Patrick put the key in the lock and pushed open the door. Immediately, he could tell someone was in the flat. Perhaps Kim hadn't yet left. Damn, he couldn't access his control centre while she was here. He'd need to get rid of her.

He knew now that it had been a flaw in the design of his apartment. With the benefit of hindsight, he should have installed a second way into the secret room that contained all of the screens he used to monitor SWY. The toilet off the hall backed onto the same room. Maybe he'd get the designers back in a few weeks to install a concealed door in the toilet and hide it behind a long mirror. That might work. At least then, whenever he had guests, he could pretend to go to the loo and secretly access the room.

"You still here, darling?" he called down the hallway.

No answer. Odd.

He entered the living room and halted abruptly, shocked to see two women standing by the dining table. Kim, as he'd expected, and DI Jenny Price, who he'd last seen in person on Monday at Kim's flat, and via webcams quite a few times since.

"W-what's going on?" he stammered, his brain rapidly processing the implications. Was her presence somehow linked to Fingal's presence in Bushey? He looked around, making sure that Fingal was nowhere to be seen. That would be too much.

The doorbell rang. What the hell was going on?

"I'll get that," said the detective, who walked past him. She opened the door and he heard her greet two more colleagues.

He looked at Kim and repeated, "What's going on?"

"You tell me, Patrick," she said, coldly, a tone he'd never heard in her voice before.

"Tell us what you know about SecretlyWatchingYou, Mr Harper," said DI Price, returning to the living room, her colleagues in tow.

"I don't know what you're talking about."

"I see. In that case, tell me, where were you this morning?"

"None of your fucking business."

Kim raised an eyebrow, surprised to hear him swear. She folded her arms and said to the detective, "He told me he was going to work."

"Work?" Price turned to Patrick. "Yes, where do you work? How does a student pay for a pad like this and drive around in a 911 like the one you've just arrived in?"

Patrick repeated his last response, enunciating every word, layering in more aggression. "None of your fucking business."

"I'll be the judge of that."

"Get the fuck out of my flat," he shouted, starting to lose control. And, pissed off at Kim, added for her benefit, "All of you. Now!"

"I don't know what you've done, Patrick," said Kim menacingly. "But I am leaving. Permanently."

Patrick could feel his walls crumbling down. Losing Kim one day was inevitable. His ears pounded. He needed to lash out.

"Fuck off then," he said through clenched teeth. "You mean nothing to me anyway." The words were out before he could take them back.

Kim's eyes bulged in terror and disbelief. "What's wrong with you, Patrick? I've never seen you like this."

Patrick clenched his fists. Involuntarily, she took a step back from him.

The detective stepped forward. "Watch yourself, Mr Harper. If you want me to arrest you, I will."

"What the fuck for?"

"About two hundred contraventions against the Human Rights Act of 1998 for a start, which, under Article 8, has provisions for the right to respect a person's private and family life."

The male detective chimed in, "And then there's the Data Protection Act of the same year."

The other female detective added, "And don't forget the offence of voyeurism, which is covered by the Sexual Offences Act of 2003."

Patrick could feel his stomach churning. They knew about SWY. But he held his ground.

"You've got nothing. Now get the fuck out."

He felt the draught before he heard the familiar low hum of the mechanism. He saw the shocked glances on all four faces, each of which looked beyond him. He knew then that his world was going to fall out from under him, but he whirled around anyway, needing to see with his eyes, rather than rely on his other senses.

The bookcase slowly parted, revealing the secret room. Patrick's jaw slackened completely. He wondered if he'd accidentally pressed the button on his key fob, but no, that was safe inside his jacket pocket. He waited as the door swung open to reach its zenith.

Out stepped Fingal.

"Crooner42," he declared, a triumphant grin plastered on his face. "You've just been pwned."

Brody couldn't keep the smile from his face.

But then Crooner42's horrified expression slowly morphed into an angry snarl and, with a guttural roar, he charged. Completely unprepared, Brody felt Crooner42 crash into him, his body lifting off the ground to fly backwards into the room. He landed on his back, his head banging heavily on the wooden floor, Crooner42's weight landing on his body, winding him. Dazed, Brody could only watch as Crooner42 pulled a fist back to strike him. Just as he let fly, O'Reilly tackled his attacker from behind. Crooner42 was knocked to one side. O'Reilly used his whole body weight to pin down Crooner42's thrashing body. Jenny and Fiona rushed in and, with a pair of handcuffs, the three officers quickly subdued him.

Brody got to his feet, rubbing the back of his head. He checked his hand for blood, but there was none. His skull throbbed and his ribs ached. The others stood up, leaving Crooner42 lying on the floor.

"What have you done?" wailed Crooner42, staring at the wall of screens.

All thirty-three of them displayed the same thing, the front page of SecretlyWatchingYou. Only, instead of the site's usual panel of webcam images, it showed a diagonal banner in large red font that spelled out, "Pwned by Fingal".

Kim, who was standing at the doorway to the secret room, demanded, "What the hell is all this, Patrick?"

Crooner42 — Brody found it hard to think of him as Patrick — looked up at his girlfriend but said nothing. He looked away, ashamed. Brody frowned. The hacker looked familiar somehow, but he couldn't place it.

Brody answered for him. "This is where your boyfriend controls SecretlyWatchingYou.com from. He set it up three years ago. Like all small businesses, he started small with just one location where he hacked into someone's private Wi-Fi webcams and broadcast whatever streams he found, for a small fee of course, over the Internet. As time went by, he opened more and more locations on the site to meet demand. And as he did, more and more paying voyeurs found the site. Classic supply and demand. Quite the entrepreneur, aren't you, Crooner?"

"Crooner?" asked Jenny.

"Crooner42 to be precise. That's his handle on the hacker sites."

"And what's your hacker handle, Brody?" Jenny asked.

And only then did Brody's feeling of triumph crash down.

"Fingal," spat Crooner42 from the floor.

O'Reilly stepped forward, measuring Brody up and down, a note of awe in his voice. "Fingal? For the life of me, I don't believe it. You?"

Brody said nothing.

"Who's Fingal?" Jenny asked the police techie.

"Fingal's one of the world's most elite hackers. In the hacking community, he's world famous."

"I'm just Brody Taylor," countered Brody. "I'm not this Fingal you speak of."

Crooner42 grunted in disbelief.

"Now, how can you say that?" demanded O'Reilly. "Look at the screens behind you. Your name's plastered all over, so it is!"

"That's got nothing to do with me."

"On the contrary, it's got *everything* to do with you," argued

O'Reilly. "You were after putting it there when you pwned the site."

"What the hell is 'pawning'?" demanded Fiona.

"It's a hacker word for 'own'. They're after using it when they break into a site and take full control. When they own it."

"I didn't pwn the site. All I did was break into this room and let you lot in. Someone else must have pwned it."

"Don't be an eejit. Your fingerprints will be all over the keyboard."

"No, they're not."

They weren't. Brody had used the tablet PC that Crooner42 had left by the reclining chair to do his work. It was securely connected to the site; no hacking required. It hadn't taken him long to disable the site and replace the front page with his message. He'd also announced it live on CrackerHack, making sure he got full credit for his crazy week's work. Once he was done, he wiped down the tablet PC and pressed the button to open the secret door. After the days of failing to crack the site from a frontal assault and the wasted time driving down the HomeWebCam false alley, the final steps to pwn SecretlyWatchingYou had been surprisingly straightforward.

"Right, this whole room is a crime scene," announced Jenny, asserting control. "Everyone except Harry out into the living room. Harry, this is all physical and digital evidence. Can you secure it properly, please."

Crooner42 shrugged off Fiona's offer to help and struggled to his feet. She led him out into the living room.

"You've got a lot of explaining to do, Brody," whispered Jenny threateningly, as she walked out beside him. "If I find out you're this Fingal character, I'll have you for . . ." She faltered, realising the rest of the phrase.

Smiling, Brody finished the sentence for her. "Breakfast?"

She elbowed him in his sore ribs.

CHAPTER 21

Brody stood at the back of Crooner42's living room, observing the police in their white coveralls follow their crime scene containment procedures. They had multiplied like rabbits in the hour since Patrick Harper, aka Crooner42, had been taken into custody. He had been asked to put on white overshoes and latex gloves so as not to further contaminate the scene.

He'd wanted to leave, but Jenny had demanded that he stay. She had even threatened to arrest him for burglary after his earlier stunt; breaking into Patrick Harper's secret room.

When he'd arrived with Jenny, he'd nosed around, admiring the original Asteroids arcade machine and the Adams Family pinball machine. What had first struck him as odd was the complete absence of any computer devices. If this were the home of Crooner42 then surely he would have IT equipment somewhere? At the very least, there should be a Wi-Fi router, but he could find nothing. He remembered that he still had the cellular activity monitor in his satchel and so he fished it out. Sure enough, he tracked plenty of Wi-Fi signals emanating from the wall behind the bookcase. Using his tablet, he jumped on the Internet and found the estate agent's original advertisement, which included a floor plan of the apartment, showing a second bedroom, accessible from a door where the bookcase now stood.

Brody made an excuse about grabbing a coffee from a nearby coffee shop, but instead he found the access hatch to the loft above the penthouse in the hallway. He let the front door slam shut and quietly climbed up, making his way by the light of his mobile phone to the approximate area above the hidden room. He had been prepared to force a foot through the plasterboard ceiling, but fortunately he found a second hatch, which he pulled upwards, gaining access to Crooner42's private sanctuary, crammed full of computers and monitors.

Like most hackers, Crooner42 had invested all his focus in protecting his site from external threats from the Internet, never expecting anyone to track him down in the physical world, where he was completely defenceless. Secure in his secret lair, Crooner42's personal tablet PC lay unguarded on a coffee table, permanently logged into the admin console of SWY. Armed with this, Brody took full advantage and, within minutes, had successfully pwned the site and brought it down. He logged into CrackerHack to announce his achievement to everyone. Fingal had won the contest against Matt_The_Hatter and retained his elite status; probably even enhancing it a little further.

As much as he was delighted to have saved his reputation, he was deeply concerned about Jenny. He could tell she was nowhere near convinced that he and Fingal weren't the same person. She'd told him quietly, with a slight catch in her voice, that she wasn't willing to trust him right now but wanted to keep him nearby, where he could do no damage.

He didn't blame her.

His protestations that he wasn't Fingal and the complete lack of evidence to prove he was didn't conceal the fact that the timing of Brody's revelation of Crooner42's secret lair and the pwning of SWY by Fingal had occurred at exactly the same time. Right when Brody had unfettered access to SWY from within Crooner42's secret room.

But admitting the truth had greater repercussions. Putting the laws he might have ridden roughshod over to one side, his greater concern was their personal relationship. He was absolutely smitten and didn't want what they had to fade into history like any other one-night-stand. And telling the truth would surely end it. How could a police officer knowingly continue a relationship with someone like him, a professional computer hacker, white hat or not?

A huddle formed in the kitchen to discuss the case. He could see Jenny, O'Reilly, Fiona and their boss Da Silva, who'd arrived earlier, upset about something, despite the major break in their case. Jenny had introduced Brody to him as a witness who came forward to help, nothing more, and Da Silva had curtly shaken his hand and moved on.

"Where are we up to?" asked Da Silva.

"The site's been taken down," said O'Reilly.

"So as long as all the equipment in there stays off, SecretlyWatchingYou is dead in the water?"

"It isn't, sir, there's a bit more to it. The site is hosted in Russia. Yer man's equipment in there was only used to administer and monitor the site." O'Reilly struggled with making Da Silva understand.

Jenny jumped in. "Sir, the site has been stopped. And its creator has been arrested. The killer can't use it to lure any new victims. That's the main thing."

"Okay, let me get this straight. We bag up everything here. We continue the cross-force collaboration I've already got going and impound all of the shadow PC vehicles located all over the country. We tell all the people who own the webcams that they've been hacked, in case they want to rethink their usage. And we put Harper in jail for whatever laws he's broken putting up that site."

The three officers nodded.

"That's it?" he demanded. "I can't go to the press with that! We're no nearer to catching the perpetrator."

"But we've cut off the killer's food supply. That's a major step forward," retorted Jenny.

"And we're still following up with Flexbase on the meeting room bookings," continued Fiona. "We've got the IP address used at the time. It was from a mobile device over a 3G network. We're working with Vodafone to get a mobile number and hopefully an address."

"It's not enough," said Da Silva.

"Well now, maybe we can bring in specialists from the NCCU to help?" suggested O'Reilly.

"Who are they?"

"The National Cyber Crime Unit. Part of the National Crime Agency."

"That's interesting," said Da Silva.

Brody couldn't bear to listen to their committee-based approach on how to move forward. The NCCU had been a huge step forward for the UK in fighting cyber-crime, but like most things it always came down to the skills of the individual assigned to the case. They might get assigned someone not much more capable than O'Reilly. And, like any police investigator, they would be hamstrung by their own policies and procedures.

They needed someone who would take a more direct approach.

They needed a hacker.

"I can help," said Brody, stepping forward.

The four officers turned to face him.

"No way," said Jenny and O'Reilly in unison.

Da Silva lifted his eyebrows. He was giving it consideration.

Brody justified his offer. "You need to move quickly in case the killer begins to cover his tracks. He'll soon know the site is down. The data you need is stored in the SWY database. All you need to do is search through it, cross-referencing customer viewing habits with the three victim locations. That will give you a short list of paying customers. From there, you can see what personal details are stored, although I suspect not much given the nature of the site, and then maybe track down who they are through their payment methods, eliminating anyone not in the UK. Once you have a shortlist, you can then go shake them down."

"Who are you again?" asked Da Silva.

"I'm an independent IT consultant. I do security penetration testing for large corporations to help them defend against cyber criminals. I am good at what I do and I can help you right now."

A long pause.

Fiona spoke up for him. "He's the one who helped us save Sarah McNeil in Watford yesterday."

Jenny shot her a murderous look.

"Did he now?" said Da Silva.

"Sir, this is wrong," warned Jenny. "This is all evidence. We have chain of custody procedures to follow."

Da Silva countered, "That may all be true. But in UK law, whether evidence is gathered improperly or not does not mean the evidence can't be used at trial."

"But if you affect the evidence contained within the SWY

website, our case against Harper could fall apart," stated Jenny.

"I'm less concerned about Harper. Our priority is to put away the culprit for the murders of Anna Parker and Audri Sahlberg, and the attempted murders of Sarah McNeil and you, Jenny."

"If it helps," said Brody, "I'm happy to have O'Reilly observe everything I do. Maybe he can keep me on the straight and narrow."

"There's no danger of that," grumbled O'Reilly.

Jenny finished freshening up in the ladies' toilets in Holborn Station and headed to the interview rooms. After having spent the night in Brody's car, she'd been desperate to freshen up. She was looking forward to getting out of the clothes she was wearing and having a proper shower when she got home to her flat later.

She and Fiona had returned to the station in her car. She'd left Brody and Harry to it after Da Silva had given his permission for them to proceed with Brody's plan. Apparently, it would take a good few hours to work through the data. Da Silva had also made his way back.

When Jenny had originally called Da Silva from Harper's flat in Docklands to give him the good news that SWY had been shut down and they had the person behind it in custody, he'd initially been annoyed, thinking it would negate the need for his high-profile coordination role with every other force in the country to shut down each SWY location. She reminded him that they still needed to gather all the evidence, which was physically present in the shadow PCs located in the cars parked outside them all. Happy once again, he'd called another press conference. Jenny was convinced that Da Silva saw the whole case as one big PR exercise for his personal profile.

The fact that he'd blindly relied on her expertise behind the scenes was somewhat reckless, but then he'd not had much choice. He was self-aware enough to recognise his own lack of experience and so he'd made a judgement call that she was his best way through it all. All week she had shouldered the SIO's decision-making burden, Da Silva acting as little more than a mouthpiece, handing out her orders to the investigation team. She had felt the pressure mounting as the case wore on, but she had come through in the end. Although she realised that most of the breakthroughs during the week had come about thanks to Brody.

Da Silva had then turned up at Docklands, with the primary motive of being seen to be in charge. And once there, he'd finally done exactly that, and stepped up and made a decision all on his own, taking up Brody's offer of assistance, despite her very vocal reticence.

She didn't know why she was so bothered. She'd relied on Brody all week herself. But a small instinctive part of her suspected that she was on dangerous ground with him. She desperately wanted to trust him, if only to warrant the intimacy they'd shared two nights ago. Everything he'd done had helped drive the case forward. But she'd been unable to shake the feeling that something else was going on.

She knew where to get some answers.

She opened the door of the interview room.

Patrick Harper looked up and grimaced.

Opposite him sat DC Fiona Jones, perfectly presented, no clues at all that she'd spent last night stuck in Jenny's Audi with Harry.

Jenny sat next to Fiona, who led them through the preliminaries, the tape running. She confirmed Patrick's right to a solicitor. He declined.

"I take it you want to cooperate?"

"Yes."

"Why?"

"Don't you want me to?"

"I'm just surprised, given you thought everything was 'none of our business' back at your apartment."

"Yeah, well that was before that bastard opened my control room and took away any choice I had."

"I see."

"So what do you need to know?"

She wanted to know about Brody, but that was secondary. If Harper was going to confess, she needed to get it all.

"Let's start at the beginning then. Tell us about SecretlyWatchingYou."

Harper stared at them both, one by one. Jenny guessed he was still weighing up the pros and cons in his mind. He knew he'd been caught red-handed and so pleading guilty and confessing was his best chance of a reduced sentence. Although what a judge would make of all this, Jenny had no idea.

She waited patiently. Years of interview experience told her that he needed to be the one to speak next. And once he started he'd not stop. After a long twenty seconds or so, Harper adjusted his glasses and opened his mouth.

"It all started with Walter Pike."

"The landlord for your girlfriend's flat in Charlton?"

"Yes, him. But it was the year before Kim moved in. If it weren't for that pervert, I'd never have had the idea for SecretlyWatchingYou."

Harper went on to explain how he had been employed by McCarthy Security Ltd back then, as one of the CCTV fitters, working part time while going to college. At the time, they had been a traditional security services company, fitting proprietary CCTV systems the old fashioned way, mostly for businesses. But Nicky McCarthy stumbled across HomeWebCam and secured their UK franchise. Harper's computer background made him the primary installation expert. Most of the IP webcam installations were innocuous enough, but Harper smelled a rat when it came to Pike, who ordered cameras for every room of an empty house. As Harper had been the installer, he knew all the passwords and went back a month later and snuck a peak. Pike had let the house out to five female third-year students from the local University and was spending nearly every waking moment secretly spying on them through HomeWebCam. Over the course of the next few months, Pike ordered four more IP webcam installations from McCarthy which Harper installed, feeling more disgusted every time.

But Pike made him realise that if one person would go to such lengths to fuel his voyeuristic perversions, then maybe there was a business opportunity. Being the expert in the webcam setup, he knew that they could be configured to multi-cast. One night he came up with the idea for the shadow PCs. He tried it out on Pike's properties and then slowly built a website to coordinate, receive and eventually monetise the webcam streams.

Patrick bought his cars from auctions cheaply and registered them to a partially fake address in Stratford where he knew someone who used to live there. It was a house split into four flats, 6A to 6D, all sharing a single front door and mailbox. In the hallway, they had four secure boxes for the post and a trust arrangement amongst the tenants to sort the mail into each other's boxes. Through his friend, Harper added a fifth and no one seemed to think anything of it, duly dropping any correspondence for the non-existent 6E into his private letterbox. The DVLA was none the wiser, the cars were all registered and not showing as stolen, and he was able to respond to any correspondence. In fact, Harper explained that his friend had long since moved out, but because Harper had kept the key to the front door, he was still able to collect his post.

Jenny, who knew about the address in Stratford, said nothing. Just let him get it all out. However, she couldn't help but admire the simplicity of it.

Once the website was launched, quietly and with no fanfare, not wanting to attract the wrong kind of attention, it slowly started to gain an audience. He knew what he was doing probably broke some laws somewhere, and so he hosted it within a bulletproof datacentre in Russia.

"Bulletproof?" asked Jenny.

"It means that the hosting company won't play ball with any law agencies. No police could ever get them to agree to take down my site. Bulletproof."

"So the website was a success straight away."

"Enough that it covered the initial outlay. I treated it as a proper business, managing the cash flow, only adding new locations as the paying subscriber count increased to match. But within about eight months, I couldn't keep up with demand. I stopped working for McCarthy and dropped out of college. There was a core audience that would pay for every location, no matter how obscure the content. Even fishcams, would you believe?"

Jenny had seen the fishcams on the site so yes, she did believe it.

"I invested a lot of time in securing the site. I realised that it would eventually attract attention from you lot. I just didn't expect it to stay under the radar for two-and-a-half years."

"Where does Kim come into all this?"

Harper paused in his flow and looked down at his feet. So far he had been happily boasting about his successes. Jenny and Fiona had played up to it, feigning admiration, oohing and aahing at all the right moments. Jenny was surprised at herself. It wasn't even that hard to be impressed with what he'd done. He'd shown impressive business initiative. If only it hadn't been completely illegal.

"Kim and Anna moved into Walter Pike's property just over eighteen months ago, along with the other four tarts. At first I was just checking the streams, not particularly being nosey. But over time, I found myself captivated by Kim. She's gorgeous, funny, sincere. And way out of my league. I couldn't stop watching her."

Something about his uncharacteristically tender admission struck a chord with Jenny. Her recollection was hazy, but this wasn't the first time in recent memory she'd heard a story like this. She said nothing, not wanting to stop him getting everything off his chest.

"I know what I am, DI Price. At heart, I'm a geek. A nerd. An anorak. I was one right through school and —" he hesitated. "Well, you'll see my juvenile record soon enough."

She had no idea what he was referring to. Earlier in the case she'd requested a search on Kim's boyfriend, just in case, but nothing had come up on Patrick Harper at all. She made a mental note to look into it.

He continued. "So, the million dollar question. How does someone like me pull someone like Kim?"

"With knowledge," stated Fiona. "Exploiting private knowledge."

"In one, DC Jones," he said, throwing a pointed finger at her as if he was a quiz show host awarding her a prize. "Yes, I studied her and fell even harder for her. Even now, I think she's wonderful. I love her completely. I'd do anything for her. But I know she's been having second thoughts about me. I listened to her over the webcam debating her feelings about me with Anna a couple of weeks ago. That cow never liked me, always sticking the knife in."

Jenny couldn't help herself. Interview be damned. "Well, thanks to you, one of your website customers really did stick the knife into her."

"Yeah, I do feel bad about that." But he wore a cold smile and Jenny didn't believe a word. He'd said it for the benefit of the tape.

"Anyway, so I planned my first encounter with Kim carefully. There was this karaoke restaurant she liked to go to. I've always been able to knock out a tune — I was once likened to Frank Sinatra and so that's why my online handle is Crooner42, Fingal was right about that — and so I stood up and belted out her favourite song. It had the desired effect and before she knew it, we were seeing each other." Adopting a sarcastic tone, he threw one hand forward limply, an over-the-top effeminate gesture. "You wouldn't *believe* how much we had in common."

"And no doubt you were able to keep refining your act based on feedback you heard through the webcams."

"You got that right. Our whole relationship has been founded on lies and deceit. It's amazing how easy it is to manipulate someone when you know her intimate thoughts. Her hopes and dreams."

"I know what you mean," agreed Jenny, deadpan, holding his eye. "There's a murderer out there using the exact same trick, only he lures unsuspecting women to their deaths."

Harper sat back in his chair. He held his tongue, but she could see that he was annoyed with her for demeaning his story. "Do you want to hear this or not?"

This time Jenny bit her tongue.

"How much money is the site making, Patrick?" asked Fiona, appealing to his ego once more.

He grinned before speaking, obviously very proud of what he was about to say. "It's been growing at about fifteen per cent per month for the last year. I've been growing the number of locations on the site at a rate of two or three per month, each one a net new revenue stream. At the moment, there are over twenty thousand monthly subscribers. And that equates to a turnover of about £100,000 a month. And costs are minimal, so profit is high."

"Hence the 911 and the penthouse apartment."

"Yeah, well. No point earning the money without spending it."

"I take it you pay your taxes," said Fiona.

"Actually, I do. I didn't want to come a cropper like Al Capone."

"But you have come a cropper, haven't you?" jibed Jenny deliberately.

"Yeah," he reflected. "That's partly my own fault. I put my head in the lion's mouth and got bit."

"What's that supposed to mean?"

"Fingal," he said, a despairing tone creeping into his youthful arrogance. "I dragged him into this and it's backfired on me."

"Go on."

"I tricked him into doing a pentest on SWY. I sent out a request for help on CrackerHack —" Noticing the confused expression on both women's faces, he explained, "It's one of the places where hackers get together on the deep web, the secret area of the net hidden under the regular Internet. Anyway, I made it look like the request had gone out to everyone, generating buzz all over the forums about it. But in reality only Fingal had received it. He took the bait. But then I pretended to choose someone else for the job, making it look like Fingal was second choice. As expected, the community did what they always do and turned the whole thing into a contest between him and the other guy. With that much focus, I knew that Fingal would give it his best shot. His elite status in the hacking community was totally at risk if he failed to hack into SWY. And to a computer hacker, status is worth more than anything. We'll do anything to protect that. Including, so it seems, " he gave a contemptuous smile, "getting into bed with the police."

Jenny's fists clenched. For a brief moment, she thought Harper's comment was alluding to her and Brody's night together. That somehow her apartment was also on SWY and he'd been spying on them. But then she realised he'd meant the police in general and not her specifically. She unclenched her fists and calmly laid her palms on the table.

"You said earlier that Fingal and Brody were one and the same. What makes you think that?" Jenny tried to ask the question in the same light tone as every previous question, trying not to let on that this, for her, was the most important topic.

"Easy. He tried to hack into SWY on Monday and Tuesday, using all the usual tricks of the trade. He attacked it with everything he could think of. But no luck. Like I said, I did a good job on the site's defences. And on Wednesday, you show up with Brody at the Saxtons' and then at Kim's. He's obviously looking for a backdoor into the site, it's the logical next step, although admittedly I didn't think of it at the time. Only he can't find a route in and that's because he's so fixated on what he can see in front of his nose, a red herring called HomeWebCam."

"That's a bit thin. Brody being there on Wednesday could be a coincidence. Nothing to do with Fingal."

"Did Brody tell you why he was looking into SecretlyWatchingYou?"

"Yes, but it's none of your business."

Jenny recalled Brody's barefaced lie in their very first meeting in the coffee house in Docklands. His story about helping out a friend whose girlfriend was being stalked because of secret webcams at work. And when she'd pressed him on it later that night over drinks, he'd changed it to a story about him and his flatmate fooling around on the Internet. But, now that she thought about it, her memory sharpening, he'd diverted her attention by saying how much he'd been enamoured by *her*. Flattered, she hadn't pursued it at the time. She felt her cheeks colour.

"Hah!" shrieked Harper. "He lied to you. No surprise there then. He's well known for being one of the best social engineers in the game."

Fiona asked him to explain.

"A social engineer is a computer hacker who hacks the weakest link in all computing systems. Humans. They're like a cross between a hacker and a conman. They gain your confidence so that you divulge sensitive information they can then use to complete the hack. Usually it's passwords and stuff. But Fingal failed to hack SWY directly, so he reverted to type and hacked the humans. In this case, it was the people in the webcams. He would have figured that if he tracked them down to a location in the real world, he could follow the webcam streams back to SWY. Only the location he chose was the Saxtons', which just happened to be crawling with police. So he did what came naturally and social engineered you lot as well." Harper sat back and folded his arms. "You've got to admit, he's got some front."

"Everything you just said is completely circumstantial."

"All right, try this for size." Visibly enjoying himself now, Harper leaned forward. "You were at Kim's the other day, tracking down the webcams. Yes, yes, I was watching you all. Well, when you lot left the room to go search for tools to break through the padlocked door hiding Walter Pike's HomeWebCam network video recorder PC, Brody took a call on his mobile. I heard his whole conversation. It was Dwight Chambers, the CTO of HomeWebCam. But get this: Brody answered the phone as 'DCI Burnside'. You remember, that dirty TV cop from *The Bill* years ago? Turns out Fingal was in the middle of social engineering Dwight Chambers, pretending to be the police to get them to check their firewall logs for connections between HomeWebCam and SecretlyWatchingYou. Of course, there were none. He was still barking up the wrong tree at that time. But the point is that he's always had his own agenda. You were just a means to an end."

"And you can prove this, can you?"

"Uh, actually I can. I recorded that little exchange." His confidence was formidable. If half of what he had told them was true, she would be devastated. To have been manipulated so totally. So completely.

He continued. "The file is stored on my tablet PC . . ." Suddenly, Harper smashed his fist on the table violently. "Fuck, fuck, fuck. Of course! It won't be there now. Fingal was in my secret room. He'll have found that already and deleted it. God, he's a clever bastard."

"Why do you care so much about Fingal?"

"Revenge. Nothing more, nothing less. When you read my juvenile record you'll see I've been inside before, well in youth detention centre. Before I was eighteen. But the reason I got caught then was because of that bastard. He tracked me down in the real world and gave my details to the police. Next thing I know, I'm arrested and my life is ruined. All thanks to him. I vowed to get revenge."

His logic was completely twisted to justify his motivation. No acceptance that whatever he'd been doing at the time was justification enough for what happened to him.

"And have you?"

The leer that split his face was deeply chilling. "Yeah, I think I have."

He wouldn't offer any more explanation. Given that he'd been open about pretty much everything else, Jenny was suddenly concerned for Brody. If there really was any truth to him and Fingal being one and the same, then whatever Harper had done sounded ominous.

"Yet you're in here. You've lost everything. SecretlyWatchingYou. Kim. Everything."

"Still worth it. Just to bring that bastard down."

Brody had been at it for two hours now, with O'Reilly observing every move. Most of that time had been spent familiarising himself with the structure of the site, focusing primarily on its underlying data model. He needed to understand how to join the tables within the database in order to be able to construct sensible queries against it.

Crime scene technicians had been working around them, processing the apartment for physical evidence. More than once,

O'Reilly had to step in to stop them touching any of Patrick's IT equipment.

"This is fierce sophisticated."

"Yeah, it is," agreed Brody. "Such a waste of talent."

O'Reilly's animosity towards Brody had subsided as he watched him work, admiring the skills of the more experienced computer technician.

"Okay, I think we've done enough reconnaissance. Let's make a proper start."

Brody queried the number of registered users on the site. They both whistled in surprise at the result displayed.

"So, somewhere amongst these ninety-eight thousand email addresses is the murderer. We just have to narrow it down."

O'Reilly nodded.

"Shame, Harper didn't set up the system to store the IP addresses of users each time they logged in. That might have made it easier."

"How come?"

"Didn't DI Price tell you? We've got hold of the IP address used by the killer when he booked the meeting rooms on the Flexbase website."

"She didn't." O'Reilly's reaction was more petulant at being out of the loop than angry.

Brody ran a query to list everyone who had ever visited the three webcam locations of interest, *Student Heaven*, *Au Pair Affair*, and *Sales Floor*, the name for the location where Sarah McNeil had worked.

"That's still over fourteen thousand email addresses," commented O'Reilly.

"I know, but watch this." Brody then modified the query to list only the account IDs that were present in all three lists.

"Fair play, although there's still two-hundred and fifty-two."

Brody scanned the list to see if anything popped out. He spotted one of his own temporary email addresses there, but kept that to himself.

He narrowed it down to visits within the last two weeks.

O'Reilly kept up his running commentary. "Nineteen accounts. That's grand."

Brody brought up the payment details of everyone in the

shortlist.

"Okay, five of them," including his own, he noticed, "paid with bitcoins. We're not going to have much luck tracing them. You'll need your friends at NCCU to make any headway there, but that will take them weeks. The rest have used PayPal, so all we've got is their email address. But at least we know it's not a disposable email address, because it's linked to that payment system."

"So now, do we just contact PayPal and ask for address details?"

"Yes, but again, it will take some time. Probably a good few days."

"What else is there?"

"Most of these email addresses are full names. Let's see how many we can narrow down by searching for them on social media."

Over the course of the next hour, Brody ran searches across the Internet based on each of the remaining fourteen email addresses. He was trying to reverse engineer the name and any associated details of its owner. Out of the fourteen, he had hits with four, three of which were people located outside the UK. For the remaining ten accounts, he ran searches through every social media site using name variations derived from each email address. The downside was that so many people shared the same names that his list got much longer. He made a spreadsheet containing all the candidates found to be living in the UK. Where any were listed on LinkedIn, he noted the company name they worked at. His plan was to correlate the candidate names and companies against the Flexbase customer database he had taken a copy of when he'd hacked in there the previous day.

It was laborious work, and Brody was starting to get dejected. His eyes glazed over. He was tired from not having had much sleep during the previous night, as he and Jenny swapped shifts during the stakeout.

"Aye, aye," said O'Reilly, impersonating an English bobby. "What 'ave we 'ere?"

Brody refocused his eyes. His last search result was listed on the screen. It was from LinkedIn.

From the picture displayed on the profile, the man looked to be in his late twenties. He had brown hair, short and cropped. The name against the picture was Ronald Keeble. But the killer piece of information was the name of the company he currently worked at.

Flexbase Ltd.

Brody recognised the man. He was the CCTV operator from the Flexbase CCTV control room, introduced at the time as Ron. The one that Ray Stone, the Flexbase Head of Security, had proudly mentioned as having come from the Bellagio in Las Vegas. Ron had coolly helped them analyse the video footage of the killer dressed as a cyclist entering the Flexbase receptions at Paddington and Watford.

The footage of himself.

CHAPTER 22

"The odds are hundreds of thousands to one. Sure it has to be yer man."

Harry's voice emanated from the speakerphone in the centre of the oval table within the small meeting room adjoining the major incident room. The core team sat around the table, DCI Raul Da Silva at the head, his hands clasped together in triumph. Flanking him on either side were DS Alan Coombs and DC Karim Malik, recently back from processing the SEAT Toledo crime scene. DC Fiona Jones sat next to Jenny. DCS McLintock was also conferenced in. She was surprised he hadn't popped down; he was only in his office three floors above.

"I agree, Harry," said Da Silva confidently. "Have we got Ronald Keeble's address yet?"

Despite herself, Jenny was almost impressed with Da Silva's transformation over the course of this week. She'd kept Da Silva afloat during the early stages of the investigation, when it was nigh on impossible to properly prioritise all the different lines of enquiry. But over the last day, as the case started to narrow to its conclusion, he had taken charge, without her help in the background. He'd even started referring to his officers by their forenames.

"Yes, it's in Basildon, in Essex," said Fiona. "Confirmed from the Flexbase staff database as well as the electoral role. He's twenty-nine, unmarried and lives alone."

"He works in the security centre in the Flexbase head office in

Docklands. Spends his day watching CCTV," offered Harry.

"And his night watching webcams on SecretlyWatchingYou," added Karim. "Talk about taking your . . . work home." He just about managed to drop the swear word he'd been about to include.

Jenny recalled the quiet CCTV operator from her visit to the Flexbase headquarters the other day. It was hard for her to accept that she had only been a couple of feet from the murderer and not realised it. Surely some police instinct should have warned her. And to top it all, he had brazenly operated the CCTV controls to bring up video images of himself walking through Paddington and Watford receptions, dressed in his cycling gear. And his disguise must have had worked because, a day later, she had come eye-to-eye with the killer herself and hadn't recognised him beneath the cap and sunglasses.

But it did explain his unexpected but creepy reaction on seeing her again.

You would have been good. That's the shame of it.

Jenny wrapped her arms around herself, shuddering involuntarily.

"What else do we know about him?" asked DCS McLintock.

"No criminal record. Born and bred in Essex. Parents live in Southend. He's been working for Flexbase for nearly three years," summarised Harry, clearly enjoying his moment in the spotlight, even though he wasn't in the room. "Before that, yer man worked at the Bellagio in Las Vegas."

"Okay, so where is he now?" demanded Da Silva. "Home? Work? Somewhere in-between?"

Jenny gazed out of the window. It was early evening, dark outside. The rain had started again. She spoke up. "He'll be arriving home about now. I phoned David Dawson, the Flexbase CEO. He got Magnus Peggler, the CIO, to check the security system. Apparently, Keeble left the office just after 5:00 p.m. It would take him about an hour to get to Basildon from there. He commutes by train."

"Okay, I'll organise a search warrant and clear things with Essex constabulary," said McLintock from the speakerphone.

"Three strands," ordered Da Silva. "Alan, Karim, you're with me in Basildon. We'll request local support from Essex as well."

Jenny looked up sharply. Why hadn't he included her in the take down team?

He continued. "Harry, now that we have our chief suspect, you can finish processing the crime scene at Patrick Harper's."

"I'm yer man, sir," Harry responded, cheerfully.

"Jenny…" She clenched her hands. "You've got a relationship with Dawson at Flexbase. We need to seize Keeble's work computer as evidence. He's bound to have logged into SecretlyWatchingYou from work, as well as home. You head over there. Take Fiona."

Jenny felt everyone staring at her, knowing they'd all be shocked that she was being excluded from the arrest. She studied her fingernails. To be given such a trivial task was humiliating. It was Da Silva finally letting everyone know who was in charge. Just as she'd suspected, he would trample over anyone on his rise to the top. She should have left him to drown at the beginning of the week. But no, she'd seen an opportunity to help herself gain more SIO level experience and had grabbed the opportunity. Except the records would show DCI Raul Da Silva as SIO *and* the arresting officer of a multiple murderer.

Not DI Jenny Price.

No one spoke up. If DCS McLintock hadn't been on speakerphone, perhaps someone would have jumped to her defence.

"Everyone clear?"

"Yes, sir."

"Right, I'm off home then," said a new, tired-sounding voice from the speakerphone. "I need a shower."

Jenny hid a smile. It was Brody, still in Harper's flat with Harry. He hadn't been announced when the meeting began.

"Ah, Mr Taylor," said Da Silva, somewhat chagrined. "On behalf of the Metropolitan Police, I'd like to say a huge thank you for your invaluable assistance today."

The windscreen wipers flew side-to-side, mesmerising him. A horn beeped behind and he realised with a start that the lights had changed to green. Brody forced himself to focus and turned into Upper Street. A few hundred yards later, he slowed to a stop in the middle of the road, indicating right, although all the resident's parking spaces outside his apartment were occupied. He glanced left and saw a car pull away from outside Bruno's. Fate was telling him something again. He flipped the indicator left, checked his mirror and drove frontwards into the spot.

His usual seat was taken. He didn't care. He was too tired for anything. Without the adrenaline-fuelled rush from his earlier exploits, the lack of sleep was getting to him. He was also starving.

"Ah, Mr Brody, Mr Brody," greeted Stefan, who then halted mid-track when he saw Brody's dishevelled state. "Mr Brody, is everything okay?"

"It's been a long day, Stefan. I'm tired and hungry, what can you do for me?"

"Here, sit, sit." Stefan showed him to a sofa in the centre of the room, facing the back of the coffee lounge. Brody dropped into the sofa and fought the urge to curl up and go to sleep. "We have good panini, Mr Brody. Prosciutto, pepper and basil, or maybe chicken, olive and artichoke?"

"I'll have one of each, thanks Stefan."

"And for drink?"

"Surprise me."

Brody pulled his tablet PC out of his man bag and lazily connected to his private Wi-Fi network across the road.

He logged onto CrackerHack. As expected, he was the talk of the town. He read through the posts congratulating him on pwning Crooner42's site. He began typing, announcing his presence.

Fingal: Thanks guys.

He waited, and his screen soon filled with congratulations and questions.

Mawrpheus: You d'man, Fingal.
Random_Ness: Great work. How'd you do it? What exploit did you use?

What exploit indeed. He didn't answer. Not answering would let the buzz about him grow. Allow his elite status, that had so nearly been ruined, to elevate to an even higher plane.

Mawrpheus: Where's Matt_The_Hatter? He's a bit fucking quiet since he's been beaten.
Random_Ness: Yeah, Matty boy. Where are you, man?

Brody laughed at their bravado now that Matt_The_Hatter had been beaten. Just the other day only he and Doc_Doom had dared to stand up to Matt_The_Hatter. But Brody had discovered something all the others didn't know. There was no way Matt_The_Hatter would be joining the conversation. He couldn't. He was currently locked up in a police cell in Holborn Station.

Patrick Harper had more than one online handle. He'd been building them up over years. Crooner42 was his primary one, but Matt_The_Hatter was one of his others. Earlier in the week, when Crooner42 had initially awarded the work to Matt_The_Hatter, everyone had been shocked, including Brody. Why would passive Crooner42 award the work to the overly aggressive Matt_The_Hatter? But Harper had cleverly awarded it from one of his personas to another. Brody recalled that Matt_The_Hatter had been the first to ask Crooner42 who'd been awarded the work. It had come across as a self-serving request designed to feed his own ego, but it had been asked to prompt the community to draw the information out, resulting in the predictable conversations that had forced Fingal into a public contest against Matt_The_Hatter.

Only there had been no contest. Matt_The_Hatter already had full access to SWY. Harper had this as insurance. If, somehow, Fingal got close then Harper would quickly login as Matt_The_Hatter and pwn the site in his name. Either way, Harper would have won, humiliating Brody. Either by Brody failing or by Matt_The_Hatter apparently winning. One of Harper's handles, Crooner42 or Matt_The_Hatter, would have risen up the ranks of the hacking community while Fingal's credibility plummeted.

The fact that Harper's original request for help on pentesting SecretlyWatchingYou had been sent to him alone had been hidden in the noise that came afterwards, all generated by Harper and the rest of the online rabble. But if Brody hadn't responded that morning, then he was sure that Harper would have tried again another time.

And Brody knew now why Patrick Harper had singled him out. Revenge. Brody had once known of him as Patrick Smith, aka Zyr0ss, when he had been a sixteen-year-old hacker behind a gambling scam that Brody had been paid to unmask. Brody had never met him then, or even seen a picture. Which was why Brody still thought it strange that he'd recognised Patrick Harper when he'd first seen him earlier.

Brody had done his job at the time and provided the information to the gambling site owner, and had never thought about Patrick Smith again. Until today, when he'd looked through Patrick Harper's computer while hiding in the secret room. Brody had discovered details about his personal history and put it all together. Then he'd found login credentials stored for multiple sites, for both Crooner42 and Matt_The_Hatter, and replayed the chat logs and worked out how Harper had put it all together.

It had been a neat plan. Brody had never been so well manipulated. And it had very nearly worked.

"Here you are Mr Brody," announced Stefan with a flourish. "Two panini and a large Coca-Cola."

Stefan placed the items in front of him.

"I bring you espresso in a few minutes."

Brody thanked him and began devouring his supper. Instantly life coursed through him once again.

Refreshed, Brody felt capable of doing what he needed to do next.

He picked up his mobile phone and dialled Jenny. He hoped she would answer.

As he waited for it to connect, he noticed another message pop up on CrackerHack.

Doc_Doom: Fingal. At last. I need to talk to you. URGENTLY. Usual place. Right now.

It took four rings before he heard Jenny's voice.

"Yes, Brody." Her tone was flat, giving nothing away. He focused his attention on her. Whatever Doc_Doom wanted, it could wait.

"Hi Jenny. Hell of a day, eh?"

Nothing. Just the background noise of a car. She was on hands-free.

"You off to Flexbase in Docklands?"

"Yes."

"Can we meet up later on? I think we need to chat."

A long pause.

"I'm not sure Brody. You lied to me. Manipulated me. More than once. I'm in no mood to repeat that experience."

She was right. He had lied to her. But the truth would damn them even more.

"Jenny, whatever you've heard about me today I need you to know one thing . . ."

He waited. Another message flashed up on the screen, but he ignored it.

Doc_Doom: Fingal. This is serious. Your life is in immediate danger. We need to talk now.

"What's that, Brody?"

"I've fallen for you. Deeply. I don't want this to end. We've only just begun."

"Is that you *social engineering* me again? Saying what I want to hear so that you get what you need?"

What the hell? This was bad.

He said the only thing he could say. "It's the truth. And I'm truly sorry if I've hurt you."

"No Brody. I don't think you know the difference between truth and lies. Between right and wrong. You live in a world of grey. My world is black and white. You don't fit in my world."

"But —"

"Goodbye Brody." The line died.

Brody sat there, immobile, blinking into space.

Stefan placed a double espresso on the table in front of him. "There you go, Mr Brody." He looked at Brody's shocked face and smiled kindly. "Cheer up, Mr Brody. It may never happen."

Another message flashed on his screen.

Doc_Doom: Fingal. You've been outed.

The written words slowly filtered through the haze of Brody's mind.

And at that moment, he remembered where he'd seen Harper before. Brody was staring at the exact spot that Harper had sat two nights ago. And again yesterday. Patrick Harper had been in Bruno's.

Which meant that, somehow, he'd tracked Brody down in the real world.

Jenny hung up the hands-free on Brody and told Fiona, "You didn't hear any of that."

"Yes, boss." And then after a moment's hesitation, "So you and Brody got it together, then? We did wonder, when you chose to stay in his titchy car during the stakeout last night."

Jenny turned and stared mutely at her colleague. Fiona suddenly shouted, "Red light!"

Jenny pressed her foot on the brakes. Her A3 noisily skidded on the wet surface but halted inches from the car in front. Through the relentless windscreen wipers, she could see the wide eyes of its driver in the rear view mirror.

"I mean, there's nothing wrong with it, Jenny. He's a good-looking guy."

"It's none of your business, Fiona."

The lights changed to green and Jenny pulled off. They were nearly at the Flexbase headquarters in Docklands.

"I guess not. But for what it's worth, I think you're being a bit hard on him. I heard everything Harper said about him and even if it was all true, and the only reason he was helping us was to further his own ends; it doesn't mean he's a bad guy. Without him, we'd never have caught Keeble so quickly. Or saved Sarah McNeil. And if his only objective was to take down the website, then why did he stay on and help us identify Keeble?"

Jenny didn't have an answer for that.

"I'll tell you why," Fiona persevered, "Because of you."

Jenny turned right and pulled up outside the Flexbase headquarters in Docklands. She turned off the ignition.

In the ensuing silence between them, she could hear the rain battering the roof of her car.

"Maybe so, but that doesn't change the fact that he lied to my face," she said eventually.

"White lies at worst."

"You're too forgiving."

"And you're being too hard on him. And yourself."

They sat quietly for a minute. Finally, Fiona spoke; bringing their thoughts back to the matter in hand. "I suppose we should head in.

The sooner we seize the evidence, the sooner we can get home. At least it's the weekend."

Neither of them had exactly rushed out of Holborn to get down here, both feeling dejected that they had been excluded from the action currently occurring in Essex. After the week-long adrenaline rush, this sedate ending to the case seemed demeaning. Jenny knew full well that all cases became laborious after the initial enthusiasm, when they had to switch modes and formalise all the evidence, prepare everything for the CPS; dot every 'i', cross every 't'. But this was particularly galling.

On the phone earlier, the Flexbase CEO, David Dawson, had been shocked to hear one of his employees was implicated in the murder enquiry. He apologised that he couldn't be there himself to help them, as he was in Austria, skiing with clients. He said he would arrange for Magnus Peggler, the CIO, to meet them. Apparently, he was planning to work late this evening, doing some system upgrades in the quiet period over the weekend. And, as Dawson pointed out, Peggler would be the best person to give them access to whatever Keeble had touched.

Her phone rang again. It was Alan. She put him on speakerphone.

"Did you get him?" asked Jenny, hoping that she and Fiona could soak up some of the arrest's excitement from afar.

"Yeah, we've got him." Alan's tone was dejected.

"What's up, Al?"

"You should have been here for this. This is your collar, not his."

"Thanks, Al. I feel much the same."

"It's worse. Da Silva only tipped off the bloody press. He even made us all wait inside Keeble's home for them to arrive. They're all outside now, waiting for him to lead Keeble out and into the police van."

It would be the crowning glory for Da Silva. Only three weeks into his newly-promoted role as DCI, he'd already caught a double-murderer. He would go far.

"Look, there he goes. Television cameras and microphones. Fuck me."

"Thanks Al. We're going to finish off here at Flexbase. We'll see you and Karim in The Dolphin later, yes?"

"As long as Da Silva's not there. Yeah, okay Jen."

She ended the call. There was nothing left to say.

They exited the car and ran through the rain into the main reception of the Flexbase building.

"Leroy? Danny? You here?" Brody flew into his apartment, shouting at the top of his voice. "Leroy!"

There was no answer. He rushed down the hall, burst into the living room and came to an abrupt stop, his heart jumping into his mouth.

Leroy and Danny were in the centre of the room facing him, on their knees, side by side, their hands behind their heads. Blood was dripping from a gash on Leroy's cheek onto his t-shirt. Danny shook his head once in warning to Brody.

Brody rushed over and was immediately struck from behind. He fell flat to the floor in front of his two friends. He felt blood start to leak from the back of his head. Leroy reached over to help Brody.

"Leave him," snarled a voice from behind.

Groggily, Brody pushed himself up and turned around.

He was facing the barrel of a sawn-off shotgun.

"Do not move." The voice came from the man holding the gun and was directed at Leroy and Danny. Other than his dark brown boots, he was dressed completely in black. Black jeans, black woollen jumper, long black leather coat, black woollen hat pulled low. He was middle-aged, trim, with dark bushy eyebrows and emotionless brown eyes.

"Kneel next to the others." The accent was Eastern European. Perhaps Russian.

Brody quickly joined the dots and realised his fate. As he moved into place, his back to the hitman, Brody whispered, "I'm so sorry," to the kneeling couple.

"Say nothing," commanded the gunman.

Brody took his place next to Leroy. His head began to throb. His body began to shake uncontrollably.

"Do nothing."

He walked over to the dining table and pulled out one of the chairs with one hand and, with the other, kept the shotgun pointed in their direction. He lugged the chair over towards them and set it down about six feet away. Absently, Brody wondered whether he was about to sit down for some kind of strange chat. Instead, he reached inside his jacket and pulled out a tablet PC. He swiped fingers, pressed something and then he positioned it upright on the chair, facing them.

A Skype video call was being made. Brody could see the vibrating icon and hear the ringing sound. Brody prayed that it wouldn't be answered.

It connected.

A face filled the screen. Mid-twenties, short blond crew cut, nose ring, ear lobe rings, and studs in his blond eyebrows. The wings of a phoenix reached up from his neck, the tattoo reaching his ears. When he spoke, a barbell piercing in his tongue flashed occasionally.

"Three?" he said, surprised. "I was expecting only one, Yakov." Definitely Russian.

The hitman, standing behind the tablet still holding the gun on them, grunted. "I kill all three."

"Yes, you'd like that, wouldn't you?"

Brody and Leroy glanced at each other in shock. Dribble escaped Leroy's mouth. Danny stared impassively out the window, ignoring the conversation.

"Which one of you is Fingal?"

Silence.

"Yakov . . ."

Yakov sauntered around the chair, still pointing the gun at them. He booted Danny in the stomach, and he immediately doubled over in agony.

"I'm Fingal," stated Brody. "Let them go. They've got nothing to do with this."

Yakov returned to his former position. Danny coughed and spluttered, but rose himself up with dignity. He resumed staring out the window.

"Ah, Fingal, it's such a pleasure to finally put a face to the name. I do so like to see my rivals in the whites of their eyes before I execute them. I'm just sorry I cannot be there in person." He slowly licked his lips, the stud protruding grotesquely.

"And who the fuck are you?" spat Leroy.

"Ah, yes, I forgot my manners. That's so important to you English, is it not?" He leaned his head to one side. "I am known to Fingal as Contagion."

"I know of you," confirmed Brody.

Online, his name was written as Contag10n. He was a renowned black hat cybercriminal, very active in the darkest areas of the deep web. He was credited as being the architect behind some of the world's most prevalent Advanced Persistent Threats such as Styx, SandWiper, and Machine_Gh0st, designed to attack commercial and government computer systems. Rumours conflicted as to his motivation. One minute he was credited with being a cyber-criminal for hire and the next he was state-sponsored, usually associated with Russia.

"Good. But what you may not know is that I am the leader of Vorovskoy Mir."

Everything fell into place for Brody. If it hadn't been clear already, he now truly understood that he was a dead man. And worse, Leroy and Danny would die too.

Contag10n's face moved downwards on the screen as he looked above their heads.

"Yakov, show me the poster on the wall behind them."

Yakov picked up the tablet and angled it at the poster on the wall. It was the framed blown-up printout of the Vorovskoy Mir Most Wanted site, offering rewards for information leading to the capture of any of the hackers listed. Fingal was third on the list, with a $1 million reward. Brody had mounted the poster to continuously remind him to take every step to remain completely anonymous online.

"Hah, this is most poetic. Thank you, Yakov." The hitman placed the tablet back on the chair. "It seems I do not need to explain why you are on your knees."

"Yes, you fucking do," demanded Leroy.

"Okay, for your friend's benefit, Fingal. He should at least know why he has to die today." Contag10n's image turned towards Leroy. "Your friend Fingal has been a fly in the ointment of my organisation for many years. He has cost us many millions of dollars uncovering our networks of APTs. Has he done this for money, something I could understand and perhaps respect? No. Does he work for the police or the government? No. So why would he do these things? The answer is simple. In English, it is only three letters for such a big thing. *Ego*. He has done these things for nothing more than the adulation of his peers in the hacking community, none of whom he'll ever meet face-to-face. This I have never understood."

Contag10n turned back to Brody.

"What is the point of doing what you do if you cannot bask in its glory in the real world? Please, tell me, I am interested."

Leroy and Danny both turned their heads to hear his answer. It was a version of the argument he and Leroy had had many times. What was the point of doing anything online when everyone he talked to were nothing more than letters and numbers on a screen?

"I do what I do because I can," answered Brody. "Could I have done it all without taking any credit and have avoided all this? Yes, of course." He turned to face his best friend and his boyfriend. "And right now I wish I had. But Contag10n is right. I always sought praise for what I've done. The applause."

"Bravo, Fingal. Yes, we all have egos. Perhaps even me. Yakov could have eliminated you without our little chat. But I wanted you to know that I am the reason you die today. And not just my name, Contag10n. But *me*. This face." He leaned into the camera, his nose ring prominent. "Goodbye, Fingal."

Yakov moved from behind the chair and stood behind them.

"Ah, very good, Yakov. I will see everything from there."

"Which one first?" asked Yakov.

"Start with the pretty one. Then the big black one in the middle. And then Fingal."

Leroy and Danny held each other's hands.

Brody bowed his head in shame.

Yakov placed the gun behind Danny's head.

It was strange being in a modern office building after working hours on a Friday evening. No atmosphere of business being done. No people striding about purposefully. No hum of noise, except the air conditioning.

The security guard on the ground floor had looked insignificant within the empty atrium. He had been told to expect them, checked their warrant cards and ushered them through to the lift lobby.

On the twentieth floor, it was the same. Quiet and empty. The lights were dimmed but not off. The low lighting drew Jenny's attention to London's breathtaking night-scape visible through the floor-to-ceiling windows, millions of lights spreading out in every direction as far as she could see, the view from this high up making the torrential rain seem inconsequential.

"What now?" asked Fiona.

"I'm sure the guard will have phoned through. If not, David Dawson gave me Magnus Peggler's mobile. Let's give him a minute."

As if on cue, Peggler arrived. He held up his pass that had been hanging around his neck to the internal security doors and pushed them open.

"Oh, there's two of you." His high-pitched voice was shrill with confusion. "David just said it would be you, DI Price."

"Well, I guess that makes me the official gooseberry," joked Fiona. She held her hand out and introduced herself. "DC Fiona Jones."

He shook it briskly. Before Jenny could offer her own, he turned and said, "This way."

They followed him. He made no small talk.

He walked them down a corridor, through a set of double doors and across an open plan office. Jenny recognised the secure door with the small glass window that led up to the CCTV control and the computer floor. He flashed his pass at the sensor and entered a code. They followed him up the private flight of stairs.

When they reached the hallway on the floor above, Peggler asked them to wait there. He stepped into the CCTV control room, leaving them in the hallway. Through the window, they watched him enter the inner office.

"Don't think I've ever felt so unwelcome," whispered Fiona. "And what's with the soprano voice?"

"Yeah, he's a bit odd. He was the other day as well."

Peggler returned holding two white plastic passes and handed them one each.

He pointed to the sensor next to the transparent circular tube with its double door system. "Just hold it to the sensor and the first door will open. They're one-time-use visitor passes so you don't need a code. Leave your mobile phones on the table, we can't have them interfering with the computer equipment."

"But we're only here for Ronald Keeble's PC."

"Oh, I thought David said you were here to interview him?"

Jenny and Fiona looked at each other.

"He's here?" Jenny felt her mouth dry up.

"Yes, of course. He's helping me upgrade the CCTV control system."

"But he's at his home in Basildon. David Dawson told us he left for home around five."

"And we've just arrested him," added Fiona.

"Well, you must have arrested someone else. He did pop out at five, but that was to get sandwiches for later. It's going to be a late night."

"He's in there?" clarified Jenny, pointing through the window at the long rows of computer racks.

"Yeah, he's behind the fifth set of racks. I'll take you to him."

"You stay here," asserted Jenny. "We'll get him."

She looked at Fiona. The blood was pumping through her veins now. "You ready?"

Fiona nodded, offering a grim smile. Jenny knew she was thinking the same thing. That Da Silva had just made a huge public mistake. And, after his behaviour towards Jenny, perhaps it was one that they could capitalise on. She knew she probably ought to call for backup before going through. Fuck it: she wanted this to be their collar.

Jenny held her pass up to the security sensor. The outer door of the tube began to rotate open.

"Don't forget your mobiles," said Peggler, his voice even higher.

"Seriously?"

He held out his hand in emphasis. Jenny reached into her back pocket and dropped it in his hand. Fiona did the same.

She stepped into the tube and the door behind her slid to a close. When it was completely shut, there was enough of a pause for Jenny, in her heightened state, to become concerned that she was trapped. But then the door in front slid to one side. She stepped into the computer hall. It was colder in here and the hum of noise from the industrial air conditioning and the computer equipment was very loud. She waited for Fiona to go through the same rigmarole, furtively looking around in case Ronald Keeble suddenly appeared.

Once they were both through the security tube, Jenny said, "You take the far wall. I'll take this one. We'll check each row one at a time. You at the bottom, me at the top."

"Sounds good to me."

Fiona headed for the other end of the first set of racks. Jenny waited at the top. She gave the thumbs up and they quietly made their way to the corridor behind the first set of computer equipment. As expected, it was empty. Fiona was at the other end. This time Fiona gave the thumbs up, ready for the second corridor between the racks of computer equipment.

Synchronised, they appeared at top and bottom of the second corridor. Again it was empty. They repeated the process for the next two corridors, both empty. It was the next one that Peggler had referred to. Jenny took a deep breath, gave the thumbs up to Fiona and rushed around the fifth rack to the corridor behind it.

It was empty again.

Jenny came to a stop. Fiona did the same at the other end of the corridor. She held her palms out to signify her confusion. Jenny shrugged her shoulders in answer and then pointed to the next one. Perhaps they'd miscounted. They repeated the process but again the next corridor was empty. There was only one more, but yet again there was no one there.

There was nowhere else to hide.

"This is fucking weird," said Fiona who had jogged up the last corridor to join her. "There's nowhere to hide ... unless he's climbed inside one of those computer racks?"

"Good thinking."

Together, they sped up and down each corridor, checking every rack in turn, always keeping an eye on the circular tube exit from the computer room, just in case Keeble made a dash for it. Each rack had transparent doors on the outside and so they could see the layers of computer equipment within. Eventually, they made it back to the open space between the first rack and the exit.

He was nowhere to be found.

They headed back to the exit.

Peggler wasn't there.

"You go first," said Jenny, still looking behind them in case they'd somehow missed Keeble.

Fiona nodded and raised her pass to the security sensor. It beeped red.

'Eh?"

She tried again. Same result.

"Try yours."

Jenny did.

Red.

And then they both stared at each other in horror, registering that something was very amiss.

Through the glass wall next to the tube exit, they saw movement.

Peggler appeared from the CCTV control room and walked to the glass window, carrying a bag. He was belly laughing as he approached.

"This is no fucking joke," shouted Jenny, banging her fist on the window for effect. It was completely solid. "Let us out of here. Now."

He shook his head, almost apologetically, still laughing.

"What the fuck is wrong with you?" cried Jenny, anger bubbling up inside her.

He bent right down, beneath the line of the glass window. She could only see his back. The wall blocked whatever he was doing with his hands.

And then, suddenly, he raised himself upright.

"Recognise me now, bitch?" His voice was suddenly deep.

He'd put on a black cap with an embroidered Adidas logo on it and dark sunglasses.

Even without the fake beard and moustache, Jenny now recognised him. She'd last seen that disguise while hanging six floors up in the Flexbase atrium in Windsor.

"Fuck."

CHAPTER 23

The bang, when it came, was much louder than Brody had expected.

Through his knees, he felt the whole apartment shake.

Then he heard multiple shots from right behind him, with the corresponding sound of bullets hitting the walls opposite, and shrapnel ricocheting in all directions. Suddenly smoke appeared in the room, followed by another almighty bang. Realising something altogether different was going on, Brody dived sideways onto Leroy and Danny, who fell backwards to the floor under his weight.

A cascade of bullets hit Yakov behind them and he was thrown backwards onto the wall, knocking the framed Vorovskoy Mir poster off its hook. It landed on top of his prone body. Blood splattered the wall behind.

"Alpha, clear."

"Bravo, clear."

And from further away. "Charlie, clear."

Brody felt himself being dragged away from his friends.

"You all right, son?" The helmeted armed response police officer stared at Brody from behind his goggles.

"Yes, I'm fine."

Suddenly a howl shook him to his soul. It was Leroy, crying out Danny's name in anguish. "Nooooooo!" It was the most forlorn noise Brody had ever heard.

Through the clearing wafts of smoke, Brody could see Leroy

trying to shake Danny awake. But half of his head had been blown off. Most of it was spread across the living room. Leroy wailed Danny's name again, over and over.

Brody sat there, immobile. Uncomprehending.

Slowly, Leroy stopped shaking Danny. He turned to face Brody. His tear-covered abject face turned furious.

"Why not you?" he shouted. "This is *your* fault! All your fault. It should be you. Not . . ." He choked on his words and the fury left him. " . . . Not my beautiful Danny." He turned and flung himself across Danny's prone body, bawling.

Brody looked around helplessly.

He saw the tablet PC, still on, still standing on the chair, despite everything. Blood and guts were splattered across it. The outraged face of Contag10n filled the screen.

Brody reached out and grabbed the tablet, so that his face filled Contag10n's screen. As he pressed two buttons together on the tablet, he spoke the warning with all the menace in the world. "Know this. I will hunt you down and destroy you. You are a dead man."

Brody flung the tablet across the room and watched it smash into the wall, flicker and die.

Sometime later, Brody sat at his dining table, shell-shocked at the events. Everything was a blur.

The armed response team had secured the apartment and retreated, only to be replaced with a more normal-looking set of police detectives and crime scene officers. Leroy had to be forcibly removed from Danny's body. As he passed Brody, Leroy charged at him like a rabid dog, but the officers held onto him. Their calm words fell on deaf ears as they led him out to an ambulance, still howling.

Another officer walked calmly through the chaos, making a beeline for Brody. He was tall and massively overweight. His suit was ill-fitting and his shoes scuffed. He was chewing gum.

"Not quite what I expected." He looked Brody up and down. "But I always knew you weren't Australian."

Brody grunted a nod of resigned comprehension. "Doc_Doom."

"I always wanted us to meet in the flesh but," he surveyed the wreckage, "not under such circumstances."

"I have you to thank for saving my life?"

"Yes. I'm just sorry we couldn't get here any quicker. The armed response unit moved as fast as they could." He looked over at Danny's body. "Not quickly enough, though."

"No."

He held out his hand. "My real name is Victor Gibb."

Brody limply accepted the handshake. "Brody Taylor."

Brody shook his head as he worked out what was going on. "So are you police, MI5 or MI6?"

Gibb sat his massive frame down opposite him. "Neither. GCHQ."

"And all this time on the CrackerHack forums as Doc_Doom you've been trying to gain my trust. Why?"

"To recruit you. The GCHQ needs your skills Brody. There's a cyberwar brewing. State funded. China. Russia. The Middle East. We could do with someone like you on our team."

"Me?" Brody couldn't believe it.

"Look, I appreciate this isn't the time or place to have this conversation. But I have waited an awfully long time to have it. You're not exactly easy to get hold of in meatspace."

"Well, today seems to be the day for it. Crooner42, Contag10n and now you, Doc_Doom."

"You can thank Crooner42 for Contag10n. He's the one who outed you to Vorovskoy Mir."

"Well, right now, Crooner42's in police custody."

Gibb raised his eyebrows in surprise but didn't ask. With his resources, he'd be able to find out anything he wanted.

At length, Gibb explained how Crooner42 had somehow gained access to Fingal's identity information and provided it to Vorovskoy Mir yesterday evening over their secure website. GCHQ picked up the resulting chatter this morning, keyed off the keyword 'Fingal'. The hit instructions had made their way through Russian Mafia channels. Fortunately it had ended up with Yakov, someone that MI5 had under surveillance. Only by following him were they able to track down the specific details. Gibb had been kept informed in real-time and the minute Yakov had entered Brody's apartment, he'd ordered the armed take down.

"So if you'd have taken him down before entering my apartment, none of this would have happened?"

"True, but the police needed reasonable suspicion before we

could act. Observing him break into your apartment gave us that. It took a good half-an-hour to get the unit here and ready to act. In the meantime, you showed up. Good job you didn't arrive earlier. Yakov would have been in and out before we got here."

Brody remembered his thought about the fates telling him something, making him to park on the other side of the road, which had resulted in him choosing to go into Bruno's before coming home. Just that small decision had saved his and Leroy's life.

But not poor Danny's.

Brody stood up and walked over to his friend's dead body, not really sure what he wanted to do or say. He felt that he needed to apologise, but no words would make it through to Danny now. Instead, he just stared at the sorry mess that was once his best friend's partner for life.

One of the crime scene officers was taking photos.

The flash caused a reflection from the ring on Danny's finger, his multi-coloured rainbow ring that had been a present from Leroy. The colours were meant to signify the six colours of the gay pride rainbow flag.

And immediately a new connection formed in Brody's mind.

He turned and ran.

Brody burst into Bruno's coffee shop, the door swinging back violently and crashing on the wall. As one, the lounge's patrons pivoted their heads to see what the commotion was. Not caring, Brody vaulted a table and then the sofa he'd been sitting on earlier. He scanned the coffee table, but his computer was no longer there.

"Stefan?" he shouted at the top of his voice, not seeing the head barista anywhere. "Stefan!"

He'd left the computer behind when he'd rushed over the road to warn Leroy and Danny that they all needed to make a fast exit from his apartment and never return. The threat from Vorovskoy Mir had always been very real to Brody, and he had prepared for the eventuality of his identity being discovered by having replacement ones lined up. As long as they never discovered the existence of Leroy or Danny, then they could all regroup in a few weeks when Brody set himself up under his new guise. It would have cost Brody his apartment and computer equipment, but that was nothing that he couldn't replace. He had no personal possessions.

But he hadn't been quick enough. Or, more accurately, Crooner42 had leaked his identity as Brody Taylor without any fanfare, and so Brody hadn't known he'd been compromised until it was already too late. Danny had paid the price of Brody's failure with his life.

It was unbearable.

Stefan stepped out from behind a door marked 'Staff Only'. "Ah, Mr Brody, Mr Brody." He pulled up short when he saw the bandage on his head and the blood splattered all over Brody's shirt. "What has happened? Are all the police out there for you?"

"My computer, Stefan. Where's my computer?"

The door swung open and Victor Gibb strode in, out of breath.

"Is here, don't worry Mr Brody." Stefan stepped behind the counter, reached underneath and pulled it out. "Here you are."

Brody sat at the nearest spare table. He unfolded his tablet PC.

"Do you mind telling me what the fuck is going on?" asked Gibb.

As Brody connected to the Internet, he explained. "Have you heard the news this week about the meeting room killer?"

Gibb nodded. Brody connected to SWY control console using the administrator access that he'd uncovered earlier that day at Harper's apartment in Docklands.

"I've been helping the police track down the killer. The website he was using to learn all about his victims so that he could set up his lures was SecretlyWatchingYou."

"The same site Crooner42 got you to pentest this week."

Brody searched through the user database for Ronald Keeble's details.

"Exactly. Well, we tracked down the killer earlier today by correlating user activity within the site. He's a Flexbase employee called Ronald Keeble. That's the company whose meeting rooms were used. As an employee, he knew their booking systems inside out and he was in the SecretlyWatchingYou user database. The police are arresting him right now."

He copied the Gmail address that Keeble had used, the same one that was linked to his PayPal account. He flipped windows and pasted the address into the PayPal login screen.

"I think they're arresting the wrong guy."

He switched back to SWY. He found the corresponding

password details. Not caring about user privacy, Crooner42 had stored them as plain text. He copied the password, switched back to PayPal and pasted it in. Pressing enter, he prayed the passwords were the same on both sites.

"And you know all this because?"

"Because the guy they're arresting is gay. A gay man is hardly likely to be going about raping and killing women."

The password worked. He was inside the PayPal account. He navigated through the account settings and brought up the bank account details linked to the PayPal account.

"And that just dawned on you upstairs, did it?"

"Kind of. Danny wears a rainbow ring. So does his boyfriend, Leroy. They bought them for each other a couple of years ago. I think the rainbow refers to the gay pride rainbow flag."

"I'm not with you."

"I was in Flexbase the other day and I met Keeble. I didn't think anything of it at the time, but he was also wearing a rainbow ring. But seeing Danny's ring just now jogged my memory."

"So how come you narrowed down on him in the first place?"

"I didn't. I narrowed down to an email address in his name. It was linked to a PayPal account."

"The email and PayPal accounts are not his then?"

"No."

"Whose are they?"

Brody turned the PC to Gibb, who bent over to look at the screen.

"They belong to Magnus Peggler, the Flexbase CIO." Brody threw his hands up in the air. "God, I'm a fucking idiot. I should have checked this."

"Checked what?"

"Hold on a second." Brody dialled Jenny on his mobile. Eventually it was answered. Brody went to speak but then heard Jenny's recorded voice. "This is DI Jenny Price. Please leave a message."

"Jenny, ring me as soon as you get this. Ronald Keeble's the wrong guy. The killer is Magnus Peggler. Please be careful. *Please*."

He hung up.

He didn't know whether she just wasn't answering him because of their earlier conversation or because she couldn't.

He texted her as well, just in case.

Brody grabbed his tablet PC and ran. As he charged past Gibb, he pointed his car keys through the window at his car and pressed the remote, then threw them back to Gibb and said, "Here, you drive."

The hazard lights flashed twice and Brody jumped into the passenger seat.

Brody reached over and opened the driver door as Gibb stepped out of the shop, halting suddenly. "I can't fit in that thing! Have you not seen the size of me?" It would indeed be a tight fit. "Wherever we're going, let's take my car."

"There's no time, come on. Jump in."

Gibb folded himself into the car, reaching down and pushing the seat back as far as it would go. With his head bent down by the car's roof, he looked like an adult trying to ride a vehicle on a child's merry-go-round.

He started the car and reversed out. "Which way?"

"That way. Drive towards Docklands."

Gibb blindly pushed out onto the road, not worrying about any passing traffic. The police had set up a cordon outside Brody's apartment, preventing any vehicles from travelling along Upper Street. He changed into first and floored it.

"You said you should have checked something. What was it?" asked Gibb.

"The bank account details within the PayPal account. They don't belong to Keeble; they belong to Peggler. The clever bastard set up the email and PayPal account in an email address that looked like it belonged to Ronald Keeble, but everything within the account is Peggler's. It's impossible to make PayPal work without a real credit check, but you can use any email address you control as the account name."

"Clever. So Peggler was able to pay for SWY using PayPal linked to an account that, at first glance, looked as though it belonged to someone else."

"Yes."

"But the police would have worked this out eventually."

"Maybe. But it gives him plenty of time to run for cover. He sees the police arrest Keeble and off he goes."

"So why have you got me driving like a lunatic towards

Docklands?"

"Because the two police officers I'm worried about have gone to Flexbase, where Peggler is waiting to meet them."

"What's the big deal?"

"They're both women."

Gibb put his enormous foot down.

You don't know whether to be angry or happy.

Angry that your source of gullible women is gone or happy that the policewoman is still alive. That she somehow survived the fall when you prised her fingers off the railing.

Angry that they've tracked down your account on SecretlyWatchingYou or happy that they've fallen for your little insurance trick that pointed them towards that disgusting homo who worked in the CCTV control room.

Angry that you'll soon need to run and hide or happy that the policewoman brought you a nice friend to play with for when you've finished with her.

The shock on her face when you put on the hat and sunglasses was comical. You laughed like you haven't laughed in a long time. You were already laughing from watching them hunt down the non-existent queer in the datacentre. That was so fucking funny. You couldn't believe they would be gullible enough to have fallen for that.

And hadn't you done well? Thinking on your feet like that. You hadn't expected two of them to show up. One you could easily handled with your massive dagger, but two? That was too risky. Tricking them into the datacentre was so damn clever of you. And making them leave their mobile phones behind, that was a masterstroke. As if phones affect computer equipment! What a joke.

You are a fucking genius, if you do say so yourself.

And your genius has no end tonight.

You watch the policewoman throw a blade server from one of the racks at the window. It bounces off harmlessly. She is swearing at you.

"Sshh," you say to her, loudly enough for her to hear. She stops shouting.

You turn your tablet computer around and place it flat on the window so that she can see it. She comes up close. You look at her cleavage while she looks at the screen. You feel the movement in your boxers below. Ooh, looks like someone wants to come out and play.

"Look at this," you say. "These are the controls for the hypoxic fire suppression system."

She looks confused. The other one too.

"It regulates the amount of oxygen inside the datacentre where you are now. It's normally set at fifteen per cent. High enough to breath but low enough to prevent combustion."

Understanding settled on her face. The other one too.

"Yes, as you can see, I've set it to lower the mix to below five per cent oxygen."

Panicking, the whores looked around the computer room helplessly.

"It might take about ten minutes, but soon you will become faint and fall unconscious. There is nothing you can do to stop it."

They shout at you. Pleading. But you ignore them.

"And when you are unconscious, I will come in there and then we're going to have some fun."

For effect, you lift your dagger in front of you. They haven't seen it until now.

You watch the horror on their faces and laugh.

You have a major hard-on now.

But you must be patient.

As they flew down Commercial Street, Spitalfields Market on the right, Brody slammed his fist on the dashboard.

He felt so powerless.

He'd already caused the death of one person close to him today. He couldn't bear to be the cause of another.

They were still at least fifteen minutes away; even with Gibb's race car driving.

Gibb had called for backup and the same armed response unit that had raided Brody's apartment was now regrouping and heading over towards Docklands. But they would take even longer to get there.

Brody had called O'Reilly, the only other number he had of anyone on Jenny's team. The only reason he had it was because of the non-existent school bullying trick he'd pulled on Wednesday morning, which had enabled Brody to meet Jenny alone. O'Reilly was still at Patrick Harper's apartment. He explained the situation and asked for Da Silva and Coombs's numbers. O'Reilly complied, saying he would head over to Flexbase immediately, as he was only a mile or so away. He'd be there fairly quickly if he were able to hail a taxi.

Brody phoned Da Silva but got voicemail. Alan Coombs picked up and listened to Brody's story. He swore a lot and then told him to leave it with them.

But they would all be powerless when they got there. The Flexbase physical security systems were top notch. Without the right access, no one could get in. Peggler would have all the time in the world to do whatever he wanted.

Unless . . .

Brody powered on his tablet PC and connected to the Internet again.

"What are you doing now?" asked Gibb.

"Hacking into Flexbase."

"From here in the car? That's impossible."

But Gibb didn't know that Brody already had full access to the Flexbase systems from his hacking session the day before when he'd got hold of the IP addresses and found the Windsor meeting room booking that had enabled Jenny to save Sarah McNeil's life.

"I broke in there yesterday. I already have the access I need."

"See, it's exactly that kind of behaviour that would go down so well in GCHQ."

"Not now, eh?"

Brody logged in and negotiated his way through to the CCTV system. He began combing through the video feeds, searching for movement. Eventually, he found what he was looking for.

"Fuck."

Jenny and Fiona were in the main datacentre, on the floor, their backs to the wall opposite the main entrance. Their eyes were shut. They weren't moving.

He found the audio, but could only hear the air conditioning system.

Then he heard Jenny cough and splutter. What the hell was going on?

Where was Peggler? He looked around and discovered him in the room outside. He was just standing there, turning a massive dagger over and over in his hands, as if he was waiting for something.

Gibb leaned over for a brief look. "That's fucking impressive."

Brody found his way through to the building control system.

He saw the fire alarm systems and, next to it, the emergency public address system for the building. He patched his computer in, selected the speakers on the datacentre floor and began talking.

He kept the two CCTV feeds playing, showing him Peggler in one, and Jenny and Fiona in the other.

"Jenny, its Brody. Can you hear me?"

There was no reaction.

Damn. He checked the settings, making sure the microphone was turned on. It was. Just as he was about to re-examine the building control system settings, he saw movement.

Jenny and Fiona both opened their eyes, looking around in confusion.

Peggler gave no reaction. He was unable to hear Brody.

Brody realised there was a time lag as video and audio made its way back over the Internet to his PC.

"Jenny, are you okay? What the hell is going on there?"

After a long moment, she replied. She said one word before breaking into a cough and splutter. "Oxygen."

And immediately Brody understood what Peggler was doing.

He quickly flipped back to the building control system, tracked down the hypoxic air control system he'd noticed yesterday and saw that the oxygen levels had been lowered beneath five per cent. Peggler was waiting for them to fall unconscious before going in. Fuck.

Brody quickly raised the oxygen bar as high as it would go, but he had no idea how quickly or slowly the system worked.

Glancing out the car window, he got his bearings. "Jenny, we're ten minutes away. There's an armed response unit on the way. I'm hacked into the Flexbase systems. I've reset the oxygen levels; hopefully you'll start to feel it come through very soon. Peggler can't hear me. Give me a sign you've heard this."

Jenny lay prone with her back to the wall. He thought he heard her whisper something, but couldn't catch it.

"Fuck, there's nothing else I can do." His voice rose in utter desperation. "I'm so sorry Jenny. For everything."

And, after a minute, he watched Fiona fall to one side.

And then Jenny.

You watch and wait. You have been patient.

You will make these good ones. You won't waste the opportunity like before. You'll make this the best one ever. Perfection. And then repeat it again with her friend. Or maybe you'll swap the order. You're not sure. You'll decide when you get in there.

You head into the CCTV control room inner office and find the emergency oxygen mask. You chuckle to yourself. You'll need that.

Once you've checked they're nice and unconscious, you'll reset the oxygen levels. After all, you want them alive when you fuck them. When you hold a knife to their throats and make them squeeze tight.

You remember you'll need rope and retrieve some from your bag. You'll need to tie them both up good and tight. Can't have one sneaking up behind you while you're otherwise engaged, can you?

With everything set, you hold your security pass up to the double doors and type in your code. The first door slides open. You're confident the additional weight of the tablet PC, knife, mask and rope is within tolerance levels. You remove your shoes and leave them outside just to be safe, to balance out the weight. It wouldn't be smart to get trapped in there. That would be silly.

The door closes behind you. After a slight pause, the door in front slides open.

You're in, breathing through the oxygen mask.

There's a strange background noise. The air conditioning sounds different. But then you realise it must be because of the oxygen mask.

You can already feel your hard-on returning in the excitement.

You walk across the empty space to the other side of the room.

You look down at the two prone bodies. They are both beautiful. This will be amazing.

But which one should you choose first? Do you want the policewoman first, the one that looks most like *her*? Or do you want to save the policewoman to last? But then you're thinking about how long you might have to wait in-between. You'll need time to get it up again. And what if you can't? It's happened before.

You kick the legs of the other one, the policewoman's friend. No reaction.

A voice booms out from all around. You look up in complete confusion.

Magnus Peggler, stop where you are! We have the place surrounded. Drop the knife.

You freeze, completely baffled. You look around, but there's no one there.

And then you are hit in the stomach and begin to stumble backwards.

Jenny threw herself with all her might at Peggler.

She was weak, she knew that, but it was the only moment when he would be distracted enough.

Brody's voice had given her the chance they needed. She could sense Fiona right behind her.

She felt a crashing blow on the back of her head and she lost her grip, falling face down to the floor. She could see Peggler's shoeless feet retreating backwards. He had dropped his tablet PC but held onto the knife.

She saw Fiona run past her and then suddenly halt.

Peggler was waving his huge dagger in front of him, side to side in slashing movements. It was a defence tactic, but it would be lethal to charge him now, unarmed as they were.

Jenny picked herself up off the floor and stood side by side with Fiona.

"Drop the knife, Peggler."

"You're under arrest."

"Nooooo!" he wailed in his high-pitch voice, retreating backwards towards the exit.

Jenny and Fiona advanced in unison, keeping the same distance.

Be careful, Jenny.

Brody's voice emanated from the speakers.

Slowly Peggler made it back to the exit. Still slashing the knife in front of him, he pressed his pass on the security sensor and furtively typed in his code. The door began to open.

Let him go, Jenny, advised Brody's voice. *He'll never make it outside.*

She wanted to charge into him, but it would be too dangerous.

Peggler stepped backwards into the tube.

She screamed out in frustration.

They had come so close only to watch him get away.

Peggler grinned from ear to ear as the door slid to a close, blocking them from him.

He locked eyes on Jenny and screamed through the glass. "I'll come back for you, *mother*! I'm not finished with you. I'll never be finished with you."

His words were chilling. As if he saw Jenny as his mother. Through her oxygen-deprived haze, Jenny faintly wondered if the women he raped and killed were all substitutes for his mother, or some similar sick design.

Peggler turned, waiting for the second door to open. The pause was longer than before. And then, instead of opening, an alarm went off along with a flashing light above the mantrap.

Shrieking, Peggler smashed his fists and the butt of the knife at the tube's glass walls. But they had no impact. He kept on smashing.

Jenny and Fiona looked at each other in surprise.

Jenny held up her hand high. Fiona high-fived it.

Nice work, Fingal, said another voice through the speaker system. Someone with Brody.

Would you believe it, Peggler? Brody's tinny voice taunted the rapist. *Someone's only gone and hacked into your personnel file and amended your weight. Oops!*

Peggler became even more frenzied, thrashing about in every direction like a rabid animal. Eventually, his lashing out subsided and he slumped to the floor of the mantrap: caught.

EPILOGUE

At least the rain had stopped.

Jenny stood by the grave while the vicar spoke his words of comfort. Not that Danny's family were taking any from them, his mother standing there stoically, tears running freely down her cheeks. His brother's head was bowed, his hand held by his wife who held a hanky to her eyes with her free hand. There was no father. She had been told that he had died some years before.

Similar to Magnus Peggler. His father had died when he was ten. He was then left with his mother, who had never got over the loss of her husband, fixating on her son as a surrogate husband, even sexually. Their incestuous relationship went on for a few years, right up until Magnus broke down to his English teacher, aged fifteen. Social services became involved and Magnus was eventually fostered. Mrs Peggler was arrested and imprisoned, where she died under suspicious circumstances. All of it was a matter of public record. But no one had ever considered the on-going psychological impact on the young Magnus who, on the surface, grew up to be a healthy, productive member of society. Underneath, he had been regressing back to his youth, searching women to fulfil his twisted fantasy of maternal revenge. Magnus Peggler would no doubt be fodder for criminal profilers for years to come.

But what had bothered Jenny the most was when she'd seen a picture of Mrs Peggler. It had almost been like looking at a photograph of herself. It had given her the creeps.

She shook her head, trying to clear her mind of thoughts of Peggler. She needed to focus on the funeral and the reason she was here. She studied the rest of the mourners.

Leroy, Danny's boyfriend of many years, stood on the other side of Danny's mother. His expression contained more rage than grief.

The only other people she knew were standing either side of her. On her left was Victor Gibb, the agent from GCHQ that she'd been introduced to that fateful night a week before. On her right, squeezing her hand almost painfully, was Brody. She could feel him taking deep breaths in an attempt to avoid tears.

He failed.

And when Leroy's angry line of sight fell on Brody, the animosity reaching right across the coffin containing Danny's body, Brody caved in completely and withdrew from the congregation. She followed him. She was here for Brody. She'd never met Danny, although Brody had told her everything about him. And his best friend, Leroy.

She caught up with him by a copse of trees.

"It'll never be the same again, will it?" he asked, wiping his eyes with the sleeve of his suit jacket.

"No."

They stood in silence, looking back down towards the graveside. They watched as the gathering took turns to throw dirt on top of the coffin.

"I've made my decision."

She nodded and pulled him close.

She knew he had. And she knew what his decision was. He would join GCHQ and he would deploy their vast capabilities to bring down Vorovskoy Mir, hunting a computer hacker called Contag10n, the man who'd been responsible for Danny's death and ruptured friendship with Leroy.

Two hours later, they sat in an independent coffee shop in the centre of Cardiff, Danny's hometown. Despite his grief, Brody had been impressed. She'd discovered it in advance on the Internet. Jenny was becoming much more adept at being online. Next thing he knew, she'd probably want to become friends with him on Facebook or something just as crazy.

They sat opposite each other, holding hands.

Two untouched macchiatos lay on the table between them.

"There's one thing I'd still like to know, Brody."

"Oh yes? I thought I'd told you everything."

And he had. Everything.

"Why do you call yourself Fingal?"

Ah, that.

He'd forgotten that.

"What's my name?" he asked her.

"Brody." And to his inquiring look she added, "Brody Taylor."

He took a massive deep breath.

"That's not actually my name." He shrugged apologetically.

She punched him playfully in the arm but then became serious. "Go on."

"My . . ." He faltered. "Jesus, this is hard. I've never told anyone this. Well, no one except Leroy."

"Brody, you know the rules."

The rules they had laid down for their relationship to function involved telling the complete truth, at all times. It was the only way she would accept him. She'd eventually got past the lies and deceit from their first few days together during the case, ultimately accepting that Brody's feelings towards her were genuine. His actions in saving her and Fiona's lives had gone a long way to Jenny giving him enough leeway to explain himself.

"Okay, okay. It's my surname that's Brody. My real surname."

She looked confused. "So what's your first name?"

"Finn."

"And that's where Fingal comes from? Finn?"

"Yes."

"Finn Brody," she said, trying it out for size. She offered her hand for him to shake. He took it.

"Well, it's a pleasure to finally meet you, Finn Brody."

THE END

AFTERWORD

Thanks for joining Brody and Jenny in this Deep Web Thriller. Enjoyed the story? Here's what you can do next.

If you loved the book and have a moment to spare, I would really appreciate a short review where you bought the book (and/or on www.goodreads.com). Your help in spreading the word is gratefully appreciated - it really helps aspiring indie authors like me. You can also sign up to be notified of my next book, as well as pre-release specials and giveaways at www.ianhsutherland.com.

In case you missed it, Brody appears in a prequel novella to *Invasion of Privacy* **called** *Social Engineer.* **More information is available at** www.ianhsutherland.com/social-engineer.

Thank you for reading this book. I've been actively procrastinating about it for many, many years. But I finally knuckled down in 2012, giving up television (well, except for my three guilty pleasures: Match of the Day, Australian Masterchef and 24!!) and got on with the job of writing it, which turned out to be a true privilege and a pleasure. I hope you've enjoyed reading it as much as I enjoyed writing, editing and publishing it. I plan for this to be a long running series featuring Brody/Fingal and each novel will expose more about the Dark Web, which is, sadly, very real.

Ian Sutherland, London, August 2014.

ACKNOWLEDGEMENTS

It's been a long journey to complete and publish my first novel and many people along the way have greatly helped me, not always knowingly! First I'd like to thank some of my earliest beta readers on wattpad.com who gave their constructive and positive feedback long before the book was finished. You gave me the confidence that what I was writing was worth reading. In particular, *deancmoore, EurekaEureka, evidents, Fakedeadgirlfriend, lkrice, Next_JK_Rowling, ricktaylor18, sauthca, Quor000* and *WilsonGill* who all stuck with me right the way through. For those of you who bought the book because of the cover — most people do despite the saying — I thank the talented Peter O'Connor of bespokebookcovers.com. Then there's the enthusiasm and professionalism of my editor, Bryony Sutherland (no relation!), who took a manuscript I, naively, thought needed little help, and found a thousand ways to improve it. This is a much better novel because of her. And lastly, my wife, Cheryl, and my daughters Laura and Raquel, who have lived my writer's dream day-to-day, always politely reminding me to get on with it. Well here we are at last!

ABOUT IAN SUTHERLAND

Ian Sutherland is a crime thriller author, living in London with his wife and two daughters. Leveraging his career in the IT industry, Ian's stories shed light on the threats we face from cybercrime as it becomes all too prevalent in our day-to-day lives. Invasion of Privacy is his first novel and was professionally self-published in August 2014.

Learn more about Ian at www.ianhsutherland.com.

Follow him on twitter at www.twitter.com/iansuth
Like his Facebook page at www.facebook.com/ihsutherland

Printed in Great Britain
by Amazon.co.uk, Ltd.,
Marston Gate.